I DON'T RECOGNIZE THIS WORLD ANYMORE

KRISTOPHER TRIANA

BAD DREAM BOOKS

PRAISE FOR KRISTOPHER TRIANA

"Like the bastard son of Faulkner and Barker, Triana trudges a grotesque literary lane all his own."
— **Nick Roberts**, author of *The Exorcist's House*

"Kristopher Triana writes beautiful nightmares, horrific fairytales, and intoxicating horrors, and however depraved and damaged his characters, you get to know them well ... whether you want to or not."
— **Tim Lebbon**, author of *The Last Storm*

"Triana's work is a volatile mixture of visceral noir and twistedly disturbing passion play that invades the reader's psyche and exposes the raw and throbbing nerve hidden within."
— **Ronald Kelly**, author of *Fear, The Saga of Dead-Eye*, and *Southern Fried & Horrified*

"Kristopher Triana is without question one of the very best of the new breed of horror writers."
— **Bryan Smith**, author of *The Killing Kind*

"Whatever style or mode Triana is writing in, the voice matches it unfailingly."
— *Cemetery Dance*

"One of the most exciting and disturbing voices in extreme horror in quite some time. His stuff hurts so good."
— **Brian Keene**, author of *The Rising*

"Triana's masterful, gripping storytelling will not let go."
— *Scream Magazine*

"Triana is a master of affecting, distressing, and immensely powerful horror."
—**Jonathan Butcher**, author of *What Good Girls Do*

in loving memory of Bear and Shadow

"If you can't be a good example,
at least be a horrible warning."
—Aileen Wuornos

CHAPTER ONE

My ex-wife was the one to send me to prison, but it was my dog that led me to crime. Crazy thing is it was in that order. Because I didn't go to prison as an inmate. I went because I needed a job.

Urgently hiring.

That's what the post said on the Good Gigs website. I didn't need any experience or special diplomas. Just had to be over eighteen, a legal citizen, able to stand for up to twelve hours a day, and have a clean record—or relatively clean, as I would soon find out. I'm not sure what the public prison hiring system is like, but American Corrections Industries—a private prison corporation—seemed not only eager to bring on staff, but desperate; even at a women's prison, which seemed preferable to their much more dangerous male counterparts.

"Starting pay is thirteen dollars an hour," the HR director told me during my phone interview. It was just above Arizona's minimum wage. "That may not seem like much, but overtime is regularly available at time and a half, if you're willing to work extra days."

"Okay."

"And there's always room for advancement. Most of our wardens are former COs."

"COs?"

"Corrections officers."

She asked about the job history in the resume I'd submitted online, but it was obvious she was just going through the motions. She wasn't the only one. I was standing in my kitchen in my boxer shorts, feigning enthusiasm for a bad job with long hours and shit pay. It was two in the afternoon, and I'd already cracked open a beer. It sweated in the spring heat, leaving rings on the particle board table. On the floor, Charlie rested on his side, his gray muzzle an inch from my bare foot. I rubbed under his chin with my big toe and his tail thumped the tile.

After the prerequisite small talk, the HR woman stopped wasting our time. "Everything looks good, Mr. Donnelly. I'll be passing along my interview notes to our people at Norrington. Whether or not we're interested in taking your application to the next step, you should hear from us within one business week."

But I received a follow-up call the next day, and less than two weeks later I was driving west through Navaho County, not far from the Four Corners where tourists like to stand in Utah, Colorado, Arizona, and New Mexico at the same time. Though only March, the abundant sunshine made the arid landscape seem to cook, the mesquite and ponderosas drooping, pale, and cracked. Exhausted cattle loitered on the open range along Interstate 40, looking dazed and meaningless. Along neighboring Route 66, long-abandoned houses sulked, broken and forgotten, the graffitied ruins of a lost age. The desert was peppered with sleepy communities, ghost towns, and Indian reservations, most of them with a population under two thousand, and from the looks of things, many residents were living under the poverty line.

Despite the vast nothingness, I passed signs warning against hitchhiking, along with gruesome billboards protesting abortion. A huge junkyard filled with the skeletons of old cars glimmered with mangled chrome. The landscape devolved into sun-bleached grassland. On the breeze, sand drifted across the pavement like scattering ants. My only company was ravens. I was beginning to think I must have passed the prison without realizing it when I spotted concrete buildings with sheds of corrugated metal. There were fences topped with razor wire, but no massive wall surrounding the property. I could see people wandering around behind the fence. It certainly didn't match my idea of what a prison would look like. If not for the signs, I would have thought it was some sort of factory.

I turned my old pickup down the pebbled road leading to Norrington Women's Correctional Facility, slowly approaching the guards at the gate. One was a lanky Black man. The other was a stout Native American woman with a face like Charles Bronson. Both wore the same beige uniform I would soon spend my work hours in, pistols holstered at their hips. A German Shepherd sat beside the female guard, dressed in a dark blue vest, making it even more intimidating, even to a guy like me who loved dogs.

The male guard approached, waving me closer.

"Mornin'," he said. "What's your business?"

I handed him my driver's license. "I'm a new hire. Here for orientation."

"Alright. Open both doors and step out of the vehicle for me, please."

I did as I was told, leaving the truck's doors open like fanning wings. I felt like I should put my hands on the hood and spread my legs for a pat down, but figured I'd wait to be instructed. The female guard led the dog to my truck. It sniffed all around the exterior before jumping inside for further inspection.

"He'll probably smell my dog," I said, groundlessly nervous. "Must be enough fur in there to build a whole other Labrador."

The woman didn't even offer a polite smile, only watched the dog finish. She probably wasn't supposed to socialize at times like this. The male guard pointed out a white building on the outside of the fence.

"That's the classroom there," he said. "Good luck, man."

Getting back into my truck, I headed toward the building and parked, stroking my beard. I'd debated shaving it off while applying for jobs, but hoped it made me look tougher for this particular gig, even if my muzzle was getting as gray as my dog's.

Forty-four and starting over. I gave myself a sad glance in the rearview mirror. *How many do-overs can one man have?*

I brushed my hair with my fingers and got out, re-tucking my shirt into my slacks before entering the building. I expected a cool woosh of recirculated air to greet me, but the anteroom was warm, the air stale with the odor of cheap coffee. A spindly woman with purple rings under her eyes was fussing around a cluttered desk, a half-eaten egg sandwich in her hand. Her blonde bird's nest of hair was in two buns on the sides of her head. She didn't greet me. Instead, she called out for someone else to deal with the situation.

"Hey, Burt," she yelled around the corner. "Got another one."

I stood silently until a man responded to her call. He looked to be nearing sixty, with a silvery head of hair and matching moustache. Despite the warm weather, he wore a long-sleeved uniform, with a coffee mug in one hand and a clipboard in the other.

"New cadet?" he asked me.

"Yes, sir. Liam Donnelly."

He checked his clipboard and made a mark. "Burt Goodman. I'll be your instructor. Come with me." I followed him through a small corridor of desks and file cabinets. Goodman opened a door for me. "Head on in. I'm waiting on two more, then we'll start. Help yourself to refreshments."

Goodman let the door close behind me. The room was lit with bright fluorescents that disagreed with my eyes. There were three folding tables lined up like a cafeteria with folding chairs behind them. Against one wall was another table with the meager refreshments Goodman had mentioned. At the front of the class was a fifth table with an open laptop, a black duffel bag, and a stack of blue folders with the ACI corporate logo on them—an eagle's head in silhouette with two golden spears behind it in an X, like a patriotic skull and crossbones. On the wall behind the table was a roll-down projection screen.

There were two other students. One was a white woman in her fifties with a haggard face and dyed-red hair. She wore a button-up shirt with the Dollywood logo on the breast pocket. The other was a gangly Latino boy who looked just shy of twenty. His arms were sleeved in cheap, blurry tattoos, with another on his neck. To my surprise, he gave me a friendly smile, and the woman didn't. I poured myself coffee in a Styrofoam cup, noticing the plastic buckets lined up by the bottled waters. I sat at the front table, diagonally across from the woman, with the young man behind me.

"How's it goin', dude?" he said. "Yo, I'm Ricki."

I shook his hand and introduced myself.

"Ever work in a prison before?" he asked.

"Nah. How 'bout you?"

He shook his head. "Naw, man. This'll actually be my first job on the books." He gestured to the woman. "That's Beverly. Says she's done this gig before."

I turned to her. "That right?"

Beverly nodded. "Yeah. Not here though."

"You transferring?"

"No," she said in a rusty voice, "I used to work at Douglas but left when things got bad. I've been workin' at a donut shop a while, but they went under, so here I am."

I recalled the Douglas riot being in the news. A small race war had broken out in the yard, resulting in a SWAT team being deployed. Picturing this older woman caught in the middle of a men's prison disturbance made me shift uncomfortably in my chair.

"This won't be all like that shit," Ricki said. "This here's just a prison for chicks. It's cake."

Beverly didn't say anything, but her lips drew tight as she looked away. Clearly, she didn't share Ricki's opinion.

I wanted to ask her more about her experience as a corrections officer, but Ricki just kept on talking.

"My aunt did six months in a women's prison in Albuquerque. Said it was like being at summer camp." He snickered. "You see that show *Orange is the New Black*?"

"Not much," I told him. "My wife used to like it, but I never really checked it out."

I reminded myself to stop calling Karmen my *wife* now that she was well on her way to being my *ex-wife*. It would be best not to talk about her at all.

"That show," Ricki said. "It's like a lesbo soap opera. Showed a women's prison for what it is, man. It's like a resort for these bitches. They just make out and have parties all day."

Now Beverly spoke up. "That's not accurate, and neither is that show."

Ricki smirked. "Oh yeah? Like how?"

"Well, just look at the kitchen situation on it. It's totally unsafe, what with the inmates having easy access to knives 'n stuff. And ain't no cook can just decide to starve somebody. Inmates don't have that kind of power. And the guards are *way* too nice. You can't be like that. The place isn't overcrowded either. Real pens are *always* overcrowded. And trans women are almost never put in a female prison. Oh, and my favorite—that one girl ratted out the main character to the Feds, and yet they're put in the same prison, on the same unit? That's just not safe. It would never happen."

"But that shit's based on a true story," Ricki said.

"I can guarantee you that part ain't. No informant is gonna be put on the same unit as the person they ratted out. It'd be putting a target on her back."

I nodded. "Makes sense to me."

"Okay," Ricki said. "But women's prisons are still pretty chill."

"Not this one, kid." Beverly gave him a side-eyed glance and shook her head. "Not this one."

The door came open. In walked a Black man and a white woman, followed by Burt Goodman. The recruits looked fresh out of high school to me, but at my age, anyone under thirty does. The woman was exceptionally petite, maybe four-foot nine, one hundred pounds. They found seats. Goodman bent over his laptop to open a PowerPoint presentation. He lit up blue, then stepped out of the way so the rolldown screen behind him revealed the American Corrections Industries logo.

"Good morning, cadets," Goodman said.

We mumbled a collective "good morning."

"And welcome to your new opportunities at Norrington Women's Correctional Facility. Today we'll be going through the preliminaries and doing a little—" Goodman stopped short, face hardening, and pointed at the young brunette as she fiddled with her phone. "Excuse me."

"Sorry, one sec."

"You want to text, go home."

The brunette looked up, paling when she saw Goodman's hard expression. "Oh. I'm so sorry." She put the phone face-down on the table. "Sorry. It was important."

"Cadet Sloane," he said. "When you're working in this facility, you are a corrections officer whether you're around inmates or not. You'll be expected to act as such at all times."

"Yes, sir. I'm sorry, I—"

"You can't be distracted. Distracted will get you and your fellow COs hurt or even killed."

Realizing her apologies weren't getting her anywhere, Ileana Sloane merely nodded, embarrassed to be called out on her very first day. She was a mousy woman with large eyes and teeth, her hair back in a ponytail. A hoodie too big for her hung upon her skinny frame like a blanket, and the bottoms of her jeans were frayed where her Converse stepped on the backs of the legs.

Behind me, Ricki snickered quietly at the uncomfortable scene.

"I suggest you *all* pay attention," Goodman said. "People seem to think ACI will just let anyone work here, that all you need is a driver's license and a pulse. But at the end of your three-week training, there will be a test. You fail, your employment contract is void. So, is everyone ready now?"

The room made a small grunt of agreement.

Goodman handed out the folders one by one. Inside were information packets, a rule book, and a pen. He began going through much of what the HR person had told me on the phone, all the basics of working in a prison that should be obvious to anyone. Then he got into some of the more interesting rules.

"Do any of you have family or friends incarcerated here?" he asked.

No one replied.

"If you do, you must report it. If one comes in down the road, you must report it. Even if it's someone you haven't seen since grade school, we need to know. Do any of you have relatives or friends incarcerated elsewhere?"

Ricki, Beverly, and the young Black guy raised their hands.

"Any in women's prisons?" Goodman asked.

The hands went down.

"Okay. We're gonna go over some of the differences between men's and women's prisons, which are many. In this country, there are over four thousand corrections facilities, but only about a hundred and seventy are for females." He changed the image behind him to the next slide, showing the statistics. "The main difference is the level of security. As you may have noticed, we don't have guard towers or a Great Wall of China here at Norrington. Most women's prisons are separated by dormitories or cottages rather than cell blocks. Because women's prisons are less violent than men's, the inmates tend to have more freedom."

Behind me, Ricki whispered. "Told ya."

"For the most part," Goodman went on, "Norrington fits this mold, but there are some differences you need to know about before we take your employment process any further." He straightened tall to emphasize the seriousness of the subject. "This is a high security women's correctional facility. Most ladies who find themselves behind bars are incarcerated because of non-violent crimes—usually drugs and theft, property offenses and the like. Norrington houses such inmates, but we also house the largest population of violent female offenders in the country. These women are here for murder and manslaughter, assault with deadly weapons, aggravated battery, sexual assaults, child abuse, and every other nasty thing you can imagine. We have lifers beyond rehabilitation; killers who will proudly tell you they live just to kill again; women who've murdered their own babies. The worst ones are delegated to a segregation unit called Sparrow."

He changed to the next slide, which showed a cell block unit.

"These inmates are kept in cells, not dorms. They don't get to wander around like the others. Some are aggressive. Many are mentally ill. I'm telling you this because a lot of cadets think working at a women's prison instead of a man's will be safe, easy work. I can assure you that's not the case at Norrington. Not in Sparrow unit, and not on cell block Raven."

"Are those the units we'll be in?" Ileana asked.

"You'll all work all units, eventually. If any of you are hesitant to be in this kind of environment, I suggest you bow out now."

He scanned the classroom for quitters. Judging by her meek expression, I expected Ileana to stand up and tell Goodman this job wasn't for her after all. But she didn't. No one did. It seemed we all needed this job, no matter the risk it posed.

"Alright then," Goodman continued. "Here are some hard rules for you from the ACA's Code of Ethics. Number one—do *not* have sex with the inmates."

Ricki snickered, but again Goodman didn't hear him.

"Anyone caught in a sexual relationship with an inmate faces serious consequences," Goodman said. "You will certainly lose your job and can be fined up to ten thousand dollars and sentenced to a year's hard labor, if not something more severe."

Ricki sighed, disappointed. "Shit… for real?"

This time Goodman heard him. He lumbered toward Ricki, and I was caught between the two men. Goodman's face was like a dynamited mine.

"Oh, I'm sorry," he said to Ricki. "Is that a letdown for you, Gonzales?"

I could hear Ricki swallow. "Uh, nah, man. I was just jokin'."

"Sex with an inmate is no joke. It's a *felony*. After the passing of the Prison Rape Elimination Act, the law now clearly states that inmates cannot give consent. Under certain conditions, a guard that has sex with an inmate may be seen as a predator and will have to register as a sex offender. Most will find themselves on the other side of those prison bars. I suggest you remember that."

He stared Ricki down, then returned to the slideshow. The image of a cartoon hamburger came up with a red bar through it like the *Ghostbusters* logo.

"Do not eat food given to inmates," Goodman said. "This is also a hard rule. It's for everyone's safety."

I wondered what guard would be stupid enough to eat a burger an inmate handed them, then realized it must have happened enough times if there was a warning about it on day one.

"Do not sell any items to inmates, even simple things like a notepad or lipstick. Do not buy anything from them. Do not fraternize or pick sides. Refrain at all times from becoming involved in the personal lives of an inmate or their family. Your job is to create a safe environment, not make friends. Prisoners will *never* see COs as equals, and frankly, you shouldn't want them to. It'll just make your life harder. Trust me, I've seen this play out enough times to know. A personal relationship between a CO and an inmate always ends badly."

I wondered if I should start taking notes, which seemed odd given the commonsense nature of the information. I played with my pen but didn't jot anything down. Neither did anyone else as Goodman went on, giving more examples of unethical behavior before getting down to employee relations.

"The job does not offer holidays off or extra holiday pay," he said. "After ninety days, you'll qualify for vacation and benefits, but there is no sick time."

"Can you use your vacation time if you get sick?" Ileana asked.

"You can, but it's discouraged. On a nice day, people suddenly decide they'd rather go fishing than come to work. Calling out of a prison job isn't like calling out of a shift at Wal-Mart. Here, being short-staffed creates danger. When I was a CO, I never once called out, even if I had the flu. I had *perfect* attendance."

The measure of pride Goodman took in this made me exhale a long breath. The man was a corporate stooge. It would be wise for me to remember that, for such lizards cannot be trusted. That he was in HR was a dark comedy.

"Shifts are twelve hours long with a half hour unpaid lunch," Goodman said. "The job also comes with regular mandatory overtime."

I could almost feel the classroom's collective flinch. Coming from retail and warehouses, I was sadly used to long hours on my feet, and frequent call-outs that caused me to work double shifts.

"Mental health is an important factor too," Goodman said. "Prison work can be very stressful. In your binders, you'll find fridge magnets with a help line number. All calls are confidential. You get three counseling sessions for free each year. ACI suggests you use them if you're feeling depressed or develop relationship problems at home. Don't wait until you're suicidal to get help."

The threat of violence from prisoners didn't worry me so much, but the mention of an increased risk of depression and suicide did. I needed this job because I'd lost my last one after a mental health crisis that resulted in my wife of nine years abandoning me. I say *abandoned* rather than *left*, because she decided we needed to separate right after I had my breakdown. I managed to recover from that breakdown, but the depression and shame set in soon after, and Karmen declared it all to be "more than she signed up for."

Sometimes the biggest lie anyone ever tells you is at the altar when they say, "I do."

"Now I'm gonna play you a video," Goodman said.

He clicked the laptop, then turned off the lights to create a darkened theater. I was reminded of my school days, back when slideshows were put up on projectors and teachers played movies when they just couldn't take another day of dealing with obnoxious kids.

After the ACI logo, a Muzak tune carried through a transition to a white-haired man in a drab suit and tie. He looked like Jack Lemmon. The company logo was on the wall behind him, and on either side was a flag on a pole— one the American flag, the other the state flag of Arizona.

"Hello, cadets," he said. "My name is Fred Meredith, and I am the proud president of American Corrections Industries. I am delighted to welcome you fresh faces to your exciting new positions within our dynamic corporation. Becoming a corrections officer is a great opportunity for you and your families."

That he said this right after Goodman warned us about the job's mental health woes made me stifle a bitter laugh.

The president went on, sugaring up the dog turd.

"I was once a corrections officer myself. I rose up to Warden in just five years, and now I'm the head of one of the fastest growing private correctional institutes in the world. ACI operates facilities for men and women all across the country, as well as juvenile detention centers in the southwest. I went from making less than forty grand a year to now bringing in a seven-figure salary." He pointed at the camera and smiled with bleached teeth. "Each of you has the potential to do the same. Sound incredible? Well, just look at me. I'm living proof that a dream of success can become reality here at ACI, and it all starts with you." Again, he pointed through the screen at us, at *me*. I felt like I was watching an Amway commercial. "We at ACI are more than a company—we're a family."

I seethed internally. I'd worked retail long enough to know the biggest line of bullshit a company gives its employees is the *"we're family"* lie. My hesitations about the job continued to rise, but I didn't walk out. Instead, I sat through this sleazy businessman's patronizing pep talk.

"Each of you are just as important here as I am," Meredith said, "because each of you comes to us with your own unique experiences and ideas. Together, we can continue to grow our company and build upon our reputation as the finest correctional institute the world has ever seen, maintaining safe, rehabilitating, productive prison environments for our fellow Americans."

I almost expected some inspiring tune to play, maybe "Pomp and Circumstance" or the national anthem. I glanced around the room, seeing lifeless faces, slumped shoulders, and fidgeting fingers. The others weren't fooled by the propaganda either. Beverly, a former corrections officer, seemed particularly insulted. When the video was over, Goodman turned the lights back on and I stirred in my seat, struggling to still appear interested.

"In the back of your binder, you'll find a waiver," Goodman said.

We cadets shuffled through our paperwork. When I found the waiver and started reading it, a chill went through me.

"Aw shit," Ricki said as he read his.

"You must understand," Goodman explained. "At any prison, there is always the risk of riot. COs are not issued pistols or batons because an inmate can potentially get their hands on them. You're only given an OC chemical spray, a vest, and your lifeline radio. Most of the time, you won't need a weapon. But when there's a serious disturbance..." He reached into the duffle bag and drew out what appeared to be a small rocket launcher, then placed a canister at the front of the table. "... we use these to restore order."

"Tear gas," Beverly said.

"Precisely. As COs, you'll need to know what tear gas is like." Goodman eyed us one by one. "Today you'll be sprayed with this canister."

The young Black man raised his hand. "Hold up, man. I have asthma."

"This is part of the hiring process, Mr. Smith."

"But you said we wouldn't be havin' no weapons anyway, 'cause an inmate could grab it and take it away from us."

"*You* won't have the tear gas. At least not while you're a rookie CO. We have special teams for that."

"So what we gotta do this for then?"

"Signing the waiver to be tear gassed is mandatory."

Smith crossed his arms. "I said I have asthma, man."

"I heard you. Did you hear me? This is a requirement. If you don't want to submit to be tear gassed, fine, but your training ends here."

Goodman and Smith stared at one another like a showdown in an old western movie. Smith stood, the chair moving back with a screech.

"This shit ain't for me," Smith said, waving Goodman away. "Y'all must be crazy."

Goodman pursed his lips as Smith rounded the table and headed for the door. When he was gone, Goodman returned his attention to us.

"Anyone else want to bow out?" he asked. "If so, do it now."

I gazed down at the waiver, tapping the tip of my pen near the *sign here* sticker. Glancing at the others, I saw Beverly signing hers. Ileana looked even paler than when Goodman had scolded her for being on her phone.

"This shit is whack," Ricki whispered. "You gonna sign it, bro?"

His desire for comradery exposed his fear.

"Unfortunately, I need this job," I told him.

I shrugged and signed my name.

We stood in a clearing on the opposite side of the fence from the empty exercise yard. I spotted a rustic, red barn at the rear of the property, the shadows of horses passing across the cracks between the boards. Ravens hopped about the roof in a black cluster. Similarly, Goodman had his cadets stand shoulder to shoulder like infantrymen. Beverly was on my left, Ricki on my right, with Ileana beside the more experienced woman. I wondered why Beverly even needed to do this. As a former CO, hadn't she gone through the tear gas treatment before? Wouldn't she already know what it was like? She made no mention of it and offered no objections.

Goodman paced before us. "Tear gas actually isn't a gas at all. It's aerosolized crystals that bind to moisture, going for the eyes, skin, mouth, and throat, and then entering your lungs. Your body reacts to it hysterically, producing tears and mucus. The panic is worse than the pain. It's enough to completely incapacitate you."

I looked to Beverly, hoping she'd have some tips for handling this, but the woman was silent. She stared at the ground. That she was bracing herself made me even more nervous.

"The trick is to not panic," Goodman said. "You must fight that urge. Do not run away. Normally, you should, but I need you to experience this. Stay on your spot until the fog dissipates. I repeat—*do not run away*."

For the first time since class had begun, I saw the hint of a smile on Goodman's face. He was going to enjoy this. Stepping back, he secured a gas mask over his head. Sweat built at the small of my back, a drop rolling past my ear. I wiped it away because it only meant more moisture for the gas to react to. Goodman raised the launcher like some discount Rambo, and the canister landed at our feet, a huge plume of white engulfing us. Instantly, my throat felt full of rusty razors. My eyes poured and suddenly I couldn't open them. I drooled all over myself, snot gushing from my nostrils. Every inch of skin felt rug-burned, and even though I knew the source of my agony, I became confused and disoriented.

You deserve this, I thought. *You deserve pain.*

Goodman told someone not to run away but I wasn't sure if he meant me or one of the others. I was aware of my stumbling, but believed I'd stayed in the same spot. Ileana sobbed. Ricki cursed. When I managed to blink, I saw Beverly had taken a knee.

I'd had my share of physical pain, including small acts of violence against me, but I'd never been attacked with a chemical weapon before. I would have preferred it to stay that way. When at last the fog cleared, Goodman congratulated us. I half expected him to shoot us with another canister as some sort of cruel test, but the punishment was over for the day. Beverly actually chuckled as she rose to her feet. Ricki was still cursing. Like me, Ileana was just regaining her composure. Goodman guided us back inside where we each grabbed bottles of water and flushed our eyes out over the plastic buckets. I rinsed my mouth and spit several times, Goodman reminding us not to swallow. The cadets shared a box of Kleenex, blowing our noses free of jalapeno-hot mucus. The agony slowly receded into a lesser, nagging pain.

"That's all for today," Goodman said. "Once your eyes adjust, go home and shower and wash those clothes. Great job everyone. Hope to see you all back tomorrow at nine."

His words suggested some of us would bail out before then. It was a fair assumption. I was certainly beginning to question what the fuck I was doing here. The rent needed to be paid, and groceries weren't free, but was being tear gassed for minimum wage really where I was at in life? I was middle-aged, on the verge of divorce, with no family or resources. "Solitary man" didn't even begin to describe the loner I'd become. All I had was a dog, an old Ford Ranger, and a beat-up house I rented in a land just a desolate as I was. If I didn't find work, I stood to lose even that.

As we walked through the parking lot, Ricki vented his frustration. "This is some bullshit, bro. That motherfucka be trippin'."

"He's just doing his job," Beverly said.

Ileana's eyes were cherries. "Never thought I'd be blasted with tear gas for a living. Guess I should've stayed in school."

"Man," Ricki said, "this job is whack. If my uncle wasn't doin' time, I'd still be workin' for him. 'Stead I gotta do this prison bullshit, gettin' mace in my face 'n shit."

"What'd your uncle do?" Ileana asked.

"He's a contractor. I done helped him work on houses."

"No, I mean why's he is prison?"

Ricki's eyebrows drew closer together. "Why ya gotta be askin' me that, girl? Ain't yo bid'ness."

"Sorry," she said, turning her head away. "I didn't mean to be rude."

Beverly glanced at Ileana as she unlocked her car. "It's sure considered rude by inmates to ask what they're in for. But hey, they're all innocent, right?"

Ileana smiled. "Well, it was nice meeting y'all. Plan on coming back tomorrow?"

"Shit," Ricki said, "I dunno now."

"You already took the tear gas," I said. "Be a shame for that to have been for nothing."

"Yeah," Ileana said. "The worst is over with."

Beverly chuckled as she got in her car. "You keep thinkin' that."

Ricki and Ileana didn't seem to catch what she meant, but I did. The worst was hardly over. How could it be when we hadn't even set foot inside the prison yet?

CHAPTER TWO

Now that I'd taken the required drug test, the sobriety I'd been practicing while seeking employment could come to an end. It'd been weeks since I'd taken an edible, relying solely on alcohol to get me through the nights. Marijuana was legal in Arizona, but that didn't mean employers couldn't discriminate against you if you tested positive for it. Though not what you'd call a pothead, I often partook in a little weed for rest and relaxation, particularly after my mental collapse. I was completely anti-social whenever getting stoned for fear of anxiety attacks and paranoia, but given my self-imposed isolation, this was never a problem. After a day of mind-numbing orientation and a dose of tear gas, a bit of THC was my way to unwind, so I took the pill and plopped my ass into the worn recliner, waiting for the leftover pizza to reheat. Meanwhile, Charlie was slurping up wet, organic dog food, eating better than I was.

Norrington was still on my mind, particularly the potential danger it posed to my mental state. Googling, I discovered some worrisome facts about being a prison guard. According to multiple studies, corrections officers suffered higher rates of PTSD than soldiers returning from Afghanistan and Iraq, and were more than twice as likely to commit suicide than the average American.

Suicide…

Stress-related burnout and a significantly shorter life span were some of the additional benefits I could look forward to. But for me, burnout was inevitable, wasn't it? And was a shorter life such a bad thing?

Suicide…

Life saves the worst for last. Your final years are the ones where you can't walk or control your bodily functions. That is the cruel punchline of being clinically depressed— though you already felt like life was unbearable, it was better than it would ever be again.

Suicide…

After a long drink at his water dish, Charlie came over, slobbering on the arm of the chair. I scratched behind his ear, and he turned his head into it, my boy having the unique ability to make me smile.

"They say your dad is crazy," I told him. "Must be if I'm willing to take this fuckin' job."

But the money Karmen and I had split from selling the house wouldn't last forever. Healthcare alone was enough to drain my bank account in a short period of time. I was physically healthy, but that could change at any moment, and my dog had regular vet visits just as expensive as bills for human doctors. Charlie was going on twelve, which was old for any dog breed but considered the finish line for Labrador Retrievers. Karmen and I adopted him when he was just a puppy, back before we were married. He was special to both of us, but while Karmen adored him, she didn't spend time with Charlie the way I did. I was the one who trained Charlie and took him hiking and wrestled with him. Karmen mostly petted him and gave him treats, loving him in her own passive way whereas I bonded with him actively. When she announced she was leaving me, she didn't try to take Charlie with her, saying she could never pry us apart. Frankly, I thought she just wanted her new start to have less responsibility. She didn't want residuals of her former life to haunt her—no reminders of me. But her motivation didn't really matter. What mattered was I got to keep my dog without an argument.

"Not a whole lot of options out there," I told Charlie now. "Not for an old man like me. There's no way I'm going back to retail or any other job in the service industry."

Charlie snorted in agreement, then did a few circles before lying down. I wondered if he thought about Karmen as much as I did, then scolded myself for thinking of her again. My mind was like some diseased carousel with my ex riding around on one of its broken horses.

I ate my miserable pizza while standing in the kitchen, staring out the window at the dull, beige grassland. The sun was setting in a sky of fire, an unkindness of ravens throwing spindly shadows across the yard. The waist-high chain-link fence shuddered in the breeze.

I watched the night come.

The edible kicked in but failed to lift my spirits.

Now I was just stoned and sad.

Everyone returned the next morning, and Goodman surprised us by starting our day with a written test.

"Don't get nervous," he said. "This isn't your big exam. That won't be for a few more weeks, remember?"

He'd gone over so much yesterday, carousing through much of it. I couldn't recall when he'd said our exam would be, but also didn't know what this test sheet was about. I'd already done an exam for my general mental acuity, with basic math and writing skills, and taken the required physical. I read the large text on the top sheet.

ACI Personality Questionnaire.

"This test will help us better understand *you*," Goodman explained, "so we can better utilize you based on your strengths. We'll see if you're dutiful or analytical, if you're creative or rule-orientated. Some of you will be better at certain tasks than others, and we need to know that. But there are no right or wrong answers. Just answer honestly."

Ileana raised her hand. "But this, like, decides what department we work? Or, I mean, what unit?"

"Not exactly. It just gives us a better idea of the raw materials we'll be molding."

I thought of what I'd read online about how working in a prison environment can change your personality, that many guards become dominating or even sadistic. Unfortunately, it's human nature for us to become draconian bastards when we're given control over others.

"This test is also designed to flag any significant personality disorders or mental illness problems," Goodman said. "Anything that would clash with the nature of the job."

I bit my bottom lip. On my online application, there'd been a question that tripped me. It asked if I'd been held in a psychiatric ward against my will by order of the court within the past year. I could truthfully check "no" because no court had been involved in my time in the behavioral health center. But would this test expose me for the broken, tortured man I was, disqualifying me for a job no sane person would want in the first place?

I cringed reading question one: *Are you easily fazed?*

I scrolled through some of the others.

How long does it take you to calm down when you're angry?

Do you often feel overwhelmed?

Do you prefer working alone?

It was as if they'd designed the questions specifically to get me fired. They dangled before me like glittering fishing lures, mocking me, bullying me over my condition. Ricki snickered behind me, and I briefly thought he was laughing at me, that he somehow knew I was too cracked to pass the psyche test. But when I looked back at him, he was just smiling and shaking his head as he filled in his answers, amused. When I looked back, everyone else had started and Goodman was staring at me.

"No right or wrong answers, Donnelly," he said.

I got started because there was nothing else to do, trying my best to answer the way I thought a normal person would. *No, I'm not easily fazed. Of course not. I'm totally in control of my emotional reactions. And no, I don't want to work alone. Only a freak would want that kind of peace.* I noticed some of the questions were repeated, only phrased differently—a trick to see if you were consistent. It reminded me of something my father had always told me. *If you're gonna lie, make sure you stick to it*—a rare piece of good advice from the old man.

Though the test had over a hundred questions, they were mostly true or false, so it only took the class about fifteen minutes. Goodman gathered the papers but did not grade them right away as I'd hoped he would, even though I knew it wasn't that kind of test. If my answers disqualified me, I didn't want to waste any more time here than I already had. For all I knew, I was going to be pepper-sprayed today or maybe put in a chokehold as part of my training.

"We're gonna talk a little more about this prison and how it is run," Goodman said. "Norrington serves all superior courts in Arizona, and reports to the Department of Corrections as well as the American Correctional Association. We are staffed with a wide variety of COs that include unit floor officers, key officers, infirmary officers, captains and supervisors, front-gate and perimeter patrol, nurses, social workers, and animal handlers, among others. We house over twelve hundred prisoners, all female, most between the ages of twenty and sixty, with a small fistful of elderly inmates."

I noticed he hadn't mentioned the number of staff compared to the number of inmates. I didn't ask about it. The omission seemed deliberate.

"As I said yesterday," Goodman continued, "these women are the baddest of the bad. For female offenders, Norrington is the bottom line. Last stop. Many are lifers. Some are on death row."

"Whoa," Ricki said, impressed. "You *execute* people here?"

Goodman gave a hard nod. "Capital punishment is the max legal penalty in the state of Arizona."

"So there's, like, an electric chair up in this place?"

Goodman smirked. "No. Old Sparky is enjoying a well-earned retirement. Lethal injection is the standard MOD, and we don't do it at this facility. We only house the death row inmates."

Ileana stirred in her seat. "So, we won't have to... you know..."

"Be an executioner?" Goodman said with a chuckle. "No, no. Besides, that's not for rookies. That's something you graduate to."

A promotion, I thought. Something to aspire to—*The Reaper*.

Getting back on track, Goodman bored us with the prison's history, programming, drug treatments, inmate classes, and community services. I kept drifting in and out of focus, my attention span just as mutilated as any other American's, only it wasn't modern technology that had turned my brain to mush, but crippling despair. Karmen did some more laps on the ol' mental carousel, waving and smiling at me as she passed by, leaving me over and over. I gazed out the window at the sunny skies, thinking Charlie and I could both use a nature walk. I hoped this would be another short day so we could get one in before nightfall. Temperatures in the desert dropped significantly once the sun went down.

Some of what Goodman told us was interesting. Private prisons made their profits off housing inmates, bringing in about thirty-five dollars per day per resident. It made me wonder why the company would ever want to let someone free and if they worked harder to make sure prisoners were written up for infractions, which would chip away at any time cut for good behavior. Again, I didn't ask. Goodman wasn't the right person for such questions. But I thought I knew who might be able to answer them more honestly.

"You really know your stuff," I told Beverly during the lunch break.

She was sitting at a picnic table eating a cheese sandwich she'd brought in a paper bag. Bits of it had gathered in the corners of her mouth, and she was either oblivious or simply didn't care. I sat down across from her.

"I'm kinda nervous about this job," I said. "I was wondering if I could ask you a little about your experience."

"Okay," she said without really looking at me.

"Goodman has to make it all look a certain way. I was hoping you could tell me what it's really like."

She slurped her can of diet Dr. Pepper. "He ain't lyin', hon. He's just not tellin' the whole truth."

"And what's that?"

She gave me a sympathetic smile. "You'll do fine."

I appreciated the vote of confidence, but it wasn't what I was after. I leaned in, elbows on the table. "What's being a CO really like, Bev?"

She took another bite and breathed deep through her nose. Crumbs fell upon the same Dollywood shirt she'd worn the day before and she brushed them away. She looked even older in the natural light, hints of gray showing within the orange dye job, her hands spotted and veiny. Her eyes were so dark it was impossible to tell where the pupils ended and the irises began.

She spoke as if someone had just run over her favorite cat. "It's trying. It's very trying."

I almost asked why she would come back if that was the case, but decided it was better to just let her speak.

"It's dangerous in more ways than you first realize," she said. "It ain't just the inmates that can mess you up, it's the job itself. You drink?"

"Yeah."

"Right. Donnelly—*Irish*. Well, prepare to drink more, hon. Best thing you can do for yourself is to not take the job home with you, but that's easier said than done. You spend twelve hours a day in a hellhole… you can't just shut that off when you walk out the gate, and you sure can't tell your mind what to dream when you go to bed."

"That psych evaluation. Is that what it was really about?"

"Part of it, yeah. But Goodman's right. They wanna know where you'll fit in best. But you give that kinda test to a rookie and it ain't gonna be valid after a few weeks workin' as a CO. Take that test again in a month and it'll have a whole new outcome. Prison changes you, no matter what side of the bars you're on."

"How so?"

Beverly looked out across the empty yard, brushing her hair away when the wind fluttered it against her cheek.

"You know," she said, "when I first started at Douglas, I thought maybe I could make a difference in the lives of those men. I thought helping to rehabilitate cons so they could live a normal life on the outside again was gonna be a big part of the job. People gotta be punished for their crimes, sure, but they also gotta have a chance to start over once they pay their dues, right?"

I nodded. I remembered one of the questions from the psych test. *Are you passionate about social issues?*

"Yup," Beverly said. "When you first start out, you wanna have some sort of humanity as a CO. You think it's important to treat cons as people first. But unless you're real stupid, that attitude changes right quick. At the end of the day, all that's really important is you *never* back down. See, inmates mistake kindness for weakness. And you can't *never*

be seen as weak in the pen, whether you're a con or a CO."
She looked me up and down. "You're a big guy. Got some
muscle. But don't think for a second that'll be enough, hon."

"You're saying I have to be mean."

Beverly shook her head. "Not mean. *Strong. Firm.* If you
come in there too mean, you'll just make enemies. You really
don't want that, and don't get paid enough for it neither. You
could be signing your own death warrant if you play cop
with the cons on your unit. Besides, some of 'em are gonna
be helpful to you, like the orderlies and the cooks. A CO's
gotta find a balance 'tween not takin' any nonsense and not
steppin' on no toes."

"Sounds like a difficult game to play."

"And just when you think you got the hang of it,
somebody comes along and changes all the rules."

Now I was the one to take a deep breath. I looked to the
others. Ricki was talking on his phone and Ileana had her nose
buried in hers, texting or playing a game, maybe updating
social media with vague hints about her new profession.

"Think we'll all make it?" I asked Beverly.

"Oh, we'll all make it *in*. ACI don't let people fail their
final exams. If you can stand and walk, you can work here.
And you gotta try pretty damn hard to get fired."

"Really?" I asked, surprised.

"People ain't exactly lining up to be prison guards, and
half of rookies drop out in their first year. These places are
always short-staffed. It's one of the biggest problems private
prisons have."

"Maybe they should pay more."

"They *definitely* should. But those decisions are made in
the ivory towers, not down here by the wardens. You know,

at the public prisons, the starting pay is a good deal higher than what ACI pays. Around sixteen an hour. And if you go to police academy for training, you get an extra five hundred *per month.* Plus, you get an extra two hundred when you pass your quarterly physical. Of course, the corrections academy you gotta go through to qualify for the job is a lot tougher than this here ACI training. It's like a boot camp, with an instructor screamin' in your face, and marching and shotgun training—the whole bit. I had to do that crap for eight weeks. This here training is a breeze by comparison. That's one of the reasons ACI don't pay us as much or give those bonus incentives, 'cause the job don't ask as much from applicants. That's why COs are always finding their own incentives, and why ACI is always short-staffed." She nodded toward Ricki and Ileana. "Them two'll get in, but that don't mean they'll last, at least not on the up and up. I don't even worry tellin' you this. Goodman knows it and would probably tell you the same thing."

"What do you mean?"

"There's four of us here, hon. At least two will end up dirty."

I swallowed hard. "You sayin' that based on us or statistics?"

"Just speakin' from experience. Half of cadets become dirty COs."

I wanted to ask if she'd gone dirty but chose to word it differently. "Is that why you left Douglas?"

She crushed the empty soda can. "Nah."

Silence lingered between us. Beverly had said all she intended to.

As if he were a football coach, Burt Goodman came out of the classroom and gave a two-fingers-in-the-mouth whistle, and we cadets filed back inside to continue our education.

Though the day involved no tear gas, the lessons were torturous enough, Goodman going on and on about details that seem unimportant—the chain of command; the checklists; the color codes and filing systems. He only kept our attention through keeping us anxious, randomly calling on us to answer questions, seeing if we'd been listening. We cadets were mentally exhausted by the end of it and barely said goodbye to each other because we were too eager to get away from the place. I considered asking Beverly if I could buy her a drink so we could talk some more about her experiences in the prison system, but I didn't want the leathery crone to think I was hitting on her. This made me consider asking Ileana out for a drink sometime with the prefix of talking about class. Though not conventionally attractive, Ileana wasn't ugly either, and despite the libido-killing side effects of my antidepressants I still maintained an appetite for physical contact with a woman, particularly after being affection-starved by Karmen for so long. But there was a wide variety of reasons I would never dare to proposition Ileana.

For one thing, I lacked confidence; at least with dating. I'd never been shy when it came to asking women out, but I hadn't been single in almost a decade, and knew I would be rusty and awkward. I also knew I couldn't keep my mask of normalcy up for long, that eventually the real me would poke through the fragile façade in an emotional drone strike that would obliterate what meager relationship had been built. Even just being in a bar for that first drink would take enormous effort, especially after the social exhaustion of being in a classroom all day.

For another thing, I was older than her. Ileana looked to be in her early twenties, whereas I was halfway to fifty. I could be her dad. It pained me to realize I was closer to Beverly's age than Ileana's. It didn't seem possible I'd grown as old as I was. Pursuing Ileana would have made me a stereotypical divorced guy, the poster boy for the male midlife crisis. And she only would've laughed at me. If she were into older men, she'd probably only date ones with money. Even if by some miracle she was actually into me, that would only make things worse, because while she didn't know the huge mistake she'd be making, I did, and I wouldn't want to subject her to the unavoidable poison that came with loving me.

That's the problem with dating young women. They still have hope. They still believe in Prince Charming and true love and happy endings.

I wasn't a bad looking guy. While no athlete or gym rat, I was in better shape than most men my age. I had no fashion sense whatsoever but cleaned up nicely when I wanted to. But my mind was a black tornado of trauma and suicide ideation, and no matter how hard I tried, what whirled within me always came out of my stupid mouth, eventually.

If I'd never shared my dark thoughts with Karmen, I might've still had a wife. If I could somehow keep women from knowing who I really was—telling them what I thought they wanted to hear, like I had with the psyche evaluation—I might be able to maintain a relationship. It would be built upon a lie, but wasn't a lie that offered human tenderness preferable to a bitter truth that offered nothing but sad days and lonely nights?

If I wanted to find out, I would first have to learn to keep my "normal guy" costume on. Perhaps becoming a corrections officer would assist me in that. The job required vigilance and tenacity. Most of all, it required confidence. If I were to have any chance at not appearing weak, I would have to swallow all my feelings of self-hatred, self-doubt, and self-pity. Maybe the inmates weren't the only ones who could be rehabilitated by a prison environment. Perhaps my time at Norrington would prepare me for dealing with the everyday world, a place that I, in many ways, no longer understood.

It would certainly give me plenty of practice talking to women.

CHAPTER THREE

My first day on the job, I was paired with a short, square-jawed young man with hard eyes. He wore a uniform one size too small, to extenuate his muscles, and a ski cap with the ACI logo at the front. He introduced himself as *Officer* Anthony Nelson, immediately striking me as the sort of guy who never smiled, afraid he might not appear macho enough if he did. Considering he was ordered to teach me, I was surprised to learn he'd only been a CO for four months. Beverly hadn't exaggerated when it came to turnover.

Before my first day on the grounds, I got a high-and-tight haircut but kept my beard. I'd started growing it after Karmen left and it represented a new chapter in my life. Putting on my uniform was sobering. My own reflection intimidated me. It cemented the reality of what I was doing with a sort of grim finality. Putting on the protective vest felt like dressing up in a Halloween costume, like I was a fake, an imposter. A "lifeline" radio was pinned to my shoulder, and my utility belt included cuffs, flashlight, OC chemical spray, and keys.

I felt like fucking Batman.

When I first stepped into Hummingbird unit, I lowered my brow in an attempt to look sterner to the awaiting inmates. My nerves mocked me, filling my gut not with butterflies but with enraged hornets.

With the opening of a door, I was suddenly immersed in a tier of inmates.

There must have been close to seventy of them—women of all ages, races, and sizes. Because of where the prison was located, many were Mexican, and there was a larger percentage of Native American inmates than the national average.

It was a dormitory-style unit with bunk beds in a communal living space, with a few mattresses on the floor. White concrete walls bore hotline numbers stamped in bold text. These were free lines to report sexual assault, and the word *"RAPE"* stood out like an assault all its own. The inmates went without shackles and were free to roam about the unit. They wore blue shirts and slacks, looking like nurses, with some just in their white undershirts. Given the number of them, I was surprised to not see any other guards besides Officer Anthony and myself.

"Rookie comin' through," a white woman with dreadlocks said. She grinned at me with meth-ruined teeth and clutched the rim of her pants.

A group of Latinas eyed me up and down, smirking and whispering. An old woman gazed up from the bible she was reading, looking over her glasses with dead eyes. Three women playing Uno stopped to size me up. Some of the inmates gave me lascivious looks while others offered only disdain.

"I smell fresh meat," someone in the back of the unit said.

A few ladies whistled from their bunks.

"Wellity, well, well," said another, drawing laughter from the others.

I wasn't sure how to react, so I said nothing. When the inmates stared at me, I stared back—long enough not to seem weak, but not so long as to seem hostile.

Balance, I thought. *You've got to find the balance.*

A Native American woman winked at me. "Hey there, rookie."

"Oh, yeah, yeah," a Mexican said to her friends, "*él es lindo.*"

A man being catcalled by women is an experience usually reserved for rock stars and male strippers. While most women see getting catcalled as harassment, men tend to enjoy it. I figured the inmates did this with all rookie COs, but I still couldn't help but relish the attention. I restrained myself from smiling.

Officer Anthony shouted above the women's giggles. "Alright, ladies! Count!"

I held up my clipboard with the count sheet, a series of names and numbers designed as a checklist to make sure no inmates were missing. The women returned to their bunks, some quicker than others, all glowering at Officer Anthony. Clearly, he hadn't made any friends during his four months at Norrington. He walked briskly and I had to pick up my pace to keep up with him. His chest puffed out, nostrils flaring, stick firmly up his ass.

"Robocop says it's count time," a heavyset Black woman said.

"This is some bullshit," said another inmate. "Why we's gotta stop and do a count now?"

Officer Anthony pointed at her. "Any more language out of you and I'm writing you up."

She pursed her lips. "Man…"

"It's a little early for this," Officer Anthony told me. "That's why they're pissy. But a proper count is the first thing you want to learn as a corrections officer. It might just be the most important."

To me, it seemed more appropriate for a cell unit than a dorm, but I did as I was told, as did the inmates. I walked down the rows, comparing the numbers on my sheet to the ones stamped on the bunks. The inmates also had to participate in the process.

"Hernandez," I said, looking at the short but athletic-looking inmate in the first bunk. "Number?"

She repeated her surname and gave me her number. I put a check on the sheet and went on, repeating the tedious task up and down each row. *Campbell, Brown, Lopez, Kindly, Anderson, Rivera, Gutierrez, Richardson, Castillo, Branham.* At least this introduced me to the inmates one at a time. The dorm's maximum occupancy was fifty, but it housed sixty-six inmates. Some seemed like they absolutely belonged here— rough and tumble mares that looked as if they'd been born in prison. They had face tattoos, missing teeth, scars, cornrows, pockmarks, and shaved heads. Others looked like any woman you'd meet on the outside, with plain features and practical hairstyles. Some were feminine, others barely resembled the fairer sex at all. Some were only eighteen. Others could have been grandmothers.

"Don't let the dormitory style fool you," Officer Anthony told me when the count was through. "Hummingbird is still a medium level unit. We've got some real agitators here."

I nodded.

"They hoot and whistle at you like that," he said, "you can write 'em up."

"Oh. Okay."

"It might give you a little thrill when they do that—'specially the cute ones—but it's disrespectful. A CO must command respect at all times." He put his hands on his hips, flexing a little. "Some of these women have been locked up longer than I've been alive. But even the ones who've only been here a few months are thirsty, know what I mean?"

"Yeah. Makes sense."

"But they don't always catcall you 'cause they like you. Just remember, they're in here for a reason. They're always sizing you up, trying to find ways to manipulate you. You can't trust 'em. Not a single one."

I knew Officer Anthony was right, but so far, the one person I didn't trust was him. The young man took himself way too seriously, building his ego based upon the power he held over others. I'd always disliked people like that. They believe they're alphas but the respect they receive isn't based on anything they've earned, but rather by a system they're employed by. They're not brave or masculine. They're small, petty, insecure boys, bullying to hide their own emotional handicaps.

At the rear of the unit stood a booth on a control platform with a barrier of bulletproof glass, just big enough for Officer Anthony and me. He referred to it as the "command post". Here we did paperwork and monitored the unit, hitting buttons when other COs needed a door opened, and using the microphone to order the inmates around if they got too rowdy or wandered off.

"They get too much freedom," Officer Anthony said. "If it were up to me, they'd all be in seg on Sparrow, or at least in cells like up on Raven."

"You work those units yet?"

"Yeah. We get re-stationed on the reg. We gotta go wherever we're needed."

"You seem very dedicated."

"Just doin' my job," he said, puffing out his chest. "I always knew I wanted to be in law enforcement."

"So how is it on Sparrow?" I asked, not wanting him to elaborate on his fascist aspirations. "Is it as bad as they say?"

He shifted his jaw. "Sparrow's a bunch of animals. You can't take *any* shit from the inmates they got up in there. Same with Raven. You let one of 'em push you just once, and they'll *all* eat you up. I think that's why the warden likes to put me there, 'cause he knows I don't let *anything* slide."

An inmate made strange gesticulations and Officer Anthony tensed, leaning toward the microphone, but she quickly settled down, paying him no mind as she talked with her friends.

"So, what do you do when you're not here?" I asked.

"You mean, like, on my free time?"

"Yeah."

"Not much. Hit the gym. Play *Fortnite* and *Call of Duty*. Go on Tinder dates."

I wondered how long he'd been out of high school. The number of young COs astonished me. Most of the people working at Norrington who were over thirty were lieutenants or supervisors or had non-CO roles.

"Tinder dates, huh?" I asked. "I've never done online dating. Maybe I should look into it."

"It's a good idea to see girls on the outside," Officer Anthony said. "You ain't careful, this job can make you hate women."

Officer Anthony had been working the morning shift, so when he left, I was paired with the second shift CO, Tanner Wyatt. He was in his late twenties and totally jacked, his football player build compensating for his face. Tanner looked like he was always taking a particularly smelly shit, his hair perpetually being blown to the left by a non-existent wind. He breathed through his mouth as we entered Hummingbird to start the shake downs. This was standard daily procedure. The COs looked through the inmates' bunks and cells and sifted through their belongings, searching for contraband.

"The warden expects you to make busts," Tanner told me. "If you don't, he'll think you're not being thorough enough in your shake downs, or that you just don't give a shit."

We put on latex gloves. Tanner advised me to go from one end of each bunk's area to another, so not to repeat myself. He worked alongside me as we opened totes and undid bedspreads, and each inmate stood and watched us as we rooted through their belongings.

Tanner led me to the bunk of inmate Sally Kindly, a comical surname for the forty-something white woman covered in black tattoos of skeletons and other scenes of horror, with a set of devil horns inked onto her forehead.

Her earlobes had holes large enough to put a finger through, the skin stretched out by the hoop earplugs she'd worn when she was a free woman. Tanner informed me that Kindly had a history of drug trafficking within prison walls and had only recently been moved off Raven after a stint for kicking a CO in the balls. She was one to watch.

"Don't y'all go makin' no mess in my house," Kindly said, hovering over me as I squatted by her tote.

"Take it easy, Sally," Tanner said, turning her pillow.

"Robocop always be throwin' my shit everywheres."

I'd learned "Robocop" was the entire unit's nickname for Officer Anthony.

"He dumps my shit out everywheres," Kindly said again. "Messed up my MP3 player last time. Don't need to be like that."

I sifted carefully, more to be cautious of anything that could cut or jab me than as a favor to Kindly, but I figured it wouldn't hurt to treat her like a human being.

"Robocop ain't got no manners," she said. "Then he wonder whys we ain't give him no respect. Yous gotta show respect if'n you wanna get it. Believe that, rookie."

"I believe it," I said.

Noticing I was putting things back where I found them, Tanner told me to just put them in a pile so not to get mixed up. When I placed a stack of letters to one side without really inspecting them, Tanner stopped me.

"Let's have a look at those," he said.

As he unfolded one, I noticed Kindly's demeanor change. She went silent, her lips drawn tight, eyes unblinking. Tanner held up one of the letters to the light.

"Here," he said, pointing at what appeared to be a small orange stain at the bottom.

He picked at it with his fingernails, revealing it was not one sheet of paper but two stuck together with adhesive. Inside the pouch was a shred of toilet paper, and when he unfurled it, a small orange square fell into his hand.

"That's a good amount of Suboxone, Sally," Tanner said to her.

Kindly immediately shook her head. "That ain't mine."

"Oh, yeah? Then whose is it?"

"I dunno but that shit ain't mine, boss."

"It's in your belongings."

"I dunno how it got there."

"You never do."

She stomped her foot. "I said that fuckin' shit ain't mine!"

Tanner stood. So did I. Kindly backed up, looking as if she were about to run though there was nowhere to flee to. The entire unit had fallen silent, everyone watching the scene unfold. It suddenly dawned on me just how outnumbered we were.

Tanner hit his radio, and for a moment I thought he was going to call for backup, but he only asked for a female officer to come down to do a strip search.

"This is some bullshit," Kindly said. "Y'all are framing me."

Tanner took her by the arm. Kindly tensed but didn't resist. She bit her bottom lip as if restraining herself from following the instinct to fight. Something told me she'd been fighting all her life.

"I'm taking her to be searched," Tanner told me. "Keep shaking her house down. I'll be back in a bit."

He escorted Kindly out of the unit, and for the first time I was alone with the inmates. The taunts began instantly. I tried to ignore them as I inspected Kindly's things.

"Uh oh," an inmate said, "Tanner left you all by your lonesome."

Giggles and whispers. Someone made kissing sounds. I held up a paper to the light, searching for more drugs. The next paper was a child's drawing reading "I miss U Mommy." That Kindly was somebody's mother gave me pause. In the drawing, a smiling stick figure girl held hands with a sticker figure woman with horns coming out of her head. It was drawn in pencil, for crayon drawings were not allowed. In training, Goodman informed the cadets that the wax in crayons could harbor narcotics. To get high, all an inmate had to do was lick the lines made by the crayons. The ingenuity that goes into prison drug trafficking is astonishing.

I didn't find any other contraband and wasn't sure I wanted to. It would appease my supervisors to make a bust but also turn the inmates against me on my very first day. Beverly had told me it was important to build a rapport with them. Kindly only had one strip of Suboxone. Just a single, personal dose to ease some of the pain of being incarcerated. I could sympathize. I didn't think it was right for her to lose privileges over something as small as that. Maybe force her into the prison rehab program, but don't punish her harshly. But I didn't make the rules and couldn't let the inmates think I'd break them.

I closed Kindly's tote. When I stood, Lilly Gutierrez was staring at me, grabbing her crotch and thrusting her pelvis in my direction.

She blew me a kiss. "Hey, Daddy."

Gutierrez was a curvy woman in her thirties with dark hair and olive skin. She had plump lips and devastating eyes, and she'd removed her smock, leaving her in a tank top that hugged her large breasts. I took a deep breath and forced myself to hold her gaze before looking away, not wanting to seem intimidated or interested although I was both.

"You got pretty eyes," she said in a thick Mexican accent. "You are, like, *beautiful*, but for a man."

"Handsome," another inmate said.

"Yeah, that's it. *Handsome*. You handsome, Daddy."

"C'mon, Gutierrez," I said. "You know you're not supposed to comment on a CO's appearance." Though I could write her up for it, I didn't threaten to. "Just settle down."

"I settle down for you, Daddy. I lay down like good girl."

The inmates hooted and laughed. I tried to focus on my shake downs, but they continued to make my job difficult, testing the new guy.

Campbell—the white girl with dreadlocks—drew closer to me, her finger between her green teeth. "You in our jungle now, cowboy."

Though I was twice her size, the inmate made me feel threatened. I noticed the litany of small scars on the insides of her arms—a cutter.

"Back to the day room, Inmate Campbell," I said firmly. I pointed to the commons area in the center of the dorm.

"Don't call me Campbell. That's my old man's name and he ain't nothin' but a dead asshole down in Hell. Everybody done calls me Cherry."

"How about this? You go to back to the day room, then I'll call you Cherry."

She huffed but backed away and sat backwards in one of the day room's chairs, still watching me.

"Thank you," I said.

I immediately scolded myself. *Why the hell did you say that?* Goodman told us to never thank an inmate for doing what you said. You were ordering them, not asking them. Thanking an inmate implied they'd done you a favor.

Don't be so fucking passive. Find the balance, Liam.

When Tanner returned, I couldn't help but sigh with relief. It didn't last long.

"Captain wants to see you," he said.

I gulped. Had Captain Clancy heard me say "thank you" through my radio?

Tanner took over the unit. Though he was younger and had a better body, the inmates didn't catcall him like they did me. They knew better. Tanner had been at Norrington over a year and understood the games inmates played. He didn't say what the captain wanted to see me about, and I didn't dare ask. I walked past the control center, down the hallway, and was buzzed in. Then I went to Captain Clancy's office. The door was partway open. I knocked.

"C'mon in, Donnelly."

He didn't sound angry. I entered. The office had the same white concrete walls as the rest of the prison. Clancy sat behind a mahogany desk, two organized bookcases behind him. There were several framed certificates bearing his name and a photo of his nuclear family. Clancy was a wide-shouldered man in his early fifties with a gray buzzcut and a nose like an eagle's beak. His uniform was navy blue as opposed to my beige one, a huge badge glimmering upon his chest.

He gave me a small smile. "How's your first day going, rookie?"

I was already tired of being called that. "Going okay, Captain."

"I'll say. You and Tanner made a bust." He pointed to a plastic bag on the desk. Kindly's tab of Suboxone was inside it, along with a small, broken pen. "I wanted to congratulate you, as well give you a closer look at the contraband."

Tanner had shared credit with me and hadn't told the captain I'd initially passed over the papers without inspecting them. I was going to like working with him, mouth-breather or not. I doubted Officer Anthony would have done the same. Robocop would have wanted all the glory.

"I'm guessing you know what Suboxone is," Clancy said.

"Yes, sir. It's a sublingual medication used to ween people off opiates. I learned about it in training."

The captain nodded. "It's one of the most prominent drugs in penitentiaries because it's small and easy to hide. It's heroin for inmates. This one piece has a prison value of six-hundred bucks."

My eyes went wide. "That little piece?"

"Sure. One tab gets cut up into thirty pieces and are sold for twenty bucks a pop."

I shook my head. Here I'd thought it was just for Kindly's personal use, but she was really drug trafficking—playing "the game" as they called it—just as she'd been busted for before.

Clancy removed the broken piece of pen from the bag. "Know what this is?"

"I don't think so, sir."

"It's a binky. Kindly's known for making them. As much as we try to monitor the inmates when they visit the pharmacy, some of the diabetics will break off the tip of a needle in their arm and sell them to junkies and dealers like Kindly. With a broken pen, a dropper from a bottle of Visine, and a paperclip, an inmate can make a prison syringe—a binky."

I nodded, wondering why I hadn't noticed Tanner finding the binky during the shake down. "Where was that?"

"Officer Rodriguez found it when she was doing the strip search," Clancy said. "Kindly had it in her vaginal canal."

I winced. "Jesus."

"Yeah." He chortled. "She's a real pip that one. You won't be seeing her in Hummingbird anymore. Not for a long while, anyway. We never should've moved her. Oh well, let's make a new spot for her on Raven."

Raven was the high security unit where inmates were kept in one or two-person cells. It wasn't as bad as being thrown into Sparrow, which was Norrington's own little supermax with all solitary confinement cells, but it was far less hospitable than Hummingbird and came with a drastic reduction in freedoms.

"Should I gather her things, sir?" I asked.

"Box and tag 'em. She's lost the privilege of personal items."

"Okay. So, everything?"

"Everything. Good work out there today, Donnelly. Keep it up."

As soon as I got home that evening, I took a long, hot shower, bringing two beers in with me. Norrington wasn't a filthy prison, but there was a grime that came with packing too many people in one place. Thinking of Lilly Gutierrez's large breasts and puckered lips, I masturbated. Getting out of the shower, I was glad the bathroom mirror was fogged so I wouldn't have to look at myself. I was a little ashamed I'd let an inmate sexually arouse me. By masturbating to thoughts of Gutierrez, I was giving in to the temptation of her, even if only on a mental level. Fantasy is how all lust begins, and some of those inmates were offering to make fantasy into reality. Women on the outside are rarely as forward. I told myself not to be too hard on myself for my arousal. This was a totally different breed of females than most men ever encountered. It was bound to be an adjustment and a test.

I popped a third beer, made a hamburger patty and a plate of potato chips, and ate in front of the TV, half the time watching the ravens outside my window rather than the show. Somehow the massive birds reminded me of my flock of inmates. When I took the dirty plate to the sink, I noticed Charlie hadn't touched the food in his bowl. Normally he was voracious. I picked up his dish and sniffed the wet food. It smelled and looked fine. Was he just bored with it? It wasn't like him to be persnickety about his meals, but maybe he'd been on this brand too long. I fetched a bag of beef jerky out of the fridge and sprinkled pieces into the dog food, hoping it would encourage him. Charlie watched me from the sofa but didn't even bother getting off it.

"What's the matter, buddy?" I asked.

He perched his ears as I approached, his eyes full of pathos. I petted his head slowly, lovingly. With my parents long dead and my wife gone, with having never had children and being estranged from my crazy sister, this dog was the only family I had left, my one solace in a world of indifference. I had a few friends, but they were busy raising their kids, working their jobs, and maintaining their marriages. The older we got, the rarer it was to hang out. I lived a rather eremitical life. Working in the prison was the most human interaction I'd had in months. The realization of that startled me.

"Not feeling so hot?" I asked Charlie.

His tail thumped once, then settled. I looked him over for injuries but found no lesions. What I did find was a swelling on his neck, just below his jaw. It felt like there were golf balls under his fur. Being an old dog, Charlie had many fatty tumors—hard little lumps on his belly, chest, and hindlegs. They were common and totally benign. I figured these new lumps were too. I wasn't worried about them but was concerned about Charlie. Maybe he had a stomach issue and that's why he wasn't eating?

"I'll call Dr. Fred tomorrow," I told him. "Might be time for a checkup anyway."

Charlie rested his head on his paws and released one of those long dog sighs. I sat down beside him and petted him while watching a *Family Guy* rerun, not wanting to watch anything serious after the day I'd had. Something told me I wouldn't be interested in true crime shows anymore. The moment I walked out of Norrington's gates, I would leave crime and punishment behind me until my next shift.

I wanted to stay up and savor my time at home, for the sooner I fell asleep the sooner I'd wake up and return to the prison. But alcohol and exhaustion got the better of me and I passed out sitting up, Charlie resting his head on my thigh. Together, we dreamed of better days.

CHAPTER FOUR

Tribalism is prominent in all penitentiaries. The ingrained politics of prison life force people to stick to their own race. This was true in Norrington, same as any male prison. But while the ladies wanted to sit with their friends during meals, overcrowding and time constraints didn't allow it, so working in the mess hall meant I constantly had to tell inmates to sit where I told them to rather than where they wanted to. If I let a single person slide, it would open the floodgates, so I had to be strict about it, no matter how sweet or nasty an inmate got about the issue. Blacks, Whites, Latinos, Native Americans—all mixed, side by side. It was about filling the rows quickly and efficiently. The rulebook said each inmate received twenty minutes to consume a meal, but the practice in Norrington was to get them through in ten. Once they sat down, most of the women shoveled the food in like lumberjacks in a hot dog eating contest.

While I moved inmates in and out of seats, Officer Anthony—wearing a fucking balaclava for Christ's sake—made sure no one tried to sneak back in line for second helpings. Just two COs orchestrating a chow line of some five hundred women. It was insane. The cafeteria sounded like a concert at a dive bar. Smelled like one too. Trays clanged like gongs as they came off the stack, and they were portioned with the day's lunch of three ounces of roast turkey in gravy, and a half cup each of green beans, mashed potatoes, and apricots. There was a piece of toast and a plastic cup of red liquid labeled "vitamin beverage." None of it looked edible and there were no substitutions. Take it or leave it and wait for dinner, just like the meals I'd endured in the mental hospital.

Some of the women in Hummingbird unit had gussied themselves up for my second day, having combed their hair and applied makeup. Some of them looked good—*really* good. Ariel Richardson caught my attention without evening trying. She was a beautiful, blue-eyed blonde with a body even her drab prison garb couldn't hide—ridiculously good-looking for a woman behind bars. I tried to avoid Lilly Gutierrez, but her eyes never left me. I felt certain Officer Anthony noticed, but he made no mention of it. When Tanner came in for his shift, I considered talking to him about it but didn't want to appear weak to my fellow officers. It was up to me if I wanted to write Lilly up for lewd behavior. During the shake downs, I could feel her staring at me with the monastic focus of a predator cat. Whenever I made the mistake of looking at her, she puckered those full lips and winked, and when she was sure Tanner wasn't looking, she touched herself.

Tanner wrote up an infraction for one of the inmates for being in possession of another inmate's MP3 player, which struck me as an odd rule because the player had been lent, not stolen.

"Write ups keep the captain happy," Tanner told me.

"It's just that Rivera said she allowed Brown to use it."

"Don't matter."

I nodded. "So, what happens to Brown?"

"It's not a huge deal. She won't be moved to Raven unit or anything, but she'll probably get some good time deducted."

"Good time" was a term for points gained for good behavior, points that gained an inmate privileges and were stacked toward an early release. Deducting Nina Brown's good time for something so trite seemed excessive, even harsh.

"Just for an MP3 player?" I asked. "She'll be docked just for that?"

"Rules is rules," Tanner said. "We don't get to make 'em, man, just enforce 'em. 'Sides, the disciplinary committee will make the call. I'm just speculatin'."

We got to talking about the inmates then, with Tanner giving me his take on their individual personalities. He was telling me what to expect—who were troublemakers and who were just trying to do their time, who were sneaks to watch closely and who had gained his trust. Once we'd gone through enough of them for it not to seem random to bring her up, I asked about Lilly.

"Inmate Gutierrez," I said. "She strikes me as one to keep an eye on."

I was fishing, acting like my interest in the inmate was based on my CO duties, as if she hadn't infiltrated my sexual fantasies.

Tanner exhaled bad breath. "You won't catch her with contraband, but you could write her up all day long for misconduct. Not that she's a fighter or nothin' like that. She's just always playin' with herself. A pervo."

"Yeah, I noticed." I decided to press. "What's she in for, anyway?"

Tanner's eyebrows raised. I suddenly felt like a child who'd said a bad word in front of his parents.

Tanner shook his head. "It's better not to ask what these ladies are in for, man. Trust me. If you really want to, you can look at their files, but honestly, you don't want to."

"They're that bad?"

"Nah, not always. Some are just thieves or female gang members. The usual. But some of 'em are killers and freaks. It makes it a lot easier to work around these women every day if you don't know what all they did to land in Norrington, and a lot easier to treat 'em equally." He crossed his massive arms. "I'll tell you this, though. One guy who done used to work here, he got interested in that hot blonde in there, Ariel Richardson. I'm *sure* you noticed her."

I nodded. "Sure did."

"Hard not to. I mean, we're guards but we're still men. Anyways, this CO managed to pull her file and when he found out what she was in here for, he was so creeped out he quit." Tanner leaned toward me conspiratorially. "Richardson was a schoolteacher. She was caught having sex with several of her students, boys as young as twelve."

"*Seriously?*"

"I know, I know. Hard to imagine a woman that pretty would result to seducing children. And it gets worse. When she found out one of her boys was bragging to friends, she seduced another boy into killing him."

Coldness went through me like a shot. "Jesus."

I looked out the control center's window, spotting Richardson sitting in the day room with friends, having a normal conversation as if she wasn't a monster.

Tanner went on. "Fourteen-year-old boy gets his face beat in with a baseball bat by a thirteen-year-old. One kid goes to prison and the other to the grave, all 'cause of this pedo. So, the CO found this out and couldn't handle the fact that he had a crush on a woman like that, so he just never showed up for work again. No call, no show. It's a good lesson for the rest of us. It's best to stay in the dark on this, man. You'll get along with the inmates much better if you don't know the evil shit they've done."

I scanned the unit, and there was Lilly leaning against the wall, her back arched, breasts pushed out against the tight undershirt. Long, dark curls fell over one eye, the other watching me, a wet smile on her face.

I was in trouble. I knew it.

So did she.

With Sally Kindly placed in a cell on Raven unit, an inmate who'd been sleeping on a mattress on the floor was graduated to Kindly's old bunk, and an hour later a new prisoner was brought to Hummingbird to fill the empty space, killing any hope the officials were trying to reduce the population of the overcrowded unit.

Zoe Hallister. Caucasian. Thirty-three years old. Average height and build; jet-black hair; moderate tattoos. Hazel eyes behind square glasses. She plucked her eyebrows and stenciled in new ones. Tough, but not butch. A pretty face not yet ruined by hard time. She didn't stare but didn't hang her head either, walking with shoulders back and jaw tight, as if she were entering a boxing ring, a subtle warning to potential predators. Escorting her down the hall, I placed my hand on her upper arm, and though it was protocol she tensed as if shocked I'd touched her.

"Easy," I said.

"Same to you, rookie."

I smirked. "What makes you think I'm a rookie?"

"Well, you are, ain't ya?"

"It's day two."

"See?" Zoe said as we walked on, side by side. "There you go."

"How'd you know I was a rookie?"

"It's loud and clear. Is in all rookies." She had a husky voice and moved with a swagger uncommon to people in cuffs. "Cons can always tell who's new and who's been around the cell block a few times."

"I can read some things too," I said. "You may be new to Norrington, but I take it you're no stranger to incarceration."

"Ain't my first prison rodeo."

"You're witty," I said. "A sense of humor goes a long way here."

"Here on Earth?"

I stifled a smile. "Guess so."

"So, a good sense of humor will get me through my time here. Got it. What about you? What's gonna get you through *your* time here?"

I wasn't as snappy with my answers as she was. I wasn't sure if I should even acknowledge the question. We rounded the corner toward the north wing, leaving us alone in the cold, white hallway, our footsteps echoing like chains on a ghost.

"Most COs quit before you even get a chance to learn their names," Zoe said.

"I'm Officer Donnelly," I told her, feeling like a dickhead.

"Congratulations. You think you're gonna stick around a while?"

"I think so."

She smirked. "Good to know."

I wondered what she meant by that. When we arrived at Hummingbird, I showed Zoe to her bed on the floor and her designated tote.

"Home sweet home," she said.

The other inmates watched us, sizing Zoe up. I got the sense she wouldn't be fucked with. She was tall for a woman, strong-looking, and had a hardness about her that was easy to see.

"Your I.D. is also your green dot card," I told her.

"When can I hit up the commissary? I could use a few things."

A green dot card was an inmate's debit card, which they could add money to by working or having friends and relatives on the outside donate. The commissary was the store where prisoners could shop for goods, including snacks, shoes, makeup, MP3 players, postage stamps, and other approved items. It was like a drab hotel gift shop. Fifty dollars a month would get an inmate what they needed. Double that, and they could live like a queen.

"I'll get you a form and see if I can get you there today instead of tomorrow," I told Zoe. "There's already a roll of toilet paper in your tote, and a toothbrush and tube of mini toothpaste."

"Any tampons?" she asked bluntly.

"There's a couple in there."

"Thanks, boss."

As I returned to the control booth, some of the inmates who'd dolled themselves up since yesterday gave me doe eyes and duck lips. Ariel the schoolteacher glanced at me without a flirt and quickly returned to reading one of her *Twilight* books. I guessed I was too old for her. Lilly Gutierrez worked yard cleanup, so she wasn't around. I considered myself lucky.

The remainder of my twelve-hour shift was uneventful but nerve-wracking. I was still learning what buttons opened what doors, and when Tanner wasn't around, I worried I was going to hit the wrong switch and the inmates would run free. I resisted the flirtations of some of the women but none of them came on too strong. They were still studying me, determining what they could get away with. When I got into my truck at the end of my shift, I just sat there. My lower back and knees were aching from being on my feet all day, my body never missing an opportunity to remind me it was decaying.

When I arrived home, I took Charlie out and fed him, then got drunk and stoned in front of the TV, *King of the Hill* reruns taking me out of my gray reality for a few hours. Petting Charlie, I noticed the swelling under his jaw hadn't gone down. It was late Saturday night, almost Sunday. I'd made an appointment with the vet for Tuesday, my next day off.

When the edible began to wear off, I took another one, trying to escape, but the whiskey had dragged me down into a nauseous, low-level despair. The familiar, quiet depression filled my head with a black haze as I shuffled about in my sweatpants and undershirt. It was a white tank top, just like

Lilly's. I thought of her huge breasts and considered jerking off, but knew I was too wasted to maintain an erection. Still, my thoughts of the women persisted.

Snarky new inmate Zoe flashed through my mind. She'd triggered my curiosity. Ariel Richardson's movie-star hotness made me sigh. Such a waste. Some of the other inmates were attractive simply because they were young. Even Cherry Campbell, with her soiled teeth and grungy dreadlocks, could be fuckable if she got her shit together.

When sober, I was ashamed of these thoughts. In my profession, they were considered taboo. But when intoxicated, I fantasized about the inmates with unabashed pleasure. I was too love-starved and lonesome to fight it. I supposed I should try to meet someone. Maybe use a dating app like Officer Anthony suggested or at least go out to a bar and be around people not associated with my job. But I hated the thought of more social activity after dealing with difficult people twelve hours a day. So instead, I sequestered myself to the dimly-lit rental I called home and the company of my only source of love—my dog, Charlie.

Days off were meandering and pointless. I accomplished nothing more significant than completing a few errands. I got high and ate junk food and sat on the back porch with the ravens and tried to avoid thinking about all the years I'd wasted on a failed marriage, and the steadily growing threat of dying alone. Sometimes I imagined myself being lowered into the ground with no mourners even present. Whenever memories—good or bad—crept into the forefront of my consciousness, I tried to shut them down. I found the most successful distraction were fantasies about the inmates. They were a handy tool when I was home alone, but the more I relied on this the more uncomfortable I became when I was around the women for real.

The inmates were lonely too, even the ones with someone waiting for them on the outside. They were all horny, all desperate, even the straight ones that had resorted to gay sex while behind bars. Their prison was made of concrete and steel. Mine was constructed of depression and isolation. But that didn't make mine any less real. I quickly came to believe I had more in common with the inmates than the other COs possibly could. I related to their turmoil with a deeper understanding. This made me more sympathetic, but I had to conceal that. If I allowed empathy to soften me, I could lose this job, and I didn't want that, especially now that I was growing attached to my girls.

CHAPTER FIVE

I was reposted to Raven.

Not permanently, only to help because the cell block had been rowdy lately. This unit was where the more troublesome inmates were restricted to single or shared cells, a higher security sublet of the prison that served as a middle ground between Hummingbird and the segregation unit of Sparrow. Raven was noisy and musky, with a faint organic odor—unwashed armpits, unflushed human waste. These inmates didn't flirt with me, only cursed, catcalling in a threatening manner. An overweight woman with spiky hair waved me toward her cell and turned hostile when I ignored her.

"What're ya?" she asked. "A fuckin' fairy?"

While carrying meal trays to the food ports (those on Raven unit were currently banned from the mess hall), I saw Sally Kindly's face pressed between the bars of her cell, her devil horns scrunched within the wrinkles of her raised brow.

"Hey, new jack," she said. "Welcome to Hell."

She looked far worse for wear than she had in Hummingbird. Raven unit had a way of pecking away at its residents. Here, an inmate had to watch her back closely. They lost sleep and their appetites suffered. When given the option to go outside for recreation, some didn't even bother leaving their beds.

Kindly was alone in her cell. She went on. "At least in this Hell you're surrounded by ass, right, rookie?"

"That's Officer Donnelly."

"Yes, sir, boss," she said with a smirk. "You come here to frisk me and check my piss? Maybe this time you wanna be the one to dig in my cunt for contraband, huh?"

"Keep it up and you'll have another infraction. You want that?"

Her smirk faded. "Okay, okay. I was just playin' around." I moved on but Kindly stopped me. "Hey, wait a sec, boss. I wanna ask you somethin'."

My curiosity got the better of me. The other CO on the unit wasn't nearby. I could wait to pass out the other dinners.

"What is it?" I asked.

"Listen... I can tell you're firm, but you also seem like one of the decent free people 'round here. Some of us feel like we can be straight with you, ya know? Not like fuckin' Robocop or the captain. You got heart."

I waited. "What's your question?"

Kindly looked both ways, speaking low. "I'm dyin' in here, man. You guys took my Suboxone away. Now, I know I ain't s'pposed to have it, I know, but without that shit, I go into withdrawals."

"Do you need to go to the infirmary?"

She shook her head. "Nah, man. They won't give me nothin' good 'cause I done played the game too many times."

"Well, whose fault is that?"

"I know, I know." She sighed. "I've made my share of mistakes. I admit that. But I'm payin' for 'em by bein' locked in this here cage. I shouldn't have to suffer in my own body too."

My brow furrowed. "What is it you want from me?"

Again, she scanned the walkway, her voice lowering to a whisper. "I was just thinkin'… maybe we could do each other favors."

I should have walked away right then. I knew it at the time and would go on to believe it even more strongly in the weeks to come. But there was a hole in me so deep that every day I was finding it harder to pull myself out of it to face the world. My daydreams of physical contact with a woman—*any* woman—had become an obsession. Was Kindly offering her body? She wasn't the most attractive woman in Norrington and certainly didn't seem clean, but could I really afford to be picky when I was this desperate?

I couldn't go through with it. I knew that. But I wanted the fantasy to continue, at least for a little while longer, so I let her go on when I really should have just written her up.

"What sort of favors?" I asked.

A spark came into her eyes, a fisherman succeeding with their lure.

"A simple exchange," she said. "Easy. No big risk. You bring me my Suboxone, and I'll cut you in. How does forty percent sound?"

My shoulders stiffened.

"C'mon, boss," Kindly said. "I know they don't pay you guys for shit. I got a friend on the outside who can supply me—supply *us*. I'll move all the product once you get it to me. No sweat. I can get you thousands of dollars in less than two weeks."

I spoke flatly. "I thought you only wanted it for yourself."

"Hey, if we're gonna bring stuff in we might as well make it worth our while."

"Surely you realize the huge risk you're taking just by asking a CO to do this. Are you crazy?"

Her smile faded. "Hey, everybody's crazy. Ain't you noticed?"

"I figured you already had your ways of sneaking things in, given all we found on you."

"Yeah, well, you try walkin' around with a plastic tube up your man-snatch all day. See how comfortable it is."

"No thanks."

"Exactly. It hurts hiding shit in my cunt. I figure there's a better way to—"

"I mean *no thanks* to your offer."

Kindly deflated, her shoulders going slack as she hung on the bars. "C'mon, boss. Everybody wins. This is easy money."

"Anything that can land me in prison isn't what I'd call easy."

"That'll only happen if we get caught, and we ain't gettin' caught."

"Then how did Tanner and I catch you the other day?"

"That was just an accident," she said. "I forgot that piece was in with my stuff. That won't happen again. Shit, I been in the game for years, man. I sneak stuff constantly."

"In that case, I should shake your house down right now."

Kindly flushed and released the bars, backing away. "Told ya I ain't got nothin'."

"Best to make sure though, right?"

"Look, boss. I… it was just a joke. I wasn't bein' serious 'bout all that." She stepped further back, trying to hide even in the brightness of the cell. "I was just fuckin' with ya to see what you'd say. Little prank we like to pull on rookies, that's all."

"That so?"

"Yeah. Honest."

Kindly's eyes grew wet. It could have been acting—she was certainly lying to me now—but I felt for her anyway. One thing I was sure she was being honest about was her physical need for narcotics. Kindly belonged in a prison drug program, but her stacks of infractions and constant lies kept her in too much trouble to get the treatment she needed. The drug program at Norrington had limited space, and inmates with bad behavior went to the bottom of the waiting list.

If I gave Sally Kindly an infraction for something as serious as propositioning a CO with a crime, no doubt the disciplinary committee would throw her in Sparrow. She'd spend twenty-three hours a day in solitary confinement, pacing a cell floor no bigger than a king-sized bed. Throwing her into a box to go insane wasn't going to help her. I saw it as a cruel punishment with no rehabilitating value. Solitary might break an inmate down enough to make them easy to control, but it wasn't an improvement, it was a crippling. Kindly was somebody's mother. Damage done to her would bring pain to her young daughter as well.

"Look," I told her. "You know where you'd go if I wrote you up for this."

Kindly said nothing.

"I'm gonna give you a break," I said. "A *huge* break. But this is the only one you're gonna get from me, got it? I don't wanna see you go to Sparrow, Sally. I'm giving you a chance, but I don't ever want to hear you talk about drug trafficking again. Got it?"

She nodded.

"Never again," I repeated. "Stay clean. Don't let me find anything during shake downs. And remember—this conversation never happened."

She nodded again. "Yes, sir."

I slid her dinner into the food port. "Eat something, will ya?"

Norrington had a video surveillance system, but many things in the prison were old and busted, including a few of the cameras. We were advised to pay closer attention to inmates who tended to gather in these areas. The women shouldn't have known what cameras were dead, but that kind of information had a way of leaking out.

One of the busted cameras was in the east hallway leading to Hummingbird, the same hall I'd escorted Zoe Hallister down. There were two cameras overlooking the rec yard, but only one was operational. When any kind of fight broke out, they were always in the far end of the yard near building C, because the inmates knew it was a surveillance dead zone. There was an elevator in the east wing used to escort inmates to the infirmary, and its camera was out too.

A couple of the cell doors in Raven were loose in their tracks. An inmate orderly showed me how she could pop it out with her foot. When I filed a report, the captain told me he was already aware of it.

"ACI sets strict quarterly budgets," Clancy told me. "Assistant warden Moore decides what money gets spent when and where."

It seemed to me that broken cell doors should've been prioritized when it came to spending, but as a rookie CO it wasn't my place to make suggestions.

One morning I forgot to remove my keys from my pocket while walking through the metal detector at the vestibule. It didn't go off. The rookie on guard looked barely eighteen and was too busy applying ChapStick to even notice when I pulled the keys out of my pocket. I asked if I should go again and he told me not to worry about it, that the machine was always screwing up.

Many of the budget cuts were more detrimental to the inmates than us. The prison library was shamefully understocked, especially when it came to textbooks. The inmates could pass the time with Harry Potter and Michael Crichton but didn't have easy access to books on law or job-building skills. If an inmate wanted something specific, it would have to be sent to them from someone on the outside, and even then, there was a long list of banned texts the COs would confiscate. Books on Black power, the prison system, *Mein Kampf*, the occult, *Tupac Resurrection*, erotica—all forbidden. The most popular banned book in Norrington was *Fifty Shades of Grey*. Sometimes we found Xerox copies of the juicier chapters.

The work programs weren't focused on having the inmates learn a trade that could help them find employment upon release. Instead, they were driven by saving the company money (using the inmates as custodians and gardeners for the grounds) and making the company more money (having the inmates do repairs for medical supply companies that paid ACI for the labor, with ACI giving the inmates just thirteen cents an hour in wages).

Zoe Hallister wanted to work. She was given a position in the shop, repairing medical equipment and lamps. It was the last stop on the list of workstations, so once I escorted the others to their jobs, I was alone with Zoe as we walked down the hall.

"So glad I was able to get this," she said. "I much prefer shop work to being an orderly, mopping floors and stuff."

"Have you always been handy?"

"My uncle was a mechanic. Taught me a lot about tools. Shop is good for me. I can earn a few pennies and kill a lot of time. Killing time is everything in here."

"Well, when your time's up, maybe you can become a mechanic too, or a carpenter or contractor. Make a brand-new start."

She snorted a laugh. "You sound like one of those inspirational posters."

"It's never too late to change your life."

"Oh yeah? Is that what you did when you decided to become a corrections officer?"

The words stung but I tried not to let it show. "In a way, yes."

"Just bustin' chops. A job's a job. America ain't easy. We all gotta do what we gotta do."

I wanted to ask her what she'd thought she'd had to do, what she'd done to land her in prison. She wasn't a foul-mouthed, green-toothed crackhead with face tattoos. Though prison life had bronzed Zoe over with a layer of toughness, she still seemed like a normal enough woman, which was more than I could say for a lot of the inmates.

"You got a wife?" she asked.

It wasn't an appropriate conversation for us to have, but I allowed it. People didn't tend to ask me about my love life. Not since I'd stopped seeing my therapist to save money.

"Divorced," I said.

"Ah. That makes sense."

"Does it?" I asked, wondering if I should be insulted.

"It's in your demeanor."

"How so?"

She shrugged. "I dunno. You just seem… *wounded.*"

I had no response to this.

"I guess we just recognize our own," Zoe said. "I was in the joint only four months before my husband left me. Went back to his high school sweetheart—can you believe that? I mean, *high school?* It's crazy, right? Here I am in prison, and he bails on me just so he can go back in time with the girl he lost his virginity too."

"That's rough."

I knew what it was like to be abandoned by your spouse when you needed them the most. I tried to find consoling words but could only come up with the platitudes people always gave me—*you're better off; there's plenty of other fish in the sea; it's always darkest before the dawn.* She'd already accused me of feeding into inspirational sap. No need to confirm it.

"Is it part of my punishment to lose my husband?" she asked. "Or should I consider it an unexpected benefit because now I know what he's really made of—dog shit?"

I chuckled. "That's a damned good question."

We drew closer to the shop.

"Anyway," Zoe said, "thanks for listening, Liam."

She wasn't supposed to call me by my first name.

"Anytime, Zoe," I said.

We entered the shop. One of the COs assigned there was Beverly Knox, the older woman I'd trained with. I spoke with her as the shop leader led Zoe to her station.

"How're things?" I asked.

"Goin' good. Glad to see you're still around, hon. You know, that boy we was in class with, Ricki—he already quit."

"That was fast."

She shrugged. "It ain't for everybody. Ain't even for most."

"What about Ileana?"

"That tiny, young thing? Dunno. Ain't seen her since training."

I'd thought of Ileana on occasion, hoping to cross paths with her and catch up, maybe even muster the courage to ask her to have a drink sometime. *Just to talk shop*, I'd tell her.

"Hope she's doing okay," I said.

"Yeah. I dunno. Girly girl like that… they don't do so well, 'less they really got somethin' to prove."

"Oh? And what about you?"

She playfully batted my arm. "Shut up."

"Whatever it is, it doesn't seem to be bothering him," I said.

With his brow lowered, the veterinarian stroked the lumps on Charlie's neck. Charlie smiled wide, tongue hanging out. Like most Labradors, he loved everyone and was gregarious even in a scary place like the vet's office—provided they didn't put a finger in his butt.

"He usually eats just fine," I said. "Though he's gotten a little more finicky, when he gets something he likes he gobbles it right up without any trouble."

Dr. Fred smiled, but it was a somber one, the kind you never want to see during a medical examination.

"Well, it might be nothing," he said, sounding like that wasn't true. "But this is a swelling of the lymph nodes. It couldt be a simple infection, but given Charlie's age and breed… I'm sorry, but there's a good chance it's lymphoma."

I suddenly went weightless.

My stomach rose as if I was on a rollercoaster, the impossible now a very real threat. I put both hands on Charlie, swallowing hard against the rising tears. Sensing my shift in mood, my sweet boy started licking me, trying to make me feel better when he was the one facing cancer.

"I'd like to do a biopsy," Dr. Fred said, "so we know for sure. It could be nothing. It could be something we treat with simple steroids."

"And if it's lymphoma?" I managed to say.

"Well, then we can discuss chemotherapy."

I hated to ask but had to. "How much will all this cost? I mean, whatever it takes, I'll do it, but… I'm going through a divorce and I'm short on cash."

"The biopsy isn't expensive. Steroids wouldn't be either. But chemotherapy is rather costly. Do you have pet insurance?"

"No," I admitted. "I can't afford it right now."

Dr. Fred looked away, pained to be the bringer of bad news. "That's unfortunate. When it comes to this sort of cancer treatment… you're looking at upwards of eight thousand dollars."

CHAPTER SIX

I almost called out of work just so I could spend the day with Charlie. I wanted to but had to be practical no matter how emotional I was. I couldn't afford to miss work, not with only a few hundred dollars in my bank account. If Charlie did end up needing chemo, I wasn't sure how I could possibly pay for it. Forget missing work. Better to think about asking the captain for overtime shifts. But that would mean less time to spend with Charlie, and I didn't know how much time we had left.

"On a positive note," Dr. Fred had said, "Charlie won't suffer. It won't be until the end that he'll feel any pain."

The end.

Those words hit me like an uppercut, the memory of them knocking me back down whenever I dared to pick myself up. My best friend was facing death. Though the biopsy results wouldn't be back for a week, I just knew they would be bad. I researched the condition online. With a diagnosis of lymphoma, a dog could expect to live for about a month. Treatment could extend their lives considerably, but it wasn't a cure. Within a year of their first dose of chemo, dogs with this form of cancer usually relapsed.

Upwards of eight thousand dollars.

The price tag was like a disease in and of itself. I was never averse to spending money on Charlie—he ate quality food, had buckets of toys, and a dog walker to take him out during my long shifts—but in my current financial situation, eight grand might as well have been eight million. I was already paying down a small loan I'd taken out to put down deposits to rent a new place as well as cover moving costs following the separation from my wife. What little money I'd made from the sale of the old house was nearly spent, because we'd still been paying off the mortgage. Just the expenses of rent and groceries are enough to bankrupt anyone who lives alone, and I'd relied exclusively on that payout while looking for a new job. I didn't even own anything of value I could pawn. I'd have to sell my old truck twice to even get close to eight grand.

I drove to work in silence. When I pulled up to the guard station, Baxter—one of the German Shepherds that sniffed all vehicles going in and out of Norrington—moved with the sort of agility Charlie used to have. Baxter had none of my dog's lumps. No bald patches or blackening of the gums. He was young and strong, his eyes sparkling with a curious wanderlust. For all the adventures I'd taken Charlie on, I suddenly felt I hadn't done enough. I wanted to take him on a trip so he could see the ocean one more time, maybe hike through Utah together or visit a Redwood forest, let him sniff mountain air and taste fresh spring water and poop in a different state each night.

Thoughts of my dog circled over me like buzzards as I went through the daily routines on Hummingbird. The tension I'd felt working the new job dissipated, depression transforming every aspect of my employment into drudgery. My shakedowns were halfhearted. I had trouble paying attention. My reactions were slow. I forgot to lock a gate—thankfully Tanner caught it before Captain Clancy did. The hours dragged and yet I hoped I wouldn't have to do any paperwork or have any unexpected duties, that I could just sit in the control booth and do as little as possible.

I escorted the working inmates to their posts, and again found myself alone with Zoe Hallister on our way to the shop.

"What happened to you?" she asked.

"What?"

"You seem down."

I straightened my spine, ashamed my despondency was showing. "I'm okay. Just been a long day is all."

"Seems like more than that. You're acting like someone just ran over your dog."

The sudden pain in my heart must have shown on my face because Zoe's lips parted. I struggled against the rise of tears, hating myself for my vulnerability. We stopped walking.

"Dude, what is it?" Zoe asked.

"My dog…" I tried but couldn't say more.

"It's just an expression. What's going on? Are you alright?"

"Not really." I smiled at my own ridiculousness. Here I was—a CO being consoled by an inmate. I knew it was a mistake, but in my desperation, I went along with it anyway.

It was too refreshing not to. "You actually nailed it. It's my dog. He's sick."

Zoe's face dropped. "Oh no. Oh, I'm so sorry, Liam. What's wrong with him?"

And before I knew it, I was telling her. Not just about my pet's possible cancer, but all about Charlie and how much he meant to me, all my bottled feelings bursting out of me in a freefall. I managed to hold my tears in but couldn't keep my mouth shut. Zoe listened, nodding and making empathetic sounds, letting me get it all out. Isolated in the hallway with the busted camera, it was the most intimate I'd been with anyone in a long time, and it just felt right no matter how wrong it was.

I didn't mention my money worries, only focused on the emotional turmoil of the prognosis. "It's just been weighing heavy on my mind is all."

"Sure it has. Our pets are our family. I've got two dogs, Bailey and Max. They're with my mom now. Not being able to see them is one of the hardest parts of being locked up."

I drew my phone from my pocket (yet another taboo in this job) and pulled up photos of Charlie. Zoe smiled as I showed her some of my favorites—Charlie cuddling with his rope toy; running through an open field; chewing on a squeaker shaped like a taco.

"He's adorable," she said. "What a good ol' boy."

"That he is."

"So… what're you gonna do?"

I paused. "What do you mean?"

"The lymphoma. You doing chemo?"

I sighed, hands on my hips. "Seems like the only path."

"*Ouch.* My sister had a cat with cancer. Must've spent ten grand."

I nodded, not wanting to admit what I could or couldn't afford.

"And even then," Zoe said, "the cat only lived six more months than it would have without the treatment. Whether or not to spend that kind of money… it's a tough choice to make. I don't envy you."

"I'll do whatever I can for Charlie, no matter what it takes."

Zoe cocked her head, smiling up at me. "Good man."

Her eyes stayed on mine, their hazel looking almost silver in the florescent light. She was prettier than I'd realized. We held each other's stare, the warmth spreading through me, refusing to let me look away. She was so close. No one was around, no one watching, and the only camera was busted. I could lean right in and kiss her.

"Well," I said, "we'd better get going. Wouldn't want to make you late to work."

"S'alright."

I managed to look away, but Zoe kept staring at me. I took her arm again, as if I was taking her to prom, and we continued down the hall. I almost thanked her for listening but remembered I wasn't supposed to. It seemed ridiculous to obey that rule after breaking so many others, but I was trying to reroute myself.

"Keep me posted on Charlie," she said as we reached the shop.

"I will."

She turned to me. "And keep me posted on you, Liam."

"Okay."

"I mean, hey—you'll always know where to find me."

She gave me a playful wink. It could have been just to emphasize her joke. It also could have been a clear flirtation. I was too stupid to know for sure.

CHAPTER SEVEN

Blood covered the bedsheets.

Cherry Campbell fought against me as I tried to restrain her while also remaining cautious of the open wounds on her forearms. She cursed through clenched, rotted teeth, her white girl dreadlocks whipping me as she thrashed about. Officer Anthony fumbled with the handcuffs. The other inmates gathered around Campbell's bunk to watch the show, some staring in surprise, others hooting as if they were at a football game. When Officer Anthony dropped the cuffs, little Fern Hernandez mimicked his clumsy attempt to collect them, the other Latinas laughing. Sex-crazed Lilly Gutierrez watched Cherry Campbell and me wrestle, licking her lips at the intimacy of the physical struggle. When we finally got the cuffs on her, Cherry instantly went from screaming to crying.

My uniform was stained with red blotches. Blood dribbled onto the toe of my boot as I kept my prisoner on her feet. On the splattered floor, Officer Anthony found the broken piece of razorblade Cherry had used on herself. She'd sliced both arms from her elbow to her wrist, then slit the wrist diagonally, making upside-down crosses in her flesh. Very thorough. This wasn't just self-harm. This looked like a serious suicide attempt.

"I don't wanna be here no more," she bawled. "I'll never get outta this place alive!"

I shushed her gently, trying to calm Cherry down as I walked her to the control booth for the first aid kit. Officer Anthony tried to restore order to Hummingbird, allowing me to patch Cherry just enough to stop the profuse bleeding so I could safely escort her to the infirmary. Officer Anthony always preferred to stay behind and make busts rather than do anything to help an inmate, particularly one that had annoyed him with an outburst.

"Please, boss," Cherry cried as I wrapped her arms with gauze. "Just lemme die. I *hate* my life! Just lemme die, boss, I *fuckin' hate* everything."

That she was hysterical didn't make hearing these words any easier. They were too familiar to me to just brush off.

Sobbing, Cherry dragged her feet down the hall, stumbling to the point that fellow officer Diana Rodriguez came to assist me, just to be safe. We managed to get Cherry to the elevator.

"Thanks," I told Rodriguez. "I can handle her from here."

Her dark eyes observed me as if she were looking for some hidden lie. "No. It's okay, I'll help you."

She joined us as we ascended to the next floor, but when the elevator doors came open, Rodriguez didn't step out. Instead, she hit the button to bring her back to her post.

Why did she only want to come with us in the elevator? I wondered.

Another guard was in the hall on the top floor, and the infirmary had a partition of bulletproof glass facing out. Plenty of other officials around. Maybe that was why Rodriguez returned to her post, but…

I suddenly remembered the elevator camera was one of the busted ones.

She was keeping an eye on you.

Rodriguez was a veteran CO, and as a female she was extra protective of the inmates. I was a male rookie. Rodriguez didn't know me well enough to trust me. She hadn't said or insinuated anything, but I was now certain she'd tagged along because the elevator was one of the few places in the entire prison that offered privacy. Did she really think I'd molest Cherry *now*, while she was bleeding and sobbing? Maybe Rodriguez thought it was all a ruse designed by Cherry and me to give us an opportunity to have sex. Either way, it would be an extreme, radical act. I wasn't the type to get turned on by mutilation.

Or maybe Rodriguez was up my ass because she had some other interest in me. I doubted it was anything amorous. She was a sturdy, stout woman with broad shoulders, her hair always back in a tight bun, her face always baring the hard expression of a defensive lineman before the snap. She didn't seem like the type to look for romance in the workplace. In fact, she didn't seem the type to look for romance at all. But tomboys need love too.

After getting Cherry to the nurses, I headed back downstairs for a replacement uniform, only to find out it would come out of my pocket, just like the two I'd had to purchase upon my hiring.

"Best to bring a backup pair of clothes and leave 'em in your car," the clerk advised as he handed me a size XL.

In the employees-only bathroom, I washed up and repeatedly splashed warm water over my face, closing my eyes and pretending I was somewhere else, anywhere else. Cherry's mantra marched through my head like a stuck song.

Just lemme die. I hate my life. Just lemme die, boss.

Refreshed, at least externally, I shuffled back to Hummingbird where Officer Anthony was cleaning up the mess, grumbling on his hands and knees. For legal reasons, the orderlies weren't allowed to handle potentially hazardous waste. In a dormitory filled with women who'd been busted for hardcore drugs, blood-borne pathogens posed a major concern.

Bagging the bloody sheets, Officer Anthony glowered. "Everybody thought Campbell was over her cutting phase. Shows what that prison shrink knows, huh?"

Across from him, Cherry's bunkmate Enola Branham, a middle-aged Native American, had turned her back to the gore and was doing a crossword puzzle.

"Didn't surprise me," she said.

Officer Anthony straightened. "You should've called us over sooner."

"Not my responsibility."

"You must've noticed what she was doing. Must've seen it before anyone else did. But you just sat there and ignored it. I thought you two were friends."

"Cherry is my friend. I care about her very much."

"But you didn't help her. Instead, Castillo and Brown where the ones who called us over to help."

Branham shook her head slowly. "You call what you did *help*?"

"She was trying to kill herself, Branham."

"Maybe that's the best thing for her." The woman's flat tone added an extra coat of dread to her grim observation. "Maybe that's the only help she really needs."

"Suicide's no answer," Officer Anthony said.

"Easy for you to say, boss. You're one of the free people. She's behind bars and she's sick."

"Don't put that on me. Cherry Campbell was a free woman, but she made bad choices, and those choices had consequences. You're all here because you chose to be."

Branham mumbled something in another language.

Officer Anthony fumed. "And don't use your native tongue around me! I know what you're saying isn't good. I will write you up if I hear it again, understand?"

Branham said nothing, her eyes never leaving her book of crosswords. Putting on a fresh pair of gloves, I assisted Officer Anthony with stripping the sheets and pillowcase, exposing the crimson spots the mattress had sponged.

"Christ," he muttered.

"Looks like we're shy one bed," I said.

"Just as well. We'll get one of the newbies off the floor and put her mattress here. Campbell's lost her house—if she's ever allowed to come back to my unit at all."

That he referred to Hummingbird as *his* unit made my stomach sour. We sealed the bags and headed out.

"Where will she go?" I asked.

"There're two cells in Sparrow reserved for inmates like her. I hope they throw the crazy bitch in there to rot."

"She needs help."

He stopped. "Take a look around, Donnelly. *All* these women need help. They're freakin' mental."

His derogatory use of the word intensified my dislike for the little man. I was about to tell him mental illness wasn't something to hold against someone when our radios buzzed. The captain wanted to see me. Mild paranoia simmered in my head. Diana Rodriguez might have said something to him about me nearly escorting Cherry Campbell in the elevator alone, but there were no policies set in place against that. I'd done nothing wrong. So why was I so anxious?

"You still looking for overtime?" Captain Clancy asked when I entered his office.

"Yes, sir."

He nodded. "How do you feel about doing suicide watch?"

Irony often amused me, but not in this case. It felt more like a cruel joke, a mockery of all I'd been through. Here I was, a man who'd long struggled with suicide ideation, assigned to watch an inmate who'd just tried to kill herself. But I needed the money, so I put a call in to my dog walker, asking her to take Charlie home with her for the evening. She loved my dog and, because he was low maintenance, she only charged me twenty bucks. I would be released from my overtime shift on suicide watch at seven in the morning (nineteen hours after I'd arrived for my regular shift) and could pick Charlie up on my way home. I was given a half hour unpaid break between the double shifts.

I entered Sparrow.

With all the inmates locked in their solitary cells, the unit was hushed and cold like a museum. Sitting on a bench, a fat CO was reading an issue of *American Rifleman*. He didn't bother to introduce himself even after I told him my name. He just led me to the cells on the upper landing. Most were sealed with white, metal doors with one small window of reenforced glass and a food port, but at the far end of the landing were three cells with bars instead of doors. Each had a single mattress on the floor with no sheets or blankets and a metal toilet with no rim. Nothing else. Two of the cells were empty.

Cherry Campbell was in the last cell, standing with her back to us, her forehead against the wall. Her arms were not just bandaged but wrapped in some harder material—casts designed to keep her from reopening her wounds. The cell was tiny and cramped despite the minimal furnishings.

A chair was placed right outside the cell, a small stack of safe-for-work magazines and a newspaper on the floor beside it. Essentially, my job was to sit there and make sure Cherry didn't try to kill herself again. That's why she had no sheets—she could hang herself with them. Of course, she had none of her belongings from Hummingbird either and nowhere to hide another blade. She'd been medicated and was expected to be easy tonight. The CO told me the only hard part of the job would be staying awake. I turned down his offer to borrow his gun nut magazine, and he shuffled back downstairs, leaving me the only officer in this section of the segregation unit. All was quiet but for Cherry's gentle sniffling.

Eventually she sat on the floor and drew her knees to her chest, still facing the rear wall. I started reading yesterday's newspaper, occasionally looking up only to see Cherry hadn't moved. She'd stopped crying, at least.

It was just past two a.m. when she broke the silence. "It wasn't supposed to be like this ya know."

I gazed up at her. Cherry wasn't looking at me, but she'd turned her head to the side so I could see her face in profile. In the punishing, bright light of her cell, the young woman looked withered and drained, a skeleton of her former self.

"I was gonna be somebody, man," Cherry said. "I wasn't never gonna be no basic bitch with the hubby and the three kids and the minivan. I was gonna be a rock star, man—a movie star. Maybe move to L.A. or even New York. Mothafuckas act like it's all my fault. Well, *it ain't.* Anybody in my shoes woulda done the same." She sniffed. "He was beatin' on me bad—way worse than before. Knocked out two of my teeth. Broke my fuckin' arm, he yanked it so hard. That sumbitch was bashin' my skull in, man. You tell me what else I was supposed to do?"

I didn't know Cherry's story any better than any other inmates, but if she wanted to share, I would listen. It was the best I could offer her. Advice was out of the question, and not just because of prison dynamics. I'd often been told that sometimes a woman just wants to be heard. Sometimes just listening *is* helping. I thought that was a crock of shit but went with it anyway.

"Self-defense," Cherry continued. "I was protectin' myself, and the fuckin' system punished me for it, man. I thought they'd give me a bullet, not a *dime.* I mean, shit, a year I can do, but fuckin' *ten?* I still gots eight to go." She looked at me now, her eyes as red as her namesake. "Them other bitches talk behind my back. I know it. They say I'm chatted out—*cracked.* They think this place got me goin' psych, but what they dunno is I been cracked since I popped outta my mama's nasty ass. This cage just be makin' me worse is all."

I held her gaze but remained mute.

Cherry glowered. "Ain't you gonna say nothin', cowboy?"

"Not sure what you want me to say."

She stood and slowly approached the cell bars. "I don't care what it is, just say somethin'."

I took a deep breath. "Life can be tough. It can be unfair. But that doesn't mean you should end it. You just gotta keep moving, keep fighting, and roll with the punches."

"What're you, a *Rocky* movie?"

Again, I was just recycling the generic pick-me-up phrases that were endlessly regurgitated in group therapy discussions. But I couldn't tell Cherry Campbell that. She'd wonder how I knew so much about what a psychiatric hospital was like.

"I'm just saying," I told her. "Taking your own life is never the solution."

I'd never felt more like a hypocrite than I did in that moment.

"Maybe I shoulda let that sumbitch kill me instead, huh?" she said. "Fuckin' junkie piece of shit had it comin'. He deserved what all he got. But maybe I shoulda just let him keep on bustin' my skull in. Cash out early instead of landin' up in here."

"C'mon. Don't talk like that."

"Why the fuck not? You think it ain't so bad here, huh? This livin' hell is just your workplace, cowboy. To me, it's home."

She had a point. No matter how draining Norrington could be on my soul, I still got to leave. My home life was pathetic, but I could eat what I wanted and shower in privacy and only had to share my living space with a dog.

"I know it ain't easy," I told her. "It's a prison. I can only imagine what it's like to be in your shoes, Cherry."

That I used her preferred nickname seemed to surprise her. Her shoulders slackened and she leaned into the bars, taking a more relaxed stance.

"Ain't just this joint, man," she said, gesturing around us. "Even if they let me out tomorrow, I'd still be fucked six ways from Sunday school. Ain't got nobody waitin' for me on the outside. Ain't nobody even come visit me no more. I stole money from my family and friends too many times, all to buy drugs I was hooked on. And I ain't never learned how to work no real job. Not that anybody'd hire me anyway, what with every application askin' if I ever committed a felony. I walk into some job interview and gotta tell the manager I caught a *hot one*? Shit, they wouldn't gimmie a job washin' bird shit off bicycles." Cherry grimaced as she gripped the bars. "That's why everybody who done gets out ends up comin' right back. It may be a cage but it's safer than sleepin' under a bridge in the cold, goin' hungry, gettin' raped by bums and cops and dope dealers. It's this whole system, man. Fuckin' ACI. Once you in, you ain't never gettin' out."

I wanted to tell her with good behavior she could be out in less than eight years, that she was still a young woman, that she could learn a trade and move on from this dark moment in her life. I wished to guide her out of this suicide watch cell and onto a path of rehabilitation and hope. But who was I to give advice? What rehabilitation had I achieved? What hope did I hold? Sometimes the only thing that kept me from killing myself was my dog Charlie, and now he was facing a death sentence of his own. What could I tell Cherry Campbell that would really help and not just be more of that inspirational blathering Zoe Hallister had called me out on? I couldn't encourage Cherry because too much of what she was saying was true. It was only dumb luck that put me on one side of those bars and her on the other.

"Killin' myself ain't takin' a life," Cherry said. "Can't take away what somebody ain't got."

CHAPTER EIGHT

I picked up Charlie on the way home. The pit-stop meant less time for me to sleep but assured better quality. I'd become dependent on him the way others would a service dog because Charlie provided psychological support even a myriad of medications had failed to. I also wanted him close to me tonight, for I had a message from Dr. Fred in my voicemail, one I didn't want to listen to until I was at home, just in case I would cry.

It was a good thing I did.

The test had come back positive.

Cancer, I thought as I lay in bed petting Charlie, tufts of hair floating in the bedroom. *My best friend has cancer.*

This harsh reality was the emotional equivalent to being kicked in the balls. That night, I cried harder than when my wife had walked out on me. I held Charlie close, my arm draped over him as his body inflated and deflated with his gentle breaths. He dreamed, unaware of his own mortality. And yet, at the same time, I sensed a sadness in him, an exhaustion of the will, as if he knew something was terribly wrong. There was a poison within him, spreading like an internal rash. This creature of pure love was trotting toward death's door, and if I didn't figure something out, he would reach it within a month.

But I knew these overtime shifts were not sustainable.

When I was in my twenties, I had a job at a warehouse. Using a manual pallet jack, I moved stacks of machine parts from the loading dock to the aisles. It was hard physical labor, and the shifts were eleven hours long, starting at six in the afternoon and running through the early morning. But the young are tireless, and I still managed to have a social life, a girlfriend, and go to the gym several times a week.

Now I was in my mid-forties.

You can't work like this.

I managed to get in five hours sleep by washing an edible down with two glasses of cheap bourbon. When my thoughts drifted away from my dog, everything that had been going on at work spun through my head. I thought of Cherry Campbell's mangled arms and Lilly Gutierrez's seductive curves.

Most of all, I thought of Sally Kindly.

Coming back into work the next day, I downed my morning's fourth cup of coffee and headed to Raven unit, the higher security tier. I'd been restationed again due to staffing shortages. Expecting to share my duties with one of the more experienced guards like Diane Rodriguez or Tanner Wyatt, I was surprised to find the only other CO on Raven was Ileana Sloane, the mousy girl I'd gone through training with. She was surprised to see me too.

"Can't believe we haven't crossed paths until now," Ileana said.

"I thought maybe they'd put you at another prison."

"It's a big facility. Just had overlapping shifts, I guess. They've had me watching the visitation room a lot."

We walked down the tier like old friends. It was noisier today, the inmates seeing what they could get away with.

"Male CO entering!" I announced to them—standard practice in a women's prison. I gave Ileana a groggy, sympathetic smile. "How've you been holding up?"

Her eyelashes fluttered. "It's a big adjustment."

"That's for sure."

Our boots echoed on the hard floor, a staccato of fascism within walls of anarchy.

"What all have you learned?" Ileana asked.

I knew what she meant but answered my own way. "I've learned that nothing in the free world can really prepare you for prison."

There was a small workstation for us—little more than a desk and two chairs in the open space of the tier floor. Ileana handed me one of the logbooks so we could begin our security checks. Looking in on the inmates was a routine COs were required to do every thirty minutes. But depending on staff shortages, security rounds could be much less frequent, allowing for more inmate shenanigans.

"I'll take the top floor," I said before Ileana could make a different suggestion.

It made no difference to her, but I'd been thinking long and hard about what I intended to do. Ileana proceeded down the tier, and I climbed the stairs to the upper landing, marking the time in the logbook as I checked on each inmate, moving quickly until I reached who I wanted to talk to.

Sally Kindly was still alone in her cell. She'd gotten lucky. Hopefully, I would too. She was pacing like a zoo animal, the horns on her forehead suiting her. I cleared my throat to get her attention.

Kindly's eyes were like ice. "Mornin', boss."

"Mornin' Sally," I said quietly. I peered over the railing. Ileana was far enough away to be out of earshot. Still my nerves tingled as I returned my attention to Kindly. "Listen… I've been thinking about what you said."

Her posture changed. There was tension there now. She crossed her arms as if to create another barrier between us.

I inched toward the bars and whispered. "A couple grand in a couple of weeks. That's what you said, right?"

I was hoping this would make her smile conspiratorially. Instead, Kindly went pale.

"Nah," she said, shaking her head. "Like I told ya the other day, I was just messin' with ya."

"No, you weren't. You only said that 'cause I turned you down. But what if I've reconsidered?"

She still wouldn't look at me.

"C'mon," I said. "I can't stand here very long. There are cameras."

"I dunno what you want."

I leaned forward. "I want *in*."

Now Kindly's eyes met mine, but her arms remained crossed, her whole demeanor standoffish. "I told you, I was just playin'."

"Listen to me, will ya? I've changed my mind. Something came up and I really need the money. And *you* need your Suboxone."

Her eyes flashed at the mention of the drug.

"You say it's a safe, sure thing," I said. "You've got a supplier on the outside, right? All we've got to do is figure out a way for me to get it in. I figure you've got ideas on that, right?"

But Kindly didn't loosen up. She tightened instead, her eyes turning to cold slits. "This is a piss poor trick."

"What? No."

"Bullshit. You're tryin' to entrap me. You're tryin' to get me to tell you how I got that Suboxone in here so you can bust me down again, ain't ya?"

My mouth went dry. I was losing her. "Sally, listen—"

"It's *Sally* now, huh? Like you're my friend all of a sudden."

"You said we could do each other favors. That's what I'm interested in, not busting you."

"Nah, you just want dirt. Well, find yourself another rat. I ain't falling for some new jack's trick, so he gets a promotion and I lose what little good time I got left."

I was getting nowhere but had to keep trying. After Charlie's diagnosis, I'd been wracking my brain for ways to raise money for his chemo treatment. A fundraiser? A loan? Both seemed impossible, given my lack of friends and already shaky finances. Kindly's offer to be a mule in the game was far from ideal, but it was a financial avenue. I'd be taking a huge risk trafficking narcotics into *a fucking prison*, but my fear of losing Charlie outweighed everything else, even my fear of being caught.

"You were willing to trust me before," I reminded Kindly. "I'm not like Robocop or the captain—you said that. I'm just a regular joe, and I'm in a tough spot and need fast cash."

She looked me up and down as if sizing me up for a fight. "Don't you have other inmates to check on?"

Her rejection stung. The longer I stood there, the more likely I was to raise suspicion, so I marked my logbook and stepped back.

"A dose of dope would feel damned good right now, wouldn't it?" I asked.

Kindly's sour face shifted between haunted and hungry. I figured if I worked on her I could wear her down, but the situation with my dog was urgent, and I also didn't know how long I'd be stationed on Raven unit where I'd be able to talk with Kindly.

"Think it over," I said. "But don't take too long."

I started moving away, expecting Kindly to call me back. She didn't. I gripped the pen harder and turned back to her.

"I could make things nicer for you," I said, "but I can also make them much harder."

I left her to consider this as I walked off.

I hadn't wanted to issue a vague threat, but I'd also not expected her to reject my offer. It only made sense to utilize what few tools I had to get Kindly to reconsider. If I was considering criminal acts, I shouldn't be above exploiting my power as a CO.

Before the end of my workday, Captain Clancy asked me to do another overtime shift. I figured this meant another night listening to poor Cherry Campbell's nihilistic waxing, but the captain wanted me back on Hummingbird. It was as if he was a master chess player, shifting his pawns all over the board. I used my half hour break to schedule another sleepover for Charlie, and relieved Tanner Wyatt of his post, which he'd been at for the past fifteen hours.

The inmates on Hummingbird seemed happy to see me, no doubt relieved it wasn't Robocop who'd picked up the shift.

Tonight, I'd be the only CO on the unit. It was close to lights-out time, so my duties would mostly be sedentary, with minimal inmate interaction. I would probably find myself wishing I had depressing Cherry around just for someone to talk to.

"Count!" I announced.

The inmates were preparing for bed. I went down the list as I strolled past them. Zoe Hallister gave me a small smile of hello. Richardson, the disgraced schoolteacher, was removing her pants, seeming to prefer sleeping in a shirt and panties. I ordered her to put them back on. She gave me a feline look I couldn't read but did as I asked. The Latinas carried on a conversation in Spanish, that little comedian Fern Hernandez nudging Lilly Gutierrez as I came by. As always, Lilly looked at me as if I were filet mignon cooked to perfection.

I gazed at the clock on the wall.

"Alright, ladies," I said. "Lights out."

I'd set the timer, so the lights turned off on their own. Some of the inmates weren't in their bunks yet, but they moved toward them as I came down the aisle toward the control center. Passing by her bunk, I noticed Lilly Gutierrez was sitting up at the edge of her bed. Fern Hernandez, her housemate, was in her own bed, facing the wall.

"Hey," Lilly said as I approached.

I looked down at the voluptuous inmate, and she smiled up at me. Her head was level with my crotch. She was in her tank top, hands on her knees, arms pressed inward to accentuate her ample cleavage.

"You need something?" I asked.

Lilly raised an eyebrow, then leaned forward and gently bit my dick through my slacks. She stopped just as quickly as she'd started, giving me no time to react, and then she plopped back onto her mattress with a girlish giggle. I thought I heard Hernandez snicker too but with her back to me I couldn't tell for sure. Just before Lilly drew her blanket over her, she looked me in the eye and slid her hand down the front of her pants, making sure I knew where her fingers were going.

A shiver went up my neck. I looked back and forth, wondering if anyone else had seen. The dormitory was dark and silent. If the inmates knew what Lilly had just done, whether they were in on it or not, they would have gone berserk, laughing and jumping on their beds. But Hummingbird was as still as moonlight. When I looked back to Lilly, she was wiggling beneath the blanket. She licked her lips, and in that instant all I wanted in the world was to tear the blanket away, spread her legs, and dive into her warm, wet embrace.

Instead, I headed to the control booth and closed the door behind me.

It was dark. The cameras probably hadn't picked up Lilly's little molestation. It could have gone so much worse. Still, I should have written her up immediately. I wished I had a better reason to not have, but the only one I could come up with was because I didn't want to discourage her advances. I liked having her mouth on me. I wanted her to keep flirting and groping—providing she could do it discretely. Considering I was trying to become a prison drug mule, why not go whole hog on corruption and get laid for the first time since my separation from my wife?

But then another thought hit me.

The more corrupt I was, the more likely it was I'd get caught. Saving Charlie was far more important than a piece of ass. As much as I needed the touch of a woman, I needed that drug money more, and I couldn't jeopardize the operation by canoodling with cons. Captain Clancy liked me because I was willing to do overtime shifts and didn't complain when he moved me from one unit to the next or gave me shitty positions like suicide watch. If I continued to build my reputation as a hard worker, it would lead my coworkers to believe I was trustworthy. Maybe even that side-eyed female CO, Diane Rodriguez, would cut me some slack. If I was going to run dope into Norrington, I'd have to do everything else by the book and not draw any unwanted attention.

If Lilly tried to get her hands (or mouth) on me again, I would write her up and see to it she was punished. I'd make sure all my superiors knew about it too, so I'd be the noble, earnest man who did the right thing, a shining example to my fellow COs. I'd be more thorough with shake downs, make more busts, write more citations, and ride the ACI brand.

The most successful criminals are the ones who can pass for Captain America. All I had to do was behave myself. I could do that.

But I didn't.

CHAPTER NINE

"How's your dog?" Zoe Hallister asked as I escorted her to the workshop.

It'd been nearly a week since I'd received the biopsy report. I hadn't gotten anywhere with Sally Kindly. She was convinced I was playing an entrapment game and stonewalled me whenever I offered to be a drug mule. I kept picking up overtime shifts and turned in more citations, making the higher-ups happy. The hours kept coming my way but, with the salary so piss-poor and the taxes on my overtime shifts so high, I barely noticed a difference in my bank account.

"You'd never know ol' Charlie was sick," I told Zoe. "He's eating well and still wants to play, even if he's slowed down some. But that comes with age anyway."

"And what about you, Liam? How're you holding up?"

That anyone cared sent a tingle through me. I felt as if I might collapse in the inmate's arms like a blubbering child.

I took a deep breath to recenter myself.

"One day at a time," I said.

Zoe smirked. "You sound like one of us."

"It's all anybody can do. Take it one day at a time."

"One thing I figured out as I became an adult is that nobody—freakin' *nobody*—knows what they're doing. The whole world is just winging it."

The truth of this made me sigh. Zoe stopped. We stood in the hall, looking in each other's eyes, creating the illusion we were somewhere other than a prison, like we were friends who were about to become something more.

"Look," she said softly. "What're you doing for money?"

I didn't catch on at first. "Working lots of overtime."

"Yeah, I know. The only people that're here more than you are the ones who're locked in. You must be fried."

"Honestly… it's killing me."

She stepped closer than what was allowed. "What if there was a better way?"

I looked up and down the empty hall.

"It's cool," she said. "We're in the cut."

"What?"

"*In the cut.* It means we're hidden from surveillance. We're alone and the cameras are broken in here, remember?"

I nodded.

"I was just thinking," she said, "maybe we could help each other out. I mean, we're friends, right?"

Zoe's smile made her seem ten years younger than she was. It reflected the girls of my youth, a flashback to when things somehow made more sense than they did now. In the smile of a certain kind of woman, a man can see a glimmering ocean. It's more than passion, lust, or even dumb love. It assures us time is not linear and fools us into thinking we can return to the happy boy the tired old man replaced. Zoe Hallister had that sort of girl-next-store smile, one that starts with the lips but finds its power in the eyes. The girl she'd been before adulthood came crashing down had peeked out from behind the dark veil of her prison image to wink at me. At that moment, we weren't a CO and an inmate in some cold penitentiary; we were mischievous kids on the first day of summer.

"Yes," I told her. "Yes, we're friends."

It started with simple stuff.

Cigarettes, tattoo ink, those airplane bottles of alcohol, better snacks and makeup than what the commissary offered. These things were contraband I could be disciplined for—okay, fired for—but nothing that could lead to a hard arrest. It was also easy to carry these items into the prison because Norrington's security checks were relatively relaxed for COs, particularly once they'd established themselves. I still had to go through the guard post when I drove in but going through the interior check line was a cake walk for a variety of reasons.

For one thing, the metal detector was old and faulty. It only worked when it wanted to and had falsely gone off several times, leading to the unnecessary searches of guards and civilians. So, the metal detector became a boy who cried wolf. And like most of the other damaged equipment in Norrington, ACI didn't want to dip into the budget to make repairs. I'd even heard from some of the veteran COs that whatever was left in the budget at the end of each fiscal quarter determined what size bonuses the captain, warden, and assistant warden received in their paychecks, but that may have just been office rumors.

Another reason the walk-through security check was easy was because we employees were always understaffed and hurrying to get to our units. Plus, rookie COs were placed at the metal detector with little idea how to even use the equipment. Some were just out of high school and had the attention span of a gnat. Establish a report with them, and you could bullshit while going through the routine, distracting them.

Accepting purchase orders from her fellow inmates, Zoe got them or their loved ones to put money on her green dot card, with any larger purchases being paid to an account her cousin handled for her. I didn't know all the details, but my service fee ranged depending on the item and quantity requested. Tobacco and alcohol were in the highest demand, and I could easily sneak the packs and tiny bottles under my clothing. Zoe and I kept coded logs and compared them regularly to make sure they matched, and I built up a collective total to be paid out to me each week. Inmates weren't allowed to have cash, but Zoe had another way to give me my share.

"My cousin Dennis," she explained on one of our slow walks to the workshop. She gave me his phone number. "He'll tell you where to meet so he can square up with you."

The thought of exchanging money under a bridge somewhere added another element of danger to what we were doing, but I couldn't think of any other way to go about the transaction. When I called the number, a fluttering voice gave me the name of a bar, and after my shift, I changed into a t-shirt and jeans and headed to Goldie's. It was just past eleven p.m. on a weeknight and the small bar was packed with men—*only* men. At a high table near the window, a skinny guy in a white jacket waved me over. He had hair like Pee Wee Herman and wore a touch of pink lipstick, his fingernails glossed.

"You Dennis?" I asked, making sure I wasn't just being hit on by a stranger.

The man nodded and gestured to the high-backed chair across from him. The music was loud, so we had to lean in to hear one another. The whole situation was nothing like I'd imagined. I'd pictured Dennis as some hardened criminal with biker tattoos and face scars. I'd thought we'd meet at some quiet, dilapidated location, not a popular gay bar. Dennis extended his hand. We shook, his boney grip harder than I'd expected.

"Beer?" he asked.

"Um, sure."

"Good, 'cause that's what I ordered you."

I hadn't planned on staying but wanted our business relationship to be a good one. Dennis drew a small envelope from his jacket and slid it across to me, making no effort to conceal the transaction from the other patrons. It didn't matter. No one was looking at us. I opened the envelope and thumbed the bills.

"Never count your money at the table," Dennis said with a smirk. "Don't you know the song?"

I slid the cash into my pocket. "Looked like more than I'm owed."

"Consider it an advance."

A waiter appeared through the crowd and dropped off our beers. Dennis had ordered us something fancy, a local brew or seasonal ale. Nerves had robbed my mouth of moisture, so I drank greedily.

"An advance, huh?" I asked.

Elbows on the table, Dennis made a temple with his fingers like a cartoon villain. "We have big plans for you."

He said it with an air of positivity, but I couldn't help but sense an aura of danger surrounding the man. The one thing that reassured me was my relationship with Zoe. We had a rapport unlike anything I had with the other inmates, and I was confident she wouldn't get me involved with anything too risky. Still, Dennis spooked me. He made sudden, twitchy movements as if he were on drugs or trying to kick them. With his feet on the rung of the seat, his legs bounced like he was playing the drums.

"Zoe tells me you need quick cash," Dennis said. "Says you're in a bind. Something about cancer."

"That's right."

I hoped she hadn't told him more than that. I wasn't pleased that this man knew anything remotely personal about me.

"Yeah, well, fuck cancer," Dennis said. "That shit's in all of us, did you know that? We've all got it. Our bodies fight it off constantly until one day the cancer just gets too strong and then *bam*—" He smacked the table. "Suddenly you're on the fuckin' chemo, puking your tits off and going bald. The cure's worse than the disease, right? It's a shit hand God lays down—more like a backhand if you ask me."

His rapid-fire speech caused me to lean back in discomfort, but Dennis didn't pick up on these social cues.

"Then," he said, "to make matters worse, we've got the American healthcare system. What a joke, right? Maybe you won't die but you'll wish you did when you get the bill. And it's all designed to rape you of as much money as they can. Doctors get rich keeping you sick, so why would they want to make you better all lickety-split, right? I'm telling you, I know. I know all about it."

I drank my beer. The sooner I finished it, the sooner I could excuse myself and go home to rest up for tomorrow's double shift.

"You're smart hooking up with Zoe," Dennis told me. "She knows what she's doing. Really plays the game right. She's told me a lot about you, Liam."

That the man knew my real name made me cringe.

"Like what?" I asked.

"She says you aren't afraid to take chances. I respect that, big time. A man's got to have balls if he's going to make it in this world. Even women need balls these days."

He snorted a laugh and downed the rest of his beer. I finished mine too and was relieved when Dennis stood, thinking our meeting was adjourned.

"Walk me to my car," he said.

I didn't ask questions even though I knew I should. We stepped out into the desert's cool night air, the sounds of the street seeming ambient after the pounding music of the bar. Dennis walked with the swaying hips of a woman, but this air of femininity did nothing to detract from his intimidating nature. Though short and lightweight, there was an unstable intensity to him that kept me anxious as we went deeper into the parking lot's shadows. I flinched when two men stepped out of a parked car, but they passed by us and headed right into Goldie's. I was alone with Dennis.

"I want to show you something," he said.

Reaching his sports car, Dennis opened the door and pulled a cardboard box into the light of a streetlamp, then tilted it toward me and opened the flaps. Cellular phones were stacked in the box like little, black bricks.

"You know how much one of these goes for in the joint?" he asked.

I bit my lip. Cell phones were high on the list of unacceptable prison contraband. Obviously, they would be pricey, and with good reason. Tens of thousands of calls went through American prisons every day, and all of them were regulated and monitored. They were also grossly expensive, costing over five dollars for a ten-minute call—no small amount of money for inmates making pennies an hour. An inmate with a private phone could speak openly with folks on the outside. To convicts, this little device all free people carried in their pockets was like a genie's lamp.

"These are burners," Dennis told me. "Disposable phones. When I buy them in bulk, they're eight dollars apiece. We could charge about seventy times that for one snuck into the joint."

"Phones all over the prison? C'mon. That's asking to be caught."

"I'm not talking about giving one to every con. All you do is sneak in a couple to Zoe. One or two just for her special, highest paying customers, and another for Zoe to keep. She can charge others to use them now and then. Simple, right?"

Looking at the plentiful box load, I shook my head. "I dunno. This isn't like sneaking in Marlboros and candy bars. Inmates can use phones to commit crimes from the inside. They can talk to their gang members or bosses… orchestrate all kinds of things."

"Shit," Dennis said through a smile. "This isn't a *men's* prison we're talking about, buddy. These ladies don't want a phone so they can order a hit on somebody. These are mommies we're talking about, right? With a phone they can talk to their children whenever they want. They can send their boyfriends pictures of their pussies. That's all it would be."

"It's still a major risk."

"That's why you'll be handsomely compensated. Take in three phones and I'll give you a grand."

I blinked. "A *thousand dollars?*"

All I'd trafficked up until this point now seemed like nickel and diming.

"You're taking the risk, right?" Dennis said. "You keep the grand and I'll take the leftover six hundred and change."

The enormity of it began to sink in. I ran my hand through my hair, eyes not leaving the box. They were just small flip phones, easy to conceal. I'd learned from doing shake downs just how inventive inmates were when it came to hide and seek. Zoe was clever. She could handle the challenges of stashing an illegal phone in Norrington. But the other prisoners, whoever they were, was another issue. They might get sloppy, and if they were caught with a phone, they might snitch. They wouldn't know I was the one to have brought the phones in, but they could rat out Zoe. I was confident she wouldn't squeal on me though. I was her supplier and friend. Every day we were growing closer and fonder of one another. It was even more reason I didn't want anything bad to happen to her.

Sometimes I even fantasized about her getting an early release. I would give positive reports about her that would go all the way up to Warden Nowak, gaining her good time and helping her make parole. Then I could take her on a proper date. We would have all the time we wanted to talk instead of those too-brief intervals in that one private hall. I imagined us having nice meals, going to the movies, and taking long walks with Charlie. Maybe we'd become an item. Maybe I'd remarry.

Of course, I'd not confessed any of these daydreams to Zoe. There'd been no amorous exchanges between us. The only hints of romance gurgled beneath the surface of whatever we had become. I saw it in a gleam of her eye or a wetting of her lips, brief flashes of tenderness expressed without the benefit of physical touch. Zoe wasn't like that sexpot Lilly Gutierrez. Zoe was girlfriend material. But unfortunately, she was incarcerated. I'd have to be patient. I'd have to wait for her, like someone whose spouse has gone off to war.

"What about Zoe's cut?" I asked Dennis about the phone deal. "She gets a piece of this too."

Dennis grinned like a jester. "Such a gentleman. You don't happen to have a gay brother, do you?" He chortled. "Hey, Zoe gets the phone. That's all she wants out of this. Besides, anything that benefits you and me benefits her too. I mean, we're a team, right?"

CHAPTER TEN

Zoe was on orderly duty. As she mopped the tier floor, I approached her, watching out of the corner of my eye for any prying inmates or COs.

"They're under the drinking fountain," I said.

Using small, magnetic clips, I'd attached the three phones to the underside of the fountain near the pipes. Zoe and the inmates who'd purchased the other two could retrieve them one at a time instead of everyone passing them by hand, which would raise the chances of getting caught.

"Okay," she said flatly. No smile. No praise.

"I also brought you that vodka you like. My treat." She kept on mopping, so I tried again. "Just consider it my way of saying thank you."

"You wanna thank me, then stop talking to me."

Her words cut like switchblades. She was painfully curt, far colder than she'd ever been before.

"Did I upset you?" I asked, hearing the weakness in my voice, and hating myself for being unable to stop it. "What's wrong?"

"We're not in private," Zoe said, still not looking at me as she dunked the mop in the bucket. "The other girls see me talking to you all the time and they'll think I'm a snitch."

"Oh."

I started walking away. Zoe was right. I'd gotten too comfortable. This wasn't a club—this was a *prison*. Certain rules applied, many that weren't written or enforced by the people in charge but by the inmates themselves.

"Better change out that water, Hallister," I said, loud enough for others to hear. "Spreading around dirty water isn't the same as mopping."

Zoe didn't reply. I wondered if I'd only made things worse by drawing attention to us. I moved through the Hummingbird dormitory making casual CO comments to other inmates just to keep up appearances, telling Fern Hernandez to stop twerking and Enola Branham to tidy up her house. Officer "Robocop" Anthony was now on yardwork duty, watching the inmates who maintained the grounds. Because of his absence, some of the inmates had gotten too lax, thinking I'd let everything slide because I was nicer than ol' Robocop.

Branham asked how her bunkmate, Cherry Campbell, was doing, and if she would come out of suicide watch anytime soon. I hadn't been keeping track of that situation and hadn't babysat Cherry since that first night, but I told Branham she was getting better and was expected back on Hummingbird within the week. I hoped making small talk with the others would make my conversations with Zoe less suspicious.

During the afternoon count, I found myself moving slowly down the line, evaluating the inmates in a different way. I wanted to know which two had paid for a phone, but Zoe told me it was better for me not to know, that it would only increase the risk of the inmates or my coworkers finding out I was involved. Besides, if I found one of the phones hidden somewhere, under most circumstances I would have to turn it in. I figured Zoe was right, but my curiosity remained, especially when I considered the phones might not be staying on Hummingbird. What if one of them found its way to Raven, into the hands of more hardened criminals? I hoped with those inmates being separated from the other units, it would be nearly impossible for someone on Hummingbird to pass a phone to one of them, but convicts were as creative with transporting contraband as they were with hiding it.

I had to trust Zoe would be discerning. I certainly thought of her as more trustworthy than Sally Kindly (I couldn't believe I'd actually considered working with the likes of that madwoman). Things were going smoothly, so I told myself not to worry about problems I didn't have. There were more than enough real ones to tend with.

I caught Lilly Gutierrez in bed with a Black woman named Jarea Madison, one of the tamer inmates in Norrington. Because she wasn't usually a troublemaker, I was surprised to find Madison between Lilly's thighs. I gave them both citations, and they were punished by the disciplinary committee. But while it made Madison colder to me, it did nothing to weaken Lilly's determination to seduce me, and the more I got away with trafficking contraband, the more I considered having sex with her. However, my delusional mind now housed fantasies of Zoe becoming my girlfriend once she got out, and this created a conflict between my heart and my loins, especially when Lilly would whisper offers to fuck me in the broom closet. It was a relief whenever I was transferred back to Raven for a few shifts. Though those inmates exhibited worse behavior, my relationships with them weren't as complicated.

With the extra money coming in, I met with an oncologist, and she started Charlie on Prednisone as a precursor to the chemo treatments he'd receive. Aside from a few potty accidents in the house, he responded to it just fine. The oncologist explained that because dogs were given less chemo than humans, they didn't suffer the upset stomach, hair loss, and other negative side effects often attributed to the treatment. The first visit cost me over seven hundred dollars, and the total I was quoted for the entire cycle was nine grand. I needed more money—much more.

"I've got something else for us," Zoe told me. "It poses a bigger risk but a much higher reward. And it would be steady business, not just a one-time sale like with the phones."

We continued down our special hallway. Today, its silence was like a graveyard. I guessed where Zoe was going with this but let her say it herself.

"Dennis can get us K-2," she said.

I exhaled. When we'd first started trafficking, I'd told myself it wasn't so bad because I wouldn't have to transport anything hard. No drugs, no weapons. Nothing that would land me in a cell of my own if I were busted. But I was rolling down a path here, gaining momentum as I hurdled downhill.

"It's synthetic weed," Zoe said. "It's the drug of choice in Hummingbird."

"I thought Suboxone was the most popular."

"Suboxone's the easiest to hide 'cause of its size, but it's addictive and shows up in drug tests. K-2 is milder and doesn't show in urine or blood."

"But it's not really weed," I said. "They told us all about that junk in training. It affects the brain more powerfully than regular weed does. It could be very bad, especially for some of the inmates who already have mental problems or are in drug recovery."

"Liam, you're sweet to care as much as you do, but these are grown women making their own choices. They're not your responsibility. And you don't know what it's like to be stuck in here sober every waking moment. Chemical release is one of the few escapes we convicts have. Besides, it's not any worse than the booze."

A couple of the mini liquor bottles I'd smuggled in had been found empty by other COs, but no busts had been made yet. The inmates were being careful. Maybe they could be trusted with K-2 as well.

"How much?" I asked.

"Half a pound can be put into a compressed package smaller than a fist. Each one would get you three hundred dollars, and you could bring in several at a time. Just one delivery could fetch a grand to put toward your dog."

"What about the *other* dogs? There are drug-sniffing Shepherds at the gate."

"That's the beauty of K-2. Canines can't sniff it out."

I stroked my beard. "You sound like you've done this before."

"I'm no stranger to the game."

The conversation stuck with me. It made me wonder what kind of relationship Zoe may have had with another CO in another prison. Had she been sent to Norrington because she'd been caught selling dope at her former facility? I thought about what Tanner Wyatt had said about not looking up what the inmates had done, that it could make it more difficult to deal with them. But I was dealing with Zoe in a whole different way now. She was my business partner in a small form of organized crime. It would be wise to investigate her past, but it would raise suspicion if I asked personnel for her file. It would also be a breach of trust between us, like a boyfriend caught reading his girlfriend's diary. It might change the way Zoe looked at me and doom our relationship before it had a chance to blossom.

"Okay," I said. "But there's just one thing I have to ask you first."

She waited. "Shoot."

"I almost hate to ask this, but if we're gonna take things to another level, I need to know a little more about you."

She eyed me curiously. "Okay…"

I bit my bottom lip, feeling like I was on a first date. "I need to ask what you're in here for."

Her blank expression fed my anxiety until she gave me a small smile. "I figured you'd already read up on me."

"I didn't want to… I dunno, *impose*, I guess."

"Fair enough," she said with a shrug. "I was a drug dealer, okay? Nothing crazy or gang related, but I was busted with enough hard stuff to be hit with intent to sell. It wasn't my first offense, so the judge threw his hammer down hard."

She left it at that. I nodded. I believed her and didn't see any reason to press for more details.

"The war on drugs, right?" she said. "What a joke."

I smirked. "Some war."

"Some fuckin' war."

We rookies were finally called in for our final exam. Instructor Burt Goodman was sporting a fresh buzz-cut and there was dried shaving cream behind one of his ears. As I entered the training room, I spotted Ileana Sloane looking as tiny as ever in her extra small uniform, and old battleax Beverly Knox sitting in the same chair she had during class. Goodman put on another video starring Fred Meredith. The CEO was in his office with the camera too close, making him appear like some geriatric Max Headroom.

"Congratulations, cadets!" Meredith said. "By now, you've lived the full ACI correctional facility experience."

I'll say.

I smirked but quickly stopped, not wanting Goodman to think I was mocking the great exalted leader.

"You are rookies no longer," Meredith continued. "All you need to do now is pass your final written test. Then you'll be dubbed official correctional officers and members of our fine family."

What're we, being knighted?

When the video was over, Goodman handed out the one-page exam and a ACI guidebook for each of us.

"The test is open book," he told us.

"Oh, good," Ileana said. "I always get nervous doing tests. Wouldn't want to come this far just to fail."

"You won't fail," Goodman said. "Nobody fails."

Most of what was on the multiple-choice test I'd already experienced firsthand, so those answers came easy, but I struggled with the ones about codes and regulations that were *supposed to be enforced* on paper but weren't in real life. The guidebook offered all the answers. This time Goodman graded the tests immediately, and all three of us passed. We were now part of King Meredith's court.

Beverly, Ileana, and I walked back to the main building together.

"Still on Raven?" I asked Ileana.

"Yeah. Mandatory overtime too. But it's alright. The captain says they're working out letting the Raven inmates return to the mess hall for meals. That'll be a load off my back. And if that goes well, they'll consider having them in the rec yard with ones from other units."

Beverly nodded approvingly. "That'll free up guards to pair together instead of us being so isolated all the time. I swear, some days I feel like I see only inmates. I've been alone in the workshop for weeks."

"It can get scary," Ileana agreed.

I glowered. "Mixing the ladies on Raven with Humming-bird or Robin could be pretty scary too."

"They won't do Robin," Beverly said. "Those women are sickly—cripples and head cases. They couldn't handle themselves 'round the hard cases on Raven. And, of course, Sparrow will stay on isolated rec time."

"Okay, but still. I think mixing Raven with Hummingbird is asking for trouble."

"What's wrong, Donnelly? Afraid of a little action?"

Ileana snickered at Beverly's jab.

What I was really afraid of was how the mingling might affect my trafficking situation. There was no doubt the contraband would start making its way to Raven now.

"Shit," Ileana said. "I'm ready for some excitement. I spend most of my shifts bored out of my mind, just sitting on my butt watching the inmates in their cells. I've done two extractions, but that's it."

Extraction was the term used for forcing an inmate out of their cell when they resisted. It involved brute force, sometimes including the use of chemical spray. I hadn't done one yet, but little Ileana with the body of a fourteen-year-old had done two. It seemed crazy to me, but many things about working in a prison are.

"Who'd you extract?" I asked.

"The last one wasn't even on Raven. I'm put on Sparrow for my overtime. We had to take Cherry Campbell out of her suicide watch cell to bathe her. She was refusing to after she'd covered herself in her own poo."

My jaw fell. "Jesus…"

"Yeah. It was nasty. I won't name names, but the CO who was supposed to be watching her fell asleep. Campbell chewed her bandages off and reopened her cuts, and tried to poison herself by rubbing feces into her wounds."

"Holy Hell," Beverly said. "Or should I say *holy shit*?"

The memory seemed to haunt Ileana, and my own experiences with Cherry Campbell made me feel even more sorry for her. Meth and madness had nuked the young woman's mind, and she'd eluded that a violent exchange with a man who'd been abusing her was what landed her in the joint. Solitary confinement was no cure for a broken psyche. She was getting worse in there.

Ileana went on. "But the first one we had to extract was on Raven—Natalia Bravo."

"Oh jeez," Beverly said. "Sorry, hon."

I remembered the name from my shifts on Raven but hadn't had much interaction with the inmate. "You know who she is, Bev?"

"Ah, yeah," Beverly said. "I've dealt with that crazy bitch. I dunno why they don't put her on Sparrow. She belongs in solitary."

"What happened?" I asked Ileana.

"She was caught fishing," she said. "Had a line running down from the cell above hers—Sally Kindly."

I nodded. So that's why Kindly didn't need me to run Suboxone anymore.

"Drugs?" I asked.

"We think so. By the time we caught it, whatever they'd been passing was gone. Kindly behaved when we did the shake downs, but Bravo didn't want to let us in her house. She said she'd only talk to the captain, but he'd gone home for the day. Bravo's roommate was removed, and I radioed backup, and Tanner Wyatt came down and tried to talk to her. He gave Bravo several warnings, but we ended up having to gas her. But she was tough. She crawled under her bed and put her face in the corner, but still didn't surrender. Tanner said he'd never seen someone stand up to the gas like that. We had to take Bravo down by hand—me, Tanner, and three other COs."

"She oughta be in seg," Beverly said again.

"Yeah," I said. "I'm surprised she's not, considering."

"There's just no room," Ileana explained. "Captain Clancy says the ones already in there are worse than Bravo. And we didn't even find any drugs when we shook her house down."

I almost said they should take poor Cherry Campbell out of her suicide watch cell and throw Natalia Bravo in there, but I bit my tongue.

"If they do let Raven and Hummingbird mix," Ileana said, "Bravo will be with her friends again. That's one thing I worry about."

"What friends?" I asked.

"The Latinas on Hummingbird. Hernandez, Ramos, Gutierrez—they're a gang, and Natalia Bravo is the leader."

CHAPTER ELEVEN

Sweat pooled in my crotch and armpits, and not just because it was a warm day in the desert. With the eight K-2 packages taped to my thighs, I approached the gate in my pickup, telling myself to relax. To the guards, this would be like every other encounter they'd had with me. Only I knew I'd become a drug mule. But no matter how I rationalized, my fears of being busted raced through my mind like electric shocks. Pulling up to the gate, I watched with gritted teeth as Teal, the Native American guard, came forward. I stepped out of the truck and fanned the doors. Baxter, the German Shepherd, sniffed it out as I stood there sweating in the arid grassland, worried they would find something, that one of the bags had popped without me noticing and spilled onto the floorboards.

I reminded myself of what Zoe had said. *Dogs can't detect K-2.*

But when Teal brought Baxter out of my truck, the dog moved toward me and started sniffing my legs. I fought my body's urge to tremble. The dog's head moved up and down my thighs, making the hairs on my ass stand up. But he didn't bark, which was the signal for contraband.

"He must smell my Charlie," I said, smiling against my terror.

Teal nodded, always a woman of few words. She leaned into the booth, pulled the lever, and the stop bar rose toward heaven, allowing me into hell. I drove on.

Already, I'd committed a crime. I'd brought narcotics onto penitentiary grounds. Not cigarettes or Maybelline or Snickers bars—illegal goddamn drugs.

Twenty-four hundred dollars.

It hardly seemed like enough to take a risk this big, but it was merely a drop in the bucket, provided I continued to play the game.

Passing through the metal detector gave me far less stress than the gate had. The teenage rookie wasn't nearly as dedicated to his duties as Teal and her canine companion. Eating a Little Debbie snack with one hand and flipping through a comic book with the other, he waved me through.

Though I'd removed my keys, wallet, and phone, the detector went off.

My heart rose into my gullet. My scrotum shrank tight around my testicles. In that instant, I was sure I was caught, that the machine had somehow picked up on the packages taped to my thighs.

But that was ridiculous. I just had to remain calm.

"This damned thing on the fritz again?" I asked the rookie.

"Man, it's always doin' that." He waved me in, not bothering to run the wand over me or even get up. He bit into his snack. "Have a good one."

As I proceeded to Hummingbird, I tensed seeing Officer "Robocop" Anthony escorting his inmate crew out for yard work. He nodded a hello but maintained his no-nonsense look. Lilly Gutierrez was among the crew, bringing up the rear. I'd been struggling with the newfound knowledge she was an actual gang member. She blew me a kiss and, because she was at the end of the line, no one else saw me when I pretended to catch her kiss in the air and stuff it into my pants pocket, shifting the bulge of K-2 as if I were jerking my dick. Her eyes flashed and she turned her head, watching me as we walked away from each other. The adrenaline of sneaking in drugs had cranked up my libido. Besides, I was tired of faking disinterest in sex. I was only human, and a man at that.

I made a pit stop in the employee bathroom and lowered my pants in the privacy of a stall. I cursed myself for using so much tape. I'd been afraid the bags might come loose, but now the tape was yanking my leg hairs out. Once removed, I stuffed the compressed K-2 baggies into my pockets, proceeded to Hummingbird, and relieved Tanner Wyatt from his post. As usual, he seemed overworked and tired, just as I'd always been before the rush of being a mule. It was better than any energy drink I'd ever had.

As I moved through the dormitory, I noticed pedo schoolteacher Ariel Richardson turn sharply in her seat, so her back was to me. She was hiding something.

Good.

As long as she was turned away, it was one less person watching what I was up to. I could shake down her house later. Lilly Gutierrez, Ramos, Brown, and Castillo were out cleaning the yards and tending to the garden. Lopez and Rivera were working in the kitchen. The unit was quiet. Branham was playing Uno with the other Golden Girls, a moniker the COs gave to inmates over the age of fifty. Fern Hernandez was listening to music, her headphones thumping with hip hop. She didn't even glance at me as I continued toward Zoe's house.

She was sitting up in bed reading a Gillian Flynn novel, but her eyes had been locked on me since the second I arrived on the unit. One corner of her mouth was turned up in the hint of a smile. Her hair hung around her shoulders in wavy, black curtains, making her fair skin look even paler. A stenciled eyebrow rose in anticipation of her presents.

We'd discussed doing the handoff in the hallway, it being a surveillance dead zone, but it would be difficult for Zoe to attach and conceal eight bags of dope in that short amount of time. If we lagged, someone might take notice; maybe that buzz killer CO Diane Rodriguez, who hadn't let me alone in the elevator with Campbell; or maybe Officer Robocop Anthony, who was always thirsty for praise from his superiors. Though the camera in the hall didn't work, the others on either end of it did, so all Captain Clancy would have to do was time how long Zoe and I went in one end and came out the other. If it was anything over a minute, I'd almost certainly be investigated.

Leaving the dope stashed in a hiding place, as I'd done with the phones placed under the drinking fountain, was considered too risky. If the phones had been confiscated or stolen by another inmate, it was a loss of only a few dollars. The K-2 was worth thousands on the street, and in here it was worth three times that. I didn't want to explain to Zoe's drug dealer cousin that another inmate made off with the goods. Dennis seemed like the sort of guy who didn't take well to losing money.

Zoe had assured me the compressed K-2 would not stay lumped together for long. She had plans for rapid distribution and wouldn't have to worry about hiding the sizable stash. And with me scheduled as the unit's only CO for the next fifteen hours, she'd run zero risk fulfilling orders.

I cleared my throat as I passed by her—our code for everything going according to plan. She pretended to read her book, her toes wiggling in anticipation as I proceeded to the end of the dormitory. All the unit's cameras fed back to the control booth, so I knew what few pockets of the dorm were dead zones—"in the cut," as Zoe called it. One such area was by the ventilation fans placed high inside the wall. Half of one fan could not be seen on any camera, and neither could the two feet of space below it. There was a standing, metal cabinet nearby which housed supplies for the orderlies. Normally, it could be seen in full on one of the cameras, but over the past week Zoe had been slowly inching it out of frame. Whenever she opened it for supplies, she causally nudged it to the right, so now only a small part of the top of the cabinet could be seen by the electric eye.

I strolled along the rear wall, making like I was checking all the cabinets, a common practice for COs. I watched the inmates out of the corner of my eye. None seemed interested in what I was doing. When I reached the last cabinet, I acted like I was taking an inventory and got down on one knee, removing myself from the cameras' view. I pretended to inspect the containers of sponges and rags and, concealing my right side behind the open door, I transferred the contents of my pocket to the plastic bucket within and buried the tight bags of K-2 in a shallow grave of detergent powder. I did it all in seconds, closed the cabinet, and proceeded down the unit.

It was hours before Zoe went anywhere near the dope. She was on orderly duty again today, and no one paid any attention when she retrieved supplies from the cabinet. Only I noticed the slight, pale blue dust on her fingertips. Only someone looking for it would have. The rags stacked in her arms didn't look suspicious either, though I knew what treasures lay sandwiched in their folds.

What she did with the baggies after that was another piece of information Zoe assured I was better off not knowing.

CHAPTER TWELVE

When Dennis called me, I was in my underwear in front of the TV, eating a bowl of Cookie Crisp. It was two in the morning. I had the night off, but my sleep schedule was non-existent, so I napped more than I slept a full eight hours. I figured if it worked for Charlie it could work for me. I stared at my vibrating phone, Dennis' name filling me with unease. Now that Zoe had a private phone, she handled things with Dennis, so I only met with him to do pickups. He'd never called me when a deal wasn't already scheduled.

Don't answer it.

It was very late. It wouldn't be a stretch to say I'd been asleep. But what if he kept calling? I would have to talk to him at some point, and the longer I waited the more anxious I would become, whereas if I picked up the phone now, I could find out what he wanted rather than allowing my imagination to go berserk. The edible I'd taken hours before had begun to wear off. I could handle a phone call.

"Hey, big guy," he said when I answered. "You up?"

"Not exactly."

He snickered. "Well, get up and get dressed. I've got something for you. Something real nice."

Zoe hadn't told me about anything, but I didn't want to mention her name on the phone. Whatever hot new item Dennis had, I figured I should discuss it with her first.

"Oh," I said. "Okay. Can you show it to me another time? It's late."

"No, sir. This must be done *tonight*. You know the White Feather Inn on Redding?"

I sat up straight. Redding Avenue was an offshoot of Historic Route 66. Most of the businesses that had once existed upon that stretch of road were now rusted remnants, long abandoned. Only two businesses remained open—a country store selling Navajo jewelry and blankets, and a single-story shithouse of a motel better known for drug overdoses than tourists.

"You mean that dump on the rez?" I asked.

The rez. A term Arizonians used to refer to the impoverished Native American Indian reservations, some of which were towns unto themselves. Quality of life on the rez was abysmal. The federal programs involved in reservation housing were embarrassingly inadequate, and most residents lived in crushing poverty. Crime was a major problem, especially in the central neighborhoods of Navajo County, with women in particular being frequent victims of violence.

Most people outside the reservations tried to avoid these places. Outsiders were warned to never get pulled over on the rez. Having not adopted the constitution, these forgotten towns in Navajo County practiced their own tribal laws and had their own justice system. Given what whites had done to Native Americans for hundreds of years—and continued to do even in a hyper politically correct climate—it was hard to blame the Navajo people for their dislike of white strangers.

"Can you meet me there in thirty?" Dennis asked.

"You wanna go to the rez in *the middle of the night*?"

"Now, now. Don't get hysterical. I haven't steered you wrong yet, have I? There's a good score here and I just need an extra hand. I could've called anybody, but I know you need money for the puppy, so I'm offering this to you. Think of it as a gift from Cousin Dennis."

The muscles in my neck tightened. I stared into my bowl at the little cookies floating in milk. By my feet, Charlie was on his side, snoring even though he was awake.

"What is it?" I asked Dennis. "Tell me what it is."

"Hey now. We're on the phone."

"C'mon…"

"Don't be a tampon. Just meet me at the motel in thirty. This goes well, and your money woes just might be over."

Twenty-five minutes later, I pulled onto Redding Ave. The streetlights were few and far between and the dilapidated remains of abandoned buildings loomed like crumbling beasts in the shadows of the night. Between them, random garbage was clustered in little dumping grounds throughout the barren grassland.

I spotted the neon sign of the White Feather Inn. Half the letters were dead and black. Pale lights shone up from the ground, turning the cacti into campfire ghosts. The building was flaky with wood rot, its white paint stained with mold and dirt. A few dusty pickup trucks and a blue Firebird were in the parking lot. I didn't see Dennis' car. No one was loitering about outside but a door to one room stood partway open, red light glowing from within. I wasn't about to investigate. I parked my truck far from the other cars and waited, biting my nails, wondering why I'd been stupid enough to come.

A few minutes went by before a pair of headlights burned through the darkness. A modern sedan. I couldn't recall the exact make and model Dennis drove, but this vehicle was different from the one I'd seen him in. But when the car parked beside mine, he was the one who stepped out. In a weird way, I was relieved to see him. At least it was someone I knew.

"Well, well," he said, shifting the backpack on his shoulder. "Big night for the Beaver."

I stepped out of my truck. "You wanna tell me what the hell we're doing here?"

Drawing a cigarette from his breast pocket, Dennis lit up, the flame from his lighter giving him a haunted visage. "Let's make a deal."

"What?"

"A *deal*. We're meeting some friends of mine for a little transaction."

He grinned and put his arm around my shoulders, guiding me toward the motel. I barely avoided stepping on a used diaper in the parking lot. The red light in the open doorway served as a lighthouse as we journeyed on.

"Just let me handle the talking," Dennis said. "You're my backup, alright? That's all."

"If these people are your friends, why do you need backup?"

He patted my shoulder. "You can never be too careful."

As if to emphasize this, Dennis shoved something heavy into my hoodie's pocket. When I put my hand inside, I felt the cold shape of a pistol. I stopped walking but Dennis pressed my back with one hand to move me onward.

"It's okay," he said in a hush. "Everything's going to be fine."

I stammered. "I… I don't wanna do this."

"Too late now. You take off and they'll notice. They'll suspect you're up to something and chase you through the desert and run you off the road. You don't want to know what they'll do after that."

"Jesus…"

"Don't be nervous. But if you must be, don't let it show."

I glanced at his backpack. "What've you gotten me into?"

"Serious loot, that's what. Now just be grateful and shut up."

As we stepped onto the walkway, a tall shadow entered the doorway. A man poked his head out into the white glow of the overhead fluorescents. He was Native American, maybe thirty years old, with long hair in a ponytail. A beaded necklace with a boar's hoof was slung around his neck. He wore an open denim vest over a smooth, naked torso, with dusty jeans and alligator skin boots. Behind him was a light haze. The smell of marijuana was overpowering.

"Hey," Dennis said to him. "What's up, buddy?"

The man looked at me. "Friend of yours?"

Dennis smiled. "He's cool. No worries, man."

I nearly extended my hand but thought better of it. Keeping names out of this was probably the best way to go. The man held the door in place. I noticed the frame was covered in dents, as if someone had broken into the room with a crowbar.

"You didn't mention any friends," the man told Dennis.

"Hey," Dennis said, "we're all friends here, right?"

The man said nothing.

"Are you telling me you're alone in there?" Dennis asked.

The man remained stoic but stepped aside, allowing us passage. Red bandanas were draped over the lamps, filling the room with a crimson glow. A teenage Navajo girl was stretched out on one of the beds, a bong in the lap of her cut-off shorts. She didn't even look at us. Sitting beside her on the edge of the bed was a heavyset Native American man dressed in all black, his hair short, arms like hams, jaw like cinder block. His dark eyes threw daggers. Slumped in a corner chair was a white man. His eyes were closed, head on his shoulder. At first, I thought he was dead, but his belly moved when he breathed. A shoelace was tied around one bicep, his forearm peppered with needle marks.

The long-haired man closed the door, and I was struck by the feeling of being trapped, like a coal miner in a collapsing tunnel. Doing as I was told, I remained taciturn, letting Dennis lead the way.

"The money?" the longhaired man asked.

Dennis smiled like a used car salesman. "The stuff?"

The other man rose from the bed. He nudged the girl, and she seemed to come out of a dream. He said something to her in their native tongue. Scooting off the bed, she plopped down on the other one, turning on her side, away from us. The muscly man raised the first mattress and withdrew a throw pillow.

Only it wasn't a throw pillow. It was a freezer bag stuffed with square, paper sheets.

Dennis's eyebrows drew closer together. "Wait… no lollipops?"

The long-haired man remained deadpan. "Out of stock. What does it matter? Fentanyl is fentanyl."

"I don't know why the kids like those lozenge sticks so much anyway. Then again, back in my day, we all took ecstasy and sucked on pacifiers while we danced, so maybe it's like that. They want something to do with their mouths." Dennis looked to the girl. "Is that what you prefer, honey?"

The long-haired man frowned. "Don't talk to her, talk to me."

"Okay, okay," Dennis said. "Let's all be cool. Don't worry, I'm not even into girls."

"The money."

"I've got it." Dennis raised his shoulder, gesturing toward the backpack. "But this is a whole different product you've got here, my friend. Sure, it's fentanyl, but we've got to settle on a new price, right? How many patches are in there?"

"Enough to keep you in business for a long time. You can sell them for forty or fifty bucks each." From the looks of it, the bag contained several hundred patches. "It's yours for the same price we discussed."

"I dunno." Dennis rubbed his chin. "College kids really like their lollipops. I might have a hard time moving these old man patches."

The Navajo's eyelids tightened. "You know you won't."

"C'mon," Dennis said, his salesman smile spreading wide, "you're asking for the same thirty for a totally different product."

I shivered. *Thirty?* Did he mean *thirty grand?*

"Alright," the long-haired man said. "Twenty-eight."

"If there're five hundred in there, I'm only looking at making twenty."

The muscly man spoke up. "There's over eight hundred in the bag."

"Okay," Dennis looked at the ceiling, contemplating. "So that's what… thirty-two, maybe thirty-four tops? My take is a lousy four grand? You've got to do better than that, my friend."

The Navajo men exchanged glances.

"I'll give you eighteen," Dennis said.

"No fuckin' way," the muscly man snapped.

My whole body went rigid. Dennis seemed completely relaxed. I hoped that was a good sign instead of one that he was an idiot.

"Okay," Dennis said. "Out of respect, I'll give you a nice, round twenty."

The long-haired man squinted. "Twenty-five."

"Twenty is my top, friend."

"I'm not your friend."

Dennis shook his head. "You know what? That's fine. We've had a good thing going here, chief, but if you don't want to be *ke-mo sah-bees*, I'll take my business elsewhere."

My heart raced as Dennis turned to leave. I wanted to grab onto his coattails and tuck my head. Maybe if I closed my eyes, I'd awake to find I wasn't really here but had passed out stoned in my chair and was having a nightmare.

"Wait," the long-haired man said.

Dennis stopped and looked back at him.

"Okay," the man said. "Twenty." The muscly man grumbled, and the long-haired man shushed him. "We need to move this stuff."

"Where'd you get this anyway?" Dennis asked.

"Don't push it."

"Alright, alright. Jeez. So sensitive."

He slung the backpack off his shoulder and placed it on the bed. The muscly man tossed the plastic bag toward Dennis as he rooted for the money, laying out wrapped bricks of fifty-dollar bills.

"Want to count it?" he asked when finished.

The long-haired man smirked but there was no humor in it. "We'll trust you… *kemosabe.*"

"That's more like it." Dennis put the plastic bag into the backpack with the remaining cash and slung it over his shoulder. "See? It's better for all of us when you play nice."

His condescension sent tremors through me. These men did not seem like the type to be trifled with. I didn't fear them because they were Navajo, but because they were clearly hardened criminals. When it came to these kinds of drugs and this kind of money, terrible things could happen—and often did. Dennis was still carrying ten grand these men seemed to think they should have. He was poking the dragon pretty hard.

"The lollipops," the long-haired man said. "You still want them?"

"Just as soon as you can get them," Dennis said.

"Maybe next week."

"I'll be around."

The man narrowed his eyes. "Then that's where I'll see you."

We exited the motel room, and the man closed the door behind us. Following Dennis, I realized he had the same swagger as Lilly Gutierrez, his hips cocking from side to side. If he'd had longer hair, he probably would have flipped it. I resisted the urge to look over my shoulder as I tailed behind him. I half expected the Navajos to come after us with guns, so I kept my hand close to the pistol in my hoodie's pocket. When we reached our vehicles, I finally looked back. The door to the room remained closed.

"See?" Dennis said. "That wasn't so bad."

"*Not so bad?* I was scared shitless in there."

"Oh, don't be such a bigot."

"A *what?* Hey, that's not—"

"Relax. I'm just playing with you a little bit."

Dennis reached into his bag and handed me bricks of cash—two thousand dollars.

"Not exactly what I was expecting," I said. "You told me my money troubles would be over."

"Patience, Liam, patience. This is just the beginning." He removed the rest of the money, put it on the passenger seat of his car, then handed me the backpack. "This is where the real money comes in."

I stared at the sack of fentanyl patches within. "You want me to... no, man, wait a sec..."

"Forty bucks a piece, that stupid Indian says. That's just the *street price.* Prison prices can be double that."

"Dennis—"

"Sixty-four thousand dollars, big guy. You manage to move these in Norrington, I'll give you forty percent. Twenty-five grand and change."

"There ain't no way."

I tried to hand the backpack to him. He wouldn't take it.

"Okay," Dennis said. "You're right, you're right. I fronted the money but you're taking all the risk, right? How about we split it then? *Thirty-two grand.* Each. That's seven grand more in your pocket."

I exhaled. "Speaking of pocket…" I took the pistol from my hoodie and extended it handle first. "Here's your rod back."

"You keep it. For next time."

"*Next time?*"

"You may never need a gun, but if ever you do, you'll be glad to have it. Trust me on that."

I shook my head, trying to make sense of the situation I'd landed myself in. Things had escalated so quickly. Was this how all criminals accelerated? Was this how so many normal people ended up in prison? Suddenly all the women in Norrington made more sense. Life swings hard and sometimes you're not fast or smart enough to duck.

"I can't sneak fentanyl into prison," I said. "Besides, how would we even get paid? It's not like an amount of money that huge can go on Zoe's green dot card."

"True. But there are other ways. The girls on the inside have people on the outside who can cover costs with sweet, sweet cash."

"Nah, man. K-2 is one thing. It's easy to get through 'cause it's hard to detect. The dogs we have at Norrington can sniff out fentanyl."

"In loose powder form. These are patches. They're probably harder for dogs to sniff out."

"*Probably?* You want me to risk my freedom for a *probably?* This bag is huge."

"So, we do things differently then." Dennis gave me a smile. It was meant to be reassuring but didn't have that affect. "We get creative. There's always a way. Always." He put his hands on my shoulders. "Remember, Liam—your dog needs you. Charlie, right?"

I nodded.

"Charlie needs you, and Zoe tells me you care about that dog like he was your own son. Isn't his life worth the minor inconvenience of figuring out how to get these stupid little patches into Norrington?"

I took another deep breath. Dennis was correct.

"Take a few days," Dennis said. "When you're at work, look for cracks in the system—frailties, loopholes, tricks. Do some redneck engineering. MacGyver that shit."

"Okay," I said with a sigh. "I'll try. But we have to be extremely careful."

"Sure. Absolutely."

"No, I mean even once I get it in there. This shit is practically heroin. People overdose on it. They get hooked."

"Well, let's hope for the latter. Better for business, right?"

"If this whole bag gets in, it'll be an epidemic in the penitentiary. It'll raise too many eyebrows. The whole joint will be put on lockdown and the warden will call in the STIU."

"What's STIU?"

"Security Threat Intelligence Unit. They're basically the FBI for prisons. We've gotta take it slow. Bring these things in a little at a time, provided I find a safe way to do it."

A short silence hung between us. I still wasn't sure I was going to do this, but if I was, I would do it my way. Dennis was in no position to argue. I was the only one with full access to the prison, the only one who could mule for him.

"It'll take longer to get that jackpot," he finally said, "but maybe you're right."

"I *am* right," I said, surprised by my own backbone.

I reached into the bag and withdrew a few of the smaller bags, maybe three hundred patches in all, then handed the rest back to Dennis.

"You take the remainder," I said, "for your college kids."

Smoke billowed from his nostrils. He went to the driver's side of his car and opened the door, grinning like a cartoon devil as he tossed the bag in.

"Have it your way, big guy," he said. "As long as it gets done."

CHAPTER THIRTEEN

The next afternoon, Captain Clancy asked to see me the moment I came in for my shift. The walk to his office took longer than usual. I was reminded of heading to the principal's office when I was in high school, something I'd done many times. Sweat cooked in the folds of my flesh. I hadn't brought anything into the prison that day but was nervous as if I had.

When I entered, assistant warden Lawrence Moore was standing near the captain's desk. Captain Clancy told me to shut the door behind me and take a seat. I did, and the cushion made a noise like a fart. We all said our good mornings, then the assistant warden got down to it.

"Do you know why we called you in here today?" he asked.

"No, sir."

"There's been an issue. On Hummingbird."

I waited for more.

"A big issue," the captain added.

"Indeed," Moore said. "You see, Officer Donnelly, we have reason to believe—hell, *we know*—that a CO has been involved in illegal activity with an inmate."

I gripped the armrests to keep from shaking. I looked to both men, as if one of them might save me from the other, as if all the overtime I'd worked, and all my team player credit, would grant me leniency. I was merely grasping for anything to keep me from falling into this pit. I knew I'd been busted. They just wanted to hear me admit it. I nearly blurted out that I wanted a lawyer, but Captain Clancy spoke before I could find the courage to open my mouth.

"Don't be offended, Liam," he said. "We're not singling you out. There've been several COs on Hummingbird in the past few months and we're talking to all of them."

I could breathe again. They knew something was up but didn't know I was the culprit. At least, not yet. A shake down must have turned up a bag of K-2 or a phone. I wondered if Zoe was the inmate they'd busted. She wouldn't confess, would she?

"You know what we're talking about?" Moore asked.

"No," I said as calmly as I could. "No, sir."

The men looked at each other as if deciding who would be the bringer of bad news. Finally, Captain Clancy folded his hands upon his desk and leaned toward me.

"Donnelly," he said, "this is about inmate Lilly Gutierrez."

I blinked. My mind scrambled to rewire. Here I'd been preparing to face questions about Zoe—perhaps even charges— and my superiors suddenly flipped the entire narrative on me. Surprise must have shown on my face.

"There's been an infraction involving her," the captain explained. "A very serious one. Between her and a CO."

My memory rattled with images of Lilly giving my dick a nibble and me miming jacking off as I passed her in the hall. Had we been seen after all? My heartbeat began to slow. These instances would bring reprimands, maybe even termination of employment, but there would be no arrest.

"What happened?" I dared ask.

Moore stood before me and leaned on the desk. "Last week, Lilly came into the infirmary complaining of stomach problems. She was given medication but came back saying it hadn't helped. Thinking drugs might be the problem, the nurses gave her urine and blood tests."

He paused, clearly waiting for me to say something.

"Okay," I said. "What'd they find in her?"

"Not what any of us expected. They didn't find drugs inside her—they found a baby."

My eyes went wide. "A *baby?*"

"That's right. Inmate Gutierrez is pregnant."

A strange combination of shock and relief rippled through me. I was flabbergasted that Lilly Gutierrez was with child, and yet happy about it because I knew I wasn't the father. I'd never even touched the woman, despite how intimately she'd once touched me.

"With no conjugal visits," Moore said, "that means she had intercourse illegally, inside our prison, which means one of two things. Either a guard in the visitation room allowed her to sneak off into a corner with some boyfriend, which I doubt given all the cameras, or a guard engaged in intercourse with her himself."

"Wow," I said with genuine shock. "Mr. Moore, Captain Clancy—this is the first I'm hearing about any of this. I have absolutely nothing to do with it."

I made sure to look them in the eye. I wasn't lying, so it was easy.

Moore crossed his arms. "You work regular shifts on Humming-bird."

"Yes, sir. It's my main unit."

"How would you describe inmate Gutierrez?"

"Well, for the most part, she's been fine. Never violent. Never been a danger to herself or others, far as I've seen. Her shake downs have been clean. But there have been some issues. Sex related infractions. I mean, I wrote her up for screwing around with another inmate."

"Yes. We have that on record. Have you noticed any other sexual misconduct?"

I could almost feel Lilly's teeth on my dick again. It'd been dark when it happened. No one had seen. If the cameras had picked it up, I would have already been disciplined for not reporting it. But not every second of surveillance footage was watched and scrutinized. Perhaps they'd only see it now while reviewing the footage to find out who'd knocked the inmate up. If they had and I told them there'd been no other sexual misconduct with Lilly, I would be caught in a lie. On the other hand, if I told the truth, I might be confessing to something they knew nothing about.

"No," I said. "I've not seen anything."

I'd decided to go with the lie. If I were caught in it, that meant my bosses knew about the dick nibble, so I was in trouble either way. A horrible silence filled the room. I knew they were waiting for me to babble like guilty people often do, watching my body language for any signs of bullshit.

Finally, the captain said, "Lilly is known for being a vicious flirt. She's been written up for making lewd comments to COs multiple times, including female officers. She even propositioned me once." He stared at me. "Surely, you must have experienced this too."

I nodded. I had to concede to something. A bit of truth could gain me a lot of trust with these men, something I could always use.

"Yes, Captain," I said. "She's made comments to me on occasion."

"But you didn't write her up."

"No."

Moore looked down at me. "And why not?"

"Well… to be completely honest, I didn't want to jump on every little thing the inmates did. I don't want to be everyone's enemy. I mean, you've both been COs. I don't have to tell you how helpful it is to have a rapport with the inmates on your unit. If I wrote them up for every little thing, they'd hate my guts and do everything in their power to make my job more difficult."

"So you let things slide?" Moore asked.

"I'm firm with them. I've turned in plenty of citations— I'm sure the captain will attest to that. But little things like Gutierrez commenting on my eyes or making a kissy face at me… yes, I guess I let that slide."

"And that's all she's done?"

"That's all. Never anything too out of line. No bad language even."

"We've heard different stories from other officers."

"About her interactions with them or me?"

Moore smirked. "With them. For what we've been told, she can be very aggressive sexually."

I shrugged. "Maybe I'm just not her type."

My superiors didn't seem to appreciate the levity. Again, I was surprised by my own backbone. Something was changing in me. Perhaps I was proud of myself for mustering the courage to be a mule and was emboldened by my success. Just last night I'd been involved in a high-stakes drug deal that could have turned bad. I had hundreds of fentanyl patches at home. I had a *fucking gun*.

"This is a serious matter, Officer Donnelly," Moore said.

"Yes, sir. I didn't mean to suggest it wasn't, and I apologize if I made it seem that way. I'm happy to cooperate with the investigation."

"I'm glad to hear that. So, answer me this. Have you noticed anything funny going on between Gutierrez and any of your fellow officers?"

There were many bad things one could have called me, but a rat wasn't one of them. It pained me to even write up the inmates because I felt like a lousy snitch, especially considering I was now a criminal just like they were. I suddenly recalled what Beverly Knox had told me during our first days of training.

Half of cadets become dirty COs.

I didn't know who'd been fucking Lilly. But even if I had, I wouldn't have given up their name to the bosses for breaking a rule I didn't agree with in the first place. If Lilly had been raped, it would be totally different, but that didn't seem to be what happened here.

"Sorry," I said, "but I haven't noticed anything."

I left it at that. So did my superiors. For the time being, I was free to go. I was needed on my unit.

Hummingbird.

I had to make a bust. That much was clear. The better the work I did, the lesser I would feel all those eyes on my back. My only solace was knowing the other male COs were being watched too, and not just the ones on Hummingbird. Lilly could have been impregnated in the kitchen or the showers or… anywhere, really. The Hummingbird dormitory was actually the least likely place a CO would have fucked her. It was too wide open, too many cameras, too many other inmates around. I doubted Lilly was that stupid. Oral sex at night with another prisoner was one thing. The other inmates didn't care. But screwing a guard would turn every head on the unit.

Make a bust, I told myself.

I started the routine shake downs. It would make me feel better to get a pat on the back for something after that little interrogation. As far as the bosses knew, I was a model ACI employee. I just had to keep reenforcing that image until this pregnancy scandal cooled.

Houses were torn apart. Totes turned inside out. Belongings scrutinized. I was more thorough than I'd ever been, using my flashlight in every little cranny, emptying the contents of each bag and envelope. The inmates pissed and moaned, but I continued unabated. I was halfway through searching inmate Ramos' belongings when I remembered something that could make the whole situation easier.

When I'd hid the K-2 in the supply closet, I'd noticed Ariel Richardson turn her back to me. I knew she'd been hiding something, but I'd been too busy with my own contraband to care. I'd forgotten about the fallen schoolteacher until now. I left Ramos' house and went to Richardson, who was sitting cross-legged upon her bed. She gazed up at me with dazzling eyes, her cheeks pink as if flushed by embarrassment, full lips slightly parted. Even in her bland prison uniform she was stunningly beautiful, hot as any movie starlet. Being a diddler of little boys would make most women less attractive, but with Richardson, it was only a reminder she was not only sexual, but perverted, which in a way made her more erotic.

"Stand up, inmate," I said.

Richardson got off the bed and stepped out of her house, standing just outside of it as I began my search. I wasn't sure what I was looking for. A tab of Suboxone? Mephedrone? A pipe or binky like the one Sally Kindly had hidden up her snatch? Perhaps Richardson had already ingested whatever she'd been hiding, but even resin or ash would be enough to bust her.

As I went through her meager belongings, Richardson watched me with dead eyes. Her face turned pinker. She had a container of Kool-Aid, and I poured the powder on a sheet of paper to sift through it. I rooted through her clothes, bras, and panties. I inspected her lipsticks and makeup kit. As I turned her pillowcases inside out, I felt something stiff inside the pillow.

I gave it a squeeze. Within the stuffing was a small, hard mass.

I looked to Richardson. Her face was red now.

"What's in here?" I asked. "Anything going to stick me or cut me?"

Richardson didn't speak, only shook her head. Inspecting the pillow, I found an opening just big enough for three fingers. Whatever she'd hidden in there, she'd tucked it deep within the stuffing. Using both hands, I tore the case open like a bag of potato chips. The other inmates were watching now. The stuffing fell about me like snow, and then the black mass dropped into my lap.

I recognized it immediately. I'd been the one to sneak it in.

Picking up the burner phone, I flipped it open. The screensaver image was a photo of a preteen boy holding his erect penis. When I looked at Richardson again, her eyes were swimming. I didn't see shame or remorse, only disappointment in losing her treasure. I opened the text messages and found she'd been in contact with several young boys, using the phone to send dirty messages and graphic photos. She must have memorized her students' numbers before incarceration. There were several nude shots she'd taken of herself in bathroom stalls. In many of them, she was playing with herself. The boys had sent her raunchy selfies in return. I couldn't help but marvel at Richardson's bare body in those porn star poses. The temptation to text those selfies to my phone was strong, but I knew better. What might I have done if the other inmates hadn't been watching? What might I have done if I wasn't desperate to make a bust?

"Inmate Richardson," I said, putting the phone in my pocket. "I need you to turn around."

She assumed the position. I slapped the cuffs on her.

I turned to the radio on my shoulder to call the captain. It was going to be a good day after all.

"Business is booming," Zoe said as we strolled down the hall. "My cousin take care of you?"

"Yeah. And then some."

I'd been paid for the K-2. Zoe had sold out and was asking me to sneak more in. I told her about the bag of fentanyl patches I had at home and how I'd acquired them. She seemed surprised.

"Dennis didn't tell you about it?" I asked.

"No."

"Wonder why."

She shrugged. "Maybe the little prick thinks he can cut me out of the deal."

"How? It's not like I can distribute the stuff myself."

"I've seen COs do it in other jails."

"No, I need you for that."

"I'm game, but how're you going to get that stuff in here?"

I shook my head. "I'm not. Not yet. There's too much heat right now."

"I heard. Lilly's got a bun in the oven."

"How'd you hear about that?"

Lilly Gutierrez had been put in solitary on Sparrow pending the investigation. Word had traveled anyway.

Zoe smiled. "Prisons are like high schools when it comes to gossip."

"Any idea who the father is?"

"No, but I wouldn't say if I did. I'm no snitch and don't spread rumors. For all I know it was you."

The words strung me like a wasp.

"Hey," I said, stopping us. "I never laid a hand on Lilly or anyone else."

"But she groped you."

My mouth went dry. Zoe knew about the dick nibble. If she knew, who else did?

"Relax," she said, "I saw you two that night, but I don't think anyone else did, and like I said, I don't spread gossip."

"I appreciate that," I said, hoping she was being truthful. "But I didn't have sex with Lilly."

"But you didn't seem to get mad at her when she put her mouth on your dick."

"Look, it's complicated, Zoe. You don't understand what it's like to be a CO here."

"You mean to be a man in power in a cage full of women?"

I exhaled. "Don't put it like that."

"What other way is there to put it?"

"I just don't want you to think of me that way. Lilly shocked me when she did that. I was too stunned to do anything, and afterward I was too embarrassed."

It wasn't exactly the truth, but it would do. I didn't want Zoe to think I'd screw around with another woman. We were developing a relationship here.

"Okay," she said. "So, who do you think the father is?"

We were getting closer to the workshop. "I have no idea. To hell with it. It's not my business. But until this thing blows over, there's gonna be a lot more focus put on Hummingbird. We need to lay low."

"Hey, I get it. Just hope Dennis does."

I almost asked what she meant by that, but just as we reached the door Officer Beverly Knox stepped out of the shop, nearly bumping into us.

"Oh, hello," she said. "Didn't mean to run you over. Just have to step out for a minute." She looked to Zoe. "Hey, Hallister. Get with Officer Rodriguez. She's in shop with us today and has some stuff for you."

Beverly moved out of the doorway, and there was Diana Rodriguez, giving me the same distrustful glance she always did when I was with a female inmate. I sensed it was even stronger after what had happened with Gutierrez. To Rodriguez, I was obviously a suspect. Everyone with a cock was. She guided Zoe into the shop like a protective mother bear. When I nodded and gave Rodriguez a polite smile, she only returned the nod. It was then I realized I'd never seen her happy.

Walking back to Hummingbird, I was intercepted by the captain.

"Liam," he said. "Got a moment?"

"Um, sure."

Thinking I was being called back into the office, a tremor of fear went through me, but Captain Clancy put his hand on my shoulder in a fatherly way. We were alone, so he spoke freely.

"I'm moving you to yard duty," he said. "We need someone to supervise the inmates that clean up the grounds. Since they're from Hummingbird, I figured you'd be a good fit."

"Sure, okay. But what about Anthony? I wouldn't want to take anything away from him."

The captain shifted his jaw. "Anthony Nelson has been suspended."

I nearly lost my footing. *Robocop? Suspended?*

Officer Anthony was the biggest bootlicker in Norrington; a by-the-books, hard-nosed douchebag. Was it possible he'd been the one to…

"Until further notice," Captain Clancy said, "you'll be taking over yard duty. It's a good place to be stationed. Fresh air and sunshine. You'll be down one crew member with Gutierrez in seg, but I'm sure we'll get another volunteer. Anyone you'd recommend?"

CHAPTER FOURTEEN

"You know where the word *penitentiary* comes from?"
Tanner Wyatt asked.

We were in the control booth on Hummingbird. It'd
been a quiet day after word started floating around about
Officer Anthony and Lilly Gutierrez. Suddenly everyone
had the dirt, but most of it sounded like utter horseshit.

"No," I said. "Where does the word come from?"

"*Penitentiary* is derived from *penance*. You know, like monks
who do their penance in a temple or monastery or wherever.
You serve your time to become worthy of righteousness."
He smirked. "I used to think that defined just the inmates.
Now I think it applies to us too. The COs, the captains, the
wardens—anyone inside these walls."

"What is it you think we're serving a penance for?"

"Ain't sure. But we've all got our sins."

"You think God put us in these jobs?"

Tanner only shrugged.

With the logbooks taken care of, I rounded up the yard workers for their chores. Ramos, Brown, Castillo, and the new hire, Zoe Hallister. I'd recommended her to the captain, and because of her good behavior he'd agreed to put her on the yard. It was an easy decision for me to make. It would allow me more time with Zoe, which was good for both business and pleasure. With the sexual misconduct case solved, things inside Norrington had returned to normal, or as normal as prison life gets. The warden and others at the top would have to answer to the Department of Corrections and the American Correctional Association, but otherwise the heat had died down, or was at least off the backs of the COs.

With bills mounting, my thoughts returned to trafficking.

It was a clear day. The warmth of spring was pushing the temperature near eighty, but the dry heat felt good as the sunshine fell upon my face. The crew carried the rakes and buckets from the shed, and I directed Castillo and Ramos to the garden where they always worked. Ernestine Castillo—one of the Golden Girls—had been a passionate gardener as a free woman. Sandra Ramos, a Latina youth with a mohawk, spoke little and worked hard at whatever task she was given. Nina Brown, a heavyset woman with a high, girlish voice, was on cleanup, so I paired Zoe with her to bag debris.

Brown was one of the few inmates who didn't insist upon her innocence. She often talked about her drug addiction and alcoholism which led her to committing armed robberies to support her habits. Now she was high on Jesus and enjoyed "working with Mother Earth to be closer to God's creation."

A few ravens flapped about, hoping the humans might offer bread. The horses in the stable huffed, and again I wondered why the warden continued to pay for their care while the prison needed so many repairs. The only purpose the horses served was to chase after escaped convicts through the desert wasteland surrounding the prison, but that had never happened here, and wouldn't all-terrain vehicles have been more affordable in the long run?

As the inmates worked, I gazed out at the sandstone formations to the rear of the building. In so many ways, the deserts of the American southwest were like another planet entirely. This was where all the sci-fi movies were filmed when a director wanted to recreate Mars. In the days when westerns ruled the silver screen, Hollywood spent a great deal of money to shoot in places like this. Now this poor county had to stay afloat by selling land to companies like ACI so they could build more prisons.

Fuck 'em, I thought. *It wasn't their land to begin with.*

Inmate Brown jumped back, dropping her rake. "Eww!"

I looked down at what repulsed her. The bird was dead but didn't have any visible injuries, and there were no insects on it, so it must not have been dead for long. Its body was peppered with black spots, but they were part of its plumage, not rot. Its pink head was bright as an Easter basket.

"Well would you look at that," Zoe said. She crouched beside the carcass. "Incredible."

Brown winced. "It's not incredible, it's gross!"

Zoe reached for the bird, cupping it in her gloved hands. Brown made a sour face but looked closer.

"You know what type of bird this is?" Zoe asked us. When we didn't reply, she said, "It's a hummingbird. An Anna's hummingbird." She pointed out the long beak. "When I was a kid, we had a feeder on our back porch. They used to come by all the time, and I'd watch them. I loved how they seemed to hover in midair."

"What happened to this one?" I asked.

Zoe's eyes were hooded in the shadows cast by the sun. "Nothing. Sometimes things just die."

"Okay," Brown said, "so throw it in the trash, will ya?"

As she pointed to the garbage bag at our feet, an idea came to me. It was a sudden burst of brilliance, and I was tempted to tell Brown to fuck off so I could share the idea with Zoe.

"I'm not throwing it out," Zoe said, "let's bury it here."

She got down on her knees, gently placed the bird beside her, and started digging with the garden hand rake. Zoe's eyes misted. Her chin dimpled. The bird's death had impacted her in a way I wouldn't have expected.

I could tell her my idea tomorrow.

There was something I needed to test first.

When I returned from Walmart, Charlie danced excitedly around me, as if I'd been gone a week instead of an hour. He was doing well with his treatments. The doctors said he was a real trooper and an easy patient to work on. Everyone who met Charlie always adored him. As a reward, I'd bought a pack of bacon to treat him with.

I'd also bought a pellet rifle.

It was sturdy and old-fashioned looking, reminding me of the rifle Ralphie wanted in *A Christmas Story*, only bigger.

The BBs were on the large side too. I'd purchased two boxes along with a bag of birdfeed. After putting the groceries away, I let Charlie outside. I filled a coffee mug with birdfeed and joined Charlie out back, sprinkling the feed throughout the yard. I chuckled as I cleared bird shit off the lawn chair with a wet rag. Sitting down, I placed the pellet rifle across my lap and loaded it, then popped the first beer of my first day off in a week and a half. Charlie sniffed at the scattered birdfeed, but I told him to leave it be and he obeyed. He sat in the shade beside me, his mouth open as he tested the air. We waited.

The first raven appeared at the edge of the property. I gripped the rifle, slowly bringing it to my shoulder. There was nothing behind my house but desert rock. Nothing to worry about hitting. The pistol Dennis had given me would be too loud and would damage the bird too much. The air rifle was silent, so it wouldn't draw attention from neighbors, and I figured it would be strong enough to do the job. Putting my eye to the sight, I watched the raven pick at the free meal. The bird was huge and absolutely perfect.

That I hit him on the first shot surprised me. I was no marksman but had a large target. Wearing dishwashing gloves, I brought the dead bird inside and put it in the sink, Charlie watching curiously as I drew a knife from the drawer. I wasn't sure how to go about this and didn't think I could find an instructional video on YouTube. Maybe taxidermy instructions would help, but I didn't want to get fancy or leave that kind of search in my online history. I'd just have to learn by doing.

I stabbed the knife into the raven's breast, then sliced it down the middle all the way to the anus. Using the knife like a pry bar, I opened the bird. Blood pooled in the sink as I began digging out the guts. When it was completely disemboweled, I gave it a good rinse and cleaned up the mess, then brought the bird to the window that received the most sunlight and placed it on the sill. It'd gone easier than I'd anticipated, and I was happy with my work.

Several hours and beers later, the raven was sufficiently dry, so I brought it to the kitchen counter and placed it beside the sandwich bags, Tightbond hide glue, and parallel clamps.

Because of the bird's size, I was able to fit three whole baggies inside its cavity.

It was a new moon, and the desert was cold and black. The lack of houses and streetlights deepened the enveloping darkness. Even I was a shadow, dressed in my black hoodie and sweatpants. I drove slowly, the only sound being Charlie's breathing in the back cab. He licked my ear. He must have sensed my nervousness.

"It's okay, boy."

My hands gripped the wheel, illuminated by the spooky green glow of the dash. I chewed a toothpick just to give myself something to fidget with. A repurposed bag from Walmart was in the passenger seat beside me. We drove past the junkyard where several cars had been buried hood-first in the sand like some strange, trashy Easter Island. Rows of rusted cars were parked behind the gate. We passed by darkened old barns and the boarded-up, graffitied remains of restaurants abandoned in the previous century. My skin turned to gooseflesh as I made the turn.

We'd be there soon. I was really doing this.

Already I wanted to shut my headlights off—stealth would be everything tonight—but without them there would be only blackness. I had to wait until I got closer.

But not too close.

The pale spotlights of Norrington Women's Correctional Facility appeared like UFOs against the night sky. The stop bar was down, gates closed, the guard booth an empty shadow. In the bright, white lights of the yard, the fence seemed to shimmer like ripples on a summer lake. I'd seen the prison after dark many times, but it had never seemed as ominous as it did at that moment. I felt like a guerilla approaching enemy lines and suddenly wondered if I should have brought the pistol, then cursed myself for such an idiotic notion. That would be taking things way too far. I wasn't that kind of criminal. Honestly, I didn't even like to think of myself as a criminal at all, only an opportunist, a soldier of misfortune, a man in dire straits doing what had to be done.

The prison grew larger as I drew nearer. My stomach gurgled.

"Easy," I told myself.

If I didn't calm down, I might literally shit my pants. I scratched Charlie's head, and he panted happily. Petting him always calmed me like a Xanax. We drove on, and I watched the prison as we passed by it from afar. No one in the yard. No towers to worry about. We were so short-staffed and overworked, especially now that Officer Anthony was suspended. The COs were burnt out. Tired officers cut corners. I couldn't ask for a better situation. I knew that, but my body was ripe with tension anyway.

Passing by the prison, I was tempted to just keep on driving. I didn't have to do this. I could turn around and go home right now and that would be the end of all this terror. But I just couldn't allow it. So, when I passed the rocky bluff a half mile from the rear of the prison, I turned off my headlights, made a U turn, and pulled the truck between the huge sandstones. Charlie got excited, thinking we were going exploring. I retrieved the chewy bone from the glovebox to keep him entertained.

"You be good, boy."

I grabbed the Walmart bag and dug out its contents. Stepping out of the truck, I put my sweater's hood up and breathed deep of the cool night air. The silence of the desert was absolute. Every scuffle of my footsteps sounded like an avalanche to me. Stuffing my bundle into my hoodie, I held it close to my body and proceeded down the slope in a hunched sprint. I imagined myself as one with the shadows, sailing through the desert plains like a vampire bat or...

Like a bird.

Hummingbird.

Jailbird.

I snuck through the grassland, and when I came upon the prison, I got low, trying to stay out of the light as long as possible. Eventually I would have to run into the path of the beams. It would be brief, and it wasn't like there were officers standing behind each spotlight. They were merely a deterrent. At the edge of the last shadow, I drew the bandana from my back pocket and tied it around my face like a bank robber.

Taking the deepest breath of my life, I ran toward the fence, trying not to think at all now. I itched to get it over with, but I wasn't Michael Jordan. I had to get closer. Moving faster than I thought my old ass was capable, adrenaline made me shake as I came within two feet of the fence. I reached into my hoodie, braced the raven with both hands, and hurled it into the air for one final flight.

CHAPTER FIFTEEN

Though I'd gotten very little sleep, my excitement was like an energy shot, and I came in for my morning shift with a bright smile. If anyone had seen me last night, the police would have come already. I'd gotten away with the first step of my plan. Time for the next. It was excruciating keeping the details to myself those first few hours. The urge to tell Zoe was overwhelming but I couldn't until we were alone, so I waited until I was doing the shake downs.

I whispered to her as I worked through her totes. "I've got something for you."

Zoe raised her eyebrows but said nothing.

"You'll get it on yard duty, so be ready."

I went back to the shake downs, doing a half-assed job because I didn't want to find contraband on Hummingbird for a while. I wanted the bosses to think everything was running smoothly now so they'd turn their attention elsewhere. I would make an extra effort to write up citations on Raven unit, the recreation yard, and in the mess hall. It would keep up appearances, keep the bosses happy, and keep Hummingbird—the home of my illegal enterprise—from being scrutinized.

Pregnant Lilly Gutierrez had moved to seg, followed by Ariel Richardson for the child porn bust I'd made with her phone. Assistant Warden Moore commended me for that little victory. But I'd taken a gamble by turning Richardson in. She would be interrogated about how she'd gotten the phone. But as I'd expected, she hadn't snitched. Zoe had become very popular on Hummingbird, and now that the inmates from Raven were allowed to mingle with the Hummingbird inmates on the yard and in the mess hall, Zoe's customer count had grown exponentially. The inmates had given her the nickname CVS Suzi, due to her ability to supply drugs and other contraband. Crossing her meant access would be cut off to everyone. By ratting out Zoe Hallister, a snitch would earn the ire of all their fellow inmates and would doubtlessly pay a penalty. With that kind of weight behind Zoe, and with my advantages as a CO, we were becoming a bulletproof duo, and that had given me the courage to take things up another notch.

On yard duty, I put Castillo and Ramos on the garden but separated Nina Brown from Zoe, sending Brown to tend to the north end of the yard and escorting Zoe to the rear. I spoke loudly about a patch of Sahara mustards I wanted Zoe to tend to, invasive weeds that weren't actually there. She picked up on what I was doing. She'd deliberately come outside overdressed in a sweater so she could remove it while working. Once we were far enough from the others, I whispered to her.

"There's a dead raven about fifteen feet ahead, near the edge of the fence."

Zoe furrowed her brow. "Um… a what?"

"It's stuffed," I explained. "Use the garden rake to undo the glue in its breast, remove the bag, then take off your sweater and ball the bag into it. Then throw the bird in the trash with the other yard garbage."

"*What?*" she whispered. "You stuffed a bird with mojo?"

"Nah. Not K-2. This is the hard stuff."

Her eyes widened. "*Fentanyl?* You stuffed the bird with those patches? How did you—"

"Never mind that now. Just collect the bag."

"Where did you get a dead raven?"

I'd wondered how she would react to this, given her tenderness when she'd found the hummingbird's corpse. I was hoping her desire for booming business would outweigh any outrage she might have over my method of transport.

"An air gun," I admitted. "It was a quick death. No suffering."

Zoe gaped at me.

"I'm sorry. I know you like birds, but this idea—"

"Is genius," she said with a smile. "Dude, *fuck ravens*. I'm only sentimental for hummingbirds and blue jays, not those black birds of death. This is a genius plan, Liam. God, I could kiss you."

A warm rush flowed through me. We couldn't kiss here and now, but I was confident one day we would. Zoe's praise—and choice of expression—had me as giddy as a schoolboy with his first crush. She beamed up at me from beneath the brim of her gardening hat, her eyes alive with this new information. I could almost see the thoughts and plans blossoming within her, and I was proud to have delighted her so, like a child making his parents laugh.

"Okay," Zoe said, "I'm on it."

"Be as discrete as you can. I'll keep the others away."

"You're the best, Liam. The absolute *best*."

Zoe moved through the grass in search of her prize, a little girl hunting for an Easter egg. I enjoyed watching her from the back, her hair shining like hot tar in the sunshine, the cherry of her ass bouncing with every excited step.

You're the best, Liam. The absolute best.

How I longed to hear her say these words under more intimate circumstances. Zoe Hallister intoxicated me more than any of the drugs we dealt ever could. Booze and edibles paled in comparison to the bliss mere thoughts of her offered me. Though our real interactions were painfully limited, I'd created a dreamworld for us with Zoe serving as the center, a sun goddess for the rest of my personal Narnia to revolve around. Smuggling drugs had started with needing money for Charlie, but I knew now that I would continue doing it even once the chemo was paid for; not so much for the money, but for the joy it brought to the woman I was falling in love with.

I walked to the garden, feigning supervision of the other inmates, and watched Zoe out of the corner of my eye as she found the bird. She removed her sweater and wiped her brow. Her undershirt was tight and hugged her slender form like gauze as she hunched over to hide what she was doing. When the yard work was finished, she balled up her sweater under one arm as we went back inside, carrying enough prison junk to kill a fleet of horses.

China White. Goodfella. Apache. TNT.

Inmates had a lot of slang terms for fentanyl, but no matter what form it was coming in, the stuff was all heroin to me. I'd been too afraid to try one out on myself. I didn't need to get hooked on something I had such an enormous amount of, especially seeing as Dennis had paid for it all. But the women of Norrington didn't have as much to lose—if anything. These patches offered an escape that far surpassed synthetic weed and were much stronger than suboxone. In training I'd learned that fentanyl was the most powerful painkiller on the market—fifty times more potent than street heroin. Inmates facing years, decades, or even life in prison were the most desperate people I'd ever met. Any substance that offered temporary alleviation from depression and boredom was seen as heaven-sent. Fentanyl promised elation, the chemical equivalent to being set free. If anyone needed a cure for pain, it was these women who'd been so crippled by it.

This was going to work out great for everyone.

"You're one slick son of a bitch," Dennis said.

He sat back in the booth and swirled his drink with a straw. It was early yet, and Goldie's bar was mellow, just three men sitting at the counter while two employees set up the makeshift runway for the night's drag show. We'd taken the booth at the back for privacy, Dennis slipping me a large manila envelope beneath the table.

"A dead bird," Dennis said with a chuckle. "What's next? You gonna throw a coyote over the fence, or are we sticking to avian? Maybe you could get fancy and use a dove for symbolism, or maybe a roadrunner just for giggles."

"Keep it simple," I said. "Ravens are everywhere in this godforsaken desert. Nobody bats an eye at one."

"Maybe not *one*, but if the prison yard becomes a graveyard for them it's bound to alert somebody."

"I won't do it often enough for that. Like I said at the start, this'll be a slow game."

Keeping it under the table, I opened the envelope to see bundles of cash packed as tightly as I'd packed the goods that had earned it. Dennis' cheeks were like pink apples as he sucked down his beverage. The gravity of my success suddenly slapped me. I'd never had this much money at one time. I'd struck dirty gold.

"Big guy," Dennis said, leaning across the table. "This is just the tip. You see that, don't you? We're going to be very rich men."

"And a rich woman," I added.

For a moment he looked confused. "Oh, right. Zoe. Yeah, her too." His smile returned. "She's getting taken care of—don't you worry about that—but we're talking about you and me here, right? I have plans, my friend—*big* plans."

I nodded. "Okay. But there's still plenty of stuff at my house to move. The remaining patches, some K-2—"

"Yeah, yeah. Listen, I'm thinking on a grand scale here. This prison narcotics gig is sweet, but we could be doing so much more. I mean, what's stopping us from expanding our horizons?"

Dennis was full of energy tonight, but while most people's excitement can be contagious, his put me on guard. I waited for him to say more but already didn't like where he was going.

"I've got something for you," Dennis continued. "For both of us. A deal so good you'll jump up and smack your grandma in the mouth with your dick." He snickered, clearly high on something. "See, our Indian friends, they're in possession of much more than fentanyl patches."

I thought of the long-haired man's grim expression and his well-built sidekick's penetrating eyes. Seeing those two again wasn't high on my wish list. I almost told Dennis so, but he slid out of the booth and patted me on the shoulder, motioning me to leave with him.

"Let's take a drive," he said.

"Dennis, I don't think—"

"You don't have to think. This is a no-brainer, believe me."

He nudged me again and I stood. I had my money. I could walk with Dennis to the parking lot, tell him I wasn't interested in the new deal, and head home. As we walked, Dennis slung an arm over my shoulder like a drunken groomsman, as if we'd known each other for years.

"Forget just paying for chemo," he said. "When we're done, you'll own the whole fucking vet hospital."

Outside, the last of the sun had made a watercolor painting of the evening sky. The darkness was nearly full but the light in the west silhouetted Dennis in pink fire. He rambled with the grandiose chatter of a manic man while we walked to our vehicles.

"Listen, Dennis," I said. "Maybe I should call you an Uber."

"An Uber?" he said. "I'm not wasted, just jazzed. You can feel the excitement, right? It's like an electromagnetic pulse. It's calling in the air tonight like Phil Fucking Collins. Surely you feel it too."

"I just don't think you should drive right now, dude."

Then I wondered why I should care. He was my drug connection, but I had a sizeable stash at home, and if Dennis killed himself in a car wreck Zoe and I wouldn't have to cut him in on the profits.

"Okay," he said. "I won't drive. You drive."

He opened the passenger door to my truck. Before I could object, he'd climbed in and slammed the door behind him, giggling like a child with a whoopee cushion. I wasn't in the mood for an argument, so I just got in and tucked the envelope of cash under the seat. Dennis had retrieved a small, plastic tube from his shirt pocket and was pouring out a line of white powder on my dashboard. He sniffed it up with a tiny straw.

"Want some coke?" he asked.

"No thanks," I said, starting the truck. "I don't do well with stimulants."

Dennis grinned. "Oh, Liam. I'll pull you out of that shell yet."

"Until then, where can I drop you off?"

He told me to take a right out of the lot. The small pocket of urban activity surrounding Goldie's included restaurants and family-owned shops, all of it packed into three blocks. We drove through them as the night crowd littered the streets, dressed to get laid, high on the release from their nine-to-fives. I followed Dennis' directions as we entered the suburbs on the edge of town, one-story homes and ranch houses spread out like checker pieces on a board of unforgiving dirt. The chain-link fences seemed aggressive now, reminding me of Norrington's yard, and I wondered if I'd ever be able to look at certain things the same way again or if my profession had permanently altered my perception of the world.

Dennis rambled on. "Nothing but good vibes, my friend—that's what I'm getting. You feel it too, right? I mean, look how well we've worked together. Life can be so brazen. Here I've been searching for a partner all this time, and suddenly my crazy cousin drops you in my lap like a Christmas present. Zoe, of all people!"

"Crazy?" I asked, taking slight offense on her behalf. "How is Zoe crazy?"

Dennis stared at me, then broke out in laughter. "Are you fucking serious?"

"What? What is it?"

"Oh, you poor thing," he said, drying his eyes with his sleeve. "You're a sweetheart, you know that, right?"

"Don't call me that."

"Relax. I'm just saying you're… well, I don't want to say *naïve*, but…"

My hands tightened on the wheel. "And just what am I so naïve about? Zoe? I think I know Zoe pretty well, thank you."

Dennis put his palm to his chest. "Oh, my. Liam… do you have *a thing* for her?"

I flushed. "You're high as a kite. Just tell me which way to go."

"Keep going straight on." He cocked his head. "My goodness. Liam and Zoe, sittin' in a tree."

"Knock it off. What're you, ten?"

"Does she know? Are you two an item or are you just crushing on her in secret?"

"You're wasted. You're imagining things."

"Oh, so you're denying it? Bitch, please."

"Let it go, Dennis."

He leaned back in his seat. "Fine. Far be it from me to get between Romeo and his jailbird Juliette. Turn right here."

As the truck rounded the corner, Dennis lit a cigarette and rolled down the window. The night air was crisp and alluring, the neighborhood growing quieter as its residents settled in for the evening. As we approached the cul-de-sac, I rode the brake, waiting for Dennis to tell me which of the houses was his, but he looked so out of place here. I pictured him living in a seedy apartment, not a quaint house in a middle-class neighborhood.

"You live here?" I asked.

He snorted a laugh. "You're adorable."

"Then what the hell are we doing here?"

"Dropping in on old friends."

"Okay, fine. Which house belongs to your friend?"

He pointed out a single-story home with no fence, a minivan in the driveway. I turned the truck around to be on that side of the cul-de-sac and stopped before the house. A sudden sense of unease rippled through me.

"Wait," I said, "this isn't where the Indians live, is it?"

"They wish." He flicked his cigarette out the window. "Keep the engine running. You got your piece?"

My heartbeat accelerated. "The *gun?* No. What the fuck are you doing?"

Dennis hopped out of the truck, not closing the door all the way. Standing in the street, he drew the pistol he'd concealed under his shirt, popped the magazine to check it, and slammed it back in.

He gave me a stern look. "You're not going to take off on me, are you?"

"Dennis, just get back in the truck."

"You take off on me and I'm not going to be very happy with you. *Zoe* won't be either. You don't want to upset your Juliette, do you?"

"Dennis, *please*, just get back in the truck. I don't know what this is, but I don't wanna do it, man."

"Oh, stop being a girl. All you have to do is drive. You said I shouldn't, so here you are. I'll be in and out in two shakes."

Before I could object any further, Dennis sprinted up the driveway. I watched without breathing as he ran around the side of the house, holding his gun low in both hands like a TV cop. *Now* I sensed the energy in the air Dennis had spoken of. I felt like a man sweating in the electric chair, waiting on the flip of the switch. Perhaps tonight would land me on actual death row. Who knew what Dennis was going in this house for? Maybe it was a simple robbery, but what if he were going to assassinate rivals or someone who'd crossed him? I'd be an accessory to murder.

Bail out! my mind screamed. *Drive away!*

But I froze in my seat. I didn't want to draw Dennis' wrath by abandoning him. Plus, he was right—I wouldn't do anything to jeopardize my budding relationship with Zoe or the steady cash flow. If her cousin ended up behind bars because I'd bailed on him, she'd resent me, and that would ruin everything.

I told myself if I heard gunshots, I'd be out of there. That would be the last straw. I had to set some limits, draw some lines.

I didn't hear a shot, but I did hear a woman scream.

My every muscle flexed. The sound of men arguing followed the scream, but I could only make out every other word. Dennis was demanding something from the couple.

He said they owed him. The other man shouted for Dennis to get the fuck out of his house, and Dennis must have hurt him for it, for the man cried out in pain. Sweat formed at my brow. If I could hear them, that meant the neighbors could too. It wasn't even late yet.

C'mon, damnit!

I gripped the wheel so hard it shuddered. All had fallen silent. I didn't like what that implied, but I'd yet to hear any shots. I prayed I wouldn't. A shadow moved quickly across the yard—*Dennis*. He carried a white, cardboard box with handles at each end. Something was on his face. When he got closer, I realized what it was. He climbed in and, before he could even get the door shut, I hit the gas. The truck roared down the avenue.

"Slow down," Dennis said, his chin dripping blood.

I tried to speak but couldn't.

"I said *slow down*. This is residential."

I eased off the gas and Dennis pointed right. "Turn here. I know a quick way out."

As I took the turn, Dennis drew a handkerchief and started clearing the blood spattered on his face. His eyes were black and crazed.

"*What the fuck, man?*" I managed to say. "*What the fuck did you do?*"

"Relax. I didn't do any permanent damage. Turn right at the end of this street."

"I didn't hear a shot."

"Of course not. Don't be ridiculous. All I used the gun for was to whip him. I'd only brought it so I'd have the upper hand, but the little pecker tried to act tough with me 'cause his bitch was with him."

"She was screaming like a horror movie."

"I know. That's why I had to hurt her too."

I made the turn. "You… you didn't…"

"I told you—they'll be fine. Now take a left out of here and get on the old state road." As I followed his directions, Dennis opened the lid of the box. "My friend back there owed me some money. Not an inordinate amount, but it's the principle. I'd given him fair warning and too many reminders already. Straight men always think they can take on a fag, that it's easy to kick our asses. Showed him." He reached into the box and drew out something rectangular in a mylar bag. "These should settle up his debt nicely."

I'd expected the box to hold cash, firearms, or drugs.

I definitely hadn't expected a comic book collection.

Each was individually wrapped with a numbered sticker in the top left corner. Dennis pulled them up to inspect them—Batman & Robin, Daredevil, Silver Surfer, Vampirella, Ghost Rider, Archie, Supergirl.

"*You* collect comics?" I asked.

"Do I look like I collect comics?" he said, still pawing through the lot. "I couldn't care less about this Marvel shit. What I care about is—ah!" He flipped one to show me the cover of an old *The Incredible Hulk* comic where the green hero was battling a man in yellow. "This is Hulk number 181. It marks the first appearance of Wolverine. I only know this 'cause my friend there liked to show off his collection to guests when he got high." He pointed to the numbered sticker. "This here is an official rating. It's only a grade six, but I looked it up, and the asshole wasn't exaggerating its value. It's worth thousands. And who knows what all these other ones are worth. I'll check and—"

"Why did you bring me along on this, Dennis?" I asked, my fear morphing into anger. "This has nothing to do with me or Zoe. It has nothing to do with our deals."

He continued pawing through the loot. "We're partners, aren't we?"

"Not for this kind of thing we're not."

"You saying you don't want your cut?" he asked, and when I started to answer him, he grabbed me by my shirt and put his face in mine. "Look, you did it. It's *done*. When you form a partnership, you stick together, Liam. We're a team, you and me. Zoe too."

I shook free of him. "I know that. But I'm not gonna let you hold Zoe over me to get me to go along with whatever crazy shit you're involved in. I'm not your monkey."

Dennis backed off and chuckled. "Okay, okay. This is all just the adrenaline talking. We're both a little amped up, right? You're not the only one freaked out, mister. It's not every day I pistol-whip somebody, you know."

"That's just it. Slinging dope is one thing, but breaking into people's houses and assaulting and robbing them... that's not something I want to get wrapped up in. With all the noise they made, somebody must've called 911. Someone might've seen my truck."

"Don't worry about all that. Even if someone did, there's no way this guy or his bitch are going to press charges. They won't say a word."

"Why not?"

"Because he's a criminal too."

I waited for more that didn't come. "That's all?"

"That's all it takes, Liam." He turned his head to keep his eyes on me. A smear of blood remained upon his cheek.

"Once you're in deep enough, there's no calling the police for help. Not for anything."

We drove on through darkness.

CHAPTER SIXTEEN

The ball launched from Zoe's fingertips, went over the heads of the other inmates, and bounced on the rim before going through the hoop. Her team was in the lead for the afternoon's basketball game, and she was a big reason why. Zoe was skilled athletically and in a great mood, laughing and smiling and encouraging the other players. After the arrival of the fentanyl patches, her popularity had only increased. Everyone wanted to be in her good graces. With her rise to glory in full swing, it seemed a shame for me to kill her buzz, but I had to talk to her about Dennis. I just needed to wait for the right time, and the rec yard wasn't the place, not with so many people around.

Some of the inmates from Raven were on the yard today too. Fellow CO Ileana Sloan escorted them out for exercise and resocialization, as if they were kennel dogs. I spotted Sally Kindly among them, her devil horn tattoos identifying her even at a distance. I also recognized Natalia Bravo, the Latina prison gang leader that Ileana and Beverly had told me about. She was a massive woman—tall and overweight and heavily inked. One of her eyes wandered, the thick scar beneath the socket suggesting it hadn't always been that way. Fern Hernandez and Sandra Ramos orbited around Bravo like gnats.

Ileana walked among the incarcerated women with a confidence out of proportion with her appearance. She was smaller than any of the inmates she supervised but seemed to have mastered how to handle herself around them. We stood in the shade of the awning as we watched the basketball game, her attention locked on those she was responsible for. Whenever someone stepped even a little out of line, Ileana barked at them about it faster than I would have, putting an end to a problem before it could start.

"Being on Raven has toughened you up, huh?" I asked.

Ileana smirked but there was no humor in it. "It's just like Goodman told us when we took those personality tests. Being a guard really changes you. I'm not the same person I was when I started here."

"Everything okay?"

She kept her eyes on the inmates. "Better than they were. I'm just glad they finally let Raven unit back to the mess hall and rec yard. They're so much worse when they have nothing to do."

"I meant are *you* doing okay."

"Honestly, I don't know anymore. Sometimes I feel like I don't even recognize myself, you know? My priorities, my ambitions, my ethics—they've all changed during my time here."

Her words resonated with me in ways I couldn't share, so I only nodded and kept listening.

"It really does take too much effort to treat these women like human beings," Ileana said. "Most of my energy is spent on showing them—over and over and over—that I won't back down. It's exhausting, but that's the whole job, at least on Raven. None of these women show compunction, so I can't either. Every day they catcall me, size me up, call me racist, and stare me down like they're about to pound my face in. But I can never let them know it gets to me, 'cause then they'll know they—" She shouted to one of the inmates, "—*Copeland*, get off the fence! *Now*!" The inmate who'd been leaning against the fence moved away from it, giving us a look filled with bile. Ileana said, "And wipe that pissy look off your face, understand?"

"Yes, ma'am," Inmate Copeland murmured.

Ileana reminded me of an angry mother shouting at her children on a playground. But there was more to it than that. The mousiness that had defined her when we'd been in training was gone, leaving behind a caustic, smoldering shell of her former self.

"I never used to shout at people," she told me. "Now it's all I do. It's become one of my favorite parts of the job. Have you noticed that too? How being a CO makes it feel good to be mad?"

It was true. Being a corrections officer meant constantly being challenged by inmates. You had to endure their endless lies, manipulations, rule-breaking, and general misbehavior. That's why Ileana reminded me of an angry mother. She was babysitting dangerous women who had to be forced to show respect and treat Ileana with basic human decency.

Most of the time, I worked on an easier unit than she did, but even I'd started to blur the line between pleasure and rage. If not for the thrill of trafficking drugs, dominating the inmates would've been my only source of happiness within Norrington's walls.

"Nothing feels better than saying no to an inmate," I admitted.

"Totally. I mean, that's our job—to limit their freedom. But it's become more than that for me. I *love* to write them up. I *love* to punish them. But then, when I'm not here, I hate myself for it. I mean… I'm not a sadist. It's the damn inmates. They're so mean, so manipulative. So lazy, gross, and violent. The lousy bitches just don't give you any other option."

"Unfortunately, that's true."

"Ol' Beverly was right about everything. She warned me from the start I'd have to get mean or go home. She told me I'd start drinking more, and boy have I. I can't get to sleep without a few glasses of wine anymore. When I'm at home alone and things are quiet, all I can hear is the constant, low roar of Raven unit. Even when I pass out, I can't escape it. My dreams are filled with broken cell bars and hair-pulling fights and women flinging used tampons down the tier at me. When it's a good dream, I get to tear gas them all."

When I looked at Ileana more closely, I saw the shade of purple that had befallen her eyelids, and the stress wrinkles that were deepening on the sides of her mouth. She was aging like a U.S. president.

"Ileana," I said, "it's none of my business, but maybe you should call the free help line. Get some counseling."

"Oh, c'mon. Talking out problems isn't the same as fixing them." She finally made eye contact with me. "Besides, after that idiot got Gutierrez pregnant on ACI property, they're probably extra careful about who they keep in their employ, no matter how desperate for staff they are. They find out what's in my head and they'll find a reason to get rid of me."

An inmate jogged over to us, and Ileana raised one hand like a traffic cop to slow her down.

"Officer Sloane," the inmate said, "about my clothes…"

Ileana sneered at her. "You hang 'em to dry in an unauthorized area, you pay the price."

"I know, but—"

"You're an adult, Inmate Ritter. You've been here long enough to know the rules. When I find laundry where it's not supposed to be, I confiscate it. End of discussion."

The inmate's face twisted. "I'm just saying—"

Ileana stepped forward quickly, her boots touching inmate Ritter's toes. Though she was more than a foot shorter than Ritter, Ileana's essence overpowered the inmate, making her cower away.

"You wanna keep your good time?" Ileana said. "Then *don't fuck with me.*"

I tensed, ready for a heated exchange, but Ritter tucked her head into her chest, then walked away silently. Ileana watched her go with eyes like razorblades.

She really had changed.

After returning from the rec yard, Zoe approached the control booth where I was bullshitting with Tanner Wyatt. She held up her left wrist with her right hand.

"Boss," she said to me. "Can I go to the infirmary now?"

I stared at her, confused.

"You said the nurse would look at my busted finger," she said, as if reminding me. "It's been killing me after I sprained it on that one ball toss."

Catching her drift, I asked Tanner if he would mind watching the unit while I transported the inmate to the infirmary. A minute later, I was alone with Zoe.

"You're not really hurt, right?" I asked.

"No. Just wanted to get you alone."

"Yeah, me too. We need to have a talk."

We were buzzed through the door to the next wing. The hallway was deserted, but I waited until we were in the privacy of the elevator before talking about what happened the night before. When the doors closed, I turned to Zoe, but before I could get out her cousin's name, she stepped into me, backing me against the wall, and raised her lips to meet mine.

Her mouth was impossibly warm and soft, a feast for a man starved too long. My initial shock gave way to delight as Zoe pressed the stop button on the elevator. It seemed she too knew about the busted camera. She reached under my shirt, running her fingernails through my chest hair and pinching my nipple. I put my hands on her hips and pulled her in, but she guided them lower to cup her ass. She removed her top, and I buried my face in the tenderness of her. We didn't speak. There was no need to. Our mouths remained locked as we fondled, exploring each other's bodies, pulling at our clothing, and in a sudden, fevered twist of flesh I was inside of her.

We thudded against the walls of the elevator in crazed abandon, and when it was over, we dressed quickly, saying nothing, for there was no time to waste. I hit the button, and the elevator made its ascent. Exiting, I released Zoe to the infirmary, both of us acting casual. I tried to maintain a professional appearance even though my face was flushed. My crotch was still moist, but I reminded myself that no one else knew that—no one but Zoe. Made of stronger nerves than mine, Zoe didn't tremble or sweat as she was admitted, only gave me a sly glance as she slipped into the nurse's station.

Walking back to the elevator, my vision blurred. The endorphins were having their way with me just as Zoe had. Tingles raced through my entire body as I struggled to process conflicting feelings of elation and terror. Everything had happened so fast. In a way, our sex was the perfect representation of the rapid pace I now had to maintain to keep from stumbling my way into an arrest. Once the elevator doors closed, I slumped against the wall and tried to steady my speeding heart.

"Oh, Jesus," I whispered, holding my chest. "What am I doing?"

But given the chance I would do it again.

The feeling of Zoe's yielding flesh against my own spoke to the most primal part of me. My ex-wife had given my masculinity a brutal thrashing. I'd feared I might never recover from it, but fifteen minutes in an elevator with a wanton partner had resuscitated the man in me.

There is no overstating the healing powers of a good lay after you've gone so long without one, even if you must make it a quickie.

I wondered if Officer Anthony and Lilly Gutierrez had used the same hiding spot for their sexual liaisons. Was that how Zoe knew the elevator's camera was dead? Had Lilly told her? Had Zoe known what had been going on between them? If so, why would she have not told me? Because she refused to be a rat? And if the elevator was where Lilly got pregnant, did Captain Clancy and Assistant Warden Moore know that, and if so, had the camera been replaced? Was it possible someone had seen us? Had Zoe and I made a little prison porno that could burn us both for good?

Stop. You're getting carried away.

It's easy to drive yourself right out of your own skull sometimes. The world's full of maybes. There was no sense in me worrying about things I had no real reason to believe had happened. It would be better to just bask in the afterglow of my first sex since Karmen left, something I'd been yearning for with a desperation that sometimes bordered on obsession.

While giving myself a whore's bath in the men's room, I daydreamed about Zoe, already plotting our next romantic interlude. I was still mentally aroused when I returned to Hummingbird. Perhaps it was my imagination, but the inmates were looking at me differently. They wore the same look they'd had on my first day—a collective coy, flirty, and yet mocking gaze, as if they knew something about me that I did not yet know about myself.

CHAPTER SEVENTEEN

They finally released Cherry Campbell from suicide watch.

I was given the task of escorting her back to Hummingbird. With Richardson and Gutierrez now on seg, there was room for Cherry's return. As we walked through Sparrow, inmates shouted from behind their closed doors, desperate for any form of human contact. They teased Cherry for being suicidal, as if depression made her weak. Ileana Sloane was right. There were a lot of cruel women in Norrington. They weren't all as easy to handle as they were on Hummingbird. If I had to work on Sparrow or Raven as often as she had, I'd probably have entered the dark mental state Ileana had reached too.

"I'm glad to see you're feeling better," I told Cherry as I walked her down the hall.

"Yeah," she said without enthusiasm.

She'd been heavily medicated the past few weeks, an anti-psychotic cocktail whipped up by the prison shrink. Some inmates faked suicide attempts just to get anxiety medication, but Cherry's act of poisoning herself with feces was no performance piece. She'd earned her meds, but I wondered just how helpful they were.

"You are feeling better, aren't you?" I asked.

She offered a weak shrug. "Just spendin' my life in sin 'n misery. Norrington's my house of the risin' sun."

"Things'll be better on Hummingbird. Your friends will be happy to see you."

"What friends?" she said flatly.

"Enola Branham has asked about you almost every day."

"Enola thinks she's my fuckin' Indian chief mama even though I'm cracker-ass white."

"I'm sure she means well."

Cherry scoffed. "Ain't you learned yet? Ain't *nobody* up in here means well. They's all cunts. They's only your friend when they want somethin'."

I had no response to that other than to change the subject. "You're out of solitary. I'd like to see you stay out. Let's see if we can get you on a work program. Would you like that?"

"Whatever you say, cowboy."

Despite her grumblings, when Cherry returned to Hummingbird she wasn't mocked and ridiculed the way she'd been while walking through Sparrow. Some inmates showed no interest in her either way, but a few offered her words of support and encouragement. Cherry even allowed Enola Branham to give her a hug. When Cherry put her arms around Branham, her sleeves inched to her elbows, revealing terrible scars.

After the midday count, it was time to take the crew to the yard. There were no dead birds to gut, but I separated Zoe from the others anyway. It was our first alone time since having sex in the elevator, and I kicked at the dirt like a shy adolescent as we spoke.

"That was really something," I said. "What we did."

She smiled. "Let's do it again sometime."

"Sooner than later."

She looked around. "Want to sneak off?"

I chuckled. "C'mon. You know I can't do that, no matter how much I'd like to."

"Nobody's looking, babe. They've all got their backs to us, working on the garden."

When I turned back to look at them, Zoe palmed my crotch. Not expecting it, I flinched and backed up a step. "Easy. This yard has cameras."

"Not even a quick handjob?" She pouted playfully. "You're no fun."

"Believe me, I want it. Just not here. I'll figure something out."

"Okay. You're the boss."

Hearing her talk like this made my loins stir. I looked her up and down, hungry to take that body again.

"So, what do you have coming next?" she asked.

"Huh?"

"The next birdy. What's going in it?"

"Please tell me you don't need more fentanyl already."

"No, no," she assured me. "I'm rationing them out to the others. I don't want anyone knowing I have a stash that size."

"And if enough inmates are caught on the nod, it'll draw attention back to the unit. We don't want that."

"Right. That's why we should mix it up. I have a lot of customers looking for other stuff—coke, molly, shrooms. Not to the mention the hardware. We need syringes and pipes and—"

"Whoa, whoa, whoa. Take it down a notch."

"Hey, c'mon, they don't call me CVS Suzi for nothing."

"But I don't have all of that stuff."

"Dennis can get anything."

I sighed. "Yeah… I've been meaning to talk to you about him. The other night—"

"The comic book raid? I know. He told me."

"Oh. He did?"

"Sorry he dragged you into that." She snickered. "Dennis can be a little wild sometimes."

"*A little wild?* Zoe, your cousin is dangerous and unstable. Honestly, I don't know if we should keep dealing with him. Maybe we can find someone else on the outside. You must know other people."

Zoe's whole demeanor changed. She took on an expression I'd never seen from her before—a cold, hard look more common to the inmates on Raven and Sparrow.

"We're not cutting Dennis out," she said.

"Look, he'll get what he's owed for what I have left to smuggle, but after that, I just think it'll be safer if we—"

"I said we're *not* cutting him out. Just because he intimidates you doesn't mean we're going to drop him. That's not how the game works."

"Oh?" I crossed my arms. "Then how does it work?"

She didn't flinch at my standoffishness. "It works like this, Liam. We stick together and watch each other's backs. We're never going to find a better supplier than Dennis. He's reliable and gives us our fair share. I know he's a little reckless sometimes, but he's careful when it comes to trafficking, and that's what's important. Besides, haven't things been going great with him otherwise? You've got money for Charlie's chemo and probably even some extra cash to throw around. You've got all the drugs you could ever want. And now you've even got me." She winked. "I *know* you're happy about that."

I suddenly recalled how Dennis teased me about my crush on Zoe. Had he told her? If so, was it before or after she'd had sex with me? I liked to think she'd made the first move on me out of sheer magnetism, not because her cousin had encouraged her.

"I am happy to have you, Zoe," I said. "More than you know."

"Good. Then don't fuck this up for us." She squatted to start work on the yard. "Now give me space. We've been talking too long."

A few hours later, when everyone was back on the unit, an emergency call came through on my lifeline radio just before lunch. Ileana Sloane was issuing a code orange, the second most extreme alert in the ACI book. It meant an inmate was unarmed but showing the strong potential for violence. I ran down the hall toward Raven, hearing the captain and other COs barking over the radio. More help was on the way, but I was the first to arrive.

Several inmates were loose on the tier. Ileana must have been lining them up to go to the mess hall. Now she was squaring off with Natalia Bravo. The massive inmate was King Kong compared to the diminutive CO. Though trembling,

Ileana was standing her ground, the chemical spray in her fist. She and Bravo shouted over each other, and I couldn't tell what the argument was about, but it didn't matter. I came beside Ileana and held my hands out in front of me, ready to grapple if need be.

The inmates still in their cells were yelling and shaking the bars. The seven that were out hooted and cheered as the situation escalated, egging Bravo on. Among them was Sally Kindly, clapping her tattooed hands. Her wide-eyed excitement set her devil horns high on her brow.

"Inmate Bravo!" I shouted. "Get down on the floor, *now!*"

Bravo ignored me and continued berating Ileana. "Fuck you, bitch! Lil' punk-ass bitch! I'll beat your pretty lil' face in 'til you ain't so pretty no more!"

"I'm giving you a direct order!" I said. "Down, *now!*"

"On the fucking ground, Bravo!" Ileana demanded. "Down or you're getting sprayed!"

Bravo bared her teeth like a hissing cat. "Don't you know who I am? You're gonna find out, bitch. You fuck with my house and your new home's gonna be the dirt!"

The sound of running turned my head. Captain Clancy and two other COs were approaching. One of them was Beverly Knox. She was moving quickly, especially for someone her age. The captain shouted the same orders at Bravo and yielded the same results.

"Fuck all y'all!" Bravo said.

The COs encircled the big woman, wolves closing in on a buffalo. Ileana kept her spray aimed at Bravo despite the backup. Her face was twitching, legs shaking, an officer on the verge of a breakdown.

Captain Clancy took center stage. "Last warning, Bravo! Don't make us do this."

Bravo pounded her chest with her fist and growled. Clancy gave the order, and the COs swarmed like hornets. Being closest to Bravo's right arm, I grabbed it and tried to twist it up behind her back, but the woman was ferocious, and I struggled to even keep my grip on her. From the top tier, someone tossed a wet roll of toilet paper down at us. Other projectiles followed. The COs piled on Bravo, all of us trying to wrestle the behemoth to the ground. It wasn't until Beverly kicked the back of Bravo's knee that the big woman buckled. The captain took Bravo's other arm and together we fanned them out, and Beverly put her weight against Bravo's back to push her toward the floor. Another CO whipped out cuffs.

Ileana was the only one who hadn't moved on Bravo. She stood over the rest of us, still clutching her spray. Her gaze had gone from nervous to furious, and she gritted her teeth as her face turned red.

She shouted at Bravo. "I told you, you fat cunt! I fucking *told* you!"

Captain Clancy shot her a look. "Officer Sloane, stand down."

We managed to get Bravo in cuffs but as we hoisted her to her feet she started writhing, and we had to work her back into her cell as a group. Bravo's housemate stood just outside the cell, watching stoically. We left the cuffs on Bravo as we forced her back inside.

Once she was sealed in, the captain questioned her. "You gonna settle down or am I gonna have to put you in seg?"

Bravo took deep breaths, nostrils flaring. "You know I don't like nobody touchin' me, boss."

"You gave us little recourse, Inmate Bravo. You know better than to defy orders. We've had this talk too many times before."

"You need to talk to your girl." Bravo nodded upward at Ileana. "She be trippin' up in here 'n shit. She gotta learn to act right. Show respect."

Ileana stepped toward the bars, but the captain gently tugged her back. Finally, she holstered her chemical spray. The captain told us we'd done a good job and released us back to our posts. I exhaled with relief. This was the most psychical I'd had to get with an inmate, and my hands were trembling from the rush. As I walked off the unit, I heard the captain talking to Bravo, being firm with her while also working to calm her down. Though she ranted about Ileana, Bravo was beginning to cool, and even agreed to turn around and put her hands through the food port so she could be released from the cuffs. Her cellmate gently rubbed Bravo's back and kissed her cheek, whispering words of encouragement.

Beverly joined me on the walk back to Hummingbird.

"First time?" she asked.

"Tackling an inmate? Yeah."

"Don't worry, hon. It gets easier. Don't get me wrong, every inmate has a different level of danger to 'em, but you get used to doing it."

"You certainly seemed at ease with it. You were kickin' ass like Clint Eastwood. I'm gonna have to start calling you Dirty Harriet."

She chuckled at the joke, then got serious. "I went at Bravo a little hard 'cause of her size and reputation. Different tactics for different inmates. I hope Ileana learns that."

"Yeah. She seemed frazzled. You know, she and I were talking the other day and, well, I think this place is really starting to get to her."

"And then some. When she started, everyone was worried she was too meek. Now she's gone completely in the other direction." Beverly shrugged. "Maybe she feels like she has to, in order to assert herself."

"It can't be easy being a CO that small."

"These convicts have tortured the poor kid. I wish the captain would move her to Robin or Hummingbird. Give the girl a break."

We were buzzed through another doorway and came into the hall connecting Hummingbird to the workshop, the same hall that offered me privacy with Zoe.

"Bev," I said, "can I ask you something?"

"Sure."

"You don't have to answer if you don't want to. I don't mean to pry. I was just wondering why you left the male prison you used to work at. What made you quit after all those years?"

Beverly pursed her lips. "Honestly?"

"Only if you're comfortable answering."

She stopped walking, so I did too. Beverly put her hands on her hips and stared off. "Guess you're worried about Ileana. I am too. But she's made it this far. That girl's tougher than she looks. I don't think she'll quit now." She sighed. "But it wasn't the violence and danger and meanness of working at Douglas that made me quit. I didn't leave 'cause I'd made enemies. I left 'cause I made a friend."

"A friend? You mean, like, an inmate friend?"

She nodded. "Lord knows I wasn't looking for one. I thought I was tougher and smarter than that. But you know how it is. You're a male CO in a female prison. You see how they act. Well, imagine bein' a female CO in a *men's* prison. I know I ain't exactly Scarlett Johansson, but we're talkin' men who've been locked up a *long* time. They said things that were out of line *constantly*. Some of those punks were vulgar and I wrote 'em up. Others were just flirty. I could ignore it as long as they were respectful. But then I met Tyler." Just mentioning the man's name made Beverly sigh again, a glaze coming over her eyes. "He was so young. Early twenties. Handsome and fit, always working out shirtless. It started small—him saying nice things about my hair or my smile. I knew he was playin' me, but I liked the attention. I've lived alone a long time. I'm old and fat. It gets lonely.

"I should've put a stop to it when he started slipping me love notes. Every day became like Valentine's Day. It was so refreshing, you know? To have someone notice me, to look at me like a woman. I felt *seen* after so many years of feeling invisible. Suddenly I was adored. I—" She stopped short and gave me an embarrassed smile. "Jeez, listen to me, goin' on and on. Sorry, hon."

"No, it's okay," I said. I wanted to hear more. In many ways I felt I needed to. "You can tell me."

"Well, there ain't much more to tell. The long-short of it is, I got too chummy with Tyler—nothing physical, mind you, just an emotional attachment. When he started asking me for favors, I knew it was time to cut it off. I wanted to ask the warden to put me on a different cell block but was too scared he'd find out about the love notes and everything. But I knew I would continue to struggle with my feelings for

Tyler. I knew I'd be tempted by him."

I thought of Zoe's hands and mouth on my body, of the taste of her flesh and the sweet feel of her insides.

Beverly went on. "I knew the only way I could stay away from him was if I quit. At least then I wouldn't have to fight my urges every day. And if I was tempted to write or visit him, I'd be stopped by my fear of being exposed for consorting with an inmate when I was a prison employee."

"So, you just resigned? Just like that?"

"Yep. Things were gettin' bad at that place anyway. It was very violent. Dangerous. I told the warden I just didn't feel safe workin' there anymore. He tried to change my mind—I like to think I'm a damn good CO—but I refused."

"You *are* a damn good CO, Beverly. I guess you did the right thing."

"Well, thanks, hon. I think I did right. But I gotta admit, I still think about Tyler all the time. He's probably been released by now. I wonder if maybe I missed out on a great opportunity to be with a hot, young guy. I mean, at my age, that was probably my last chance." She grinned to cover up her misting eyes. "I'll tell you this much—if I'd known just how shitty workin' retail is, I probably never woulda quit bein' a CO!"

Beverly laughed and we continued down the hallway.

The captain asked Tanner Wyatt to stay a few extra hours so Hummingbird would be covered in my absence. He had me finish the remainder of my shift on Raven, covering for Ileana Sloane so she could leave early.

"She's not in any trouble," Captain Clancy explained to me in private. "She just needs to take a mental health day. I insisted upon it."

After lunch, I escorted the thugs of Raven unit back into their cages. The block was still buzzing from the day's entertainment. Natalia Bravo had to eat inside her cell. She'd not been moved to segregation as punishment for her outburst—at least, not yet. Surely there would be an investigation. I never questioned the captain's decisions, but considering she'd threatened an officer, I wasn't happy about Bravo not being immediately thrown on Sparrow for a long stint in solitary. Often the choices made by ACI's upper management left me confounded but I was too bogged down in my own misconduct to make waves.

A true scoundrel knows how to pick his battles.

Because the outburst had been Bravo's alone, I didn't see any reason to punish the entire unit by locking it down, so I let the inmates enjoy an hour of tier time to socialize and release some of the collective pressure. The walls of Raven seemed to hiss like cold water on a hot pan. The energy here was always different from Hummingbird, but today it was especially intense. As I monitored the inmates, I sensed it was more than just the midday drama that had churned this witches' cauldron. It'd been some time since I'd pulled a shift on Raven, and something had clearly changed, further deteriorating an already seedy environment. The cell block seemed more of an animal house now, the vibe akin to New York City's 42nd Street at midnight back in the 1970s. The inmates were louder, their cells smellier. The very walls seemed to sweat. A thin coat of grease lingered on everyone's faces, giving the women an oily sheen that intensified the dark rings under their eyes. Some of them had constricted pupils.

"Back into Hell," a raspy voice said.

I turned to see Sally Kindly had approached my workstation. Her hair and clothing were messed. Her skin was so pale it almost appeared blue, giving her facial ink an almost 3D effect. I noticed a new design on her cheekbone in the shape of a rose, its thorn pricking a drop of blood like a prison tear tattoo. The last time I'd tried to talk to her, Kindly had seemed nervous around me, afraid I was entrapping her. But whatever hesitation she'd felt was now gone. She was showing me her best yellow smile, a look of mischief about her like a Halloween prankster about to hit the streets with rotten eggs.

"Clancy is the captain of this shipwreck," Kindly said, "but you're everybody's first mate, ain'tcha, hoss?"

I furrowed my brow. "What're you babbling about?"

"You ain't no new jack no more. You done learned how shit really goes down up in here."

"Look, I'm not in the mood for… whatever this is."

"Guess I shoulda got ya while the gettin' was good, huh? You don't need me now. Got somebody else to ride this mule."

My jaw tightened. "What're you saying to me?"

Kindly sniffed. She looked both ways, then leaned in. "Used to be I was the drugstore in this joint. But there's a CVS Suzi who done moved in. Pissed me off at first, but this bitch has got stuff I never coulda got past the gate noways, so I can't complain too much. I mean, who needs suboxone when I can have fentanyl?"

I glowered. "Watch it, Kindly."

"I'm just sayin', if you had someone livin' here on Raven too, you could cut out that Hummingbird middleman."

"*Shut up,*" I hissed through clenched teeth.

"Ohhhh, or what, huh? You gonna write me up? Gonna open an investigation? I doubt that shit. This whole cell block is on the nod now. Sort of dope comin' into Norrington these days, ain't no way CVS Suzi doin' it all by her lonesome. She's gotta have a CO in her pocket." She sniffed again. "Wish I'd known you were for real."

"Shut your mouth, Kindly. And don't open it again."

"Relax, your secret is safe with me, as long as—"

I stepped into her. "I don't have to write you up or report you to make your life a nightmare. You know that, don't you?" Her smug smile began to dissipate, and I seized upon her weakness. "You think this place is Hell *now?* Imagine just how much worse I could make it for you if I was so inclined. Not just as a CO, but as someone who is, you know, *connected.*"

Kindly went even paler. Her cockiness crumbled under the weight of my vague threat. She tried to smile it away but failed, so she shrugged, suddenly friendly.

"Hey," she said, "I was just jokin'."

"That must be why I'm laughing so hard."

"Listen, I—"

"Save it, Kindly."

I struggled with what to say next. I needed to do more than just assert my dominance as a CO. I had to intimidate Sally Kindly just enough to assure her mouth stayed shut. My time as a prison guard had taught me much about mind games and power struggles. It was ideal to never let an inmate get away with anything, but *essential* to never let an inmate intimidate you or put you in a place of bargaining. It would be easy to bribe Kindly with free dope, but that was not the way to play the game.

"Here's how it's gonna be," I told her. "From now on, I own you. Even when I'm not posted on Raven—even when

I'm at home, enjoying the life of a *free person*—even then, I've got eyes on you now, understand? So you just lay low, bitch. Low as the fucking dirt. Because that's what you are, Kindly—you're dirt. You're toilet scum and everyone knows it—even you. So just sit in the turd bowl until I call on you for something, and when I do it's none of this 'new jack' or 'hoss' shit. It's 'yes, sir, Officer Donnelly' and that's all. Got it?"

Her face hardened. "Yes, sir."

"Good. Now get the hell away from me. People see you talking to a guard too long they'll start thinking you're a snitch, and we all know what happens to snitches, don't we?"

CHAPTER EIGHTEEN

If I wanted to get paid, I had no choice but to meet with Dennis. But after our last encounter, I didn't want to travel with him outside of Goldie's bar. We sat with our beers and Dennis handed me two envelopes.

"What's this extra one?" I asked.

"I got twenty grand for that box of comics. That there's your cut. I figure you earned forty percent."

"What's that… eight grand? Just for driving?"

"Well, I did spring the whole thing on you, right? Guess I was a bit of a pill." He gave me a self-deprecating smile, his purple lipstick glittering. "I was a little high that night. Sorry if I made you uncomfortable. We cool?"

"We're cool," I said, though I wasn't so sure. "I just don't want to be involved with any more home invasions or robberies. *No violence.* Okay?"

"Understood. We'll stick to our main order of business. How're you on supplies?"

"Good enough to stuff one more bird. I'll be sending it over the fence soon. After that, we'll need more."

"Gotcha. I've got enough of that fake weed shit to stone Woody Harrelson to the grave."

I shook my head. "The mojo is fine, but the fentanyl is where the real money is."

"Well, well," Dennis wiggled his eyebrows. "Looky here— Liam the businessman."

"I just want the most bang for our buck. If we're gonna take the risk, might as well go big."

"I like this attitude! There's just one problem, big guy. I already sold the rest of the fentanyl patches to college kids. We're tapped out."

"What about your connection?"

Dennis laughed. "You mean Chief Kemosabe? He hasn't even been able to get his hands on the lollipops I asked for. Those Indians aren't the most consistent when it comes to inventory. I spoke with him earlier this week and all he had to offer was grass. I had to remind him it's legal in Arizona now."

"He has no other fentanyl?"

"If he'd had any he would've tried to sell it to me, right? The poor chief is tapped out. Lately he can't even score Percocet."

My shoulders sagged. Business in Norrington was turning a high profit. Zoe was moving product swiftly and stealthily, and while there had been the occasional possession bust by another CO, none of the inmates caught with dope ever revealed their source, and so far, only the synthetic marijuana had been found. The fentanyl patches were the hot item despite their hefty price tag of twenty-five dollars for half a patch. Most inmates wanted to make sure they got every last drop of dope, so when they were finished wearing the patches, they swallowed them. This was beneficial because there was no concern over used ones being discarded throughout the prison for anyone to find. They'd proven to be the perfect product.

"There must be somebody you can get them from," I said. "You must know someone other than the Indians."

"I know lots of people. I'm a popular guy. But fentanyl patches aren't joints. It's not like every dope dealer in the desert is going to have them on hand." Dennis leaned across the table to me. "However, maybe there's someone *you* know."

"Me? What do you mean?"

"You work in a prison. Plenty of those women in there have connections on the outside, right?"

My mouth fell open. "Are you *nuts?* What're you saying? That I should go around asking inmates if they can hook us up?"

"No, no. I'm not saying you go shopping. I'm saying maybe you've already got one or two you know for sure could connect us."

I thought of Sally Kindly. I'd essentially kicked the legs out from under her, having felt I had no other choice. I thought of Natalia Bravo and her reputation as a gang leader. There were many inmates I could proposition but I just wasn't comfortable with the idea.

"And what about Zoe?" I asked.

"Don't worry. I haven't forgotten your baby girl in all of this. We won't be cutting anyone out, just expanding our network."

"Well, I don't have anybody anyway."

He smirked like he didn't believe me. "You know, half of these customers we've got on the inside have their husbands and boyfriends paying me for the dope Zoe gives them. Maybe those guys—"

"They're our customers, Dennis. Let's leave them at that. Besides, they're way too close to the situation."

"I don't know if I agree with your logic on that, but…"

"Zoe told me you could get anything."

Dennis puckered his lips. "Oh, a challenge? Is that what this is?"

"I'm just saying—"

"And I'm just telling. To be clear, yes, I *can* get anything. But some things require risk, which means I'll need assistance. If I'm going to take risks for our enterprise, I'll need you to make those risks less dangerous by assisting me."

"Assisting you how?"

"By being there."

My stomach tightened. "If you're suggesting another home invasion…"

"No, I'm talking about working with new suppliers. I'm not stupid enough to bring a fat sack of cash to a stranger without backup."

"But you're the professional here. Don't you have, like, henchmen or something?"

He nearly spit up his drink. "*Henchmen?* Christ, you sound like one of those comic books. No, I don't have *fucking henchmen*, Liam. Jesus. Despite how professional you may think I am, I'm not exactly Tony Montana, in case you haven't noticed. The only guys who accompany me on deals are directly involved in them. Bottom line: if you want me to go fentanyl fishing, you're getting in the boat with me."

The meeting was set up sooner than I'd expected. I wasn't sure if that was a good thing or a bad thing. It might have meant Dennis rushed into things. But Zoe needed product. I'd sent the last of the narcotics over the fence in another raven stuffed like a Thanksgiving turkey. It was important to all of us to keep the supply chain strong.

I'd begun considering what my long-term goal was with all of this.

With the last two envelopes Dennis had given me, I'd met my fundraising goal. Charlie's chemo treatments were now paid for, so I didn't need the money the way I had when this all started. There would be other vet bills to worry about—monthly follow-up visits and any future treatments if Charlie relapsed—but while taking care of him was my priority, it was no longer the only reason I was playing the game.

The kind of money I was bringing in by drug trafficking was unlike anything I'd ever had before, and because I was so poorly paid as an ACI employee I almost considered this a self-instated raise. Considering all the stress and trauma that came with being a CO, it was no wonder so many of us embraced corruption. It was all that made the job worth doing.

I wasn't sure how long this could go on. The more dope I brought into Norrington, the greater the risk became. But we'd also not been caught or even suspected of anything, as far as I knew, and that only encouraged my desire to make as much money as I could while I could. I was building a financial safety net for myself, a cushion to help me avoid ever struggling again the way I had when I'd first gotten divorced. I'd scraped by on the meager income of the lower-middle-class since childhood, and was ready to get through life more comfortably, especially in twenty-first century America where the very concept of the middle class was becoming a relic.

Perhaps it was greedy of me. Perhaps it was unethical—it was certainly dangerous, not only for me and my partners but the inmate customers too. But the world is a greedy, unethical place where one's survival counts on their ability to bend the rules to their favor. By my way of thinking, society had no business setting such rules in the first place. The American prison system in particular was not one to wag fingers. While I had no personal stance for or against capital punishment, it was stunningly hypocritical for a system to condemn illegal drug dealing while they legally executed human beings. In some states, death by *firing squad* was still an option, due to difficulties obtaining lethal injection chemicals. As recently as 2022, South Carolina had made a death row inmate choose between sitting in the electric chair and being shot in the head. This from a society that calls itself civilized, a country that calls itself the land of the free yet has the highest population of incarcerated people on Earth.

Working in a penitentiary had thoroughly schooled me on many grim realities. Humanity likes to delude itself into believing it has matured, that it has evolved from the dark ages of torture and persecution. But anyone who has spent time in prison on either side of the bars can tell you just how brutal human beings remain at their core. Under the right conditions, we go right back to ripping each other's guts out with hot irons.

Dennis picked me up as planned. It was a BMW—a different car than the others I'd seen him drive. I figured he was enjoying himself with all the money we'd been making, splurging on new toys. We headed to I-40, the new Route 66 that stretched from California to North Carolina. Navajo trading posts and sun-bleached billboards sparsely decorated the roadside. It was four in the afternoon. The sunshine was merciless, the asphalt ahead blurred by heat waves, and the forsaken desert stretched out before us like a dust-caked circle of Hell.

I shifted in my seat, discomforted by the bulk of the pistol tucked in my waistband at the small of my back. Dennis told me it was a SIG Sauer P365 with a ten-round magazine, ideal for conceal and carry. I also stashed a small canister of mace in my pocket. Incapacitating a potential threat seemed a better solution than killing them, and I remained hopeful violence wouldn't make an appearance in my life today.

"Tell me again how you know these guys," I said.

Dennis played with the cigarette in his mouth. "Just a couple of assholes who run in the same circles as us."

Us.

That he included me in his street hood associations made me a little queasy, but there was no denying my status as a criminal now. No matter how I tried to justify my actions, I was a drug dealer.

"Ever do business with them before?" I asked.

"Not as such, but a friend of mine has. I don't know about their pharmaceuticals, but I can at least vouch for the quality of their cocaine and peyote. It's good stuff. But I can't say how they do business. They might be on the up and up with us, or they may try to pull some shit."

"What kind of shit?"

"Bamboozling. Scamming. You know, the behavior of your typical drug-dealing scoundrel."

"Is that what you expect?"

"I don't know what to expect. All I know is it's wise to be prepared for anything. That's why we bring backup." He raised the bottom of his shirt to show the butt of the .22 revolver sticking out of his jeans. "They have us meeting on the rez, but they're not Indians. They're a couple of white cowboys. Word has it, they were run out of Oklahoma by a cartel. Now they're trying to rebuild their narcotics ring here, but they're still small time. Because of that, I figure the risk is relatively low, right?"

I took a deep breath. "So where exactly are we meeting them?"

"I was given an address. Some country store in the middle of nowhere that only survives off tourists going to The Painted Desert."

"A country store in broad daylight seems an odd place to do a drug deal."

"I'm sure it won't be right on the fucking sales floor. It'll be in some back room. One of the guys owns the place, I think."

"A *white guy* owns a store on the rez? That can't be right."

Dennis exhaled, his lips making a fart sound. "Okay, maybe not *owns*, but he works there or at least operates out the back. Maybe he has some kind of deal with the owner, gives them a percentage of any backdoor business."

"But you're not sure?"

"Listen, man. Drug dealers don't like it when you ask a lot of questions, okay? Now are we doing this or not?"

I stared out the window. "Yeah. Yeah, we're doing it."

We exited the highway, taking a road so crumbled it would have been better as dirt. The country store appeared among the dry grassland like an oasis, the only option for food and gas in many miles. Dennis was right. Places like this only stayed in business thanks to travelers who came to this part of the state to see the natural wonders the desert had to offer. They filled their tanks and stocked up on overpriced bottles of water and snacks, maybe grabbing a refrigerator magnet as a souvenir.

A large board advertising the gas prices stood before the turn off to the parking lot. Going around it, Dennis pulled the car to the storefront. I wondered if it would be better to park around back, given the nature of our visit, but I let it go. A dusty jeep was out front, with an old pickup parked along the side of the building, an ATV in its bed. The country store was painted brown with yellow letters advertising cold beer, tobacco, and Navajo jewelry. On the porch, a wooden statue of an Indian in full headdress held cigars, and a sort of dreamcatcher hung above the open front door, spinning slowly in the hot breeze. As we got out of the car, I squinted against the daylight, trying to see what was behind the storefront windows, but my eyes couldn't adjust enough.

Dennis hung his backpack over one shoulder. We went inside. It was like any other country store. Rows of shelves with chips and automotive supplies. Impulse buys on the top shelves and dusty canned goods on the bottom. At the counter, a tray of hot dogs and egg sandwiches were kept warm by a Sterno.

Standing behind the counter was a young Navajo woman. She gave us a quick glance but said nothing. I stared at her. She looked a lot like the girl from the White Feather Inn, the one who'd been stoned out of her skull during the drug deal with the Indians, but I wasn't sure if it was her. I was about to ask Dennis if he recognized her when a lanky white man stepped out of the bathroom, drawing our attention. He was in his twenties but had retained his teen acne. His cowboy boots clacked upon the hardwood floor, a nice pairing with his too-tight jeans and oversized belt buckle. A straw cowboy hat was titled back on his head as if he'd just wiped sweat from his brow.

He gave us the once over. "Can't bring that backpack in here."

"We're here to see Dwight," Dennis said.

The kid's expression changed, a novice thug trying to appear tougher than he was. "You got the cash?"

"Is he here or not?"

The kid put his hands on his hips. He eyed us and we eyed him right back. Waving us to follow, he led us past the souvenir spinners to the short hall at the rear of the store. He knocked on a cracked-open door.

"Bring 'em in, Kyle," a voice said from inside.

Kyle pushed the door in, and we followed him into a small office where two other men were waiting. One was standing by the back wall with his arms crossed. He looked just a little older than Kyle, with a wide jaw and beady eyes. A John Deere trucker hat was on his head, a wad of dip bulging his bottom lip. Sitting at the desk was a man in his fifties with a grayed Magnum P.I. mustache and a suede cowboy hat set properly upon his head. His western wear looked more expensive than those of his young friends, with a bolo tie and gold watch rounding out the ensemble.

"You must be Dennis," the older man said. He stood and extended his hand. "Dwight McCracken."

They shook. Then it was my turn. I gave Dwight my first name only, and he didn't seem to mind. He had Kyle shut the door. The room seemed to constrict around us. It was a little too small to offer breathing room to five men. Dwight stepped around to the front of the desk to be face to face with us.

"This here's my oldest, Hank," Dwight said, pointing out the man in the trucker hat. "Ya'll already met my youngest. I like everybody to know everybody. Keeps things friendly, I tell ya."

The gesture would have been more assuring if he hadn't sucked his teeth afterward. That the man ran a drug ring with his children—no matter how small the operation or how adult his sons were—made me leery of him. Though I'd only been in his presence a minute, he struck me as smarmy and shifty, putting me on edge. I told myself it was just nerves making me paranoid, but I couldn't shake the bad impression. It lingered like a sour taste.

"Our mutual acquaintance tells me you have what we're looking for," Dennis said.

"Sure do," Dwight said. "Wouldn't wanna waste you gentlemen's time."

We waited for him to produce the goods, but no one moved.

"So where is it?" Dennis asked.

"First things first," Dwight said. "You got the cash?"

Dennis shrugged the backpack, pointing at it with his head but not putting it down. "Wouldn't want to waste your time either."

Keeping his eyes on us, Dwight raised two fingers, and Hank opened the bottom drawer of the desk. I kept my hand close to my side in case I needed one of my weapons. Hank placed a paper grocery bag on the desk and slid it to his father.

Dwight picked it up with both hands, a smile curling his mustache, and tilted the bag so we could see the little plastic packages within.

"Six hundred patches," he said. "A steal at just twenty grand."

"Can I get a closer look?" Dennis asked.

Dwight exchanged glances with his sons, then extended the bag toward us. We leaned in. The patches didn't look exactly like the ones we'd been peddling in Norrington, but still appeared legitimate. They were blank white squares, factory sealed.

"Let's open one," Dennis said.

Dwight shook his head. "Let's see the cash."

"Pretty standard to inspect the goods first, friend."

Dennis' firmness impressed me but did not amuse the cowboy one bit.

Dwight's nostrils flared. "I ain't wasting one if ya'll ain't got the money to buy. This ain't no free sample at Costco."

"I'm not going to put it on," Dennis told him. "I just want you to open one of the packages so I can see what's inside."

"Sounds like you're sayin' ya'll don't trust me."

"We don't. Not yet."

Tension flooded the room, making the stuffy air feel hotter. Hank and Kyle kept glancing at each other as if giving subtle signals. It filled me with the urge to flee, but I remained locked where I stood.

"Look," Dwight said, slow and soft, "we ain't got no reason to trust you boys neither. But if we're gonna work together, we're gonna have to extend that olive branch, now ain't we? There's gotta be a give 'n take, am I right or am I right?" He looked to his boys, and they nodded to back him up. "We done showed ya'll our goods, but so far, ya'll ain't shown us diddly squat. Now are ya gonna pony up or ain't ya?"

Dennis slung the backpack off his shoulder just enough to unzip the top, giving the cowboys a quick view of the green bundles within before zipping it up again.

"There," he said. "You've seen it. Now open a patch."

Dwight sucked his teeth some more.

"Please," Dennis added, trying politeness. "We just need to see."

With a wry smile, Dwight reached into the bag and drew out one of the packets, but Dennis stopped him before he could tear it open.

"Not that one," Dennis said. He slowly reached into the bag and selected one from himself. "This one."

Dwight's smile vanished. Dennis held up the packet to the light, then tore the perforated edge. The vapor hit us instantly, a mentholated odor that stung the air.

Dennis furrowed his brow. "What the..."

The cowboys looked about nervously before Dwight ironed on a fresh smile, the look of an unctuous preacher. "It's high-quality stuff."

"Bullshit," I said, speaking for the first time. I took the packet from Dennis and ran a finger over the patch. My skin began to tingle. "This isn't fentanyl."

Dwight frowned. "The hell it ain't."

"Fentanyl is odorless. This here is some kind muscle rub." I frowned right back at the cowboy. "You're trying to sell us patches of Icy Hot."

Things happened quickly after that.

Everyone got loud, talking over each other. Fingers were pointed. Dwight put the bag on the desk and stood up straight, yelling at us, and when Hank started for the backpack, Dennis reached into his waistband for his gun. The bravery I'd had a moment ago suddenly disappeared to be replaced by cold, hard terror. Dennis barely got the pistol out of his jeans before Dwight dove for it. I reached behind my back for my pistol, but in their struggle the other three men crashed into me, and I fumbled the gun. It spun under the desk. Dwight slammed into me. I took a swing, catching the shit-kicking patriarch under the jaw. The shadow of Kyle darted across the room as the rest of us wrestled on the floor. He was going for the cabinet. A fist hit me, but I wasn't sure who it belonged to. Dennis raised his revolver high, trying to keep the other men from getting it.

A sudden blast deafened me, pain stabbing my eardrums. I thought it was Dennis' pistol that had gone off, but the shot was far too loud to be a .22.

I got low.

Kyle stood above us with a huge revolver he'd drawn from the cabinet. Dennis didn't appear shot, and I didn't believe I'd been hit either. Had Kyle only fired a warning shot? Indoors? I was vaguely aware of him yelling demands, but my injured eardrums made him impossible to understand. The young man looked terrified, his hands shaking around a gun too big for them. When he aimed at Dennis, I was sure Kyle would blow us all to bits without even meaning to, so I reached into my pocket, drew the plastic tube, and squirted the young man with mace. At first, Kyle only flinched, not realizing what had happened. Then the pain set in. He dropped the gun and vigorously rubbed his eyes, screaming as he turned red.

"You son of a bitch!" someone hollered.

The office was too tiny. The residual mace in the air began stinging the rest of us. Going for broke, I squirted Hank but missed his eyes, the chemical going into his open mouth. He gagged and hissed, his hold on Dennis loosening, and Dennis managed to knock the larger man off him. Dwight was still twisting Dennis' arm for his gun, but Dennis head-butted the cowboy in the face, causing him to fall into the desk. His nose bloomed with blood and his blazer opened, revealing he had a pistol of his own.

Dennis sprung up with the backpack and looked to me. "C'mon!"

Before following him, I pawed under the desk and snatched my pistol, not wanting to be outgunned on the way out. I prayed the cowboys wouldn't chase us but knew better than to expect that. Dennis flung the door open, and we charged out to the sales floor, blinking away mace tears. I knocked over a spinner and keychains scattered. Seeing our guns, the clerk backed against the wall of cigarette cartons with her hands up. I was now almost certain she was the same girl from the motel, but I didn't know what to make of it.

Dennis was faster than I was. He'd already made it outside just as I reached the front door.

A stack of Pepsi bottles was beside me, and one of them burst.

I spun just enough to see Dwight—red-eyed and teeth clenched—pointing his hand cannon at me. It was just as big as the one his son had brandished, maybe a .44 Magnum. I stumbled through the doorway and bolted down the porch steps just as Dennis started the car. I feared he was going to speed off without me to save his own skin, but he waited for me to jump in before peeling out.

Gunshots rang. Bullets struck the rear of the BMW.

"Shoot back!" Dennis told me.

In the rearview mirror, I saw Dwight bound down the porch steps and aim the pistol with both hands.

"Get down!" I said, pushing the back of Dennis' head as I hunched in my seat.

The car swerved, tires screaming as we fled gunfire. Crouched in the driver's seat, Dennis took us to the edge of the parking lot, toward the gas prices sign, and just as we were turning out of the lot another car came in. With the sign there, the driver of the other car must not have seen us any better than we saw them.

We collided head-on.

The BMW shuddered as the front end indented, the fiberglass no match for the factory steel of the older model Cadillac. Having not put on our seatbelts, I was slammed into the dashboard and Dennis bumped his chest against the steering wheel. I'd dropped my pistol on the seat, clutching my bruised ribs with both hands.

Dennis tried to start the stalled engine. It only gurgled. Smoke rose from the hood like an erupting volcano.

"Fuck!" he shouted.

I blinked something wet from my eyes, unsure if it was blood or sweat or Pepsi. Through the fractured windshield, I could see the woman in the Cadillac. She was close to sixty and overweight, probably some kid's favorite grandma. She was fumbling with her purse, and while her glasses were askew, she seemed unharmed. I looked back. Dwight had been joined by Hank and they were climbing into the jeep. We had to do something—*fast*.

Dennis grabbed my gun before I could, and carried the backpack out of the BMW, yelling at me to move my ass. I wasn't sure what exactly we were doing, but I got out of the car anyway, disorientated, shaking.

"Are you both okay?" a voice asked.

The woman stood just outside her car, her driver's license and insurance card in hand, her purse slung over her shoulder. Her pink shirt declared: *Grand Canyon National Park.*

"Get out of here," I told her. "Now."

The woman went pale. "But… we should exchange…"

She trailed off as the jeep screeched in reverse. The woman inched a little behind the driver's door of her Cadillac. Dennis ran over to us, and when the woman saw his pistol, she shrieked. Baring his teeth like some rabid animal, Dennis fired off three shots at the jeep as it turned around. My stomach bottomed out as if I were falling. The woman put her hands over her ears and wailed, and Dennis pushed past her and got into the driver's seat of the Cadillac. The keys still dangled in the ignition.

"Move, move, move!" he shouted.

Whether he was talking to me or the woman I did not know, but I ran around to the passenger side of the car, barely making it to my seat before the Cadillac spun free from the wreckage, both doors still open. The chaos seemed to distort the world around me, blurring the rules of time and space, leaving me in a strange fugue state as the screams and smell of burning rubber invaded my senses.

I was only vaguely aware of the woman's presence when we raced out of the parking lot. It wasn't until we were rocketing down the road that I realized how she was still with us.

Dennis had shoved her out of the way, and he was the one driving. The driver's door was still open, and the woman appeared to be holding on to it. I couldn't understand why she would be doing that. Fearing for her safety, I screamed at her to let go, but as I leaned across the seat, I got a better look and realized why she hadn't.

While getting out of her car, the strap of her purse had become twisted with the seatbelt, and now her arm was caught between the two. She was tangled, stuck, and being dragged across busted gravel.

"Stop!" she begged. "Stop!"

Her legs thrashed in her shorts, the broken road skinning her bare flesh as Dennis sped away. I shook him, yelling at him to stop the car, but something on the Cadillac popped as bullets struck it. The cowboys were gaining on us.

Dennis accelerated.

The woman shrieked as her body was tossed about, slamming into the wedge of the doorjamb and bouncing off the potholes, blood and flesh misting the air. The woman's face ran red, eyes bulging in horror.

The cowboys' jeep pulled alongside the passenger side of the Cadillac. Hank was at the wheel. His father was standing in a crouch, readying his aim. Dennis cut the wheel in a sharp left, and the Cadillac went off the road, bouncing through the grassland and hauling the woman through cactus plants and jagged rocks as we tried to get out of the shooter's range.

Everyone was screaming. My lungs burned. A bullet struck the door and passed through it, narrowly missing me as it hit the backseat.

Dennis shoved the pistol at me. "Shoot them!"

I took up the gun, my every muscle flexed, sweat pouring down my face. With both arms out the window, I took aim at the cowboys. Being in an open jeep, they were totally exposed—nothing to hide behind, no shields. Hank slammed on the brakes just as I opened fire. My bullets hit the front of the jeep, a tire popping, and as we came back onto the road, Dennis picked up speed, leaving the cowboys in our dust and gun smoke.

I realized the woman wasn't screaming anymore.

When I turned to look for her, I immediately wished I hadn't. The bloody door was still flapping about on its hinges. The woman's arm remained tangled in the seatbelt, but the woman was gone.

CHAPTER NINETEEN

I gripped the bottle with both hands, trying to stop them from shaking. I felt like I should be in a hospital—not so much for my injuries, which were minor, but for my fractured sanity. I'd recouped from madness in psyche wards before, and while I wouldn't necessarily recommend them, the treatments did have some benefit. At least I'd been able to sleep after several days of wide-awake mania. The craving for a sedative was now hitting me like a form of starvation. I wanted chemically-induced darkness, a bed-ridden oblivion where my mind could process all that had happened, without my engagement.

Taking another swig from the bottle of Beam, I gazed up at Dennis from my seat at his kitchen table. He'd just come out of the bathroom wearing a fresh set of clothes, the woman's blood cleaned off his face.

"Don't get too drunk," he said. "We need to be sharp right now."

I didn't reply. It was as if I'd lost the ability to form words. Dennis took a seat across from me. His house was dim, the blackout curtains drawn tight. It smelled of cigarettes and cats, like an ashtray had been dumped out in a litter box. We'd come here in a panic after losing the cowboys. My guess was they'd given up after the woman we'd been dragging snapped free from her arm and rolled down the street behind us like she was no more than a squirrel.

"We've got to get rid of that Cadillac," Dennis said. "Damn desert. There are no trees to hide it behind or lakes to dump it in. Any ideas?"

I just stared at the bottle.

Dennis raised his voice. "I need you to snap out of it, Liam."

"*Snap*…" I said. "That woman's arm *snapped* right off at the shoulder."

"Yeah, I know. I was there."

"Why didn't you stop the goddamned car?"

"Because then we'd be dead too. Those hicks were about to blow a hole in your skull the size of a half dollar, remember?" He lit a cigarette. "Look… this whole disaster… it's not our fault. I didn't know those bastards were gonna try and rip us off, and certainly didn't think they'd try to kill us over a lousy twenty grand."

I shook my head. "I never should've gone with you."

"Hey, neither of us should've gone, but it's a little late for shoulda. Let's just be happy we got away."

"You expect me to be happy at a time like this?"

He blew smoke in a huff. "You're alive, aren't you?"

"That's more than can be said for that poor woman."

"Hey, it's just an arm, right? She might still be alive."

I squinted at him in disbelief. "You fucking know she's roadkill."

"Well, if she is, that's a lowdown, dirty shame, but right now we need to be more concerned with ourselves. Not only do we have to worry about those cowboys, but we also must think about the cops. I doubt those rednecks would call the law, but—"

"What the hell are we going to do, Dennis?" I seethed. "Tell me what we're going to do!"

He narrowed his eyes at me. "First of all, Liam, you're going to calm the fuck down and stop glaring at me like I ruined your life. You think I wanted any of this? I'm in the same dire straits as you. Instead of assigning blame, maybe we should work together to fix the situation."

I took another drink. He had a point. Even if I wanted to hold him responsible, which I suppose made me feel better about my own involvement, Dennis had done the best he could, given the circumstances. The nightmare at the country store had been a frantic mess. There'd been no time to contemplate the best way to handle the situation. We'd barely had enough time to save our lives.

"Okay," I said. "So what do you think will happen now?"

He shrugged. "I've got no idea what those rednecks will do about the body—if they're going to make up some story to the cops or bury her themselves. They'll want to come for us, but they only know our first names. I doubt they'll be able to find us. Even our mutual connection knows little about me."

"What about your car? We left it behind. Isn't your registration in the glove box?"

"The BMW?" Dennis smirked. "No worries there. It was a hot car."

"It was *stolen?*"

"You don't think I'd drive my own car to something like that, do you?"

"But… where'd you get it?"

"Relax. I deal in lots of hot cars. Little side business of mine. I thought you knew."

"No, I didn't. But I guess that's good it can't be traced back to you. Still, our prints are all over it."

"Prints?" Dennis chuckled. "Fingerprinting may look cool in the movies, but it doesn't work so well in real life. Cops can dust a whole house and never find a single complete fingerprint from the owner. The BMW isn't an issue, big guy, the Cadillac is."

I downed my drink, contemplating. "So we burn it. File the VIN numbers off and torch it in an abandoned lot. There's plenty of 'em off 66."

"I dunno. A burning Caddy is bound to draw attention, suspicion. I'd rather hide it than try to destroy it. But where?"

Suddenly it came to me. "I know a place."

We waited until after dark.

The junkyard was far from the interstate, no other buildings nearby. It stood alone in the desert like a huge rust stain—rows upon rows of busted cars, trucks, washing machines, and other hunks of garbage. Out front, a few cars were buried hood-down in the sand in a strange display of roadside Americana. I always passed it on my way to work and back, often at night. It was ripe with shadows, offering plenty of cover.

Using a garden hose, we'd sprayed down the Cadillac's driver's side door before hitting the road around one in the morning. The temperature had dropped considerably, the cool air of night making me think of long-ago Halloweens when I'd trick-'r-treated in the streets, enjoying life in a way I never would again. Thinking back to the little boy I'd once been, I doubted we would recognize one another now. I was so far removed from him. How could I ever explain to my childhood self that I was driving a stolen Cadillac with a severed human arm in the trunk, going to a junkyard to cover up drug-related manslaughter?

Seeing blood in a car again was traumatizing enough. It dug up the memory of the worst night of my life—my wife Karmen screaming in pain, her bodily fluids drenching the passenger seat of our car. The trauma of that horrific moment would never fully fade. There was only so much the shrinks and their pills could do to ease recollections of ruin.

As I headed toward the junkyard, Dennis tailed me in one of the other cars he kept in his garage. I didn't bother asking if it was hot. What did it matter anymore? With our headlights off, we pulled in front of the gate and got out of our vehicles. The junkyard was still, silent, and black—all but for one small light at either end of the lot. Dennis popped his trunk and retrieved the toolbox. I unscrewed the license plates from the Cadillac and put them aside. The chain-link fence was tall but climbable, but we needed to get the car in. The gate was closed off with a length of chain and a padlock the size of a paperback book. Dennis started on it with the hammer while I wedged the crowbar between the gate's doors, trying to pop the chain.

Dennis suddenly froze. "You hear something?"

I listened. A scuffling sound made my skin pimple. Something was coming on—*fast*.

"I thought this place would be empty," Dennis whispered.

"So did I."

Dennis drew his reloaded revolver.

A dark mass sped out of the shadows, coming toward us. We backed away as the Rottweiler jumped at the fence, his jaws snapping.

"Jesus Christ!" Dennis said.

"Good thing we didn't bust the gate open."

The huge dog was on his hind legs now, his front paws on the fence. Slobber dripped from his fangs, spraying when he barked.

"Let's just get outta here," I said.

"Fuck that," Dennis said. "This place is our best bet."

"But the dog…"

"Fuck him." Dennis raised the pistol at the Rottweiler.

I lunged. "No!"

I forced his gun arm down, getting the dog out of the sights. Dennis struggled. Though skinnier than me, he was strong and wiry and mean—a difficult man to dominate.

"You're *not* killing the dog!" I demanded.

Dennis stomped on my foot. Pain exploded through it, but I kept my hold on him. He tried to headbutt me, but I ducked away and put my shoulder into him and charged like a linebacker, slamming him to the ground. While trying to break his fall, Dennis dropped the gun. I snatched it. The wind knocked out of him, Dennis lay in the sand, staring up at me with fury in his eyes.

"You know how I feel about dogs," I said. "You wouldn't want me to kill a junkyard cat, would you?"

"I wouldn't give a flying fuck!"

I extended my hand to help him up, but he smacked it away and rose to his feet on his own. He dusted himself off and shook his head in disapproval. All the while, the dog raged on behind the fence.

"So what then?" Dennis asked. "How're we going to do this, smart guy? Are we really going to risk prison just to spare the life of a rabid dog?"

"He's not rabid. Don't be ridiculous. He's just a guard dog."

"He's a monster, but fine. You can't bear to hurt a pooch even to save your own candy ass, so you tell me where we go from here."

I rubbed the back of my neck, thinking. I was exhausted and yet still rattled over everything that had transpired. I just wanted to go home and cuddle up with Charlie, get wasted, and watch a comedy in the hope of raising my spirits. If only I had some drugs with me, I could sedate the guard dog, but even if I had some, I'd need food to hide it in. If I had a bone, I could preoccupy the dog with it, but where was I going to get a bone at this time of night?

An idea rose out of the darkest crypt of my mind. It made me hate myself, but I went along with it anyway.

I popped the trunk of the Cadillac and picked up the dead woman's arm. The top of the humerus bone stuck out of the wound where it had busted free from the shoulder. The torn meat was still tacky with blood. As I placed the arm on the Cadillac's dented hood, Dennis furrowed his brow at me.

"Knife," I said.

Dennis drew the pocketknife from his toolbox and tossed it to me without a word. I sawed at a piece of flesh and ripped it off the arm—wishing I had gloves—and slowly approached the gate. The dog barked but must have caught wind of the meat. He settled to a low growl.

"It's okay, boy," I told him. "Want a treat?"

The dog tested the air between him and the chunk of flesh. I tossed it through the gap in the fence's doors. The Rottweiler sniffed at it, gave it a lick, then started chewing. Behind me, I heard Dennis gag. I returned to the Cadillac, got in, and put the arm on the passenger side floorboard.

I poked my head out the window. "I'm going in. This guy will be more interested in food than me."

"*Food?*"

"You know what I mean. He'll eat all the flesh off, so we won't have to worry about her fingertips identifying her. Maybe he'll even bury the bones. Even if he doesn't, this place is huge. We stand a good chance of the arm and the car not being discovered for a while. Even with the fence busted open, they'll probably just think it was kids screwing around. Vandals. There are so many cars in here it'll be forever before someone notices the Caddy, if at all."

Dennis let loose a sardonic laugh. "This is batshit crazy. You know that, right?"

"Yeah, I know." I stared at him. "That's why this is the end of it, Dennis."

"What do you mean?"

"I mean I'm done. Things have gotten *way* out of hand. We hide this car, and you drive me home. After Zoe sells the rest of the patches, you give me my share of the money, and then you and I never see each other again."

Dennis narrowed his eyes. "You're saying our arrangement is null and void?"

"I am."

"Horseshit. This isn't the end of anything, Liam."

"I'm telling you it is."

He scoffed. "Yeah? Try telling your girlfriend that. See how it goes and get back to me."

"I can handle Zoe."

"You keep thinking that."

His cocksure attitude left me uneasy, but I'd made my decision. Risking landing a drug charge was one thing—a murder rap was something different. And putting my very life at risk for money was an act of madness. Those cowboys had nearly killed me. I never wanted to be in a situation like that again. It simply wasn't worth it.

"Just get in your car," I told Dennis. "Keep the windows rolled up in case the Rottie takes an interest in you, but I don't think he will. I'll keep him busy."

"He comes near me, I'll run his ass over."

"You do that, and I'll put a bullet in you."

He flushed. "You son of a bitch, are you *threatening me?*"

"I've got your gun. Hurt the dog and I'll shoot you with it, I swear to God."

The scary part was I meant it. I never would have thought I had it in me to shoot someone, but I'd been pushed well past my limit. My stress was turning into rage. I couldn't go through all of this to save my dog and let someone else's dog be killed in the process. I absolutely would not tolerate that.

"Just be ready," I told Dennis. "I'll hide the Caddy, and you tail behind so you can pick me up."

"How do you know I won't just leave your ass here? Maybe a walk home will set you straight."

"You do that, and you'll be upping my chances of getting caught, which means you'll be upping your own too. Be pissed at me all you want, Dennis, but let's not be stupid about this."

"Too late."

"We're in this together."

He stared at me, smirked, and lit a fresh cigarette. "Whatever you say, partner."

I started the Cadillac.

Taking it slow, I pressed the grill against the junkyard's front gate. The dog was barking again, but as I inched the car forward, creating more pressure, he backed away from the fence. I pressed the gas pedal. The lock and chain pulled taut. I pressed further, the tires spinning in place. Finally, something snapped, and the gate opened like an invitation.

As I coasted in, the Rottweiler trotted alongside me, barking and frothing. Dennis slowly followed me, and we wound through a labyrinth of rust, rubber, and erosion. Twisted chrome shined in the moonlight like battle swords. Windshields that had burst into spiderwebs greeted me in an ominous omen. I drove deeper into the maze of garbage, through rows of cars that stretched into the black horizon like a dozen funeral processions.

I picked a spot far from the main gate and parked. The Rottweiler had kept up with me and was barking at my door, but he didn't seem as ferocious as he had at the start. He didn't want to maul me—he wanted more meat. I waited for Dennis to pull up behind me, then rolled down the window halfway and picked up the dead woman's arm, sliding it through the gap. The dog picked it up in his jaws and trotted off into the shadows. Despite the grossness, I couldn't help but laugh a little.

I hopped into Dennis' car. We exited the junkyard, closed the gate, and draped the chain as if it hadn't been broken. Then we drove away in silence, heading for the lonesome highway, heading for home.

CHAPTER TWENTY

"Are you being serious right now?" Zoe asked.

We were out on the yard. Ernestine Castillo was on her knees in the garden, with Sandra Ramos helping the old woman stir the soil. Nina Brown was yanking weeds, her large body soaked in sweat though we'd only been outside a few minutes. Zoe pretended to rake as we conferenced at the edge of the fence.

"I'm sorry," I said. "But this is it. I'm out."

Not wanting to frighten her, I'd not gone into details about all that had happened. I felt it suffice to simply say I was done. I'd never planned on this drug trafficking lasting forever.

"Babe," she said in a soothing voice, "I know it gets scary sometimes. We're both taking huge risks here. I get it. But we're also doing so well right now. We've really hit our stride, baby."

I apologized again and told her the situation had gone too far for comfort, that we'd had a hell of a ride, but conditions had changed. Though Zoe continued to smile and said assuring things, I detected a glimmer of irritation in her eyes. I wondered if she'd already talked to Dennis and just wasn't telling me. Would he have given her all the gory details? Wouldn't it be better if no one else knew about the dead woman and the Cadillac?

"I know what you need," Zoe said, raising an eyebrow. "You need to get rid of some of that stress. Clear your head. Maybe I can help with that."

She stepped into me suggestively, close enough for me to smell her, an aroma of femineity that dizzied me. She wet her lips.

"Easy," I reminded her. "We're not alone."

"Not yet."

She placed the rake against the fence and drew her pruning shears from her tool belt. I thought she was getting to work, but instead she opened the sheers and put the points of the blades to the inside of her forearm.

I stared at her. "What're you—"

I didn't get to finish. Zoe dug the blades into her flesh—no easy task considering they weren't very sharp. She dragged them up to the crook of her elbow, drawing blood. Looking at her arm reminded me of a certain Rottweiler's chew toy, something I preferred to forget. I grabbed her wrist to stop her from further mutilating her body.

"Jesus, Zoe! What're you doing to yourself?"

She giggled. "Relax. It's just a flesh wound. I'm not some wacko cutter like Cherry Campbell."

"Then why're you cutting yourself?"

She rolled her eyes. "*Duh*." She raised her bleeding arm, speaking louder. "Oh, Officer Donnelly, I seem to have cut myself while working. Can you wrap my arm and take me to the infirmary, please?"

We were in the elevator less than thirty minutes later, with the stop button slammed down. Zoe was ferocious, coming at me like a wild animal, her hands everywhere, my shirt coming open, her teeth nibbling my skin, her tongue in my chest hair. I tried to take her in my arms, but she pushed me back against the wall and grabbed my belt and undid my slacks.

"Let me change your mind about things," Zoe said.

She put her hair back before dropping to her knees.

Never underestimate the power of a good blowjob.

After dropping Zoe off at the infirmary, I returned to Hummingbird in a relaxed stroll, still flushed with endorphins. She'd been right. That was just what I'd needed. I still had my doubts about the drug trafficking, and definitely didn't want to work with Dennis again, but now, instead of quitting completely, I was contemplating ways to keep working with Zoe without him.

If I gave Zoe an ultimatum of choosing him or me, surely, she'd choose me, right? I was the one on the inside, the only one who could mule product into Norrington. Besides, we'd developed an intimate relationship. That's why I wanted to keep her happy. If I cut her off completely, she might cut off the physical touch, and I needed that almost as much as the money. I couldn't go back to the sexless loneliness I'd suffered before Zoe Hallister had come into my life. It would be too dangerous to my fragile mental health. There had to be a way we could continue enjoying ourselves without having to endure innocent bystanders being turned into roadkill, not to mention threats to my life.

I started my shake downs on Hummingbird, sifting through totes and bunks. If a CO was going to find one of the hundreds of fentanyl patches circulating through the prison, I wanted it to be me, so I could bury it without documenting it. The only problem with that was the inmate would know I'd let it slide. They'd wonder why. Rumors would abound. Considering the quantity of contraband floating through Norrington now, it was nothing short of a miracle that the other COs hadn't made any substantial busts, only small ones for mojo and alcohol. I attributed this not only to the inmates swallowing the fentanyl patches when they were done with them, but also to a general apathy on behalf of the guards. Overworked, underpaid, and unhappy, the COs weren't as thorough in their shake downs as they were supposed to be. With Officer "Robocop" Anthony on suspension, the company kiss-up was gone, and things had gotten laxer on the unit, perhaps a little too lax.

As I pawed through her belongings, Nina Brown hovered close to me. She'd been antsy lately, always fidgeting and biting her nails. Though still a heavy woman, she'd been losing weight. Something was up.

"You ain't gonna find nothin'," she said.

I kept searching. "Okay."

"I've been straight a long time now. The crack and heroin that done landed me in here ain't got a hold on me no more."

"That's real good, Brown."

She rung her hands. "Boss… can I ask you something?"

"Alright."

Brown looked each way, making sure no other inmates were listening. She hesitated. Whatever she had to say, it was paining her to get it out.

"You and Zoe Hallister…" she began.

The hairs on my neck stood up. I looked at Brown now, waiting for more, not wanting to hear it but needing to know how much she knew.

"I've seen you two," Brown said. "In the yard, talkin'. Seems like you get along good."

I stared at her. Stoic. Silent.

"I was just gonna ask if… well…"

"What, inmate Brown?" I asked firmly.

She gulped. "It's just that… well… I don't think Zoe likes me."

Some of the tension eased from my neck. "Oh?"

"I just want her to like me. I don't know what to do. I'm desperate."

Now the situation was revealing itself. I didn't have as much to worry about as I'd thought. Brown wanted an *in* with the prison's CVS Suzi but had been struggling to bond with her. I wasn't sure why, but it seemed Zoe wasn't doing business with Brown. For all her talk of getting clean, Brown was still a junkie at heart, and sober against her will.

"I'm not sure what you expect me to do about that," I told her.

I did not want to get involved. Zoe could choose who she wanted to make deals with. I was sure she had her reasons for turning Nina Brown away, and the less I knew about it, the better.

"Okay," Brown said in a sigh. "Can I ask you something else then, Officer Donnelly?"

I wanted out of this conversation. "Okay, what?"

She rubbed her arms. "I been real anxious. Can't sleep none. I need help."

"Are you saying Zoe is harassing you?"

"Naw, naw. Ain't like that. I'm just anxious in general. I think I have, like, one of them panic disorders."

Now I saw where this was going. Unable to buy drugs from Zoe, Brown was trying to get something from the infirmary. If she could convince people she had anxiety, she could get a subscription.

"You'll have to take that up with the doctors," I said.

Brown seemed disappointed, but she thanked me. I left her house and went on to the next one, sorting through Fern Hernandez's things while she lay in her bed listening to her MP3 player, Imagine Dragons' "Thunder" coming from her earbuds. She paid me no mind. Cherry Campbell slept as I went through her things. Golden Girl Ernestine Castillo asked me about her gardening equipment, but I told her it would have to wait. When my shake downs were completed, I went to the control booth where Tanner Wyatt was reading a magazine with his feet up, further confirming my belief that all the COs were fed up with this shitty job.

"You hear 'bout Anthony?" he asked.

"Funny, I was just thinking about him. What's up?"

"He's being charged for knockin' up Lilly."

"Oh shit…"

"Yeah. He is *screwed*, man. His career is over. He may even be looking at jail time."

I shook my head even though I didn't give a fuck about the guy. "That's a shame. He was so dedicated to the job. I figured he'd be an assistant warden within a couple of years."

Tanner nodded. "He was on that track. Kind of an annoying little prick though."

"Man, I'm glad you said it, so I didn't have to. Anthony's bad fortune is his own fault."

We shook our heads.

"How about Ileana?" I asked. "When's she coming back?"

"Don't know, but the sooner the better. If I pull any more overtime, I'm gonna drop dead. I'm so burnt out, man. Fried as a potato. I can't even focus on what I'm doing anymore, you know?"

"I hear ya. It's gotten so I let a lot of things slide just because I'm already so bogged down with other work that I don't want to write the girls up for every little thing."

"Yup. And then the warden comes down on us for not doing enough citations."

I rolled my eyes. "It's like the higher-ups live for those damn things."

"Well," Tanner said, "they actually kind of do. See, these private prisons give double the infraction write-ups that regular prisons do. That way, they lengthen the stay of each inmate. Helps ACI avoid paying an occupancy fine. Not to mention the rent they get for each inmate housed here. The more citations we write, the more money ACI makes."

"Christ. They really run this place like a business."

"That's 'cause this *is* a business."

"But they're playing with these women's lives."

Tanner shrugged. "That's capitalism for ya."

Enola Branham came running at the booth. For a woman her age, she moved fast.

"No running!" Tanner shouted into the microphone.

But Branham kept coming. We exited the booth as she reached it. Tears were rolling down the woman's cheeks.

"It's Cherry!" she said in a panic.

We followed her back into the dormitory. Cherry was still in bed. While doing the shake downs, I'd though she was merely napping. Now I could see there was a blue tint to her skin, her eyes sunken, lips dry. I checked her neck for a pulse. Then I checked her wrist, getting the same result.

"She's not breathing," Branham cried. "She's so cold."

"What the hell happened?" Tanner asked.

"I dunno. She's been laying there a while. I tried to wake her up, but she won't respond."

Tanner called in the emergency. A nurse was rushing down. I put my arms under Cherry and lifted her, feeling something under her clothes. I heard crinkling plastic.

"Did she cut herself?" Tanner asked.

He went for her sleeve and rolled it up. There was nothing I could do to stop him, no way to hide what I feared was coming.

A fentanyl patch was on Cherry's arm, and I could feel several more stuck to her back. I lowered her onto the mattress and began CPR. Cherry remained unresponsive. When help arrived, the nurse discovered a patch on each of Cherry's breasts, tucked under her bra.

The nurse tried to resuscitate the inmate right there in her bed.

Tried and failed.

CHAPTER TWENTY-ONE

We're fucked.

I was sure I was about to end up just like Officer Anthony, only worse—a disgraced CO staring down a long stint in prison for smuggling dope, which had led to the death of an inmate.

I should have known this would happen. Cherry Campbell was suicidal. She'd already tried to kill herself in horrific ways. Compared to poisoning her blood with feces, an overdose of fentanyl was a peaceful way to go.

She never should have been taken off suicide watch.

Why hadn't I told Zoe not to serve her? How did Cherry end up with so many patches? Zoe had assured me she'd been rationing them out.

"This is bad," Captain Clancy said.

We were in the warden's office, Captain Clancy and Assistant Warden Moore standing on either side of the warden's mahogany desk. The office was tidy, unlike nearly every other office in Norrington.

Warden Sam Nowak stood behind his desk, his fists pressed down on the wood, leaning toward me and Tanner Wyatt. Nowak was in his fifties with a salt and pepper flattop, like a police chief out of an '80s movie. His suit appeared pressed, an American flag pin in his lapel. His expression was deathly serious.

"This is *very* bad," Nowak said, reiterating the captain's words. "Gentlemen, I need to know how Inmate Campbell managed to get *five patches of fentanyl.*"

That they already knew what the patches contained surprised me. Not enough time had passed for them to have the things tested. Someone must have known them by first glance, or perhaps the nurse came to the assumption based on how Cherry died. Or…

Or one of the inmates snitched.

Tanner and I remained speechless.

"I'm going to have a lot of explaining to do," Nowak said. "So, I need some answers from my officers. You two are responsible for the inmates on Hummingbird, are you not?"

"Yes, sir," we both said.

"Cherry Campbell overdosed under your watch. I need you to tell me how something like this can happen."

Tanner said, "We don't know, sir. She must've kept them hidden very well."

"Did you complete the afternoon shake downs?"

"Yes, sir," I said. "I did them shortly before Inmate Branham brought Campbell's condition to our attention."

"You didn't notice anything out of the ordinary at that time?"

"No, sir. Or, I mean, Campbell was in bed, but I thought she was just napping."

"*Napping?* That didn't seem odd to you?"

"No, sir. Not for Cherry Campbell."

"And why is that?"

"Campbell suffered from severe depression. She never wanted to do anything. It was like pulling teeth getting her out of her house."

"Perhaps that's because she was doped up on fentanyl all the time."

I nodded. "I suppose that's possible, sir. But she was suicidal."

Captain Clancy backed me up. "She was recently taken off suicide watch."

The warden turned his stern gaze to the captain. "It looks like mistakes were made then, doesn't it?" No one responded, all eyes downcast. The warden went on. "The drug-related death of an inmate is a very serious problem, gentlemen. That narcotics are being trafficked into my prison only adds fuel to the fire. Norrington just got out from under the microscope after that whole pregnant inmate fiasco. Now there are going to be *major* investigations all over again. The Department of Corrections, the ACA... hell, the secretary of corrections is going to have my head! This isn't even to mention having to explain all of this to our CEO. That's right—Fred Meredith himself. Do you realize just how much trouble we're in?"

Silence hung over the room like a damp sheet.

"The STIU is coming in—*again*," Warden Nowak said. "Twice in so many months. I would like for us to offer useful information without them discovering it on their own. If either of you have anything you want to tell me, now is the time to do it."

Tanner spoke up. "With all due respect, sir, we've been extremely understaffed and overworked. Things are bound to fall through the cracks."

The warden's face twitched. Tanner had surprised us all with his blunt honesty.

"Officer Wyatt," Nowak began.

Tanner kept talking. "We work hard—*very* hard. We make busts all the time and keep the inmates safe and in line. But with a hundred inmates to every CO, we're more than a little outnumbered. We can't possibly see everything that happens." The warden tried to interject but Tanner was heated now. "We bust our asses for this place while you cut every corner. It's one thing to be underappreciated, but I don't take kindly to being accused of whatever it is you're trying to pin on us."

"That's *enough!*" Warden Nowak said, finally silencing Tanner. "You don't tell me how things are going to be, Wyatt. This is *my* prison. *You* work for *me*."

Tanner's nostrils flared. "Not anymore."

"What's that now?"

The captain interjected. "Tanner, just calm down."

"Sorry, Cap, but I've had it. Sixteen-hour shifts, with night shifts followed by morning shifts. No sleep, no peace of mind, no work-life balance. And now *this?* It's just not worth it."

"Tanner, you're a great CO, no one is accusing you of—"

The warden cut the captain off. "Save it, Clancy. If he wants out, he knows where the goddamn door is."

"But, sir—"

"I will not abide a CO who doesn't value his position." He glared at Tanner. "I surely won't abide one whose incompetence puts *my position* at risk!"

Tanner removed his badge. "Fuck this."

"Good," Nowak said. "Leave. Just don't think for a second that quitting will exempt you from this investigation."

"Do what you gotta do, man," Tanner said, tossing the badge on the desk.

"I will. You can count on that."

Tanner turned to go, and Captain Clancy went to him, trying to talk him out of resigning. The captain was more even-tempered than the warden, and smart enough to value a CO who'd been with ACI as long as Tanner had, especially with the company already struggling to keep officers. Warden Nowak was in an understandable tizzy—facing the very real possibility of being fired himself—but that didn't mean he should blow up at what remaining staff he had.

Though I respected the way he'd stood up for all of us, I didn't like seeing Tanner Wyatt go. He was a good guy and a fine coworker. I'd lucked out sharing Hummingbird with him. Who knew what changes the captain would have to make to keep all units covered now? The forced overtime would be crippling.

Perhaps Tanner had the right idea. If not for my involvement with Zoe, I might have turned in my badge too. Norrington was tearing apart like wet tissues.

"Captain Clancy," Nowak said. "I want this whole place on lockdown. I want every cell and house turned inside out. I want every inmate questioned. Get every female staff member we've got and have them start on strip searches. We're going to get to the bottom of this."

The first extensive shake down was on Hummingbird.

The captain came with Beverly Knox and Diana Rodriguez, who performed the strip searches while Captain Clancy and I turned the unit inside-out. I knew the women on Hummingbird weren't foolish enough to leave contraband in plain sight after something as heavy as a death. We wouldn't find any patches here now… I hoped.

I took it upon myself to go through Cherry Campbell's things first. Her possessions were meager, little more than a shoebox of junk to represent a life snuffed out too young. Under her mattress, I discovered a small journal. I opened it. Instead of using it for diary entries, Cherry had filled it with creative writing, poems, and musings. I flipped through to the last entry, my breath seizing as I read.

I can't recognize my own face
Alive, I'll never get out of this place
Nothing brings joy and at last I am sure
I don't recognize this world anymore

Closing the book, I was tempted to keep it to read the whole text. Not for any incriminating passages about Zoe or the fentanyl, but because of how profoundly her simple rhyme struck me. I too had always held a certain fascination with (and even respect for) those who followed through with killing themselves. Suicide was something I'd fantasized about but never achieved.

I thought of the man I'd been before I started working at this penitentiary. He was a different person entirely. The bearded, tired-eyed man I saw in the mirror was so far removed from the smiling, cleanshaven young man in my wedding photos that it would be hard to convince anyone it was the same person. Everything that had happened—

everything with my wife and the baby and the breakdown that followed—had led to this moment. I was standing outside of myself, looking in, and couldn't comprehend what I saw. It was not just I who had become a stranger; it was everything around me, every bizarre, alien element of my reality. This was a different world from the one I'd grown up in. Life hadn't passed me by—it had stabbed me in the back.

I don't recognize this world anymore.

"Shit happens," Zoe said.

That she could be so cavalier left me dumbstruck. We spoke in whispers as everyone on Hummingbird lined up for the walk to the mess hall, the noise cloaking our conversation. Since the lockdown was ordered, meals were some of the only times the inmates were allowed off their units. Time on the recreation yard was suspended. Many of the work programs were also put on hold. But what the inmates were grumbling about most was the temporary ban on visits. The warden had set a hard rule. No one other than ACI staff was to go in and out of the prison until further notice.

"How?" I asked Zoe. "How did this shit happen? How did Cherry—"

"Look, I don't know how she got all those patches. I never would've given her that many. She must've bought them off other people I'd sold to. That, or she stocked up over time without me realizing it."

"You're lucky I was the one to shake down your house and not the captain. Where're you hiding your phone?"

"Don't worry about it."

"Well, I don't know where you've kept everything hidden," I whispered, "but you have to get rid of it. *All* of it."

"Can't. Most of the dope has been sold already. Everyone's freaking out. Our houses are being ripped to shreds. We're being strip searched. I'm sure everyone's eaten their patches by now just so they won't get caught with them."

"Those STIU pricks are bound to find something soon enough."

"And just what do you want me to do about it? Fuck, Liam, if one of these bitches gets busted, *I'm* the one they'll rat on, not *you*. You ever think of that?"

"Christ… this is so bad."

I wanted to talk more, but the inmates were all lined up for chow. I guided them to the mess hall, the clamor of deprived women echoing off the concrete in a bitter choir. They'd been denied the few things that made life behind bars tolerable. Their energy was dreadful, brimming with the bile of discontent, and for the first time since my earliest days at Norrington, being around these women made me fearful.

Captain Clancy informed me that orderly and yard work would resume because we needed those hands to take care of Norrington's hefty workload. He was keeping me on yard duty, but the warden insisted I be transferred to Raven. Diana Rodriguez, the CO who didn't trust me (or any man) to begin with, was taking over my position on Hummingbird. When I asked the captain who'd be replacing Tanner Wyatt, he told me that was still being worked out, but I knew the truth.

There was no plan.

The staff was stretched too thin to keep me off Hummingbird entirely. I figured if they wanted me on Raven, that was fine, but having Rodriguez on my old unit—on Zoe's turf—made me uneasy. What would that stern, bullheaded bitch uncover?

"If you have any questions or need anything, just ask," I told her when she came to the control booth.

"Thanks," Rodriguez said flatly, "but I don't think I'll need you."

Her hair was back in a tight bun, her no-nonsense eyes as dark as midnight. She was a thick, sturdy woman, and a veteran CO. I hoped I hadn't insulted her.

"I know you know what you're doing," I said. "I just meant if you're looking for something or had any questions about the inmates, I'm always available."

She barely made eye contact as she went to the logbooks. "Alright. Thank you, Officer Donnelly."

She remained standing—a sign that I should leave.

On my first shift back on Raven, I went about my job as dutifully as possible. I fluctuated between being extra respectful to my superiors and acting insulted over what the warden had said to me and Tanner Wyatt. I couldn't decide which behavior would seem the most normal if I were innocent. I didn't want to draw suspicion by shining the boss' shoes but also wanted to show him I was a model employee. It was a difficult balancing act.

The inmates on Raven greeted me with indifference at best and malice at worst. Sally Kindly gave me the stink-eye from her dank cell, our last discussion having not gone well for either of us. She knew what Zoe was up to—what *I* was up to. She'd made that clear, and I'd made it clear how easy it would be for me to make her life a tour through Hell if she dared snitch. So far, she'd kept her mouth shut. I wondered if Cherry Campbell's death would change that. Kindly could turn rat. She didn't seem like the type to ever cooperate with prison officials, but she also didn't seem like the type to shy away from petty revenge.

As I walked the top tier, Natalia Bravo leaned on the bars of her cell, staring at me with a blank expression. I'd not had any contact with the leader of the Latinas since the outburst that caused me and other COs to take her down and led to Ileana Sloane taking time off for her mental health. Bravo's eyes followed me like the Mona Lisa's.

"What?" I asked.

"Just wonderin' how you's holdin' up, boss man."

"Mind your own business, Bravo."

"Lil' girl dies in my prison, it's gonna be my business. Believe that shit."

"*Your* prison?" I scoffed. "You sound like the warden… or Robocop."

Her face scrunched. "Don't go talkin' 'bout that boy 'round me. He took advantage of one of my girls. Course, he so short and ugly, it's about the only way that motherfucka coulda get laid. But that don't make it right, him takin' advantage of her."

"Lilly?" I asked, remembering how the trollop had once nibbled on my dick. "I find it hard to believe anyone could *take advantage* of Lilly."

"Girl's got a sex addiction. Ain't her fault. You say Robocop didn't take advantage of her? Ask the commission of prison rape. They'll tell you somethin' different. Inmates can't give no consent."

"I know, I know."

I started moving on, but Bravo had more to say. "You don't think this is *my* prison? You can ask *anybody* here. They'll tell ya just how wrong ya are. Nothin' goes down in Norrington without me knowin' 'bout it. Know what I'm sayin'?"

I stopped. I had to at least act the part of the investigative CO. "No. Just what are you saying, Bravo?"

"I been in Norrington six years. Before here, I was in New Mexico Women's Prison. So 'round here, I'm Queen Shit. Anything goes down in Norrington, it's only 'cause I know 'bout it, I approve it, and I get a taste." Her tone sent a shiver up my back. "Even a CVS gotta pay their landlord."

"What're you telling me?"

"I think you already know." Bravo narrowed her eyes. "The real question is—where do we go from here?"

"Why're you so glum?" Zoe asked while raking.

It was a gray, overcast day, promising much-needed rain. I had the strong desire to go home, sit on the back porch with Charlie, and just wait for the storm and some beers to souse me. Instead, I was pulling my eleventh shift in a row.

I'd been trafficking nothing and throwing no dead birds at night. In those rare moments we could talk, Zoe tried to nudge me back into being a mule, but today she seemed genuinely concerned about me.

"I'm not glum," I said.

"Bullshit. You've been a human Eeyore since Cherry died. I know it's sad, but it was her choice. Not everybody can make it on the inside. Cherry saw her way out and she took it. I'd say that's a God-given right if anything is."

I shook my head. "Suicide…"

The word had a way of luring me in, like a familiar song I hadn't heard in a while. It was always with me—sometimes buried in the cobwebs of my thoughts, other times screaming so loud I could concentrate on nothing else.

"Is suicide a touchy subject for you?" Zoe asked.

A memory flashed upon empty bottles of antipsychotics, of bathwater gone cold. It went back further, rewinding like the most terrible home video, giving me glimpses of Karmen I wished to forget, unearthing the sensation of madness I'd worked so hard to suppress.

Zoe leaned in. "You know you can talk to me, right?"

I believed I could. I certainly wanted to. But how do you unload years of a disintegrating marriage made toxic by tragedy? The story was too complicated to go into, especially with our interactions being so brief.

"This whole thing," I said. "It just digs up bad memories."

"About what?"

"Stuff with my ex-wife. I told you I was married once, right?"

"You mentioned it. But you don't talk about her much. Does she weigh heavy on your mind?"

I shrugged. "Sometimes."

"Are you still trying to get over your divorce?"

"No, it's not that. It's… well, it's just complicated."

Zoe worked the rake, but it was more for show, in case the other three inmates were looking. "Liam, if your ex-wife is causing you trouble, just say the word."

A cold wind blew, storm clouds rolling in like a black tide. I felt so very lost.

"What did you say?" I asked.

"Your ex-wife. If she's giving you a hard time, ripping you off for alimony or making your life miserable—if she cheated on you or did you wrong—just say the word. I can take care of it. I'd be happy to."

I couldn't blink, couldn't breathe. This was not the Zoe I thought I knew. She wasn't the sexy, spunky hustler I'd fallen for, but a dark shadow of a woman, some aberrant variant totally foreign to me. I had no doubts she meant what she was saying. Knowing she could make good on her promise chilled me most of all.

She smiled in a motherly way. "I just want you to be happy, babe, so things can get back to normal. You do so much for me. Let me do this for you."

"Jesus, Zoe. Don't talk like that. Don't ever say that again."

Her brow furrowed. "I was just trying to do something nice for you."

"You think doing harm to my wife would—"

"Ex-wife."

I stared at Zoe then. Her gaze did not waver from mine. I didn't like what I now saw beneath her surface-level beauty. That loveliness was merely concealer for something broken and twisted, something I wished I could unsee.

"Just leave her alone, okay?" I said, sounding more submissive than I'd intended.

Zoe shrugged it off. "Okay. Whatever you want. Just trying to cheer you up." She crossed her arms under her breasts, shelving them as she puckered her lips at me. "Maybe you could use another trip in the elevator, huh? That always puts a smile on that handsome face."

"Not now. There's way too much heat. The STIU has been completely up everyone's ass."

Zoe smirked. "I'd rather you be up mine."

Normally this sort of talk would get my loins boiling, but today it only made me more nervous. I felt like a male mantis about to have his head snacked upon by his mate. The sudden shift in my feelings for Zoe left me rattled, and I decided it would be best to just walk away. I had to get my head straight.

"We have to be on our best behavior," I said, turning toward the garden. "No fooling around and no contraband."

The coy smile left her face. "We might have to make an exception."

"No. I can't."

"Just one thing. I really need it. It's important."

"Zoe…"

"It's important for both of us."

I looked back at the garden. Castillo and Ramos were tending to their plants and vegetables, but Nina Brown was looking right at us—at least, until I caught her. Then she looked back at the ground where she was working. I thought about what Brown had said about seeing Zoe and me being chummy. It gave me indigestion.

"Babe," Zoe said. "I need you to sneak me a knife."

CHAPTER TWENTY-TWO

A snitch.

The thought filled me with acid. The very notion that one of the inmates was working with the bosses was enough to make me throw up. I wanted to go home sick but knew better. It would be too suspicious, even if I had the vomit to back me up. It was just nerves.

What Zoe told me on the yard ran through my head repeatedly.

"I'm close to knowing who it is. I've been careful, you know that, but that new CO they got on Hummingbird—Rodriguez—she's a real cunt, and she's been singling me out. Someone's been telling her about me—about CVS Suzi. I think Rodriguez is just waiting to find proof, and the snitch is helping her do that."

I'd only groaned. "Jesus…"

"I won't do anything crazy. I just need to put the fear of God into this stinkin' rat. Sneak a knife from the kitchen for me."

"No way. All the kitchen tools are counted between shifts. If one is unaccounted for, the prison will go on lockdown until it's found."

"I won't need it that long. I'll give the snitch a good scare, let her know I'm on to her."

"Zoe…"

"I won't hurt her. Won't have to. Once that bitch knows I'm on to what she's doing, she'll behave, 'cause if it gets out that she's a snitch, she'll get her head kicked in. The Latinas alone make *any* snitch's life miserable in here."

"Then what do you need a *fucking knife* for?"

Zoe had sighed, exasperated. "You just don't understand the politics of being an inmate. If you're going to threaten somebody, you have to bring all you've got. This ain't just about the snitch keeping her mouth shut. It's about everyone I've dealt dope to keeping their mouths shut. Everyone on Hummingbird needs to see I'm not to be fucked with."

Looking at Zoe, I'd wondered how anyone could think otherwise. Our time on yard maintenance was almost finished for the day, so I'd told her I'd think about it just to end the conversation, and then went over to Ernestine Castillo and Fern Hernandez for small talk, hoping Nina Brown would take notice and think I was chatty with everyone, not just Zoe.

Brown acted like she wasn't watching me, but I could see her spying through the corner of her eye.

It made me think about what Zoe had said a little differently.

"He's responding to it well," the oncologist said. "The lymph nodes have lost their swelling, but unfortunately there've been some other issues."

I petted Charlie as he lay on the examining table, his tired, drugged eyes looking up at me with a crushing combination of pitifulness and unwavering love.

"The echocardiogram revealed heart irregularities," she continued, "so we'll have to monitor that, and because of the cancer in his organs, I think it's best if we put him on a special diet."

I nodded, petting my good boy. I wanted to switch him to a diet of hamburgers and steaks and peanut butter and whatever delicious human food he'd ever dreamed of. I wanted him to spend his golden years in joy. As sick as he was, you'd never know it by how he'd been acting. Though he was anxious being on the examining table, otherwise he remained happy. He ate well and still barked excitedly when the treat bag came open. But I had a responsibility to not only be a fun dog dad but a good one too.

If Charlie needed special dog food, he would get it, but the costs were adding up again. The echocardiogram alone had cost over four hundred dollars, and the specially formatted canned food was three times more costly than his regular stuff. I tried not to think about the expense as the vet went on with all the other things she suggested, each of which I agreed to, even when she admitted the high price tag.

It was a sunny day. I took Charlie to the park. No one was around, so I let him off leash on the hiking trails. Red dust rose around his paws, his hanging tongue making me laugh despite my blues. Thoughts of Norrington kept my mind in chaos.

Zoe was right. If there was a snitch in our midst, we had to act before they could destroy us. I just disliked the tactic she'd proposed. A knife leaving the kitchen was a major offense. A bigger concern was what might happen if things went wrong and the snitch started a fight. Zoe assured me that wouldn't happen but...

I believed the culprit was Nina Brown. She'd had trouble getting on Zoe's good side. She'd complained of high anxiety. Perhaps that was due to ratting out her fellow inmates. Brown was also trying to come into favor with the bosses so she could get her junkie hands on a prescription for Xanax. To add to all that, I caught her watching any time I talked to Zoe.

Though I hated to admit it, Zoe was right about prison politics. She had to make an impression on Brown—on everyone. An inmate only has two things: their word and their reputation. Both must be forged of iron.

After the park, Charlie snoozed on the back porch while I stretched out in a lawn chair and got shitfaced. Beverly Knox was right about the job making you an alcoholic. She'd been right about a lot of things. I tried to keep my mood positive, playing AC/DC and The Cars and other upbeat music, but soon found myself sinking into the void in my soul again. As the whiskey wrapped its arms around me, I thought about what Zoe said about taking care of my ex-wife Karmen, whatever that meant.

Though I did harbor resentment toward my ex-wife for leaving me the way she had, I didn't wish her any physical harm. Sure, there were times when I hoped her life would be terrible without me, but these were just passing moments of vindictiveness and self-delusion. It'd taken me a long time to accept this, but our marriage had been doomed long before Karmen departed.

The night I drove her to the hospital had been the beginning of the end. She'd had complications with the pregnancy, but we'd still expected things to turn out okay. We'd been too hopeful, too naïve. Young newlyweds always are. While rushing to the emergency room, we'd thought the baby was being born premature, a risk the doctor had warned us about. But after Karmen's water broke, she began to bleed. We'd not even made it off our street before the passenger seat was soaked red. I ran through stop signs as my wife shrieked in agony, desperate to get her to the hospital as soon as possible, and when I raced through a red light, I just didn't see the other car coming until it was too late.

The other driver couldn't help but slam into our passenger side door, sending us skidding across the intersection, my pregnant wife falling into me, our heads colliding, busting open my forehead and filling my eyes with blood. Because of her condition, Karmen had left her seatbelt undone, and was only stopped from flying through the windshield when the airbag shot out.

We could never be sure if it'd been the crash that caused it or if it had already been happening before we'd even got in the car, but our baby was born dead while we were still stuck in the wreckage. The firemen had to cut us out with the jaws of life as Karmen screamed and screamed in our cage of knotted metal.

The death of a child—even an unborn one—is a lot for a marriage to endure. Add blame to that, and the erosion accelerates.

Though Karmen never said she blamed me for the accident, her behavior said it for her. Her affection was cut off. She slept as far away from me as she could while still remaining in our bed. She only spoke to me when it was necessary, kissing me back but never taking the initiative to kiss. But as harsh as her behavior was, the way I treated myself was worse.

I was certain our child was dead because of me. If I hadn't run the red light and caused the accident, Karmen could have held on until we got to the hospital. Our baby might have been born premature, but premature babies survive all the time. My recklessness—however well-meaning—had murdered our unborn child and sent a dagger through the heart of our marriage.

This started me on a voyage into a depression so foul and thick it transformed into madness, ultimately costing me my job, and forcing me to commit myself to a mental health hospital for observation. Karmen supported me initially, but even when she visited her lack of genuine affection only made me feel worse, like I belonged there instead of in our home where we were becoming strangers under one roof. I was released from the psych ward after a brief stay, was told to see a shrink twice a week to monitor my condition, and was given a cocktail of prescriptions. Three days later, I got into the bathtub and ate every single pill I'd been given all at once.

I always wondered if Karmen had hesitated to call 911 that night. Had she considered letting me die? It would have been an easy break from a man she no longer wanted to be with. If she had thought about it, it wasn't for very long, because the medics were able to keep me alive long enough for my stomach to be pumped. After that, it was months of therapy, some of which was spent back in the psych ward. Once I was as back to normal as I was ever going to get, Karmen decided it was high time to put an end to whatever we had become.

You're never really cured from something like that.

You simply learn to live with it—if you can call that living at all.

CHAPTER TWENTY-THREE

I ignored Dennis the first four times he called.

It was just past ten at night and I was coming down from an edible high, zoning out on *South Park* reruns in my boxer shorts. Dennis didn't leave messages. He only waited fifteen minutes and called back.

Zoe had been pressuring me to bring *any* kind of dope into the prison. If our relationship had been strictly business, I would have flatly refused, but I'd mixed business with pleasure and gotten myself stuck. Though we didn't put a label on it, I'd come to think of Zoe as my girlfriend. Though she sometimes worried me, I had a need for her that came straight from my heart, so despite everything else that was going on, I didn't want to let her down.

Investigations were still underway. The STIU was grilling everyone, from the most simple-minded cripple on Robin unit all the way up to the warden. There'd been several contraband busts and meetings held before the disciplinary committee. Offending inmates were harshly punished. Everyone was on edge, the ACI employees fearing for their jobs and livelihood, the inmates getting crazier because they were no longer allowed to do anything but sit in their houses and cells. The boredom was so grueling they begged to mop the floors and clean the toilets just for something to do. The overall atmosphere in Norrington was one of paranoia and rage, of suspicion, secrets, and cynicism. The prison had become a pressure cooker.

ACI remained hesitant to spend any money on improvements. They didn't offer better compensation to potential employees and didn't give raises or bonuses to reward those of us who'd stayed on. They didn't repair the off-center cell doors on Raven. They'd been fined for the faulty metal detector, but instead of fixing it they just called in the handyman, a fat redneck who never really fixed anything but only kept it running long enough to be called in to repair it again.

Work was rotten and my home life wasn't much better. Except for taking Charlie to the park, I only left the house when I had to. I got drunk and stoned all the time, ate too much junk food, and watched an appalling amount of TV. Though I had a substantial sum in the bank, it was amazing how quickly it was disappearing. It was costly enough to live alone, and all the vet hospital visits and medications were eating through my new nest egg.

The phone rang a fifth time.

I picked up the phone. "What the fuck do you want?"

Dennis chuckled. "Easy, killer. How 'bout a hello?"

"I said *what* the *fuck* do you *want?*"

"Alright, alright. I know the last time we saw each other things got a little… heated."

I'd been checking the local news obsessively. Though the search was on for Gale Whitman, a retiree who'd gone missing on her way back from the Grand Canyon, no mention of a body or her car found in a junkyard had been made.

"I told you I wanted to go our separate ways," I reminded Dennis.

"And what did Zoe say to that?"

I gritted my teeth but said nothing.

Dennis snickered. "I hate to say I told you so."

"We can't work together. At least not right now."

"I heard. Conditions have worsened for our customers. But that gives us an opportunity, right? If those bitches are bored, they'll be looking for relief and entertainment, right?"

He was speaking vaguely because we were on the phone, but his point was clear. The inmates were restless. They would be extra thirsty for drugs.

"Things are too bad right now," I said.

"Listen, I'm meeting with our Kemosabe at the inn. You remember. He's got something special for us. I want you to come by and take a look, be my extra man."

The thought of playing backup for another one of Dennis' harebrained drug deals made my head hurt. After leaving the junkyard that night, I'd insisted we get rid of the guns too. Both had been fired at the cowboys during our escape, leaving behind ballistic evidence. Not trusting Dennis to do anything properly, I refused to give him his pistol back and buried them in a small patch of wilderness where I liked to take Charlie hiking. But knowing Dennis, he had brand new firearms for us to bring to the meeting with the Indians, and probably stolen ones at that.

"No fuckin' way," I said.

"For real, it's good stuff."

"I mean there's no fuckin' way I'm going with you."

"You don't have to. You can meet me there.'

"Dennis—"

"Hey, this way you'll have your own vehicle, right? You can head out if you end up feeling uncomfortable."

I refused repeatedly, but he kept chiseling away at my resolve. Finally, he threw down his ace. "C'mon, big guy. You don't want to have to tell Zoe you passed on this, do you?"

An hour later I was pulling into the White Feather Inn. The window to the Native Americans' room was lit red again. Dennis arrived on a motorcycle, dressed in red leather pants and matching jacket, with albino alligator skin boots on his feet.

"Are you pimping now too?" I asked.

"What?"

"Your clothes. You look like you've stepped out of a *Dolemite* movie."

He gave me a Joker's grin. We headed to the motel room and the long-haired man let us in. The heavyset man was there too, sitting in the chair in the corner, smoking a cigar. He seemed even more muscular in a shirt with the sleeves ripped off. This time, the long-haired man was more cordial with me, which took me by surprise.

"I'm Ron," he said, extending his hand.

We shook. I gave him my first name, unsure if I had the last time.

"This is Buffalo," Ron said, gesturing to the heavyset man.

Buffalo nodded at me and blew smoke from his nostrils.

Dennis smirked. "We through with the meet and greet? I'd like to get down to business."

"Why?" Buffalo asked. "You got a hot date tonight?"

"Yeah, your dad finally drew my number from the hat."

Buffalo started to rise from his seat, but Ron put up a hand like a crossing guard. Again, I was offput by Dennis' recklessness. His behavior endangered both of us, and I despised him for it. It was enough to tempt me to leave the motel, but I feared it would only further insult the men we were dealing with.

Just as Ron was closing the door, the teenage girl showed up, a two-liter bottle of orange soda in her hands. Seeing her up close, I was now positive she was the one who'd been at the country store during the shootout with the cowboys. We locked eyes. Hers were bloodshot, the pupils dilated. She had the tired, lost look of someone who'd exceeded the limit of what they could handle. If she recognized me from that bloody day, it didn't show. She squeezed past Ron, chugging her soda, and sat down on the bed, stretching out her long, bronze legs. She wore cut-off jeans shorts that barely covered her entire ass and a crop top Nirvana sweatshirt that showed off her smooth midsection and belly button ring. Not for the first time, I wondered what her relation to these men was.

Ron did not bother introducing her, and she showed no interest in Dennis or me. Reaching under the bed, Ron produced a WinCo Foods tote bag stacked full of plastic bags containing crystalized, off-white nuggets.

There was nothing pharmaceutical about this. Whatever it was, it was street junk.

Dennis eyed the goods. "That's a shitload of crack you've got there, friend."

"Yours for a song," Ron said.

A tingle of dread slithered up my spine like a conquering worm.

Did Dennis really expect me to sneak *crack cocaine* into a fucking *prison?*

Fentanyl was hardcore, but the patches were easy for inmates to hide and dispose of. Crack required hiding pipes, which also left behind resin. Inmates would be ten times as likely to get busted. Sneaking it in would be almost impossible. Was I supposed to stuff dead birds full of crack *and* the hardware required to use it?

I zoned out as Dennis negotiated with Ron. None of it mattered. I was drawing a line. Let Dennis buy and sell this garbage on the street, I thought. Regardless of the money it would bring in, the risk involved outweighed any potential profit. Besides, the last thing Norrington needed was to be overrun with crackheads. Things were crazy enough as it was, and while I couldn't say I was concerned for every inmate's wellbeing, I didn't want them all to suffer. I'd done enough damage with the damned fentanyl. Once the deal was over, I would make it clear to Dennis that he was on his own. I would find a way to break it to Zoe. She would understand. After all, this was fucking *crack* we were talking about.

When the deal was done, Ron lit up a joint and passed it to me. I thanked him but declined. I was only comfortable getting stoned alone. I expected Dennis to make some offensive peace pipe comment, but he only took a hit and passed the joint to the girl. She took a long, slow drag, gliding her bare legs over each other like she was riding an invisible bike. Ron popped open the mini-fridge and handed me a beer.

"Are we partying now?" Dennis asked.

"You're welcome to," Ron told us.

Dennis accepted a beer. "I can't stay long."

Unlike the last time I was in this room, the atmosphere was relaxed. I remained on my toes but didn't feel in danger. My nerves began to cool, the beer mellowing me further. I sat down on the bed opposite the one the girl was stretched out on, and the room filled with conversation, Dennis and Buffalo seeming to make peace as they discussed potential endeavors. Ron fetched two more beers and sat down beside me, speaking low.

"It is good to have friends in this business," he said, "to have connections."

"Sure."

"You seem more professional than your partner."

I scoffed. "He's not my partner."

"Perhaps we could have our own dealings then," Ron said, handing me the next beer. "I prefer professionals."

I didn't tell him I wanted nothing to do with the crack cocaine, or that I'd been considering getting out of the game completely. Maybe Ron and his outfit were just what I needed to circumvent working with Dennis. If the heat ever died down at Norrington, which it was bound to eventually, I could work directly with Ron to supply Zoe. She hadn't been keen on cutting out her cousin, but if I explained my position to her…

When Ron got up to use the bathroom, the teen girl gave me a long, hard stare. Her eyebrows drew closer together as if her intoxicated brain was trying to process something. I feared I knew what it was. When she spoke, I was proven right.

"I know you," she said, quietly enough that the others didn't notice.

I tried to play it cool. "I just have one of those faces."

"Nah, I know you, man."

"Where is it you think you know me from?" I asked, still hoping to evade recognition.

She stared a bit longer, and then her eyes went wide. She pointed at me with a cherry red fingernail, then turned her hand into a finger gun and pulled the trigger.

"Bang, bang," she said.

The girl giggled, driving nervous sweat from my pores.

"I think you've mistaken me for someone else," I said.

"Naw, it was you. I remember your face. Down at the store." She took a puff on the half joint she'd drawn from the ashtray. "Stupid rednecks. They messed up bad."

I remained silent. The girl was clearly wasted. Hopefully no one would believe her if she shared this information with the others. Hopefully she wouldn't mention it to Dennis either.

"That store belongs to my family," the girl said, slurring. "Those cowboys had a deal with my uncle, working out the back door. But they messed up bad that day. We had to take care of 'em."

I gulped. "What do you mean?"

She leaned across to me, nearly falling out of bed. "They broke the trust—no guns, no violence. We took care of that dead lady with the one arm. Then we took care of those stupid cowboys. Took care of 'em for good." She giggled and shot me with the finger gun again. "Bang, bang."

My cold sweat continued as the girl rolled back into the bed. She fluffed her pillow and drew the blanket over her, and when she closed her eyes, I took the joint from between her fingers and stubbed it out. By the time Ron returned from the toilet, she was asleep. I could only hope she wouldn't remember any of this.

When Dennis decided it was time for him to go, I went with him. On the way out, Ron shook my hand again, giving me a look that told me to remember what he'd said about connections. I nodded, silently assuring him I would, and realized he'd slipped a piece of paper into my palm. I put it in my pocket so Dennis wouldn't see.

When we got to our vehicles, Dennis tried to hand me the tote of crack. I backed away with my hands up in refusal.

"That's all you, man," I said.

Dennis' face darkened. "*What?*"

I explained my stance and concerns, but he was having none of it. He gave me the same old arguments about how much money I'd be turning down and how Zoe would be furious with me, that it'd been too long now since we'd moved product into Norrington.

I climbed into my truck.

"Don't do this," Dennis said. "Don't you dare fucking do this."

"You threatening me again?"

"It's a warning. For your own good."

I slammed the driver's door closed and turned the engine on. "I'm not afraid of you, Dennis."

It was a lie, but an important to tell. Much like Zoe and the snitch, I had to stand my ground and make sure Dennis understood I wasn't one to be messed with.

"You're opening a door here," Dennis said. "One that would be better off left closed."

I put the truck into gear, not even making eye contact with him as I pulled out of the parking lot. I watched him in my rearview mirror. Dennis stood still, watching me until I was out of sight.

I checked the slip of paper Ron had handed me. As I expected, there was a phone number on it, nothing more.

Sleep didn't come easy that night.

I slid the knife out of the leg of my work slacks. Zoe was kneeling on the ground beside me as she worked the yard, and she pocketed the blade quickly. It was a small butcher's knife I'd shoved through the gaps in the fence the night before. I'd purchased it at Wal-Mart based on it looking like the ones used in the prison cafeteria, which would cause confusion if it were discovered.

"When?" I asked.

"Soon enough."

"Just remember our talk. No violence." Saying this reminded me of what the Native American girl had said about the cowboys' broken trust. "You only scare the snitch."

As I said this, I looked across the yard at Nina Brown. When she saw me looking, she averted her gaze.

"So, you know who it is?" I asked Zoe.

She grumbled. "Don't worry about it. Let me handle it."

Her tone assured she wasn't too happy with me right now, despite me having supplied her with a weapon—no easy task.

"Okay," I said. "What's going on?"

Zoe stood. "I should be asking you that."

"Asking me what?"

"Just how long must this go on." Obviously, she'd talked to Dennis before I could explain things to her. "This abstinence from the game. How long are you gonna keep the war on drugs going?"

Her words stunned me. "Zoe, this isn't a temporary thing. We have no choice but to cancel our—"

"Like hell." Darkness moved across her eyes. "*We're* not canceling anything—*you* are. Or at least you're trying to."

"What does that mean?"

"You don't get to decide when we're done. We're a team, remember? Dennis and I want to keep playing the game. You're outvoted."

"Look, I'm starting to get mad here." But really, I was afraid. "I never said we'd be doing this shit forever."

"Hardly seems fair, does it? You got what you wanted, Liam. Your dog's chemo is all paid for. What about what I want? What about what Dennis wants?"

"I honestly don't know what it is you want and don't give a rat's ass what Dennis wants."

"No, of course not. You're only concerned with your own needs."

"Zoe—"

"You're forgetting that without me and Dennis, you couldn't afford to keep your dog alive. *I'm* the one who sold everything. *I* got you that money. *I* helped saved Charlie's life. You better think about what that means."

We stared at each other long and hard. The dreadful side of Zoe I'd only glimpsed before was rearing its ugly head again.

"Zoe," I said, "are you... are you threatening my dog?"

Her eyes were cold moons. "I'm just saying I take care of problems on the outside as well as the inside. I don't want to hurt your dog, but Dennis might if you refuse to play ball."

"You tell that son of a bitch to stay away from Charlie," I hissed with rage. "You hear me? If he so much as—"

"Calm down. He hasn't even mentioned your dog."

"Don't tell me to calm down. You can say what you want about me. Dennis can threaten me all he wants. But if he even thinks about touching Charlie, I will fucking—"

"What, Liam?" she asked, mocking me. "What will you do? Beat him up? Kill him?"

"Keep your voice down."

"Or what? You gonna write me up?"

"I'd rather not, but…"

Zoe rolled her eyes like a spoiled child. Not getting her way made her more than unpleasant to be around. Her personality seemed to flip a switch, unleashing that foul demon she usually hid so well.

I should've just walked away. Instead, I tried to reason with the beast.

"I just need a little more time," I said. "We're still on lockdown, remember? Things are too dangerous and difficult right now."

She gave me the silent treatment, raking the yard.

"Maybe soon," I said in a pathetic attempt to bring back the Zoe I preferred. "Once the STIU finishes their investigation and get out of here already, once the lockdown is lifted and inmates can mingle again, then we can revisit this. I've made some connections on the outside and—"

"Connections?" she asked, still sour.

"Look, I know you want to stick with Dennis, but he's too volatile. You can't expect me to keep working with someone who constantly puts me in danger."

Zoe went back to her directionless raking, stonewalling me with eyes downcast. I decided it was best to not press her and moved on. We'd been talking too long too often. At the garden, Ernestine Castillo and Sandra Ramos looked up at me as I approached.

"Feels so good to have something to do," Castillo said. "It's worth dealing with my arthritis just to be outside on a picture-perfect day like this."

The old woman smiled up at the clear, blue sky. Ramos looked up too, her mohawk fluttering in the breeze. I took in the warm day, but when I caught Nina Brown staring at me again, whatever comfort the weather might have offered was torn away.

"When do you think they'll lift the lockdown?" Castillo asked.

I didn't have an answer for that, but Ramos thought she did.

"Same day they break out the parkas in Hell," she said.

But Ramos was wrong. That, or the Prince of Darkness was building a snowman.

Word among the COs was the warden was being pressured to ease restrictions. Who was doing the pressuring was kept clandestine, everyone having their own take on the rumor. It wasn't until Captain Clancy mentioned it in passing that I took it seriously.

"I understand why all units were put on lockdown," he told me. "But it can't go on like this. No visits, no exercise. The inmates are climbing the walls. And you know what they say about idle hands."

I nodded. "The devil's workshop."

"Anyway, keep a lid on it for now."

I assured him I would, though I was anxious to share the good news with the inmates. They would rejoice, and after Zoe's coldness, I could use a little human warmth. A return to normal would lighten the collective mood of the whole prison, making everyone's lives easier. Just the thought brought a smile to my face.

That night, the killings began.

CHAPTER TWENTY-FOUR

The heels of my boots made an echoing percussion in the hallway. People were shouting over the radio, saying things I desperately did not want to believe. Even in the hall, I could hear the bloodcurdling cries emanating from Hummingbird like the soundtrack to a horror film.

Zoe, what have you done?

No one had mentioned her name. I had no way of confirming my suspicions until I saw for myself. Still, I felt certain Zoe was behind the commotion. The darkness within her had reared its demonic head, and this time, she'd sunk her teeth into prey.

Please, let her victim be alive.

The door buzzed open, and I bound into Hummingbird.

The unit was in anarchy.

Inmates were lined up with their backs to the wall, many crying into their hands, others watching with wide eyes. Some of the Latinas were failing to hide the smirks on their faces, but Fern Hernandez was biting her nails, showing anxiety that was uncommon to her. Jarea Madison had turned away, sobbing with her forehead pressed against a concrete pillar. Ernestine Castillo was pale-faced and whispering with rest of the Golden Girls who'd huddled together.

The Captain, Beverly Knox, and a rookie CO were at the end of the first row of bunks, blocking my view of the terrible scene. The floor beneath them was awash in blood. There were red smears from slippery footfalls. My mind thrummed with nightmarish possibilities. I imagined Nina Brown sprawled out in her bed with her throat slit, the snitch permanently silenced. Through the commotion, I saw someone was being restrained but couldn't tell who.

Oh, Zoe... Zoe, what have you done?

But as I drew closer to the scene, I noticed a small group of inmates standing by the utility closet. Among them was Zoe Hallister. She wasn't being restrained by the COs, wasn't spattered in blood, and held no dripping knife in her hand. Instead, she was watching the chaos like everyone else, her eyes placid and empty. She didn't even look at me.

Instead of being the victim, as I'd expected, Nina Brown was the one being held down with her arms behind her back. Diana Rodriguez, who had taken over the unit in my place, was on top of Brown, driving a knee into her spine. Rodriguez was speckled with blood, some of which appeared to be her own. A cut wept upon her neck. Her tight bun had unraveled, the dangling strands dripping blood. Her hands were soaked.

The captain was saying something. His words didn't register with me. It was as if a bomb had gone off, everything muted and moving in slow motion. I noticed the bloody kitchen knife in his gloved hand.

Stunned, I turned to see the lifeless mass that lay halfway out of the bunk.

Enola Branham—the sweet Native American woman who'd been Cherry Campbell's housemate, always asking about her wellbeing when she'd been on suicide watch—was shredded. She was on her back on the floor with her legs up on the bunk. Her shirt was in tatters, so rich with gore it was purple. Her torso was covered in puncture wounds. She'd been stabbed repeatedly, viciously, her killer having gone into a frenzy. Branham's hands and arms were covered in defensive wounds from trying to protect herself, and there was a stab wound where her neck met the shoulder, the meat gnarled and twisted. Another slash had taken off the tip of her nose. Her left eye had been driven deep into the socket. I only had to glance at poor Branham to know there was no chance of saving her. I'd never seen anyone so dead.

The captain pointed to me, then at Nina Brown struggling on the floor. "Hold her, Liam."

I came over so Diana Rodriguez could step off the large woman. Brown was already cuffed. As we switched places, Rodriguez slipped in the blood, and I caught her before she could hit the floor.

"Thanks," she said in a daze.

I straddled Nina Brown, prepared to fight her like a bucking bull, but the inmate had gone still. She wept and mumbled softly to herself. There were fingernail scratches on her arms and neck, and a bruise forming on her cheek, but she appeared to have no serious injuries.

Captain Clancy ordered Diana Rodriguez to go to the infirmary to have her wounds tended to, and the rest of us waited for him to tell us what to do next. For once, he didn't seem to know, and that frightened me. I'd always found Captain Clancy to be the strongest and most levelheaded person in Norrington. Seeing him at a loss was disheartening.

I looked to Zoe again. This time she met my gaze, but there was nothing in her eyes to read. She had all the emotion of a department store mannequin.

"What happened?" I asked the captain.

"Brown had a knife." He gave me a closer look at it. There was no doubt it was the same one I'd snuck to Zoe on the yard. "She attacked Branham while she was asleep. Officer Rodriguez intervened, but it was too late."

Beneath me, Nina Brown was still shaking, her eyes shut tight against the tears. Among the ruckus on the unit, I could just make out something she mumbled to herself.

"I'm sorry," she said. I wasn't sure if she was talking to Branham, me, or herself. "Please... can I have my stuff now?"

"On your feet," the captain told her.

I hoisted the woman up, her heaviness testing my strength. Brown swayed, hanging her head and weeping. She was almost as drenched in blood as the corpse she'd left behind. The captain started giving orders to Beverly and the rookie, so I was the only one who heard what Nine Brown whispered next.

"She'll sell to me now... she's got to."

After a shower and a visit to the infirmary, Nina Brown was put in solitary. I was the one to escort her. Though she'd been given a sedative, she continued to weep all the way down the block to her cell, mumbling and cursing at herself.

I was still trying to understand what had happened.

I'd thought Zoe was going to intimidate Brown with the Walmart knife, to threaten her into not being a snitch. How had Brown ended up with it, and why had she murdered Enola Branham, one of the nicest, gentlest women on Hummingbird?

"What the hell happened, Nina?" I asked when we were alone.

She only cried. I asked her again.

"I can't help it," she explained. "It's the sickness. It's… it's not my fault. I'm *sick*."

"You said you had anxiety. You didn't tell me you were homicidal."

Brown shook her head. "That ain't what I mean. I ain't no psycho. I'm dope sick, boss. CVS done cut me off."

"What?"

"I tried to get on her good side, so she'd gimmie somethin'. But she done told me no more junk… not 'til I did somethin' for her."

The coldness in my stomach spread, a black knot of fear beginning to strangle me.

"Nina," I said, "are you telling me this was an ordered hit?"

Brown hung her head again, and though she wept all night, she spoke no more. She knew she'd said enough already— too much.

Nina Brown wasn't a snitch after all. The only reason she spoke this freely with me was because she'd ascertained that Zoe and I had an inappropriate friendship. Did she know I was part of Zoe's business too? Brown had been made crazy by addiction, but she was no fool. She'd lied about Jesus replacing her need for drugs, though I suspected she wished that were true. What else had she lied about? Who would believe her if she did turn rat?

As I returned to Raven unit, the inmates prodded me for answers regarding what had gone down on Hummingbird. I ignored them, but in many of their hard faces I detected a secret knowledge, as if they'd come to the right conclusion on their own. How much drama had gone unnoticed until this bloody finale? Were some of the inmates already aware of Nina Brown's desperation and Zoe Hallister's refusal to deal dope to her? Had any of them known what was coming?

Sally Kindly's tattoo-blue arms were slid through the bars of her cell, and she cracked her knuckles as I walked by. She wiggled her eyebrows, making her devil horns move like Slinkys.

"Another fun night?" she asked.

I didn't reply.

Sitting at my workstation, I imagined the eruption that must be going on in the warden's office. There wouldn't just be a resulting shitstorm, but a goddamned shit hurricane. The admonishment would be universal. Warden Nowak would want to chain every last inmate to the floor and blindfold them with their mouths gagged. He couldn't do that, of course, but he would make things as oppressive as possible, provided he didn't get terminated by ACI first. The way things had been going, I figured we were all at risk of losing our jobs. Norrington wasn't a correctional institution anymore—it was hellscape of drug abuse, forbidden sex, suicide, and brutal murder.

And my dumb ass was at the center of it all.

I'd brought in the drugs Cherry Campbell killed herself with and provided the knife Nina Brown used to murder Enola Branham. That I'd not intended for my actions to have these results did not excuse me from guilt. I was an officer who delivered dope and weapons when he wasn't busy having dirty prison sex in elevators. I was a total scumbag and knew it. The sort of self-disgust I'd harbored after the death of my unborn child returned to me in a crushing wave.

This has to be the end.

Maybe I would get caught—the probability had only continued to rise—but even if I managed to sneak by yet again, I couldn't be a part of this any longer. When it all began, I'd felt as if I was in control of the situation. I'd decided what levels of the game to take part in, and how the game was to be played. But whatever rules I'd tried to set in place had been consistently broken. Risk had gone up while happiness had gone down, and now there was only sadness and horror and pain.

Zoe, I thought, *what have you done?*

I couldn't just blame Dennis anymore. Clearly, I never should have put it all on him in the first place. My attraction to a dangerous woman had blinded me. I should have known better than to get involved with Zoe or any other inmate in Norrington. This place was where the worst of the worst female offenders came to serve their sentences. No matter how friendly or attractive they might be, most of them had done terrible things. That Playboy centerfold of a schoolteacher, Ariel Richardson, was gorgeous enough to be in movies, but she'd also sexually abused children and continued to do so whenever she could. Cherry Campbell had seemed like the sort of troubled teen you'd want to lend a hand to, but she'd also been an unhinged killer. The women of Norrington were a sordid conglomerate of deviants, misanthropes, and maniacs. Somehow, I'd allowed myself to dismiss that reality.

I recalled what Zoe had told me about herself.

"*I was a drug dealer. Nothing big or gang related, but I was busted with enough hard stuff to be hit with intent to sell, and it wasn't my first offense, so the judge threw his hammer down hard.*"

Thoughts of her persisted until my relief arrived so I could go home. To my surprise, it was a familiar face.

"Hell of a time to return," I said.

Officer Ileana Sloane was back in uniform after a leave of absence, one we'd all begun to think she'd never return from. That the captain put her back on Raven was perplexing, considering this was where Natalia Bravo was housed, the very inmate who'd pushed Ileana over the edge. But lately it seemed like no part of Norrington was any safer than the other.

"I heard," Ileana said. "The captain filled me in on everything."

"And you still wanna come back?"

She shrugged. "My time off wasn't paid leave. I'm behind on my bills. Besides, that first day in training, I swore to myself I wouldn't let anyone break me."

"I wish I could congratulate you for your determination, but I don't know if it's the right choice to make."

"Then why're you still here?"

She wasn't being standoffish. She was only asking what all the COs had been asking each other, what we'd been asking ourselves every day.

"I dunno," I said, truthfully. "I just don't know."

On my way out, I passed by the disciplinary committee's office. It was late, and the office was empty, the lights out.

Using my key card, I entered the small room and approached the filing cabinet where copies of each inmate's records were kept, separated by unit. I opened the drawer for Hummingbird. The truth was long overdue.

Nina Brown.

Armed robbery. Assault and battery. Burglary. Drug possession (multiple offenses — Adderall, crack cocaine, fentanyl, heroin, LSD, morphine, oxycodone, tramadol). DWI. Prostitution.

Brown's RAP sheet was alarming, but she had no priors for homicide, despite multiple convictions of assault and battery. Was it possible Enola Branham was Brown's first murder?

The records of Sally Kindly and Lilly Gutierrez had not been moved from Hummingbird's files even though they'd been moved off the unit.

Elizabeth "Lilly" Gutierrez.

Assault. Disorderly conduct. Drug possession (Adderall, cocaine, MDMA). Indecent exposure. Internet Sex Crimes. Prostitution. Sexual abuse. Sexual battery. Sexual harassment. Stalking. Statutory rape. Theft. Vandalism.

The sex crimes were hardly a surprise, but Lilly's involvement in gang activity was more serious than I'd expected. Like many of the Latinas in Norrington, Lilly had ties to drug rings in New Mexico and had been an accessory to heinous crimes. Her sheet was sordid, but Kindly made Lilly look like a shoplifter by comparison.

Sally Anne Kindly.

Aggravated assault. Bribery. Burglary. Credit card fraud. Drug manufacturing and cultivation (multiple offenses). Drug possession (fentanyl, methadone, methamphetamine, toad venom). Drug distribution (multiple offenses). Identity theft. Manslaughter: Voluntary (one count). Murder: second-degree (two counts).

I skimmed the reports, gathering the personal information of each inmate—cliff notes to hellish biographies, grainy snapshots of shattered lives. These women I'd been spending fifty to sixty hours a week with had histories more disturbing than I could have imagined. I'd grown too comfortable around them. I'd begun to think of many of the inmates as relatively harmless, but they weren't just broken street hookers and mistreated orphans who'd turned to gang violence to stay alive.

Ernestine Castillo, the Golden Girl with the green thumb, had poisoned the mentally challenged tenants of her boardinghouse to collect their social security benefits. Fern Hernandez had executed two gang rivals, putting them on their knees in an alley and planting bullets in backs of their heads. Jarea Madison, who had always seemed so sweet and fragile, had murdered her boyfriend in a jealous rage after discovering he'd been unfaithful. She'd crushed his skull with a clawhammer right in front of his bedridden mother.

When I found Zoe's file, I hesitated to open it. I no longer cared about breeching any unspoken trust between us. I just didn't want to face whatever horrors awaited me in that thick manila folder. When it came to Zoe, I'd been turning a blind eye when I should have been whipping out a magnifying glass. I'd allowed myself to be caught in the webbing of her charms. Snared by the hooks of her sexuality, I'd deluded myself with abstract fantasies, my forlorn daydreams merging with erotic desires to completely dismantle my better judgment. Instead of learning the truth, I'd taken a hardened criminal at her word. I'd created my own truth.

Eventually, we all must wake from our dreams.

I awoke to a nightmare.

Zoe Hallister. Known aliases: Nancy Hollister, Zoe Graham, Sherilynn Hollister.

Aggravated assault. Aiding and abetting. Arson. Assault and battery. Child abandonment. Child abuse. Criminal contempt of court. Drug manufacturing and cultivation (multiple offenses). Drug possession (multiple offenses). Drug trafficking and distribution. Extortion. Forgery. Identity theft. Insurance fraud. Kidnapping. Manslaughter: voluntary (one count). Money Laundering. Murder: second degree (two counts). Murder: first degree (three counts).

I nearly dropped the folder. My stomach twisted in a gaseous knot. Zoe's remaining charges rolled past my blurring vision like a swarm of wasps.

Perjury. Probation violation. Racketeering. Robbery. Theft. Wire Fraud.

What should have been shocking convictions paled in comparison to the killings. Five murders and one count of voluntary manslaughter.

Zoe Hallister had taken *six lives.*

And these were just the ones she'd been convicted of. Any RAP sheet this stuffed suggested additional crimes that had never been prosecuted or even discovered. What evil deeds had this habitual offender successfully gotten away with? Had there been other bodies left in the wake of Zoe Hallister?

I was just starting on the details when the light turned on. Spinning around, I slapped the file closed and held it close to my chest.

Captain Clancy stood in the doorway, gray and wan and defeated. He eyed me with a look of pity. "That won't do you much good."

My entire body tingled with the certainty I'd been caught. I suddenly believed Nina Brown had snitched, that Zoe had been interrogated and finally gave up my name, telling the STIU everything. I thought everyone had spread out to look for me. The charges would be legion and all of them would stick. I was a dead man walking.

"I used to do that, you know," Captain Clancy said. "I'd read the file of every inmate who came into Norrington. I thought the more I learned about them, the better I would understand the way they thought and acted. I'd be able to communicate with them better to create a healthier environment for everyone, and I'd know who the troublemakers would be, who to keep an eye on and what to look for." He shook his head. "I was overly ambitious and dead wrong. Reading their files only made it harder to be around them. Knowing what they'd done to land in a place like this… horrible, horrible things. And it didn't help me anticipate any of the bad things they were going to do here either. In a place like this, everyone's capable of atrocity."

Realizing he wasn't there to bust me, I relaxed a little, but quickly put the file in with the others, not wanting him to see which one I'd been reading. I wanted to say something unassuming but feared if I opened my mouth something moronic would come out, raising the captain's suspicion. I nodded in agreement, figuring it was the best move.

"These things happen," Captain Clancy said. "Brown had it in for Branham, for whatever reason, and she managed to get her hands on a weapon. Rodriguez did the right thing."

I wasn't sure what he meant by that last part. "She did?"

"It's what I'd expect from any of you," he said. "We all want to step in and be the hero, to save the day. That's why we're in law enforcement, right? But rules are rules, and they exist for good reason. *Never* approach an armed inmate alone. Rodriguez was right to wait to intervene until she had backup. If she'd tried to get between Brown and Branham before the rest of us arrived, we might have two bodies going to the morgue instead of one."

I envisioned Enola Branham being butchered by Nina Brown while Diana Rodriguez stood just a few feet away, screaming into her radio for help, the other inmates watching on as the slaughter continued.

No wonder Branham had been stabbed so many times. No one had tried to stop Brown until it was too late.

"It's important to take your job seriously," Captain Clancy said, "but it's not worth risking your life. None of these women are worth dying for, Liam. Not a single goddamn one."

I nodded again as the weight of what he'd said hit me. "Yes, sir."

The captain patted my shoulder as we left the office. He flicked the lights off and the door slowly closed on its own as we walked down the empty corridor. The prison had gone eerily quiet.

"I want you to know I'm still pushing for the lockdown to be lifted," he said.

"Seriously? After everything that's happened?"

"I know it may seem counterintuitive, but I'm not the only one making this argument. If we don't ease some of the tension in this place, violent attacks are only going to increase in number. The inmates need to go out and exercise in the sun. They need to visit with their families. They need stuff to do. If things stay as they are, we risk a rebellion we aren't adequately staffed to handle."

Riot, I thought.

He was dancing around the word so not to frighten me, but the captain seemed frightened himself. And he was right. The warden's method of punishing the entire population for the actions of a few had neither solved the prison's problems nor made the inmates any less likely to commit crimes. The only person who'd started behaving themselves was me—though the bosses didn't know that—but I'd been scared straight, not punished.

"The STIU will investigate and make charges accordingly," Captain Clancy said. "It's out of our hands now. We're not intelligence unit officers; we're correctional officers. There are more things to concern ourselves with than a handful of isolated incidents, regardless of how unfortunate they are."

CHAPTER TWENTY-FIVE

My best course of action was inactivity.

For the next three days, I tried to be The Invisible Man, doing my job with my mouth shut, avoiding any unnecessary conversation with the inmates on Raven. Yard duty was only twice a week, so I didn't see Zoe, only caught glimpses of her in the mess hall. She looked at me but never approached. I didn't gossip with the other COs and only spoke about the murder with the warden and those hard-nosed pricks from the STIU. Hummingbird hadn't been my responsibility during the stabbing of Inmate Branham. That honor belonged to Diana Rodriguez. I wondered if she would storm out of Warden Nowak's office the way Tanner Wyatt had or take a long leave like Ileana Sloane. I doubted she would do either. Though she'd sustained minor injuries tackling Nina Brown, Rodriguez hadn't even asked to go home early that night. She took the job and herself way too seriously.

I needed to take things more seriously too. I couldn't be a part of Zoe and Dennis' tornadic world any longer. My partnership with the gruesome twosome was off. I'd known that for some time, but my partners didn't want to accept it. They seduced me, tempted me, and even threatened me, determined to retain me as their dirty delivery boy. This was no partnership. I was more like a prostitute with two pimps.

To make matters much worse, I'd learned the truth about Zoe—or at least the bloody broad strokes. Fearing I'd be caught again, I'd not returned to the disciplinary office to read her entire file, but I knew more than enough. The woman was a vicious, diabolical sociopath, as ready to kill as she was to lie. I wondered if I'd ever been in her actual presence at all, or if every interaction we'd had was simply a performance, including the times we'd had sex. Had the real Zoe Hallister been there? Was there a real Zoe Hallister left inside her at all?

I wanted it not to matter, but it did. But what mattered more was getting out of this nightmare before I ended up in handcuffs or a shallow grave. The question was how to escape it without repercussions.

Meanwhile, Norrington continued its freefall.

Nina Brown was formally charged with the murder of Enola Branham. She claimed to have acted alone and refused to say how she got the knife. All the inmates who worked in the cafeteria were interrogated, as were the orderlies who cleaned the mess hall, but all the knives and other tools were accounted for. ACI's regional leaders paid Norrington a visit and held a series of long meetings for the COs, recycling the same garbage we'd been told in training, as if all of this had happened because we'd simply forgotten the rules. Representatives of the state met with the warden, as did officials from the American Correctional Association. I was not privy to those conversations, but I had a pretty good idea of how they must have gone.

The shake downs were random and merciless. Inmates from every unit were busted with contraband. Some of it was stuff I'd brought in, but not all. The crackdown was unsparing. Even minor infractions were written up. Examples were being made, rules underlined.

I ignored calls from Dennis but didn't block his number just yet. I tried to formulate a plan. The foundation was there, but I needed materials, and before setting anything in motion, I wanted to talk with Zoe one last time, just in case there was any truth to what I'd thought we'd shared. I owed it to both of us to hear her out.

On our first day back on yard duty since the murder, I kept my distance from Zoe, too nervous to speak with her. Once she was far away from Castillo and Ramos, she called out to me, waving me over as if for help with something.

"Yes?" I asked.

"I dunno," she said. "Just thought we should talk. What's going on?"

"Jesus, Zoe."

"We've got to talk about this sometime."

"So talk."

She pouted. "Don't be hostile."

"Enola Branham is dead. Somehow, she got the knife. You want to explain to me what happened?"

The pout was replaced with a stern expression. "It's simple. We had a snitch. Now we don't."

I felt as if gravity failed me. "Wait... what?"

"Branham was the snitch. She was planning to rat me out to the captain once she got evidence of me trafficking dope."

"Why would she want to do that?"

"Because of what happened to Cherry. She overdosed on fentanyl, and Branham blamed me. Seems she had something special with Cherry. Not like lovers or anything, more like a big sister friendship. When Cherry died, Branham starting snooping. She had to be taken care of."

"You told me you were only going to frighten the snitch."

Zoe arched a penciled eyebrow. "She was pretty damned frightened, believe me."

"She's fucking *dead*, Zoe."

"Look, I'm sorry I lied to you, but I knew you'd never go for it if I told you violence was necessary."

"You're damned right I wouldn't."

"Exactly. You're one of the free people. You don't understand the code of inmates. *Rule one* is you *never* rat. That's, like, a capital offense. You know the rhyme about snitches."

"What? *Snitches get stiches?*"

She shook her head. "Maybe that applies on the schoolyard. But in prison, the saying is *snitches go in ditches*."

The ferocity in Zoe's eyes left me feeling so cold and small. There was no soul in them, only an existential void where a human being should have been.

"I was still careful," Zoe insisted. "I didn't personally do anything to Branham. I kept my hands clean by having Nina take care of it. See, I cut her off from buying dope. Without drugs, she was climbing the fucking walls by the end there." She snickered at this. "Junkies are so easy to manipulate. When they're jonesin' hard enough, they'll kill their own mother for a nickel bag. Fuck Nina. She knew what she was getting into."

My mouth dried as I listened to this confession. There was no remorse in it. If anything, Zoe seemed proud of her masterminding.

"You're a killer," I said.

"I didn't kill Branham. Nina Brown did."

"And what about those other six, huh? The ones that landed you in here?"

Zoe's smile faded. "What did you just say?"

"The six lives you took on the outside, Zoe. Five murders and one manslaughter, wasn't it?"

"You… you *spied* on me?"

That she was already trying to flip this and put the guilt on me was astonishing.

"I read your file," I said. "You lied to me about why you're in here, and you lied about what you planned to do with that knife. How many other lies have there been?"

Zoe didn't have a snappy comeback for that. She crossed her arms and looked away angrily, a child denied candy.

"This is it," I said. "We're done."

I turned to walk away, proud of myself, but Zoe wasn't going to let me off so easily.

"I say when we're done," she said, causing me to turn around. "You hear me? You don't get to just shut it down, even if you're the CO. You're crooked, same as me."

"No, not like you. I—"

"Save it. Let me tell you something instead. I've never snitched on a fellow inmate or ratted out any of my accomplices to the police. But you? You're a special case, Liam, 'cause you're *the law*. Crooked or not, you're a pig, just like all the others out there who make life a living hell for people like me. The no snitching rule doesn't apply to ratting out pigs."

"You wouldn't. You rat on me, you're screwed too."

She chortled. "I won't rat on you for the dope. I'll rat on you for fucking me."

I tried to stay strong but felt like throwing up. "No… no one will believe you."

"They won't have to take my word for it. I have *evidence*. Your DNA is on a pair of my panties. I've stashed them away for safe keeping, just in case. Combine that with the fact I know you have a mole just above your dick, and I think I've got plenty of proof."

"You… you…"

"I know what you're gonna say. If I rat on you, you'll rat on me and Dennis about the drug dealing, right?" She shook her head with a smile. "I don't think so. If you do that, you'll only be burying yourself deeper. You'll add a whole new stack of charges to your arrest, including being an accessory to the murder of an inmate."

A bead of cold sweat rolled down my neck. All I could do was stare at her, dumbfounded by the intensity of the threat. She'd obviously been planning it for some time. I had my answer now—Zoe had never cared for me the way I did her. To this woman, I was nothing but a stupid mule and occasional fuck toy, and I doubted I was even her first. I might have been one in a long line of COs she'd manipulated.

"If I were you," Zoe said, "I'd do everything I could to keep my partners happy, and I'd be sure to remember who was really in charge. I can crush you like an ant if I want to, Liam. You and that mangy mutt of yours."

Fear.

Raw and cutting. A blood-red cyclone of fear that made me physically ill.

I hit the bathroom after returning the inmates from the yard, punishing the toilet with runny terror-shits. My stomach was twisted like a braid of tobacco. Whatever limp plan of escape I'd been plotting had been reduced to smoldering ashes. Zoe had bested me. I was hers now, a puppet, just like Nina Brown had been.

When I got home from work, I drank hard liquor until I cried. Charlie nuzzled into me, trying to give me comfort, but I was inconsolable. I was such a stupid fool. A failure at everything.

And I'd done this to myself.

All I'd desired was the touch of a woman, and it had cost me dearly. I'd only wanted to save my dog's life, but I'd ruined my own life in the process. I should have just taken out a loan or maxed out my credit cards to cover the chemo. The debt would have crippled me, but at least I wouldn't have to fear prison… or worse.

I now fully understood what Zoe was capable of. If she was so inclined, she might just have me taken out too.

My drug trafficking sabbatical was over. If I didn't start working with Zoe and her insane cousin again, they would punish me. They might even punish Charlie.

But I was their mule, their only avenue to sneak dope into the prison. Therefore, I wasn't as expendable as Zoe tried to make me out to be.

Maybe I should just call her bluff?

No. It was too big a risk.

I was on the back porch when the phone rang.

The sun was going down, the firmament twisted in a psychedelic swirl. Charlie was snoozing at my feet. An unkindness of ravens was holding a meeting on the roof of my house, hovering overhead like harbingers of doom. The phone continued to ring. I stared at it, avoiding the inevitable for just a few more seconds of peace.

Then I picked up.

"Heard you had a nice lil' talk with my cousin," Dennis said. "Wouldn't you know it, she told me you were willing to reconsider carrying our new line of products."

He sounded like a rep for a skincare line. This cavalier attitude made me want to hurt him even more. I wondered if I could take Dennis in a fight if it ever came to that. I was bigger, but he was meaner, and in a fight it's usually wise to bet on the crazy one.

"I can't tonight," I said, stalling.

"Day after tomorrow at eleven in the morning. And don't tell me you're working 'cause Zoe already told me you're pulling midday shifts. I have a little spot picked out for you and me, friend. Not the bar or the motel, but somewhere a little more private."

I didn't like the implications of this. "Where?"

"Take Redding Ave but go past the White Feather. In about a mile, you'll see the turn off for a dirt road. Take it until you see me."

I breathed deep. Dennis was talking about the middle of fucking nowhere. He was luring me out to the desert.

"What is this?" I asked.

"Relax. This is just in case you give me trouble. But you're not going to give me any trouble, right?"

I sighed. "No. No trouble."

"Good. Then there's nothing for either of us to worry about. Friday at eleven. Don't be late—and come alone."

He hung up before I could say anything else. That was fine. I couldn't think of what to say anyway.

I sat in the lawn chair, watching as night fell in full, thinking about my life and what I'd made of it. Instead of finishing my beer, I poured it out over the dirt. It was time to sober up. I had to get my shit together and finalize a plan, however imperfect it may be. Going back inside, I put on a pot of coffee and ran cold water over my face. Charlie followed me from room to room, sensing I was in trouble. He mewled. I patted him on the head to assure him I was okay, but he didn't believe that any more than I did.

Pouring coffee into my thermos, I gathered my keys and camping shovel and hit the road with Charlie. I was still a little buzzed, but I needed to get this errand done *now*. I just hoped I could remember the right spot.

When we arrived, Charlie found it for me.

Though we normally hiked the trail by day, my dog was very familiar with it. He bounded up the pathway and into the thicket, tail high and wagging. I followed behind with my flashlight and camping shovel. I brought Charlie to the general vicinity, and soon he put his nose into the dirt and pawed, following my scent, showing me where I'd buried the guns.

"You must be joking," Ileana Sloane said. "With everything that's happened, they're letting them out for recess?"

I shrugged. "I'm sure the warden doesn't want this, but other people at the top have been pushing for it. The captain just told me the lockdown has officially been lifted."

I'd just arrived for my shift on Raven, which would free Ileana up for other tasks. Norrington was so hurt for staff that all the COs were being shifted about like horses on a merry-go-round. Now the visiting room and workshops were being reopened as well as the exercise yard.

"I don't know how we're expected to cover all of this at once," Ileana said.

"I don't either, but those are the orders."

"Christ. Drugs and murder and *still* these miserable bitches get pampered. If it were up to me, they'd never see the sun again."

"The general concern seems to be that without stuff to do, the inmates' behavior will only get worse."

"Worse than *murder*?"

I shrugged again.

"I never should've come back to this craphouse," Ileana said. "What was I thinking?"

"Probably that it's either the craphouse or the poor house."

She smirked. "Well, either one is just barely better than the cemetery."

Ileana left for her break. I started my rounds. Whenever beginning a shift, I liked to get a look at every inmate I was responsible for. Today, I felt like a lion tamer. The inmates on Raven had the hardest eyes of them all.

Wanting to get the word out, I went to the inmate with the most connections—Natalia Bravo.

"The lockdown is ending," I told her. "You all will be able to return to work and see visitors. You'll even get your rec time back."

Bravo watched me from behind the bars. "That's what I heard."

"Wait… you… how did you already know? I'm just finding this out myself."

"Shit. I done told you, man. Ain't nothin' goes on up in here without the Queen knowin' 'bout it." Bravo's devilish grin made her cheeks swell like plumbs. "I know all kinda things—includin' 'bout you."

"Oh yeah?" I said, trying to play it cool. "What do you know about me?"

"I know you had a little spat with your girl."

My eye began to twitch. Another inmate was on to me and Zoe. How many others knew?

I looked away from Bravo. "I don't know what you're talking about."

"Sure, you don't. That's fine, boss man. But you know 'bout that bitch Nina Brown and what all she did to Enola, now don't ya?"

"What're you saying, Inmate Bravo?" I said firmly. "Do you have something to tell me about the murder? Are you telling me you knew about the killing in advance?"

"Nah. See, that's the problem. Ain't nobody run that shit by me. People in here know better than that. Must be trippin'." She leaned on the bars to get closer to me. "Somethin's goin' on 'round here and Imma find out what."

"Yeah, well, when you do, you just let me know."

"Oh, I will, boss. And if you come up with somethin' for me, just holla."

I walked on, leaving Bravo and her vague musings behind. I had more immediate problems.

Making my way across the tier, I found Sally Kindly alone in her dank cell. She was standing up against the bars, watching me—*waiting* for me. She wasn't giving me the evil eye today. Instead, she seemed rather amused.

I cleared my throat. "Something funny, Inmate Kindly?"

"Funny?" she asked, feigning surprise. "Why no, officer. I was just thinkin' what a shame it is when somebody's got two choices and they end up goin' with the wrong one. Ain't that a bitch?"

I stood closer to the bars, speaking softly. "Just spit it out, Sally. I'm in no mood for games."

"I'm sure you've had your fill of that, huh? Fuckin' women and their games, man. Always fuckin' with a guy's head, making 'em do things they don't wanna do. It's a shame how easily a cunt can spoil everything." Kindly waited for me to confirm but I only stared at her. She whispered. "That whole mess with Enola Branham was a damned shamed. She was a good woman—at least good by Norrington standards. But she got what was comin' to her, being a snitch and all. What really ain't right is what happened to Nina."

"Nina?" I said, confused. "But she killed Enola."

"What other choice did she have?"

"What are you saying?"

"That goddamned CVS," Kindly said, her face going grim. "Somebody really oughta close it down."

I looked both ways. The cellblock was a chorus of conversations. No one was paying us any attention, but if I lingered too long, they would. I had to make this quick.

"Maybe you're right," I said.

Kindly smirked. "Trouble in paradise?"

"Trouble all around. You say it's a shame when someone makes the wrong choice, but the only real shame is not owning up to your mistakes to make things right again. That little offer you made some time ago, about working together… I'd like to take you up on it now."

She raised her eyebrows, constricting her devil horns. "Oh, really? Shit, things must be worse than I thought. I don't know if I wanna get involved with no—"

"Free stuff."

Kindly blinked. "Free?"

"I'll get you the *good* stuff to sell on Raven and hook you up with enough free samples to keep you high 'round the clock."

A glimmer of thirst befell Kindly's dark eyes. Her mischievous smile returned, the wet fangs of a T-Rex. "You serious?"

"Yeah, I'm serious. But if we're gonna do business, I'll need to know you're tough enough to handle it."

She scoffed, and rightly so. I recalled some of the offenses in her file.

Aggravated assault. Manslaughter: Voluntary. Murder: second-degree.

Kindly was certainly tough enough, but I needed her to believe she had to prove it to me.

"Okay?" she said. "I'm listenin'. Whatcha want me to do?"

CHAPTER
TWENTY-SIX

Ileana Sloane stood in the shade of the awning, watching the inmates exercise. I stood on the other end of the yard so we could keep both ends covered. The women from Hummingbird and Raven were lifting weights, doing yoga, and tossing around the basketball. After so long in isolation, they were jovial and full of energy, like children at recess.

Zoe was doing stretches, her foot up on a bench. We still hadn't spoken. Dennis must have told her about our upcoming deal because she didn't bother pressuring me anymore. Besides, she'd made her point clear.

It was high time I made mine.

Sally Kindly strolled about, making small talk with other inmates, all the while keeping her eyes on Zoe. She was marking Zoe's movements, learning her routine, studying. Nothing would happen today—but soon. First, I had to bring some of those free samples I'd promised Kindly, to show her

I would hold up my end of the deal. A little taste of things to come, provided she did what I asked.

I was concerned about having to sneak in another weapon, but Kindly assured me I needn't deliver one.

"I'll take care of it," she'd told me. "Just gimmie a little time."

"How much?"

"Not long. Don't ask when or where. Just know it'll happen."

I was trying to be patient, but I had a rendezvous with Dennis coming up. Time was in short supply.

"The far end of the fence," I'd told Kindly. "Against the wall of building C. That's where the dead zone is."

"Yeah, yeah. I know which cameras are busted. We'll see what happens, but obviously I'll try and be in the cut."

Standing in the yard now, I watched the spot closely. Natalia Bravo was leaning against the wall, surrounded by other Latinas including Fern Hernandez and Sandra Ramos. That the known gang was loitering in a surveillance dead zone was a concern, so Ileana had been keeping an eye on them. It would be a good distraction when the time came.

So it's come to this, I thought bitterly.

But much like Nina Brown, I had no choice. Things had spun too far out of my control, and now the only escape was to go whole hog.

I'd never been a violent man. After grade school, I never even got into fist fights. But that was back when I'd been civilized. Now that I was on this animal farm, I had reverted to a more primitive human state, just like the inmates of Norrington. There'd been a recall inside my head, the modern man ejected so the reptilian brain could return to power.

Kill or be killed.

A basketball game was coming together on the court. I made my way around to stand beside Ileana. It was a bright day, and she wore mirrored sunglasses which, like everything else, seemed too big for her.

"It's too hot to be out here," Ileana said.

I smiled. "You just want any reason to lock the inmates back up."

"Can you blame me? Trying to supervise this many at once is nearly impossible. It's like trying to potty train an entire litter of puppies at the same time. You need a hundred eyes in your head."

That's exactly what I'm counting on.

"Well," I said, "when they're allowed out, there're more opportunities for them to get into trouble, but it also creates more opportunities for us to write infractions. The more citations we give, the better for our careers."

"And the better for ACI. I think that was a major influence on the decision to lift the lockdown."

"You're probably right."

"This company doesn't care about the safety of its officers any more than it does its inmates," Ileana said bitterly. "We all should strike or something. If all of us refuse to work, what would they do then, huh?"

"I'm amazed this place hasn't been shut down already."

"I never would've thought a prison could operate this way. But being privately owned makes all the difference. That's why I've been looking into other jobs within the DOC. Get out of the privately run system and work directly for the state."

"Oh yeah? What're you thinking?"

She sighed. "Hell, I'm willing to work in a men's prison if it means getting out of ACI. The bitches in here have certainly toughened me up for it. I'd like to work on a SORT unit someday and handle the most dangerous situations the prison system can hurl at me. See some real action, you know?"

I shook my head. "Ileana, I swear, you probably take guys skydiving on the first date, don't you?"

This managed to get a smile out of her. It was important for me to be casual like this, to be a normal person. It reminded me I was still human.

When my shift was over, I placed the call.

At first, he didn't know who I was. I had to remind him of our previous encounters and how he'd slipped me his number at the motel because I was more levelheaded than my associate, Dennis.

"What can I do for you?" Ron asked.

I told him what I was interested in. He said it wouldn't be a problem.

On my way home, I made a detour to the White Feather Inn.

I hovered over the toilet bowl, sweaty from nerves and the day's rising temperatures. The air conditioning vents in the employee bathroom had been malfunctioning, just like so many other things in Norrington, and the trapped air was still and fetid. I pushed harder, wishing I'd put more lube on the balloon of heroin, wondering if it would have made this final step any easier. I'd thought getting it up my ass was going to be the difficult part—and it was. Except for medical needs, I considered my sphincter *exit only*. I'd put thought into getting the wad in there, but not enough thought into the expulsion. I just sat on the john, business as usual.

"C'mon," I said, feeling it break the horizon.

When the heroin balloon finally left my colon, I breathed a sigh of relief. I'd been terrified the container would bust and I'd be anally toxified. Using latex gloves, I sifted through the mess, withdrew the baggie from the balloon, and flushed the remaining evidence. I cleaned up and proceeded to Raven where I held the package in my pocket for three hours, waiting for a safe moment to make the delivery.

I was working the unit with a rookie CO. Once he finished his shift, I went to Sally Kindly's cell and opened it as if I were doing a surprise shake down. She complained loudly about being harassed, a performance for any prying ears.

I slipped the baggie into her folded towel. "Getting a syringe will be difficult. I figured you could snort it for now."

"Nah," she said. "I got a binky."

"Oh," I said, surprised though I shouldn't have been. Kindly had hidden the homemade syringes very well before, including in uncomfortable body holes.

"I also got my hands on some nail clippers," she said.

They were a coveted tool in prison because they could be used to cut metal, which I assumed was exactly why Kindly obtained them.

"Soon?" I asked.

"I'll get 'er done."

"Just don't go on the nod and spend every day passed out."

"Chill. I said it'll get done."

Kindly took the towel with the contraband, holding it close like she was breastfeeding a baby. Her arms were flaky from eczema, her tattoos looking worn and blurred.

"You know," she said, "you could use some of this dope yourself. Clear your mind. Learn to relax."

I almost laughed. Here was a convicted killer with devil horns tattooed on her forehead telling me to mellow out. My life had become a David Lynch movie... or perhaps a Zucker Brothers one.

Closing the cell door, I started my security checks, which consisted of filling out the logbook without even bothering to walk the tier. I was not the only one who did this. Unless DOC officials were visiting, the COs of Norrington cut corners wherever we could. The logbooks were audited, but the cameras and employee punch cards weren't, so fuck it. I was sitting at the station filling it out when Ileana Sloane came in unexpectedly.

"You're early," I said.

"Clancy asked me to be. Said he needed you for something else."

I stood. "Oh. Did he say what?"

Ileana shrugged. Given the gravity of all I was undertaking, I couldn't help but feel like I was tiptoeing through a field of landmines.

"Should I go to his office?" I asked.

"I guess. He didn't specify."

So I did the long walk. My eyes stayed on my feet as I moved through the corridors. I'd once read that you could tell how successful a man was by the way he walked. If he looked straight ahead, he was a businessman or manager, and if he hung his head, he was a lower-level or "unskilled" worker. Even my own walk certified me as a loser.

The captain was in the hallway just outside his office, flipping through papers on a clipboard as I approached, his reading glasses on the end of his nose. He glanced over them at me.

"How's it going, Liam?" he asked.

His casual demeanor put me at ease.

"Officer Sloane said you needed me," I said.

He made a notation with his pencil and grumbled.

"Sir?" I asked.

"Sorry," he said. "I'm not groaning at you. It's these damned expense reports. Every time I try to push for repairs, our assistant warden hands me these itemized lists and…" He shuffled through them, giving me glimpses of the files. "Lilly Gutierrez's pregnancy is already hurting us. She needs regular doctor visits—quite an expense for an inmate that brings the company less than forty bucks a day. ACI has already been spending too much money on healthcare—it's fifteen percent of our entire budget."

"That's crazy," I said, trying to seem interested.

"Thirty-eight percent of the inmates here have a chronic disease, and eight percent of those are communicable. We're treating everything from asthma to HIV."

The mention of sexually transmitted diseases made the hairs on my neck stand up. I'd been unsafe with Zoe in every sense of the word.

"But this pregnancy is gonna cost us big time," Captain Clancy said. "Our prison nurses can only do so much for Gutierrez here. She needs specialists, and when it comes time for her to deliver, that'll be a whole other fiasco. The cost of the hospital stay, plus the cost of posting guards there… it's gonna blow the whole damned budget."

I nodded, unsure what to say.

The captain clasped my shoulder. "The reason I'm telling you this is I don't want my officers to think I'm just ignoring all the problems we have here. I hope you all realize I'm doing everything I can."

"We do, Captain," I said, truthfully. Of all the higher-ups in Norrington, Captain Clancy was the most respected and well-liked by the COs. "We appreciate you."

He smiled, but it was a sad, muted smile. He seemed just as burnt out as the rest of us. I couldn't remember ever coming into work and the captain not being there. It was as if he lived here along with the inmates.

"Anyway," he said, "I asked Ileana to cover for you on Raven so I could move you to Sparrow. I need a strong CO for that unit right now."

I thought of Sparrow's main guard, Dale Woods, who had been transferred to Norrington from another ACI prison.

"Dale is out with a stomach bug," the captain explained, "and the new hire he was training was a no-call-no-show today and won't answer her phone. I guess one week on the job was enough for her."

He started walking, so I followed. I wanted to ask how long he expected me to be on Sparrow unit but didn't want to raise any eyebrows. I preferred to be on Raven or Hummingbird to oversee business, but perhaps it would be better to be on Sparrow. It would further distance me from what Kindly was going to do. While solitary confinement units could be intimidating, the inmates spent twenty-three hours a day in their cells, so I would have more time to sit and think, which could be good or bad, depending on my mood. My mind had a way of sabotaging me. But I wasn't about to argue with the captain about relocating. In his opinion, I was a model employee. I needed it to stay that way now more than ever.

"There are two million Americans incarcerated," the captain said as we made our way to Sparrow. "But ACI says it's not enough."

When we arrived on the unit, the captain went through a few procedural changes and updated me on some of the inmates. It was prison officials, not judges and juries, who decided who went into solitary and how long they had to stay there. That the seg unit was always at or near capacity said more about ACI than it did about the criminal element.

When the captain finally left, I strolled by the solid steel cell doors with their small windows and food ports. I peaked in to check on the inmates. Many of them seemed mentally ill, which was to be expected. If you weren't crazy before going to seg, it would make you that way. This form of confinement was known to cause actual brain damage.

I looked in on Nina Brown. She was curled up on her cot, facing the bare wall and shivering despite the heat. I doubted she would be leaving solitary any time soon. She might just spend the rest of her life in this concrete box. I wondered if her shivers were due to being forced to go cold turkey against the very addictions that had, in a way, landed her here. Having only one hour per day to engage with other people must have made it much more difficult to get a fix. Poor Brown had believed Zoe would take care of her. In that regard, I knew how she felt.

Lilly Gutierrez was housed at the end of the tier. When I first looked through her window, she was dancing without music, her eyes closed, lips parted in a coy smile. The woman was sexy even when nobody was looking. She wasn't even startled when she opened her eyes and spotted me watching. She kept swaying and gyrating her curvy body, so much like a stripper I expected her to disrobe. I wondered if she was showing yet. Her eyes were dark and hungry as she came closer to the door.

"Put your dick in the food port," she said, muffled by the glass.

The food port was the cell door's only opening, a sort of mail slot used for sliding in trays of food or having the inmates put their hands through to be cuffed before opening the door.

I only stared at Lilly, spellbound by the oddity of her. She winked and licked those plump lips, tapping her fingernails upon the door in an alluring percussion. I gripped the front of my belt. The temptation was surprisingly strong, my stupidity joining forces with my deep need to relieve all this compounded tension.

How damaged does a man have to be to even consider sticking his dick into a prison glory hole?

"C'mon," Lilly said. "Give it to me, daddy. Lemme have it."

The sound of my radio buzzing dragged me out of Lilly's web.

"Code red!" Ileana Sloane said over the speaker. "Requesting backup in the rec yard! Inmate is armed!"

Sloane's words sent a chill through me. Was Sally Kindly making good on her word already?

Hearing the radio, Lilly grinned. "They all busy now. Nobody gotta know but us. Give it to me, daddy. Gimmie your fat dick."

Other voices buzzed over the airwaves, Captain Clancy and additional officers responding to the high-emergency call. It sounded even more intense than when we'd had to take down Natalia Bravo.

"Violent altercation!" Ileana shouted through the speaker. "Inmate has a—"

She grunted. Then there were screams.

I ran down the tier and buzzed open the door to the south corridor. The other inmates hollered and cheered, excited by any form of entertainment. Officers continued to shout over the radio, and as I rounded the corner on my way to the yard, Officer Beverly Knox darted by wearing a helmet and carrying a riot shield. A pale, sweaty rookie tailed behind her, his eyes wide as hubcaps.

As we exited into the rec yard, daylight hit my eyes like an assault, and I struggled to adjust as I followed the sound of chaos. The blurred shapes became inmates jumping and shouting like the crowd at a rock concert. They were gathered around the wall of building C—the dead zone. Beverly yelled at them to move and plowed through with her shield like she was catching cattle, knocking away those who reacted too slowly.

Ahead, two inmates were rolling on the concrete. Blood was everywhere. The two women were so thoroughly covered in it that it was hard to make out their faces, but Kindly's tattoos and Zoe's intimately familiar body made them instantly recognizable to me. They were both in their tank top undershirts, the white cotton now crimson tie-dye. Kindly punched Zoe in her side and Zoe screamed, and when the blood began to flow, I realized she'd not been punched— she'd been stabbed with something. Kindly moved swiftly, putting her arm down on Zoe's throat to pin her, and this time when she raised her fist, I spotted the jagged piece of steel just before she drove it into Zoe's belly again and again, pummeling her gut with the jagged tip. Zoe punched and scratched but Kindly had the upper hand, and just as we reached them Zoe curled into a ball to keep from being disemboweled by the shiv.

"Drop your weapon!" Beverly Knox demanded.

But Kindly didn't. The shiv came down again and again, knifing Zoe from all sides as she tried to make herself as small a target as possible. Blood erupted from her shoulder, back, and upper arm, the jagged blade opening her in a mist of blood.

I heard the captain's voice but was too stunned to make sense of what he was saying. The COs swarmed. Kindly was sprayed directly in the face, and though she shrieked against the pain, she still stabbed Zoe twice more before Beverly slammed into her with the shield, pinning her to the concrete as Captain Clancy seized the arm holding the shiv. Having to join them somehow, I put my weight on Kindly's legs, but she wasn't even thrashing against us. It wasn't that she'd been intimidated into submission. Kindly was merely exhibiting some of the Zen she'd been encouraging me to find, however dark and deranged. Though her eyelids had turned pink and swelled shut against the chemical spray, she giggled as she licked the blood from her lips.

A nurse arrived but bolted right past Zoe. I watched him, confused, and it was then that I saw the other body, which had been hidden from my view by the crowd. I gasped, recognizing the CO uniform. I rose off Sally Kindly, and Beverly put the cuffs on her as I went to Ileana Sloane.

She was sprawled out on the bloody concrete, her eyes rolled back, a gash carved across her cheek, going from mouth to ear. Her tiny body was as crooked as a swastika. Stab wounds peppered her chest. She'd lost a shoe. Staring down at her now, I was struck by just how young she looked. It was as if I'd completely forgotten.

"Call an ambulance," the nurse told the captain. He looked to Zoe, who was still curled in a ball, clutching her decimated belly. "Better make it two."

A second nurse arrived for Zoe, along with Warden Nowak and Assistant Warden Moore, who came running through the yard like they were fleeing a bomb. Voices called out, but it all blended into one great wall of noise. Some inmates laughed. Others cried. Natalia Bravo and the Latinas watched with cold indifference. Kindly was pulled to her feet. She wobbled as she walked. Zoe had bruised her up. A foul dread slithered through me as Kindly continued to giggle over what she'd done—what *we'd* done.

CHAPTER
TWENTY-SEVEN

"What the *fuck* was that?" I asked.

I was escorting a cuffed and shackled Sally Kindly to her new holding cell in solitary. She'd had her minor injuries tended to—what I'd at first thought was a bruise was actually just her eczema acting up—and she was being moved pending her meeting with the disciplinary committee. She'd been calm since the fight breakup, so I was allowed to walk her down the tier alone.

"Takin' care of business," she said.

"You must be crazy."

She chortled. "That's what all the doctors say."

"You stabbed a *guard*."

"Fuckin' cunt got in my way. 'Sides, she had it comin'. Bitch was always pickin' on us. Showed no respect. Well, I done taught her respect."

"You're lucky she's alive."

"No, *she* is. I coulda killed her ass real easy."

"And what about Zoe?" I whispered, hoping Kindly would lower her voice too. "I thought you were going to take care of things in the dead zone without a big show. What the fuck happened to that?"

"Hey, you weren't there, man. I had her in the cut and tried to do it quick, but the bitch is tougher than I thought."

"Did you say anything?"

"Nah. Just shanked her ass. She put up a good fight for bein' unarmed, I'll give 'er that."

"She also survived," I grumbled.

"But she'll be fucked. I turned her guts inside out, man. Bitch might still die."

I shook my head. "They're saying it's not as bad as it looks. No major organs were hit. You screwed it up, Sally. You—"

She shook her arm from my grip. "Hey, fuck you, man!"

"Keep your voice down."

"You think it's so easy? Do it your own self." She lowered her voice. "And don't be skimpin' out on me. I want my dope."

I grabbed her by the arm again and we continued down the tier.

"Then you better find a way to finish what you started," I said.

"What? *How?* Ain't like theys gonna let me outta fuckin' seg *tomorrow*."

"Figure it out," I said firmly. "Until then, no more sugar."

Kindly seemed surprised by my toughness. I couldn't blame her. I was a little surprised myself.

I was changing.

My time as a criminal was altering my personality just as much as my time as a CO. I had to be tough. It was that or perish.

After getting Kindly settled in her broom closet of a cell, I stomped down the tier in a frazzled state, raging and terrified at the same time. Kindly claimed she'd not said anything to Zoe during the shanking, but what if she'd let something slip to another inmate? What if we'd been seen conspiring? A simple rumor could become an axe in my back, not just from my superiors but from Zoe herself. If she found out I had anything to do with this...

That I was more concerned with my own wellbeing than I was for poor Ileana Sloane made me feel like an even bigger piece of shit. The young CO had been stabbed six times by Kindly's shank, a weapon she'd forged with nail clippers from a metal piece of wheelchair taken from the workshop. Kindly also shoved the shank into Ileana's mouth and pulled the blade through her cheek, tearing her face in a half Joker smile that would scar her for life.

I wondered who'd snuck Kindly the materials to forge the weapon. Not that it really mattered. I had enough steaming shit on my plate.

I was meeting with Dennis in the morning.

I drove deeper into the rez.

The White Feather Inn rolled past like a fading dream, the busted lamps and soiled mattresses behind the building shining bright under the Arizona sky. The day was simmering. Waves of heat blurred the dirt road ahead like a fever dream.

I carried on, my truck flanked by cacti and scampering lizards. The corpse of a huge whiptail lay belly up, cooking in the sun. Buzzards hovered like war planes, and I couldn't help but think they might know something I didn't, that they expected me to be their next meal.

In the truck bed, the cans clamored as they bounced in their crates. The SIG Sauer P365 automatic pistol was stuffed into the rear of my waistband, slick with sweat. I ground my teeth without realizing it as I pulled off the road and into the clearing where Dennis sat in a red Corvette, listening to Rammstein at top volume.

Real inconspicuous, I thought.

I approached slowly, unable to keep my limbs from shaking.

Am I really doing this?

I supposed I was. I'd been thinking about it a lot. I'd even practiced in the mirror like some Travis Bickle wannabe. But now that I was here, my heart was racing. I struggled against the urge to just peel out and head home. I had to power through. This had to be done.

As I pulled up beside him, Dennis got out of the Corvette. He wore heart-shaped Lolita sunglasses and was dressed for the beach in flipflops, short shorts, and a tank top. Despite his appearance, I was afraid of him.

I got out of my truck.

Dennis flashed his crooked smile. "Look what the cat dragged in."

I hadn't slept a wink and it showed.

"Another new car?" I asked.

"Not bad, huh?"

"I assume it's stolen too."

Dennis smirked. "Drives just the same."

He reached into the car, drew out his backpack, and tossed it upon the sand between us. I guessed he hadn't heard about Zoe. She was still in the infirmary, or maybe even the hospital, and didn't have access to her cell phone, which she kept hidden somewhere on Hummingbird.

"Those redskins finally got me my lollipops," Dennis said. "I threw some in with the crack rocks, so now we've got an upper and a downer. We're gonna make bank off those convict sluts."

He stepped forward. I stepped back.

"Would you mellow out?" he said. "Jesus."

"How am I supposed to do that? I'm being threatened into trafficking dope."

"Don't pull that innocent little boy act with me. Your hands are as dirty as mine or Zoe's and you know it. Be happy we're still cutting you in as an act of good faith. We're hoping things can get back to normal. Put all this bitterness behind us. Water under the bridge, right?"

I exhaled. "Yeah, sure."

"You're not convincing me, Liam."

"What do you want me to say?"

He huffed, chuckled. "Have it your way. I suppose these things take time. Just remember, you holding a grudge hurts you more than it does me."

Hurting you is why I'm here, I thought.

"Why this place?" I had to ask, gesturing to the arid wasteland all around us.

"My friend Tommy doesn't want me doing business in the bar anymore. Such a diva. And besides, I wanted us to have a little privacy, you know? Just in case."

His words lingered, carrying a thinly veiled threat. We were in an isolated area in case he felt it necessary to murder me.

Looking down at the backpack, I put my hands on my hips, so they'd be closer to the gun stashed behind my back.

"You gonna pick it up or you gonna stare at it all day?" Dennis asked.

I looked up at him now, my eyes going tight, jaw clenched.

"Hey," he said in a mocking tone. "How's that dog of yours?"

My move was quick but clumsy.

I pulled the gun out of my waistband, but it got caught for half a second, which was all the time Dennis needed to react. He charged me like a linebacker, and for a skinny man he packed a wallop. We fell into the sand, plumes of orange dust rising about us as I struggled to press the gun barrel against him. Had I not been shaking so intensely I might have stood a better chance. Dennis slammed my gun arm down, my elbow hitting a rock so hard I feared it may have broken. Pain ran a river through my arm, my fingers going numb around the pistol's handle.

"You stupid bastard!" Dennis shouted in my face.

I tried to roll him off, but he punched me, and the back of my head ricocheted off the ground, flooding my vision with stars. I swung at Dennis with my free hand, clipping his chin, but other than losing his sunglasses the blow had little effect. He kept coming, a wolverine in frenzy, and when he slammed my arm on the rocks again my grip on the gun loosened.

My heart entered my throat as Dennis snatched up the pistol.

"You just had to do it the hard way," he said.

I winced, sure I was done for.

Perhaps this was for the best. Better the oblivion of death than a life of constant anxiety and terror. I had little to live for anyway. If not for thoughts of Charlie, the threat of death might have given me a sense of peace, but I envisioned him sitting by the window, waiting for me to come home, waiting forever. I couldn't let him face cancer alone. I had to survive this.

Dennis tried to pistol-whip me, but I managed to block his swing. That he hadn't shot me right away told me I maintained a slight advantage. He didn't want me dead. He still saw me as his cash cow. Killing his only gateway to his prison customers would be a poor business decision.

But that didn't mean he wouldn't hurt me.

He swung again, and I grabbed his arm with both hands. We struggled over the pistol. I put all I had into bucking Dennis off and managed to get out from under him, and we rumbled in the dust like scorpions trying to sting each other. I punched him under the chin and this time I dazed him. I bounced back to my feet as he rose to his knees, trying to steady the gun.

Dennis groaned. "Don't you move."

I kicked him square in the chest.

The pistol went off as he flew backward. I flinched, unsure if I'd been hit. I dove at Dennis, the adrenaline pounding like a piston, and grabbed for the gun, managing to wrench it free.

The thrill of victory was immediately interrupted as I heard something click, and then a sudden, sharp sting ran hot through my side.

I pulled back, warm wetness trickling down into my underwear, and spotted the bloody stiletto in Dennis' fist. The blade gleamed in the sun like a floodlight.

Dennis laughed.

I shot him in the face.

CHAPTER TWENTY-EIGHT

The world seemed to vibrate. The sky fluttered like TV static. The shot had left me momentarily deafened, dooming me to move about in a silent nightmare.

Dennis was flat on his back. The bullet had entered his forehead, making a much larger show on its way out. The back of his head had burst like a watermelon. Brain matter and scraps of skull littered the surrounding sand in a headdress of gore.

I vomited. My fear was at full tilt, a horror so intense I'd almost forgotten I'd been stabbed. Blood continued to pour from my love handle, and when I took a step, pain coursed down my side like an electric shock. I'd never felt so scatterbrained. Thoughts ran circles around each other, none of them sticking long enough for me to process. The only recurring notion was one of utter surprise.

You did it. You actually fucking did it.

The pistol was still in my hand.

You fucking killed him.

But what choice did I have? Even before he stuck me with the stiletto, I'd intended to put an end to my problem with Dennis—permanently. It was the same with Zoe. The only way to free myself from these human jackals was to end them. But I still couldn't believe I'd gone through with it. I supposed everybody felt that way after they'd killed someone. I couldn't think of a more life-changing moment.

Get moving.

I picked up the stiletto and pocketed it. After opening the door to the Corvette, I dragged Dennis to the car by his heels, then tried to maneuver his corpse inside. He was surprisingly heavy, and when his head dropped forward blood gushed from his nostrils and trickled out of his ears and eye sockets. I gagged but kept struggling with the body until I'd gotten it into the car, then slammed the door shut. Turning around, I looked at the backpack. A few drops of blood had been sprayed across it. I carried it to my truck and threw it in the back, then withdrew the gas cans I'd brought along with this in mind. Things hadn't gone exactly as I'd hoped, but now that Dennis was dead, I could return to the plan.

I drenched a rag with gasoline, popped the Corvette's gas cap, and stuffed the rag inside. I then soused the car inside and out and lit the rag with the barbeque lighter I'd brought from home.

It was another stolen car. That would make it harder to identify the body.

As the Corvette began to burn, I kicked sand over the blood on the ground.

The buzzards circling above me would take care of the rest.

The drive back seemed much longer than usual. I'd removed my shirt and held it against me to absorb the blood from my stab wound, and when I got home, I tended to it to the best of my ability, sterilizing the wound with alcohol and patching it up with bandages that instantly soaked right through with blood. I decided to take a long shower to wash everything away—the sand, the blood, the gun powder, the horror.

I had to be at work in a few hours.

Call out sick, I kept thinking.

But I couldn't do that. I needed the alibi. But it wasn't like I could limp around Norrington, wincing with every step as the wound wept through my uniform. I also couldn't go the emergency room and have it stitched. They'd ask too many questions, and I was far too rattled to lie convincingly. Did it even need stitches? I wasn't sure. I also wasn't sure I was tough enough to go cauterize it with a hot knife.

I put my head beneath the shower nozzle and closed my eyes.

I stayed in there for a long time.

After taping another wad of gauze in place, I had a double shot of whiskey. My fingers trembled upon the glass. Slowly, the bleeding lessened, or at least congealed enough within the dressing. Charlie followed me around the house as I tried to find a way to walk that didn't hurt. The pain had dulled to a mean throb. Numbness would soon follow... I hoped.

When I arrived at work, I did everything I could to act casual, only talking to other COs when necessary. Of course, the lockdown was reinstated. Hiding my limp was difficult to do without wincing, so I was a little lazier than usual, spending most of my shift sitting at the workstation on Sparrow. With all the unit's inmates in solitary, things were much easier. I just had to hope the captain wouldn't force me to do overtime. I'd never wanted to go home so badly in my life, and that was really saying something for a virtual hermit.

The only CO I had a brief conversation with was Beverly Knox. She informed me that Ileana Sloane was still in the hospital. Zoe Hallister was there too but was scheduled to be released tomorrow morning. It was as if she were a slasher from a horror movie—unstoppable, unkillable, and unrelenting.

The following day was my day off. I spent it getting high to kill the pain, both physical and mental. I tried to watch TV but couldn't focus on the simplest programs. Even game shows proved too much for me to follow. I stocked up on supplies at the drug store and tended to my wound, which became manageable. I could move around okay, so I took Charlie for an easy hike despite the heat. I wasn't sure how many more chances I'd have to do this with him. He might die still. I might go to prison. Zoe might discover all I'd done and have another inmate do to me what Nina Brown had done to Enola Branham.

Perhaps life is precious. For sure, it is agonizingly fleeting. My life didn't matter to anyone except Charlie, and at this point, his life mattered more to me than my own.

I checked in on the news but didn't see anything about a burning Corvette with a crispy corpse inside it, nor did I find any reports on the dead woman's car in the junkyard. Though tempted to Google both, I knew better than to put that in my search history. I expected the police to kick my door down any day, but several weeks passed without incident. I went to work and came home—the all-American march.

The lockdown at Norrington was absolute. I remained on Sparrow, so I didn't even see Zoe, but knew it was only a matter of time. She would be trying to contact Dennis without success. Would she put two and two together? I was confident Dennis had enough enemies to keep Zoe guessing, but she wasn't stupid.

I brought nothing into the prison. Sally Kindly hissed at me from her cell, threatening to rat me out if I didn't bring her dope, so I lied, assuring her I'd get her something as soon as the lockdown restrictions were eased—the old "when the heat dies down" routine. It didn't really satisfy her, but at least it kept her big mouth shut.

The other inmates were more vocal. They screamed and cursed and complained all day long about the lockdown, even the ones in solitary that were locked up day and night to begin with. Some inmates on Sparrow received limited tier time when they could be out of their cell but had to stay on the tier. This was supposed to be rehabilitative. The lockdown had stripped that away too. Norrington was set to explode.

"Ain't nothin' for us here," an inmate shouted at me as I slid her meal tray through the food port. "Ain't got no jobs, no rec time, no nothin'! What do you think's gonna happen when ya'll do this to us?"

While entering another woman's cell for a shake down, I noticed a foul odor just before she flung her feces at me. I wrote her up for it, but she was already in solitary, the prison was on lockdown, and I was told she was serving three life sentences, one for each of her children she'd slaughtered. What possible punishment could she receive?

The only inmate who didn't treat me with absolute loathing was Lilly Gutierrez, but even her sexual advances became more aggressive. When I caught her fingering herself, she flicked the wetness at the window. She exposed herself to me frequently, pulling down her pants and spreading her cheeks to flash me her asshole. The acts seemed more violent than sexual, like visual assaults. They left me anxious and uncomfortable.

The lockdown didn't even make sense. This wasn't like the other incidents where every house had to be shook down for drugs. Yes, a guard had been viciously attacked, but the inmate responsible had already been thrown in seg. The entire prison population was being punished for the actions of a single inmate, and the longer it went on, the more I started to side with the prisoners, but they would never see it that way. When these women saw a uniform, no matter who was wearing it, they saw an enemy, particularly when the CO was a man.

With Ileana Sloane out, I was eventually put on Raven shifts again. The unit had become too hostile for the new rookies, and one had quit after an inmate with hepatitis C shoved him to the ground and spat in his eye. When I arrived on the unit, things were even worse than I thought. The stench was heavy—piss and menstrual blood and whatever other noxious stuff the women could leave around as retaliation for the lockdown.

One of the other guards made a joke about it. "Hey, Liam. What do inmates say when they hear a toilet flush?"

"I dunno. What?"

"The say: *What the hell was that?*"

The COs were bounced from unit to unit. A rumor spread that the lockdown couldn't be lifted because we didn't have enough staff for the prison to function properly, and it gained so much traction the assistant warden sent out a memo stating it wasn't true. Few of us believed it.

Then the day finally came when the captain asked me to work shifts on Hummingbird. After weeks of no contact, I was going to see Zoe. The lockdown had everyone eating in their houses and cells, so I hadn't even glimpsed her in the mess hall. Even yard work had been put on hold. Considering Zoe had been so brutally attacked, I'd half expected the warden to put her on Sparrow so she'd be protected from anyone out to finish what Kindly had started, but if he'd offered, Zoe must have turned him down.

Unlike Sparrow and Raven, Hummingbird was an open dormitory, so while the lockdown was in effect and they couldn't leave the unit except for showers, the inmates were still free to move about the unit itself.

Zoe was sitting on her bed when I entered Hummingbird. She got up immediately and started toward me. Her eyes were hard, her mouth downturned. For someone who'd been stabbed several more times than I had, she moved much quicker than I could, and even though there were other inmates all around, she approached me directly.

"Officer Donnelly," she said. "I need to speak with you. *Now.*"

CHAPTER TWENTY-NINE

I pulled Zoe aside and talked to her near the control booth, surprised she wasn't worried about being seen chatting with a CO. Any fear of being suspected of snitching had been superseded. Perhaps she was powerful enough now to not have to worry about it. As CVS Suzi, the hold she had on Hummingbird was more like a strangulation.

"Have you talked to him?" she asked.

"Dennis? No. Not in weeks."

She narrowed her eyes. "What happened at the drop?"

"Hey, he never showed up. I waited over an hour. I called him a few times, then gave up. He never answers or calls back."

Zoe stared at me, judging my answer. I forced myself not to look away. Finally, she eased off.

"I'm worried," she said. "I think those fucking natives did something to him. Dennis told me they didn't like him.

He thought it was funny, but I warned him never to deal with redskins. You can't trust them. They're still bitter."

I wasn't sure what to say to that.

"Anyway," Zoe said, "bad shit is going on here too. That Sally bitch who stabbed me used to be one of the big drug dealers in this place. I took her business away and she came at me for it. I should've seen it coming."

Relief flooded through me. That Zoe believed the attack was related to rival drug dealing was the best assumption she could have come to.

"I'm glad you're okay," I lied. "I know we've had our differences, but... you know."

She narrowed her eyes again. "Yeah, sure."

"I'm just saying things are crazy right now. I think it's best if we put our differences aside and work together to protect both our asses."

She seemed to buy into my lies a little more, but this was Zoe, so any kindness came with a horrible price tag.

"Okay," she said. "So, are you back on Hummingbird for good?"

"No. Just covering some shifts so Rodriguez can get a day off once in a while."

"You're still working on Sparrow too?"

"There and Raven both."

Her smile worried me.

"When is your next shift on Sparrow?" she asked.

"Why?"

"Why do you think? The bitch who tried to kill me is on there. You don't think I'm gonna let her get away with what she did, do you?"

That familiar, hollow feeling in my gut returned. "Zoe..."

"You just said we have to look out for each other."

"Yeah, but—"

"No buts. This is happening. I need you to prove to me we're on the same side, especially after Dennis going missing. If you're really with me in all this, fucking prove it."

"By doing what, exactly?"

Her smirk was sinister. "You won't have to do anything. That's the point. When it happens, you just sit back and let it happen. You don't interfere or call anyone on your radio. Not until it's over."

"Jesus…"

"The only thing you have to do is deliver a package and a message to our friend Nina Brown. She'll handle the rest."

I looked around the unit. Many of the women were watching us but trying to act like they weren't. The feeling of total exposure left me antsy.

"Brown can't get to her," I said. "They're barely allowed out of their cells."

"Except to shower, right?"

I exhaled. "Zoe—"

"I'll put the package in my tote. Don't worry, it's small. You can pocket it during your shake downs."

"For Christ's sake, I'm a male CO. I don't supervise the showers. They bring in Beverly Knox for that. Besides, they—"

"Knox won't break the golden rule. She won't approach an armed inmate without backup like that idiot Sloane did— not that she had much choice. You'll be the only other CO on the unit with Knox, right? When she calls for help, you fake a fall to slow your response. Brown won't need but a minute."

"Zoe, you don't understand. The inmates in solitary are *always* isolated. There is only one shower stall and each of them use it alone, taking turns one by one. Brown *never* has access to Kindly or anyone else."

Zoe crossed her arms in sour defeat. "There must be a way."

"Sorry, but there isn't. Now will you get the hell away from me? You know how fucking suspicious this looks, us talking like this."

"I don't care," she hissed.

"Well, I do. Now get back to your house, I have work to do." Realizing my aggression, I backed off. "We can chat later, okay?"

Zoe stormed back into the dormitory. When she passed by Fern Hernandez, the Latina smiled at her.

"Trouble with your boyfriend?" Hernandez teased.

Zoe punched Hernandez in the mouth, causing her to stumble backward and trip over a chair. The other Latinas approached. I intervened, but I noticed the Latinas didn't go for Zoe's throat as intensely as they would have before she'd made a name for herself. They wanted to stand up for Hernandez but were hesitant to mess with Zoe Hallister. I wondered if Bravo had something to do with that, if they needed permission before making a move.

Ramos helped Hernandez to her feet, and while she cursed in Spanish, she didn't retaliate. No one even demanded I give Zoe a citation. The cameras on Hummingbird were functional, so I should have written Zoe up, but I didn't. There weren't enough employees to monitor the recordings anyway.

Back in the control center, I thought about what Zoe said. What if there was a way to get rid of Sally Kindly? Perhaps it would be worth doing. I didn't care about quenching Zoe's thirst for revenge, but Kindly was getting more aggressive about demanding dope from me, and her threats wouldn't stay mere threats for long. She was too volatile, too crazy, and vindictive as hell.

The fury of a woman scorned.

If I didn't bring her drugs, eventually she would snitch on me, as promised, and like any junkie, she would always want more. Though I'd needed her as an assassin, she couldn't fill that role in solitary. She'd become more trouble than she was worth, a dangerous liability. Kindly had become almost as big of a problem as Zoe. So why not take her out too?

But I'd been honest with Zoe about the inmates in solitary having no contact with each other. Brown couldn't get close to Kindly while they were both in seg, and even if the lockdown was lifted, I doubted either of the murderers would be offered tier time by the wardens, especially considering Kindly's attack on a guard. She would be left in there to rot. Taking out a hit on Kindly was asking the impossible. The only people she encountered were...

Officers, I thought with dread. *COs like you.*

When I performed the shake downs, I found the small package Zoe had mentioned in her tote. I could have reported it. Perhaps I even could have gotten her moved to a higher security unit where she belonged. But I couldn't turn on her and she knew it. Therein lied her hold over me. Zoe stood close by, blocking me from the other inmates' view. I pocketed the package quickly and discretely.

"So then... you can do it," she said.

She'd come to the same conclusion I had.

Somehow, Zoe was still successfully hiding contraband. The contents of the package were proof of that—confirmation that she could get her hands on things she wanted even without my help.

Inside the package was a binky, the same sort of homemade syringe Sally Kindly had been known to hide in her vagina. It was filled with a murky, brown liquid that was supposed to pass for heroin. Perhaps there was some in there too, but I knew there had to be more to this cocktail than that.

Zoe had handed me a lethal injection.

My first thought was that it just might work. I was becoming increasingly ruthless. The shame I'd once felt over my vile acts was now manageable.

This could be so easy. Zoe must have planned something different for Brown's package. It probably would have included a shiv and a baggie of dope for her trouble. But this package had been made specifically for me. In a weird way, it was almost thoughtful, but it was also a demand. Zoe was ordering me to kill. This added a whole new dimension to our relationship. She was asserting dominance again, just as she had when she'd threatened me and Charlie. Did I really want to submit to her this way? Would it be best for me to let her think I was doing it for her? And what would happen if I refused?

All I had to do was pass the needle to Kindly and tell her it was some of the dope I owed her. She would inject herself. It seemed simple, but I also had to consider that she'd been stripped searched—including a cavity search—before being thrown in solitary. My superiors would suspect a CO must have given her the binky, because she had no contact with other inmates, but would that be traced back to me? Was it better to risk that than risk Kindly ratting me out?

Tomorrow was my next shift on Sparrow. I had a lot of thinking to do.

Before heading home, I stashed the binky in the employee bathroom.

An ace in the hole.

"You got my fuckin' stuff yet?" Kindly barked.

The window's glass muted her, but she was too loud for comfort.

"Calm down," I said.

"Don't tell me to fuckin' calm down. You owe me, mothafucka, and I'm sick of your excuses. C'mon, I'm dyin' here! I'm fuckin' dyin'! If you don't pony up, I'm gonna—"

I put my finger to my lips in a hush. Kindly watched me curiously. I gave her a wink, then looked at the clock on the wall. She looked too. It was almost time for dinner. Kindly smiled a little, picking up on my hint.

When the meal trays arrived, I stacked them with my back to the camera and shoved the binky into Kindly's mashed potatoes.

This is it. You're killing an inmate. You're killing someone's mother.

I went down the tier delivering dinners. When I reached her cell, Kindly pulled the tray in greedily, brought it to her cot, and started pawing through the food. When she found the binky, she held it up, staring in awe as if it was an artifact from some lost civilization. I walked on, handing out the rest of the trays and making small talk with the other inmates so my talk with Kindly wouldn't stand out on the surveillance video, which would be thoroughly reviewed when this was over.

I wondered what the toxicology report would say, if one was done. What exactly was in the binky?

Another inmate was shouting nonsense, causing some of the others to shout back at her to shut up. Most of the time, noise on the unit irritated me, but today I welcomed it. If Sally Kindly cried out in pain, I had an excuse to not notice.

I let an hour pass. I heard nothing from Kindly and guessed she was on the nod, on her way to death if not already there. I told myself it wasn't really me who had killed her, that she'd injected the junk herself, but of course that was utter bullshit. I was just as responsible as Zoe Hallister. This was premeditated murder, my second one in just weeks. That wasn't even counting my involvement in the accidental death of that woman during the country store car chase.

This time I performed the security checks instead of just writing them in the logbook. I wanted a peek. I strolled up the tier, looking in on each inmate. They gave me the finger, ignored me, yelled for things they wanted and needed. Lilly Gutierrez shook her massive mammaries and tongued the inside of her cheek to simulate sucking a dick. I blew her a kiss just to make her as anxious as I was, then walked on to Kindly's cell.

She was flat on her back in bed, one arm dangling over the side, her chin slick with drool. I knocked on the door, demanding a response. She didn't offer one. I unlocked the cell and went inside, noting the vomit on the floor. I said the inmate's name. I shook her. Nothing. Checking for a pulse, I swallowed hard when I didn't find one, even though I'd expected that.

The goddamned bitch had left the binky in her lap, right out in the open. I had another decision to make. I could pocket the binky, but after the autopsy revealed a drug overdose, my bosses would want to know what happened to her hardware. That would put eyes on me, because I was the one on shift when Kindly died and discovered her body. But if I could hide the binky somewhere they *would* find it, suspicions would abound as to when she'd gotten it and who had given it to her. With so many COs being moved about from unit to unit, that left a wide range of suspects, including several rookies who hadn't established the good reputation I had.

Putting on gloves, I grabbed the waistband of Kindly's prison slacks and pulled them down along with her panties.

I could have spit in my hand to make this easier, but that would have left behind my DNA. Looking around the cell, I found Kindly's eczema cream. It would have to do.

Once the syringe was stuffed up her dead pussy, I called in the report.

CHAPTER THIRTY

Assistant Warden Moore became the new warden.

Nowak was terminated after the death of Sally Kindly. It was the last of many straws, and ACI needed a sacrificial lamb to offer the DOC, which was threatening to shut down Norrington permanently. There was talk of the inmates being transferred to other penitentiaries for as long as it took to replace every CO in our prison and make major changes. I was grilled by the investigators, the new warden, and everyone else above me. Even the captain approached me with heavy scrutiny. They all kept asking the same two questions.

How did Sally Kindly get a binky, and why did she inject heroin cut with rat poison?

It helped that I didn't have to fake surprise. That Zoe had obtained both substances without my help astonished me, but she made deals with just about everyone, and many other inmates had their own ways of getting contraband.

There was talk of suspending all the COs who'd worked on Sparrow since Kindly had been taken there, but it was an empty threat. There was no way they could handle that kind of staff shortage.

Beverly Knox had been the one to strip search Kindly before she was taken to solitary. She was suspended without pay while the whole matter was being investigated. I even saw her being walked out by the captain, a sight that pained me. Her trouble was an unfortunate side effect, but I was confident she'd survive.

The only thing that kept Norrington running was the termination of Warden Nowak and that Kindly's death was a drug overdose and not another violent murder. Still, that the prison faced so little repercussions in the grand scale of things was a grim example of just how broken the American penile system really was. Warden Moore held a meeting with the COs where he laid out his new deal with all the fire and brimstone of a snake-handling preacher, but otherwise things continued in Norrington as if another inmate hadn't died.

And there was still one more death to go.

Zoe was the final domino that had to fall. Then I could be done with all of this. I could quit my miserable job. Maybe I would even move as far away from this terrible place as possible. Start a new life for me and Charlie in Hawaii or Alaska. He loved the beach and the snow, so either place would be a good for him to spend his golden years. Zoe was the final threat to that future. Well, that and the police discovering all I'd done. I'd taken every step to prevent the latter. Now I had to finish what Sally Kindly had started. I just had to figure out how.

At least Zoe wasn't in solitary or locked in a cell. Being in a dormitory left her exposed. There were over sixty other inmates on Hummingbird—plenty of potential assassins. But regardless of all the options, shopping for one was going to be dangerous. Sally Kindly had approached me about working together. I'd already known she was up for anything when I'd proposed the job to her. I couldn't just walk around Hummingbird asking inmates if they wanted to kill Zoe for me. I had to figure something out.

Zoe continued being chatty with me when I worked Hummingbird. I knew the other inmates suspected something and could only hope they just thought she was a snitch. I wasn't so much worried about them noticing as I was the other COs, particularly Diana Rodriguez. That cunt gave me a dirty look whenever she spotted Zoe talking to me. I did my best to avoid Zoe, but she was adamant, prodding me for any information I might have about Dennis and the Indians she thought had done something to him, and insisting she needed more drugs from me to keep her business going. She was getting desperate. Without drugs to deal, her power was fading. If she couldn't control dope and money here, and the others thought she was a snitch for always pulling me aside, another inmate might just kill her for me without being asked. I doubted Zoe would let it come to that though. She'd made it clear she'd snitch on me if I left her out to dry too long.

I was at an impasse.

But then the new warden lifted the lockdown.

Considering the piss-poor morale and general outrage within Norrington Women's Correctional Facility, Warden Moore made the executive decision to kill with kindness. Instead of issuing draconian restrictions the way his predecessor had, he took a more friendly approach in the hope of easing the pressure off inmates and COs alike.

Moore even went a step further, moving several of the women in solitary out. Killer Nina Brown was kept on Sparrow, but the statutory rape schoolteacher, Ariel Richardson, who'd been on her best behavior since her last bust, was moved down to a private cell on Raven. Lilly Gutierrez—who, as an inmate who'd canoodled with a guard, was technically a *victim* of a crime—was returned to Hummingbird unit, where she could be happier and more comfortable, which would benefit her pregnancy.

The other Latinas were thrilled to have their friend back. The Golden Girls fawned over her too, excited to talk babies and wax nostalgic about their own pregnancies and grandchildren. That Lilly's baby would be taken away from her upon birth seemed to elude everyone. She was now the center of attention.

And I had my eye on her too.

When it came time for her doctor checkup, I escorted her to the infirmary. She talked dirty to me all the way to the surveillance-free elevator, and when I finally got her inside with the door closed, I hit the stop button and stared at Lilly. Her eyebrows wiggled, tongue darting out. Because she was a groper, she was always escorted in handcuffs. I removed them. Her smile deepened. I stepped into her and slid my hand between her legs, rubbing her groin over her slacks. She moaned and leaned in to lick my lips, so I slid my hand down the front of her pants and fingered her while pressing her against the wall. I wrapped her hair in my other fist, bringing her nearly climax, and then I withdrew, releasing her. Confused, she reached for my crotch. I snapped the handcuffs back on her.

"What is wrong?" she asked. "You gotta fuck me, daddy."

I shook my head. "You want more, you have to earn it."

"I do anything and all for you, daddy. Make it real sexy for you. Make you cum so good, all over my face and tits."

"No. That's not what I want. Not yet." I leaned in close, my lips to her ear, and she breathed deep of me. "I have a job for you to do."

"Blowjob," she said, "I blowjob daddy so nice. You cum in my mou—"

"Later. I have a different kind of job, understand?"

She rubbed up against me. Between her sex addiction and her limited English, I was struggling to get through. Her horniness was voracious. It was like trying to talk to a dog that's humping your leg.

"Zoe Hallister," I said. "I want—"

"Threesome," she said excitedly.

"No." I took her by the shoulders to stop her grinding. "Now listen. I read your file. Mostly sex and drug offenses. But you have an assault charge too."

She nodded, still smiling.

"I want you to hurt Zoe," I said, testing the waters.

Lilly gave me a quizzical look. "You want me fight her?"

"Not just fight. I want her gone. *Muerto.*"

She shook her head, correcting me. "*Muerta.*"

"*Muerta.*"

Lilly stepped back from me now, the look on her face more serious than any I'd seen on her before. "You want Zoe hit. No, no. I no do that."

"I'll have sex with you if you take care of Zoe. I'll even get you some drugs too."

Her face soured. "I am *with baby*. No fighting. No drugs. *Mi bebé*."

"I can make it easy for you to do. Get you a weapon…"

"*No*."

I changed course. "And I didn't mean *you* would take the drugs. I wouldn't want that, of course. I meant you could sell them. Make some money. *You* could be the new CVS Suzi."

I knew I might very well be creating one problem to solve another. Lilly could end up blackmailing me just like Kindly and Zoe had, especially if I quit my job after she'd taken care of her part of the deal. But I wouldn't welch. If she offed Zoe, I'd have sex with Lilly and give her a dope package. I had plenty of crack and fentanyl lollipops at home.

"You talk like fool," Lilly said. "I no deal drugs here. Not for you."

Now I realized why she was so reluctant.

"Ah, of course," I said. "You're with the Latinas. You can't do anything without the okay from your boss, Natalia Bravo."

Lilly averted her chocolate eyes.

"Look," I said. "I *know* Bravo is running dope in here. I'll bet she's the one circulating the heroin that killed Sally Kindly. Don't you think she'd like some free stuff? She'd be proud of you for getting it, right?"

Lilly didn't respond or even look at me.

"Fine," I said. "Forget I said anything. I'll go to Bravo myself. But then you get nothing. Understand? No dope, no money. And I won't be fucking your tits off."

That brought her eyes back to mine. There was a moment of silence between us, then I hit the button to make the elevator move again. Lilly shifted about anxiously. As we reached the landing, she spoke just before the door opened.

"Is okay," she said. "But I must check first."

With the rec yard reopened, the Latinas on Hummingbird and Raven could mingle again. That meant Lilly had access to Bravo and could fill her boss in on my proposition. It was easier to let them talk it out amongst themselves than for me to sneak private conversations with Bravo and her henchwomen. Knowing Bravo disapproved of COs taking advantage of Lilly Gutierrez's sex addiction, I hoped Lilly wouldn't mention what I'd offered her in exchange for this, but I figured Lilly wouldn't want the boss to know about it either. Bravo might forbid her to take any more dick off a guard, and that was the last thing Lilly wanted.

It didn't take long to get a response from the self-proclaimed prison queen.

Bravo approached me on the rec yard, her expression blank and unreadable. Her eyes were like black holes, pulling me in with their mystery and danger.

"You must be crazy," she said.

"No. Just at my wit's end."

"My prison just got off lockdown, and you wanna take out a hit? Don't you know how that'll set everything back?"

"I can make it worth your w—"

"You got some balls even askin'."

"Like I said, I'm desperate. Besides, you said it yourself—Zoe is a big fucking problem. This would be a win for us both. Just think about it. You kill the competition *and* get a nice bundle *and* get a CO on your side. I can make things much better for you in here."

"Is that right?" she said, mockingly.

"Okay, I'll admit another lockdown would be a big inconvenience, but we both know they never last. Besides, the new warden wants to avoid another one at all costs."

"I can get my dope without you."

"Better to have an alternate source though, right? Especially one that's a CO."

She smirked. "You still don't really know how things work in here. In so many ways, you're still a rookie."

"Yeah, well this *rookie* made it possible for Zoe Hallister to become your biggest competitor. I'm more powerful than you realize. I can offer you and your girls protection while you take care of Zoe. And I'll reward you with a bag full of so much crack and fentanyl it'll make your head spin."

This gave her pause. "You got *crack?*"

"Several ounces. Maybe even pounds."

"Where you get all that?"

"Never mind. The point is it can be yours—all of it. I won't even ask for a cut of your sales. All I want is Zoe out of the picture. You finish her and I get you the rocks and pops. Then our business is done."

"Done?"

"That's right. I'm getting out. There will be no long-term partnership, got me? One big score and we split ways."

"You sayin' you're leavin' Norrington?"

I sighed. "Hell, Bravo. Wouldn't you if you could?"

She slowly smiled. Hands on her enormous hips, Bravo gazed upon the desert hellscape surrounding the prison. Her power and influence made her as deadly as any man. If I pushed her too far, I'd have to watch my back not only around her, but around Hernandez, Ramos, Rivera, Gonzales, and all the other inmates who were either in the Latinas gang or wanted to be. Bravo also had ties to cartels in New Mexico—brutal men who beheaded their enemies and mailed the skulls to the loved ones of their victims. I wasn't playing with fire. I was playing with an atom bomb.

But it seemed I drew a good hand.

"Here's how it's gonna be," Bravo said. "You deliver the dope first. If it's good quality and as large an amount as you say it is, then…"

"Then what?"

Though Bravo smiled, her dark eyes were soulless. "Then we tear that skinny white girl to pieces."

This was the plan.

Using four of the biggest ravens I could shoot down, I would perform my makeshift taxidermy on them, stuffing them so full of crack rocks and fentanyl lollipops their bellies would barely close. I'd do as I'd done before, tossing them over the fence late at night, this time to be collected by Sandra Ramos, who was still on yard cleanup.

Bravo would not accept a mere sample. She wanted the bundles upfront.

Of course, Zoe Hallister was back on yard cleanup too, so I had to make sure she wasn't out there on the day the birds were delivered. This would be as simple as giving her orderly duties instead—having her mop the floors, clean the bathrooms, and dust the air vents. If she copped an attitude, I'd give her a citation, which would also keep her off the yard. Let the bitch get mad. If everything went smoothly, I wouldn't have to worry about pissing her off. Ramos would snatch the baggies from the birds and pass them to Bravo and the other Latinas. Once Bravo was satisfied, the assassination would commence.

This was a huge gamble. I had no reason to trust Bravo. Once she got what she wanted, she might back out on her part of the deal. I just had to hope she still saw the benefit offing Zoe would give her crew, and that she had enough honor not to stiff me.

No honor among thieves.

If Bravo screwed me over, I wouldn't leave Norrington. I'd request more shifts on Raven, where she lived, and do everything I could to make her life miserable. I'd frame her for having contraband. I'd write endless citations. I would do all I could to get her fat ass thrown in solitary. I'd find another way to take care of Zoe, and then I just might take care of Bravo too.

I was through fucking around with these bitches.

Some time ago, Ileana Sloane had confessed to me that the job was making her loathe and distrust women, that she feared working at Norrington was forever altering her opinion of females, even though she was one. I now understood what she meant. Being around America's worst female offenders— the worst women in the country—was pure misogyny fuel. It had gotten so I looked at all women as threats to be dealt with firmly, even when I wasn't at work. When I saw females in stores, I was sure they were shoplifting. When I drove past bars where they were all dolled up, I saw only diseased sluts who would hurl their feces and used tampons at me if I dared to say hello. I hated the women of Norrington and hated the free ones too. I hated my ex-wife for what she'd done to me, and what I'd become as a result. If my own mother had been alive, I probably would have stopped talking to her. In my mind, the opposite sex had become monsters.

And they call us pigs.

Getting the dead birds onto prison property was, once again, all too easy. The nerves that made me sweat the first time I'd tossed a drug-filled bird were gone. I wasn't sure if I'd gotten tougher, more careless, or had just come to accept what would be would be. I was tired of worrying. It never helped matters.

"Why do I have to clean the shitters instead of working outside?" Zoe demanded.

She'd been on edge as it was, daunted by mounting concern over her missing cousin and a mild paranoia that people suspected she was responsible for Sally Kindly's death. She was high more often than not. She'd grown withdrawn, underperforming in the workshop and rarely finishing her food. Offing Sally Kindly had put me back in Zoe's favor, but she was still pressuring me for dope. I'd asked her to give me more time. With Dennis gone, I told her I no longer had a dealer, and as far as Zoe knew I was fresh out of goods. She'd agreed, but with each passing day her patience was wearing thinner. She started talking about some criminals she knew on the outside that might be willing to deal with us, but I rejected the idea.

"People have been talking," I whispered. "About you and me."

She paled. "What? No."

"What did you expect? You approach me constantly, right in front of everyone. They're bound to suspect something's going on. I'm putting you on toilet duty so they might start to think otherwise."

Zoe pursed her lips. I was proud of my lie because it made perfect sense.

"Okay, fine," she said. "But next time I want the yard. I want that extra sunshine, and I want a little bird to visit me real soon."

"We'll find a way. But right now, it needs to look like I'm not giving you any special treatment."

On the yard, I took Sandra Ramos off the garden, having Ernestine Castillo tend to it herself. Ramos moved swiftly around the permitter, discretely tossing the dead birds into the trash bag. Again, the nervous tension that had once tortured me was no longer present. Was I numb or just cocky? Was I so tired of all this blood and death that I subconsciously wanted to get caught, just to put an end to it? Or was this recklessness pointing to a more serious concern—the rise of my mental illness?

That evening when I did my shake downs, Fern Hernandez leaned in while I sifted through her things. As usual, her headphones were on, the MP3 player in her hand. She was bobbing her head, but there was no music coming out of the ear buds. She pretended to be singing as she whispered to me.

"Tomorrow," Hernandez said. "On the yard."

Her instructions were brief. She didn't detail what the Latinas were going to do, only that Zoe would be handled during rec time. I was scheduled to be the only guard on duty. Somehow the Latinas knew that without even asking me. Perhaps Natalia Bravo hadn't been exaggerating about knowing everything that went on inside this penitentiary. I was not asked to provide a weapon. The best weapon I could give them was turning a blind eye.

CHAPTER THIRTY-ONE

Storm clouds hovered above Norrington. Even the Earth's atmosphere was in allegiance with us.

Though I still hadn't been given any details—and never would—I was part of the Latinas' hit squad. Because I was working solo today, only the inmates from Hummingbird were on the yard. Those on Raven would be given separate rec time because it was easier for a single CO to wrangle smaller groups. But this also meant Natalia Bravo and the other inmates on Raven wouldn't be present when the assassination was attempted. I hoped the Hummingbird Latinas could handle this right without Bravo's supervision. From what I could tell, spunky Fern Hernandez had been put in charge. That Zoe had previously punched Hernandez in the face gave her additional motivation.

Lilly Gutierrez stood by the wall of building C, her arms crossed, watching everything while pretending to watch nothing. She seemed to be posted as a lookout, even though I was the only CO present. Hernandez and Ramos were doing yoga stretches nearby, close enough to the wall to be in the surveillance dead zone. Rivera and Gonzales were further away, playing basketball.

Zoe Hallister was an island of a woman. She stood alone by the fence, friendless now that her drug supply had dried up. She'd ripped off, manipulated, and hurt so many inmates during her reign as CVS Suzi. The women on Hummingbird no longer wanted anything to do with her. Many no longer feared her, especially because the holes Sally Kindly had put in her were still healing.

Zoe had her fingers in the chain-link and was watching the coming storm. Her black hair fluttered in the breeze. She looked like a lost little girl to me then, and I couldn't help but wonder who was out there for her now that Dennis was gone. She'd mentioned a mother to me once, hadn't she? Or maybe a sister? Someone who was taking care of her dogs while she was in the joint. But that may have just been lies she'd told me at the offset of our relationship, saying she was a dog-lover too so we could bond over a shared interest. Not since those early days had she mentioned the dogs or her family. Who was this woman's parents? Where was her true home? Her file said she'd abandoned a child, but I'd never asked her for details. Who would come to claim Zoe's body when at last her broken soul was set free? These thoughts were almost enough to make me want to call the whole thing off—*almost*.

There'd been a time I'd believed we would be together, that I might find love again in Zoe's arms. But those arms had thrown only fists. I imagined she'd been swinging most of her life. I'd tried to be something more to Zoe, someone who could be closer to her than all others, but my kisses had been repaid with blood spat in my face. I vowed that this was the last heartbreak I would allow a woman to give me.

One of the Golden Girls moved along the fence, slowly approaching Zoe. It was Ernestine Castillo, the gardener. I was too far away to hear what was being said, but Castillo gestured toward Fern Hernandez, discreetly pointing her out to Zoe and whispering. I watched Zoe's face go from woe to pure malice. Her eyelids drew tight, staring at Fern Hernandez just across the way. Still doing stretches with Ramos, Hernandez's back was to Zoe, a welcome target.

Zoe started toward the Latinas, getting closer to the dead zone with each step. Whatever Castillo had said left Zoe pink with rage. I glanced back at Castillo, wondering what was going on. The old woman's expression was lifeless, her downturned nose reminding me of the beaks of those dead ravens. There was a darkness to Castillo I'd never detected until that moment. Her age and soft-spoken demeanor had made her invisible. Now I was given a glimpse of her true form, a window into the evil that had put her here in the first place.

The Latinas paid her to do this, I realized.

As Zoe drew closer to the Latinas, Rivera and Gonzales left the game and followed behind her. I moseyed further away, putting distance between us. I pretended to be watching the basketball game, but watched the encounter unfurl from the corner of my eye. Though most of the inmates were too caught up in the noise of the basketball game, I was just close enough to hear Zoe yell out to Hernandez.

"You talkin' shit about me, cunt?" Zoe said. "I ain't no snitch!"

The attack was swift.

Ramos dove toward Zoe's knees while Rivera grabbed her from behind. Gonzales stood guard. Zoe was restrained within a second, and Hernandez moved in close, her expression calm, her arm rocking back and forth as if she were poking Zoe with her finger. But fingers aren't forged of scrap metal.

Before Zoe could get out a scream, Hernandez covered her mouth with her free hand, still moving her other arm back and forth in a rhythmic pattern. Zoe struggled but Rivera held her arms tight, and Ramos locked her legs so she couldn't run away. Hernandez stabbed over and over and over again. Ramos had to let go to avoid the blood pouring from Zoe's abdomen. It came in such abundance that it appeared purple.

Zoe looked my way.

Her eyes pleaded for help. I held her gaze with dead eyes. I wanted her to know I was letting this happen, that I was behind it.

As Zoe buckled, Hernandez jabbed her in the throat and twisted the blade.

Lilly Gutierrez stepped away from the wall, crossed past the others, and Hernandez handed her the shank. Lilly walked away with it.

The whole thing took mere seconds. The Latinas casually strolled away from their victim, and Zoe collapsed on the pavement. Other inmates were screaming in horror. Some were laughing and taunting. Some were calling out my name. I pretended not to notice for a few more seconds before running over. Inmates had gathered around Zoe's sprawled body, more to watch the show than to help.

I knelt beside her.

Dozens of stab wounds wept red. Zoe's breasts and belly were peppered with deep punctures and there was a hole in her throat like a back-alley tracheotomy. Blood oozed from the wide hole and trickled from the corners of her mouth. Her chest heaved. She was gagging on her own blood.

I touched my lifeline radio but only pretended to hit the call button, calling for assistance on a muted line, waiting for it to be over before I would call it in for real.

I didn't yell out for any of the Latinas to get down on the ground. I played it as if I hadn't seen who'd done this. *I didn't see a damned thing, Warden.* And with the area's only camera out, none of the other prison officials would see it either.

"She's fuckin' dyin'," someone said.

"Bitch got what was coming to her," said someone else.

I got lower so Zoe could see my face. I wanted it to be the last thing she saw before she went to Hell—a journey from one nightmare world to another. Her eyes were wide, staring into mine with what may have been understanding of what had just happened, or may have been simple, dumbstruck horror. She couldn't have spoken, and she didn't even try. Zoe only stared. Stared until there was nothing left to see.

CHAPTER
THIRTY-TWO

The captain leaned back in his chair. We were alone in his office. It'd been the same old routine—the questions, the investigations, the visits from several law enforcement agents and officials from the Department of Corrections.

Poor Warden Moore. He'd only just started in the role and already had a dead inmate to answer for. I'd been questioned about what I'd seen, which I insisted was nothing. I told them by the time I'd noticed anything Zoe was dead, and her attacker had vanished into the crowd. No murder weapon was recovered. And though many inmates were questioned, no one talked. The code of silence was taken very seriously among the women of Norrington. It was one of the reasons many felt Enola Branham had gotten what she deserved.

Now the captain called me into his office for a private chat. No warden, no investigators, and no other prison employees. I felt like a kid about to be lectured by his old man. I wondered what he could possibly say or ask that hadn't already been gone over a hundred times a hundred ways.

Captain Clancy opened the box of cigars on his desk.

"Cigar?" he asked, holding one up.

It seemed an odd gesture.

"No, thanks," I said.

The captain lit up and blew smoke from his nostrils. It coiled about him like wraiths.

"I've received a report," he said.

"Oh?"

"A very serious report, I'm afraid."

I gripped the armrests. "What about?"

Captain Clancy raised his eyebrows. He sighed, shaking his head. "It's not good, Liam."

Optimistically, I was only about to be fired. Termination for gross incompetence. I could handle that.

"The report was turned in by another CO," Captain Clancy told me. "They've documented you having several conversations with inmates, and they consider this highly suspicious. Also in the report are logbook records of safety inspections you filled out that the cameras show were never done. But perhaps most concerning is the footage from Hummingbird of Fern Hernandez being punched by Zoe Hallister. You're right there in the video, and you did nothing. You didn't even write it up."

Sweat was forming at the small of my back. I stared straight ahead, as if looking through the captain and the wall behind him and into the black void that awaited me.

"You have anything to say about all of this?" Captain Clancy asked.

I shook my head. "No, sir."

He leaned forward, giving me a sympathetic look. "Well, you should. It's just you and me in here, talking man to man."

I didn't say anything.

"Are you catching my drift?" he asked.

"Captain," I began, "I've tried to be a good CO—"

"And you have been."

I breathed deep. "Thank you, sir."

"You're one of my best men. Why else would I have covered for you this long?"

The room seemed to spiral. "Covered for me?"

"C'mon, man," Captain Clancy said with a smile. "You don't really think I'm oblivious to what you've been up to, do you? I may not know all of it, but I know enough." He leaned in closer. "We have more in common than you might think."

A strange sensation coursed through me. My mind expanded—part confusion, part relief, and part anticipation. I wondered if I was being set free or caught in a trap.

"I've been monitoring you for some time," Captain Clancy continued. "You're a great worker, always going where I need you to without complaint, always willing to do overtime or deal with the most insufferable inmates. The reputation you've built has been a tremendous help to you and me both when it comes to covering up certain... indiscretions."

My tongue became an anvil, impossible to move.

This was it. Busted, at long last.

"Man to man," the captain said. "Tell me—it's great, isn't it?" It was more statement than question. "It can be scary as all hell when things get hairy, but when they're running smoothly, you feel like a fucking god."

I stared blankly. "Sir, I... I don't know what..."

"No need to deny it, Liam!" He laughed. "Jesus, don't you get what I'm telling you?" He chuckled again. "Oh! Of course. I get it. You probably think this is some sort of sting, huh? That I'm saying all this so you'll relax and confess. Well, let me assure you."

He reached for the phone on his belt and started scrolling. I watched his face. The smile never left it. When he found what he was looking for, he turned the screen toward me.

It was a photograph—a pornographic one.

Ariel Richardson, the sexy former schoolteacher, was naked and bent over a stall toilet, holding the camera out for a selfie. Behind her was Captain Clancy, his pants down around his ankles as he thrust into her. My eyes went wide, and the captain snickered. He scrolled to the next image. Ariel Richardson was sucking his dick, her blue eyes looking right at the camera, right at me.

"She is one hot piece of ass, am I right?" the captain said. "I'm a little too old to be her type, but the sick bitch is at least smart enough to know who's in control here. I run every facet of her miserable life. One hand washes the other. She knows that. And so do you. Tell me... how was Zoe Hallister? I mean, you did fuck her, right?"

"Um..."

"There are more places to fuck them than you might think. Zoe was a nice piece of trim. I planned to get around to that one, but when I realized you had something going on with her, I decided to hold back. I wanted to wait and see what you were capable of, and man, you did not disappoint." He smiled like a proud parent. "How much fentanyl did you bring in here anyway? I'll bet it was thirty times the amount we confiscated during shake downs."

I was torn between wanting to deny everything and wanting to let it all out. "Captain... are you..."

"Dirty?" he asked. "Such a nasty term for doing what we must to survive in this shitbox. Is it dirty to stay afloat, to stay *sane*?"

"No, sir. I guess it's not."

"You're *fuckin' A right* it's not." He chewed his cigar like a fat cat. "Back in my day, we ran so much dope into the prisons it was like Woodstock. I've gotten more pussy working in women's correctional facilities than I ever could on the outside."

I couldn't help but glance at the framed photo on his desk—Captain Clancy with his wife and family. Busy talking, he didn't notice.

"You've seen how things are nowadays," he said. "Women out there in the free world act like even *mentioning* sex is some kind of crime. You buy a girl a drink and she treats it like an assault. Men are being told their natural instincts are wrong, that we're born bad. But here in Norrington, the dynamic is the way nature intended. Men are the ones in control. We tell these whores when to eat, when to sleep, when to wash their assholes. Instead of all those uppity, overly sensitive bitches on the outside, we have women who either know to obey, learn real fuckin' quick, or wind up in solitary confinement the rest of their worthless lives. And if they complain, nobody cares. *Nobody.*" He puffed an ominous cloud of cigar smoke. "These women are some of the worst convicts in the nation. They don't even qualify as women anymore. They're just murderers and pedophiles. Dope fiends and thieves. They've killed their spouses, their parents, their own children. They've voided their humanity, so now humanity wants nothing to do with them. So society hands them over to us. No one cares what happens to male convicts, so why should these women be treated any better? We can do whatever we want to these cunts."

His words shocked me into numbness. What surprised me most was how much sense this was all making to me. The captain had managed to put into words some of the angry, disjointed thoughts that had been swimming through my head these past few weeks.

These inmates really *didn't count* as actual women. I'd thought I'd been telling myself that just to excuse my own bad behavior, but now I could see it was a clear, undeniable truth.

"Yeah," I confessed. "I fucked Zoe Hallister."

The captain guffawed and reached out to pat my shoulder. "Hell yeah, you did! You hit Lilly Gutierrez yet?"

"No. But I've come close."

"That's some low hanging fruit. Lilly is community cock wash around here, but she's such a good lay. Biggest titties I've ever seen, and all natural at that. Too bad that kiss-ass Anthony Robocop ruined it for the rest of us. But hey, the slut's out of seg now. You should get a piece of that ass before her pregnancy makes her unfuckable."

I couldn't help but snicker.

"There you go," the captain said. "Laugh! Relax, man."

I'd started to, but this was a lot to take in.

"By the way," Captain Clancy said, "we've got not one but *two* new inmates coming in this week. They're being transferred from juvenile detention centers now that they've turned eighteen. I've got a little birthday present for them—*right in my pants*." He laughed smoke. "That'll be a nice welcome package for 'em!"

"Eighteen," I said, my eyes going wide. "Wow. I'd thought my days of having sex with women that young were far behind me."

"I'll bet their pussies taste like spring water. It'll be a good time all around. I've got heroin moving through these halls like an underground dope railroad, and from what Natalia tells me, you've got some quality product too."

My eyebrows rose. "Natalia Bravo? You work with her?"

"*With* her? Fuck no. She works *for* me. She's what a pimp would call his 'bottom bitch'. I let her play Queen of Norrington around the other inmates, but behind closed doors, I call all the shots, at least when it comes to money and drugs. If she and her wetback friends want to go around killing and getting killed, that's their business. Best to stay out of that kind of shit, believe me. Keep things simple. Do some deals, make some dough, get your dick wet—all without taking any shit from inmates."

I grinned a little. "Makes sense to me."

"I can tell. Remember when you first started, and you caught Sally Kindly with that suboxone?"

It seemed a lifetime ago. "Yes."

"I was happy because Kindly had been operating on her own and was taking away some of my customers. Suboxone is a substitute for heroin, as you know, and heroin is the main thing I push. I was glad to have an excuse to kick her off Hummingbird. And then, when I first caught on to what you were really up to, I worried you might be too successful. Bravo was ranting about how Zoe Hallister had taken so much of our business away, but I told her to wait it out. I wanted to see what the two of you would do, what you had to offer.

"And then, when things got crazy, I saw how the DOC came down hard on Warden Nowak. I did everything I could to cover you then, 'cause I wanted him out. Nowak was a prick who made what we do more difficult. He was a mean, petty, little asshole. Our new warden is a pussycat. Things are going to be easier than ever with Moore at the helm. He's not dirty, but he's a pushover. We can really amp things up now, pal."

"Glad to be of service."

"The only thing you did that irked me was helping Bravo get her hands on a phone. I figured you must've smuggled those in, and Zoe sold it to her. When that fat bitch has phone access, she gets it in her head she can do business on her own and cut me out."

"I didn't know."

"Of course not. But value this lesson. Never, *ever* trust these cunts. Not one of them is worth the flesh they're made of."

I nodded. "So I've learned."

"This is only the beginning of what we can do together, Liam. Like I've always said, I see real potential in you. You know how to move product, you know how to keep the inmates in line, you never call out sick or give me any trouble when it comes to the job. And best of all, you know how to do your trafficking discretely. You know how to play the game. I could do a thousand interviews and still not find another like you." He reached into the desk drawer and withdrew a manila folder. "That's why I'm destroying this report Rodriguez wrote up."

Diana Rodriguez, I thought. The stern female officer who'd never cut me an inch of slack. *I should have known.*

"I've been trying to get rid of that nosy, man-hating bitch for a while now," Captain Clancy said. "After all that's happened, I'd hoped she would quit or ask to be transferred, but she's on some moral crusade to fix things around here, so much so that she actually wrote up a fucking report on a fellow CO. Unbelievable. If there's one thing I can't stand, it's a rat."

I smirked. "You know what they say about snitches."

"They get stitches."

"Maybe that applies to the schoolyard," I said, quoting Zoe, "but in a place like this, *snitches go in ditches*."

The captain chuckled. "You've got a dark side, Liam. I like that. You've got to have a dark sense of humor in here."

"So, you're going to bury the report?"

"Right in the trash. But that only puts a Band-Aid on a much bigger problem." Smoke swirled about his head, making him appear subhuman, like a creature crawling out of a swamp. "Rodriguez took this to me first. No one else has seen it, but if I fail to act, we can bet our asses she'll go over my head. And if this thing with you blows up, it could expose a whole lot more than just what you've been involved in. We must make sure that doesn't happen. *You* must make sure that doesn't happen."

The chill returned. The captain stared at me, long and hard, his eyes like glaciers. He slid a sheet of paper to me.

"Home address," he said. "Rodriguez lives alone. Gee, imagine that, huh? That miserable cunt has no husband. Surprise, surprise."

"You…" I gulped. "You want me to…"

He put up a hand to stop me. "I'm not telling you how to live your life, but if I were you, I'd take care of it sooner than later. I know it's not a pleasant thought. It has its danger. But it's her or you. You know that. And you don't have to do it yourself. See, I made some connections when I worked at the men's prison in Phoenix. A couple of the inmates I dealt with are on the streets now, and they're always looking for work, if you know what I mean. There's a number you can call on that paper."

I exhaled. "This is a lot to process."

"I hear ya, but again, time is a factor." He tapped ash. "Better her than us."

I looked out the window at a world I no longer understood. I thought of what Cherry Campbell had written before she'd killed herself.

"I don't recognize this world anymore," I said aloud.

"Tell me about it," Captain Clancy replied. "You see the news lately? That woman who went missing a while back? They found her car in a junkyard. I doubt anyone's ever going to see her alive again. Every day we get more inmates coming in, more crimes being committed. I read in the paper that some guy with a rap sheet a mile long was found burned to death in a stolen car out on the rez. The great state of Arizona is falling apart. Hell, the whole country is." He shook his head. "What's this world coming to?"

CHAPTER
THIRTY-THREE

I used the same bathroom stall the captain had.

He'd told me about a few other dead zones no one knew about, a sort of gift to toast our new partnership. The camera mounted before the door to the private, handicapped toilet on Hummingbird was one of the dead ones.

Lilly Gutierrez's lifetime as a pervert paid off handsomely for me, as I'm sure it did any man who fucked her. Alone in the stall with Lilly, I discovered she had no inhibitions, no scruples, and no gag reflex.

"You still think 'bout leaving us?" she asked when we were done. "I hear you think to quit. Say no."

I zipped up my fly. "I'd considered it before, but… well, things change."

And they really had.

Lilly smiled up at me. She put her pants back on but remained topless, my semen dribbling down her ample breasts.

"You fuck me again, daddy?" she asked.

I kissed the top of her head. "If you're good."

I left her to clean up and strolled back to the dormitory with a spring in my step. Things had been tense on Hummingbird since Zoe's murder but were slowly returning to normal, and with Diana Rodriguez having not shown up for work the last few days, it was easier for me to relax because I didn't have to look over my shoulder for her. Rodriguez also wasn't returning the warden's phone calls. Of course, she never would.

The cost had been high, cutting into my nest egg, but it was worth it not to have to worry about her. Besides, there was plenty more money to be made.

I'd put in a request with Captain Clancy to divide my shifts between Raven and Hummingbird. I could take care of more business that way.

My connection with Ron and Buffalo impressed the captain. The Natives were happy to work with me without Dennis, and delivered on product quickly and efficiently, all while offering a fair price that me, Captain Clancy, and Natalia Bravo could mark up through the sky.

Working both units also gave me access to twice as many horny inmates. The law said they couldn't consent, but the captain and I disagreed. Some of these women had been deprived of a man's touch for *years* and were more grateful for dick than I'd ever imagined.

I was pulling a double shift, so a few hours after my rendezvous with Lilly, I was relieved by Ileana Sloane, who had returned to work after her facial reconstructive surgery. Though she still had a bandage covering up the cheek Sally Kindly had mutilated, it was easy to tell she was never going to be as cute as she'd been when I'd first met her. But at least she'd been relieved of the psychological torture of working on Raven. She was placed on Hummingbird, which was a sleepover party by comparison.

As I entered Raven unit, the contraband in my pocket shifted and I had to reposition it before I got to the station to relieve the rookie on duty. Once he was gone, I walked the tier, taking in deep breaths of satisfaction despite the foul odor that permeated every corner of the unit.

Ariel Richardson looked up at me as I approached her private cell at the end of the tier. I unlocked the door, stepped inside, and closed it behind me.

"Really?" she said. "Another shake down? That rookie just did one and—"

"Shut the fuck up."

Her pretty face froze with shock. I reached into my pocket, then showed her one of the many burner phones I had left over from when Dennis had first given them to me. A glimmer entered the disgraced teacher's eyes.

"I bet you miss all your little boyfriends," I said. "It's so hard when you can't get the sexual release you need, am I right?"

She looked at the phone in my hand, then at me, then back to the phone. I shook it back and forth the same way I did a tennis ball with Charlie.

"What do you want?" Richardson asked.

"The same thing you do—satisfaction."

The inmate sighed but wiped the scowl off her face, replacing it with an ironed-on smile as she got on her knees in front of me. She was going to play nice after all.

Pride painted a big smile on my face.

I was finally getting the hang of this job.

ACKNOWLEDGEMENTS

Thanks to Nick Justus and Chandra Claypool for their feedback and edits, and for being the first people to read this book. Thanks to Scott Cole for his incredible cover art and laying out the interior. Additional thanks to my good friends Aron Beauregard, Gregg and Suzi Kirby, C.V. Hunt, Ryan Harding, Daniel J. Volpe, Bryan Smith, Jonathan Butcher, and Mona Kabbani. Biggest thanks of all to my awesome fans. You all make what I do possible.

Special thanks to Tom Mumme—always.

ABOUT THE AUTHOR

Kristopher Triana is the Splatterpunk Award-winning author of *Gone to See the River Man*, *The Old Lady*, *Full Brutal*, *They All Died Screaming*, and many other terrifying books. His work has been published in seven languages and has appeared in many anthologies and magazines, drawing praise from *Rue Morgue Magazine*, *Cemetery Dance*, *Scream Magazine*, and many more.

He lives in New England.

Get signed books and other merchandise at:
TRIANAHORROR.COM

Visit him at: **KristopherTriana.com** and on Substack, Instagram, Facebook, and TikTok.